# BLACK SCIENCE

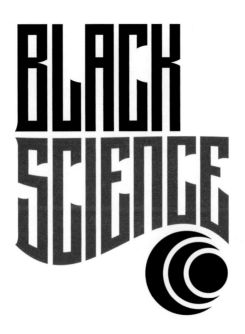

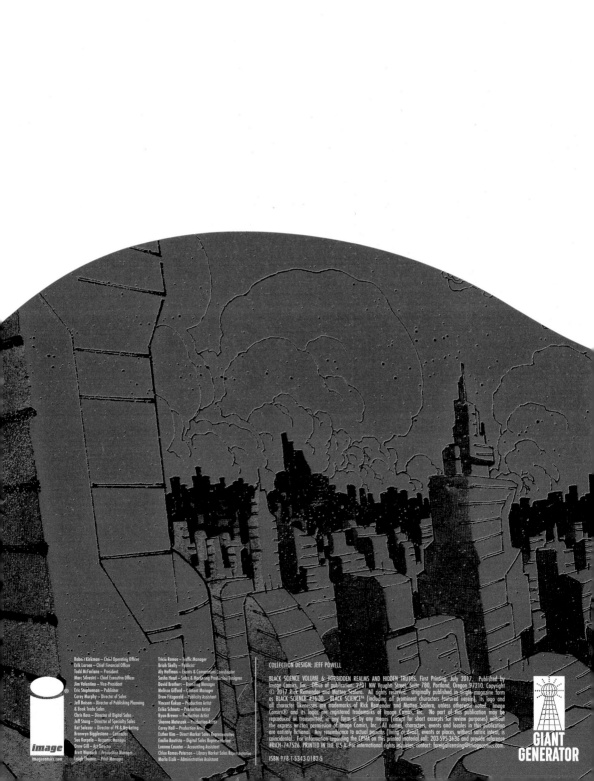

COLLECTION DESIGN: JEFF POWELL

BLACK SCIENCE VOLUME 6: FORBIDDEN REALMS AND HIDDEN TRUTHS. First Printing. July 2017. Published by Image Comics, Inc. Office of publication: 2701 NW Vaughn Street, Suite 780, Portland, Oregon 97210. Copyright © 2017 Rick Remender and Matteo Scalera. All rights reserved. Originally published in single magazine form as BLACK SCIENCE #26-30. BLACK SCIENCE™ (including all prominent characters featured herein), its logo and all character likenesses are trademarks of Rick Remender and Matteo Scalera, unless otherwise noted. Image Comics® and its logos are registered trademarks of Image Comics, Inc. No part of this publication may be reproduced or transmitted, in any form or by any means (except for short excerpts for review purposes) without the express written permission of Image Comics, Inc. All names, characters, events and locales in this publication are entirely fictional. Any resemblance to actual persons (living or dead), events or places, without satiric intent, is coincidental. For information regarding the CPSIA on this printed material call: 203-595-3636 and provide reference #RICH-747526. PRINTED IN THE U.S.A. For international rights inquiries, contact: foreignlicensing@imagecomics.com.

ISBN 978-1-5343-0182-5

GIANT
GENERATOR

RICK REMENDER
WRITER

MATTEO SCALERA
ARTIST

MORENO DINISIO
COLORS

RUS WOOTON
LETTERING + LOGO DESIGN

SEBASTIAN GIRNER
EDITOR



BLACK SCIENCE CREATED BY
RICK REMENDER & MATTEO SCALERA

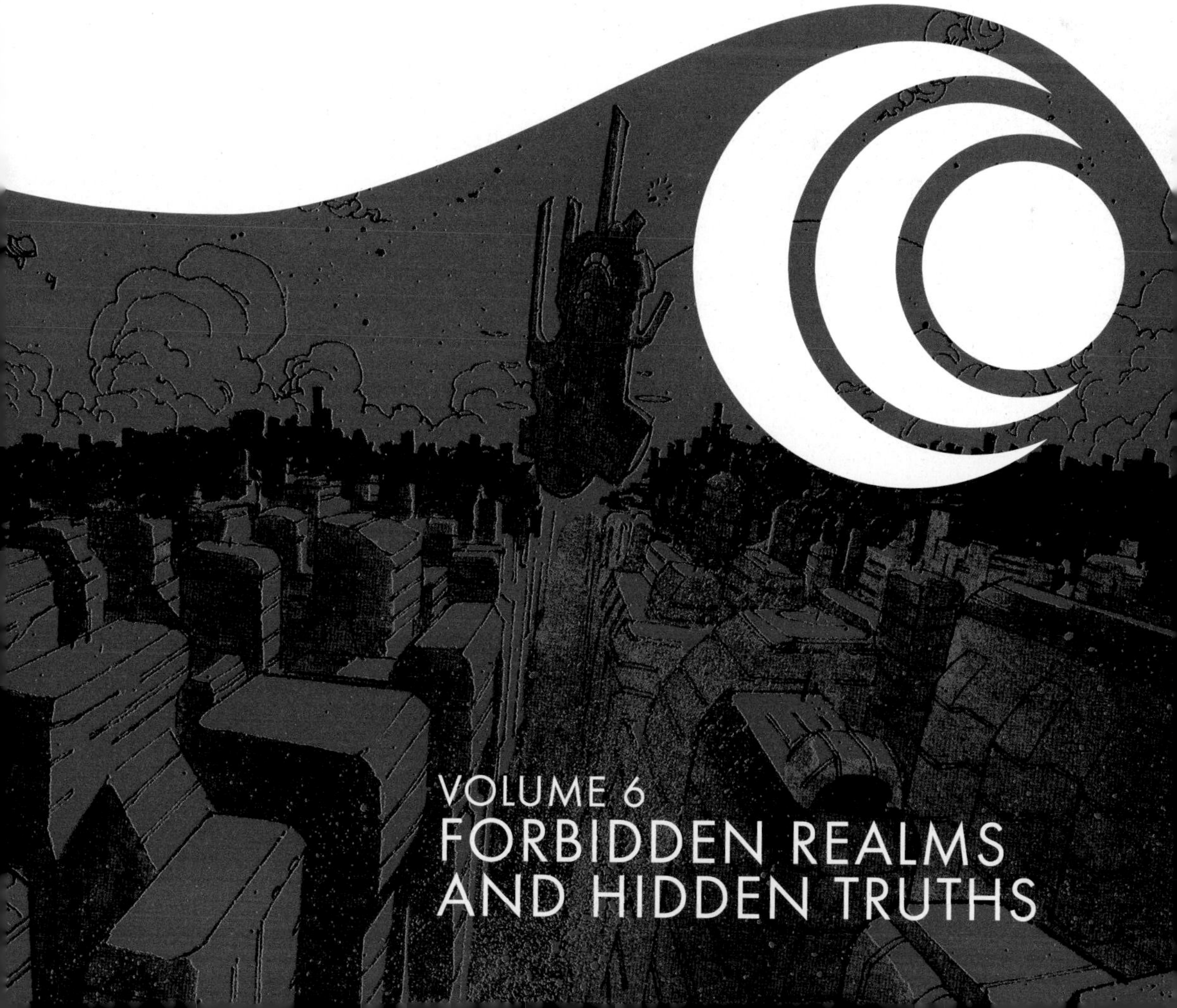

VOLUME 6

# FORBIDDEN REALMS AND HIDDEN TRUTHS

26

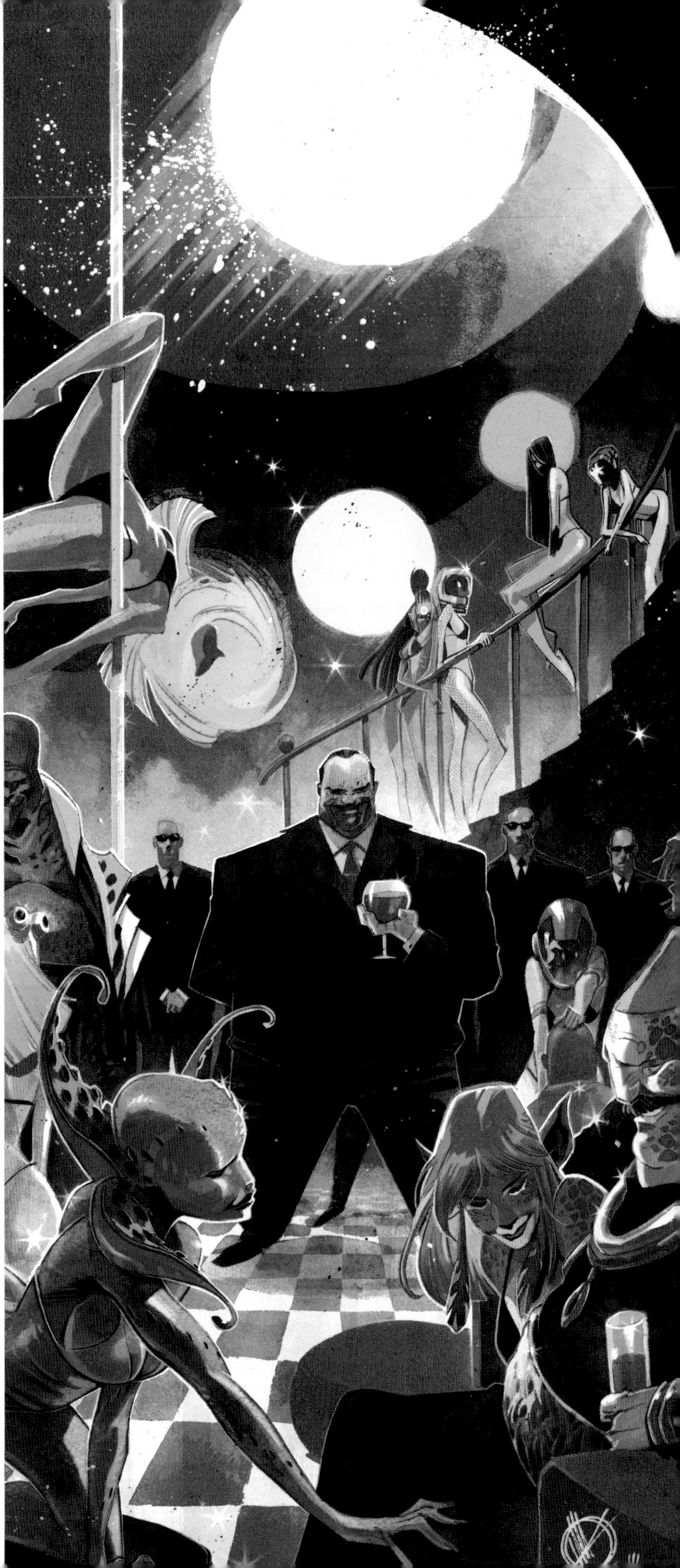

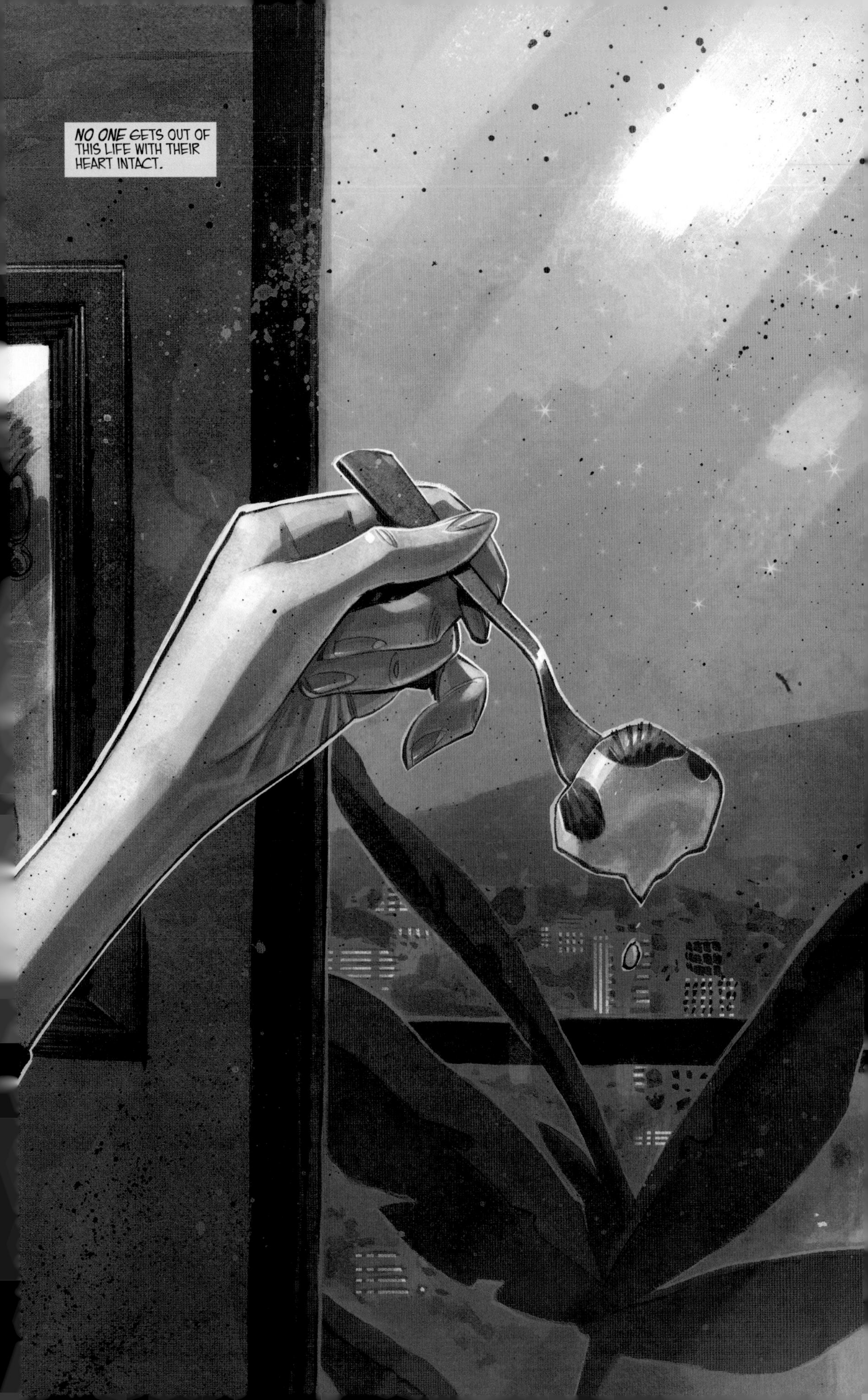
NO ONE GETS OUT OF THIS LIFE WITH THEIR HEART INTACT.

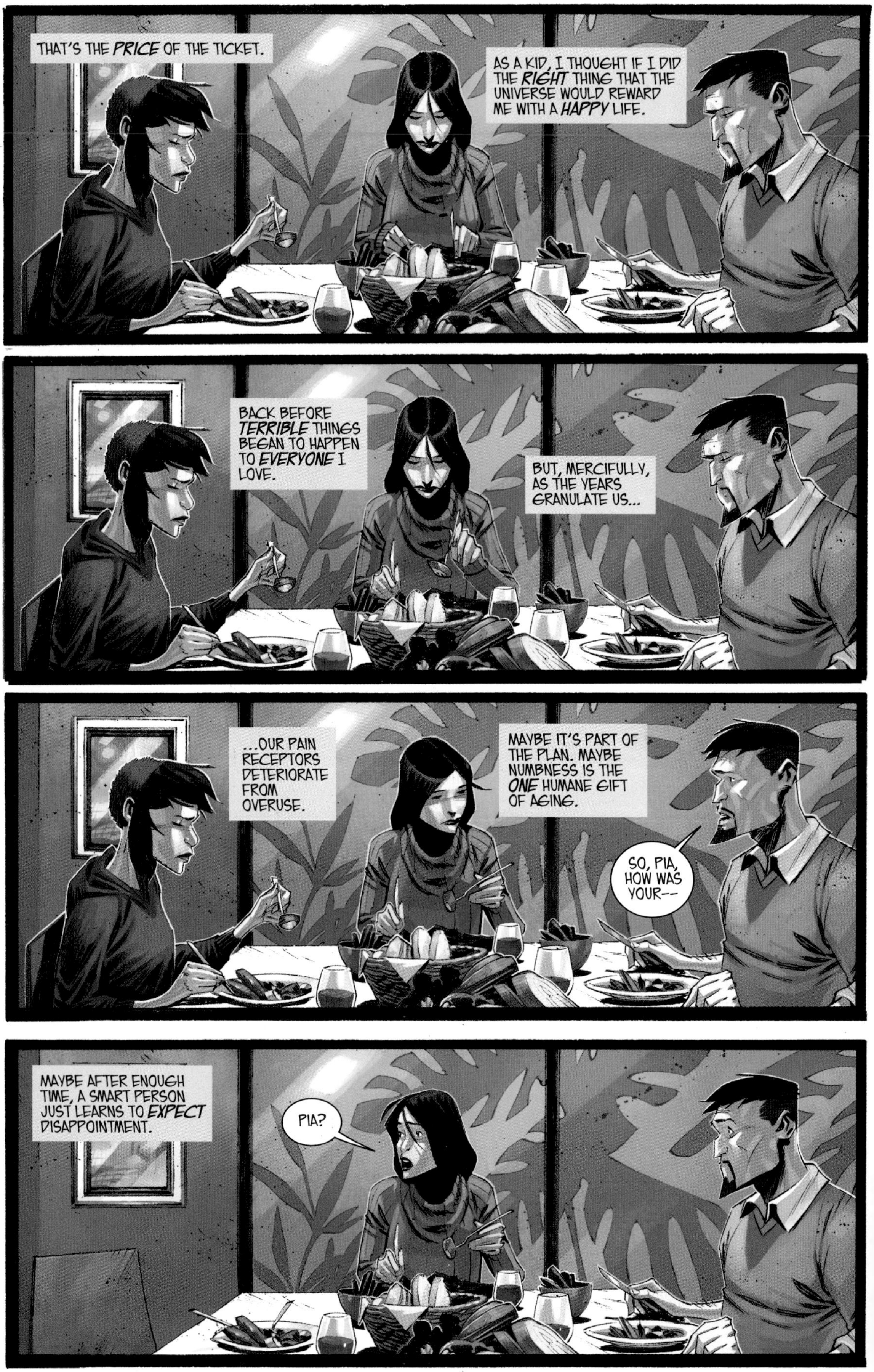
THAT'S THE PRICE OF THE TICKET.
AS A KID, I THOUGHT IF I DID THE RIGHT THING THAT THE UNIVERSE WOULD REWARD ME WITH A HAPPY LIFE.
BACK BEFORE TERRIBLE THINGS BEGAN TO HAPPEN TO EVERYONE I LOVE.
BUT, MERCIFULLY, AS THE YEARS GRANULATE US...
...OUR PAIN RECEPTORS DETERIORATE FROM OVERUSE.
MAYBE IT'S PART OF THE PLAN. MAYBE NUMBNESS IS THE ONE HUMANE GIFT OF AGING.
SO, PIA, HOW WAS YOUR--
MAYBE AFTER ENOUGH TIME, A SMART PERSON JUST LEARNS TO EXPECT DISAPPOINTMENT.
PIA?

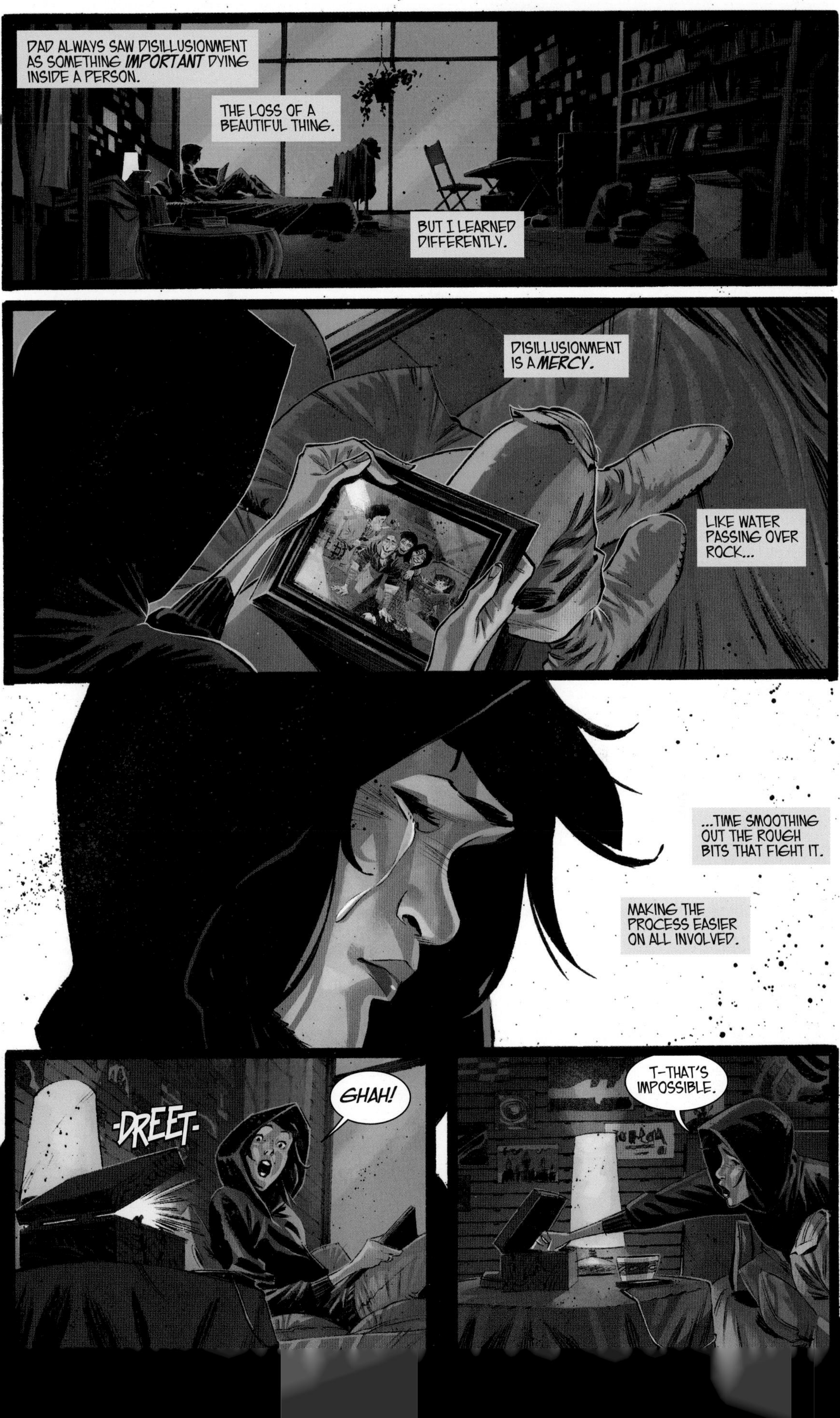
DAD ALWAYS SAW DISILLUSIONMENT AS SOMETHING IMPORTANT DYING INSIDE A PERSON.
THE LOSS OF A BEAUTIFUL THING.
BUT I LEARNED DIFFERENTLY.
DISILLUSIONMENT IS A MERCY.
LIKE WATER PASSING OVER ROCK...
...TIME SMOOTHING OUT THE ROUGH BITS THAT FIGHT IT.
MAKING THE PROCESS EASIER ON ALL INVOLVED.
-DREET-
GHAH!
T-THAT'S IMPOSSIBLE.

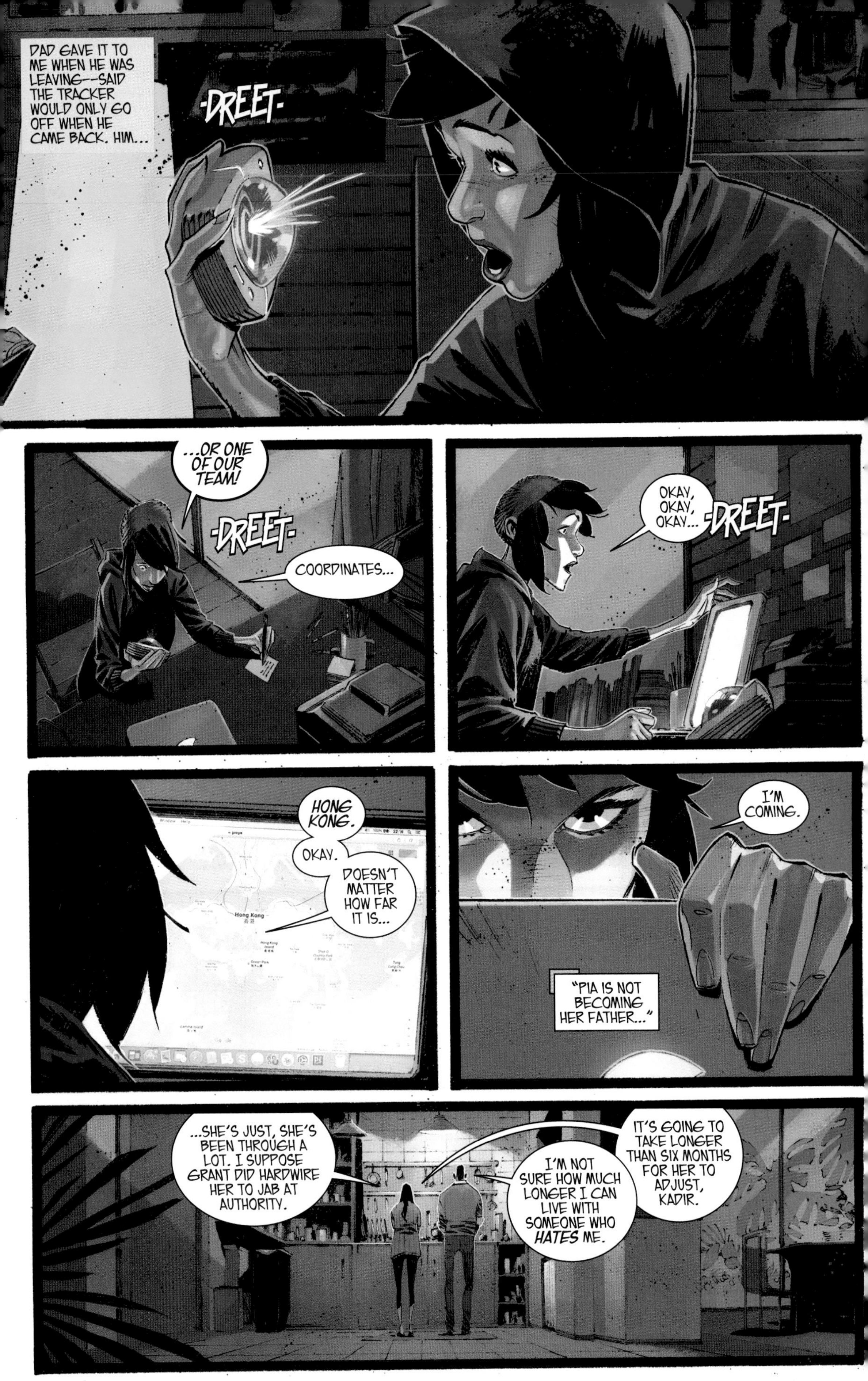
DAD GAVE IT TO ME WHEN HE WAS LEAVING--SAID THE TRACKER WOULD ONLY GO OFF WHEN HE CAME BACK. HIM...
-DREET-
...OR ONE OF OUR TEAM!
-DREET-
COORDINATES...
OKAY, OKAY, OKAY...
-DREET-
HONG KONG.
OKAY.
DOESN'T MATTER HOW FAR IT IS...
I'M COMING.
"PIA IS NOT BECOMING HER FATHER..."
...SHE'S JUST, SHE'S BEEN THROUGH A LOT. I SUPPOSE GRANT DID HARDWIRE HER TO JAB AT AUTHORITY.
I'M NOT SURE HOW MUCH LONGER I CAN LIVE WITH SOMEONE WHO HATES ME.
IT'S GOING TO TAKE LONGER THAN SIX MONTHS FOR HER TO ADJUST, KADIR.

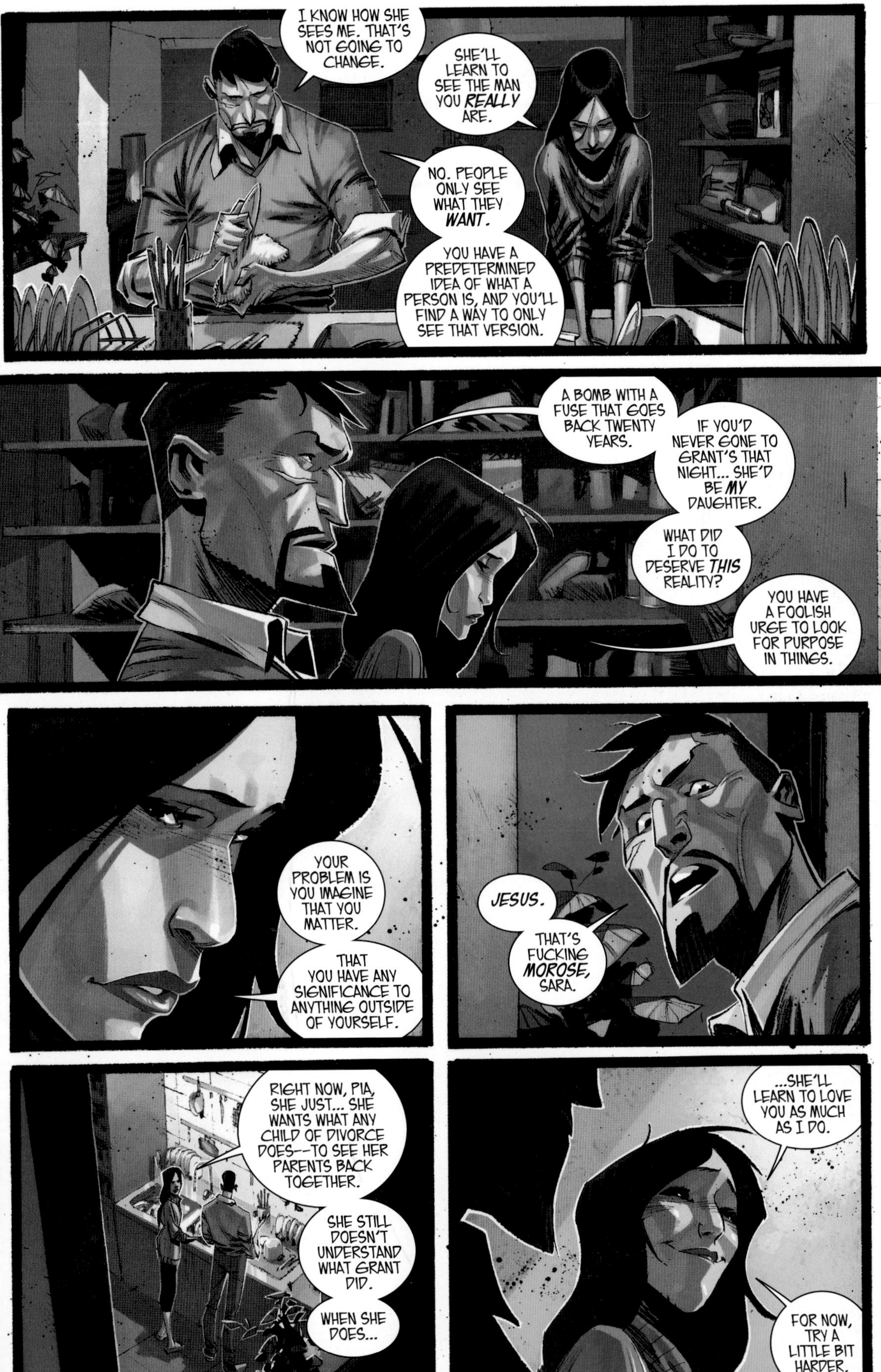
I KNOW HOW SHE SEES ME. THAT'S NOT GOING TO CHANGE.
SHE'LL LEARN TO SEE THE MAN YOU REALLY ARE.
NO. PEOPLE ONLY SEE WHAT THEY WANT.
YOU HAVE A PREDETERMINED IDEA OF WHAT A PERSON IS, AND YOU'LL FIND A WAY TO ONLY SEE THAT VERSION.
A BOMB WITH A FUSE THAT GOES BACK TWENTY YEARS.
IF YOU'D NEVER GONE TO GRANT'S THAT NIGHT... SHE'D BE MY DAUGHTER.
WHAT DID I DO TO DESERVE THIS REALITY?
YOU HAVE A FOOLISH URGE TO LOOK FOR PURPOSE IN THINGS.
YOUR PROBLEM IS YOU IMAGINE THAT YOU MATTER.
THAT YOU HAVE ANY SIGNIFICANCE TO ANYTHING OUTSIDE OF YOURSELF.
JESUS.
THAT'S FUCKING MOROSE, SARA.
RIGHT NOW, PIA, SHE JUST... SHE WANTS WHAT ANY CHILD OF DIVORCE DOES--TO SEE HER PARENTS BACK TOGETHER.
SHE STILL DOESN'T UNDERSTAND WHAT GRANT DID.
WHEN SHE DOES...
...SHE'LL LEARN TO LOVE YOU AS MUCH AS I DO.
FOR NOW, TRY A LITTLE BIT HARDER.

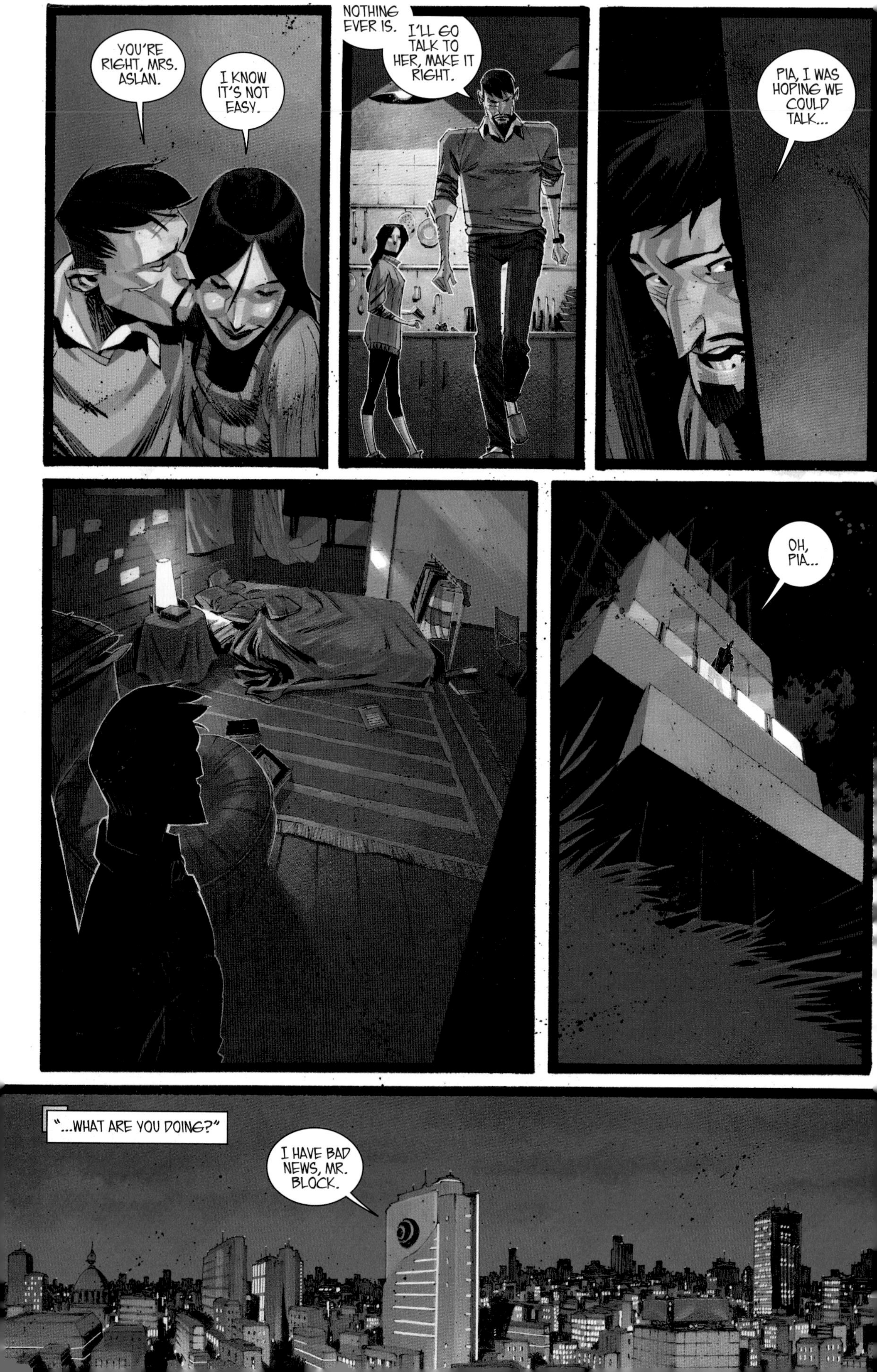
YOU'RE RIGHT, MRS. ASLAN.
I KNOW IT'S NOT EASY.
NOTHING EVER IS.
I'LL GO TALK TO HER, MAKE IT RIGHT.
PIA, I WAS HOPING WE COULD TALK...
OH, PIA...
"...WHAT ARE YOU DOING?"
I HAVE BAD NEWS, MR. BLOCK.

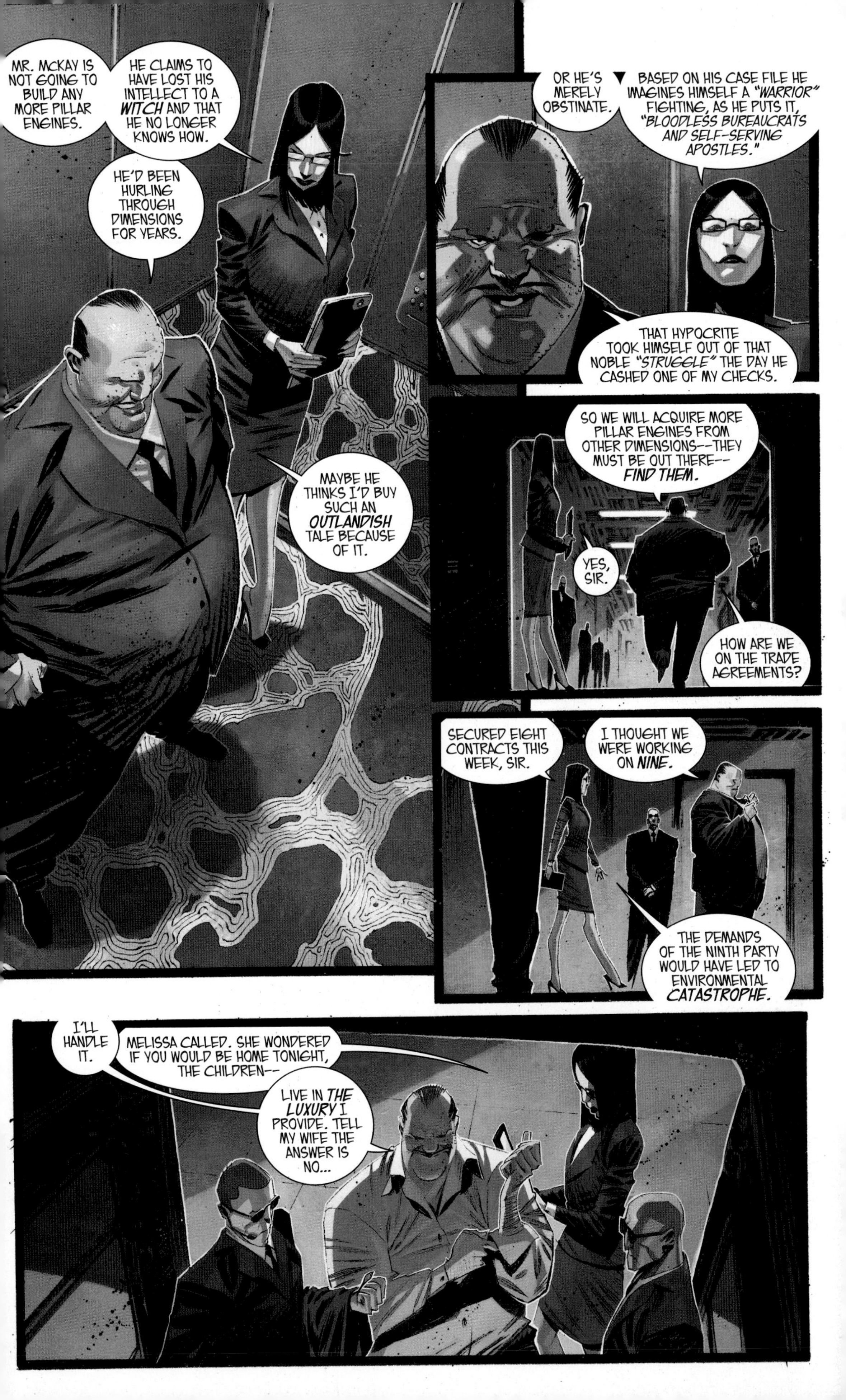
MR. McKAY IS NOT GOING TO BUILD ANY MORE PILLAR ENGINES.
HE CLAIMS TO HAVE LOST HIS INTELLECT TO A WITCH AND THAT HE NO LONGER KNOWS HOW.
HE'D BEEN HURLING THROUGH DIMENSIONS FOR YEARS.
MAYBE HE THINKS I'D BUY SUCH AN OUTLANDISH TALE BECAUSE OF IT.
OR HE'S MERELY OBSTINATE.
BASED ON HIS CASE FILE HE IMAGINES HIMSELF A "WARRIOR" FIGHTING, AS HE PUTS IT, "BLOODLESS BUREAUCRATS AND SELF-SERVING APOSTLES."
THAT HYPOCRITE TOOK HIMSELF OUT OF THAT NOBLE "STRUGGLE" THE DAY HE CASHED ONE OF MY CHECKS.
SO WE WILL ACQUIRE MORE PILLAR ENGINES FROM OTHER DIMENSIONS--THEY MUST BE OUT THERE--FIND THEM.
YES, SIR.
HOW ARE WE ON THE TRADE AGREEMENTS?
SECURED EIGHT CONTRACTS THIS WEEK, SIR.
I THOUGHT WE WERE WORKING ON NINE.
THE DEMANDS OF THE NINTH PARTY WOULD HAVE LED TO ENVIRONMENTAL CATASTROPHE.
I'LL HANDLE IT.
MELISSA CALLED. SHE WONDERED IF YOU WOULD BE HOME TONIGHT, THE CHILDREN--
LIVE IN THE LUXURY I PROVIDE. TELL MY WIFE THE ANSWER IS NO...

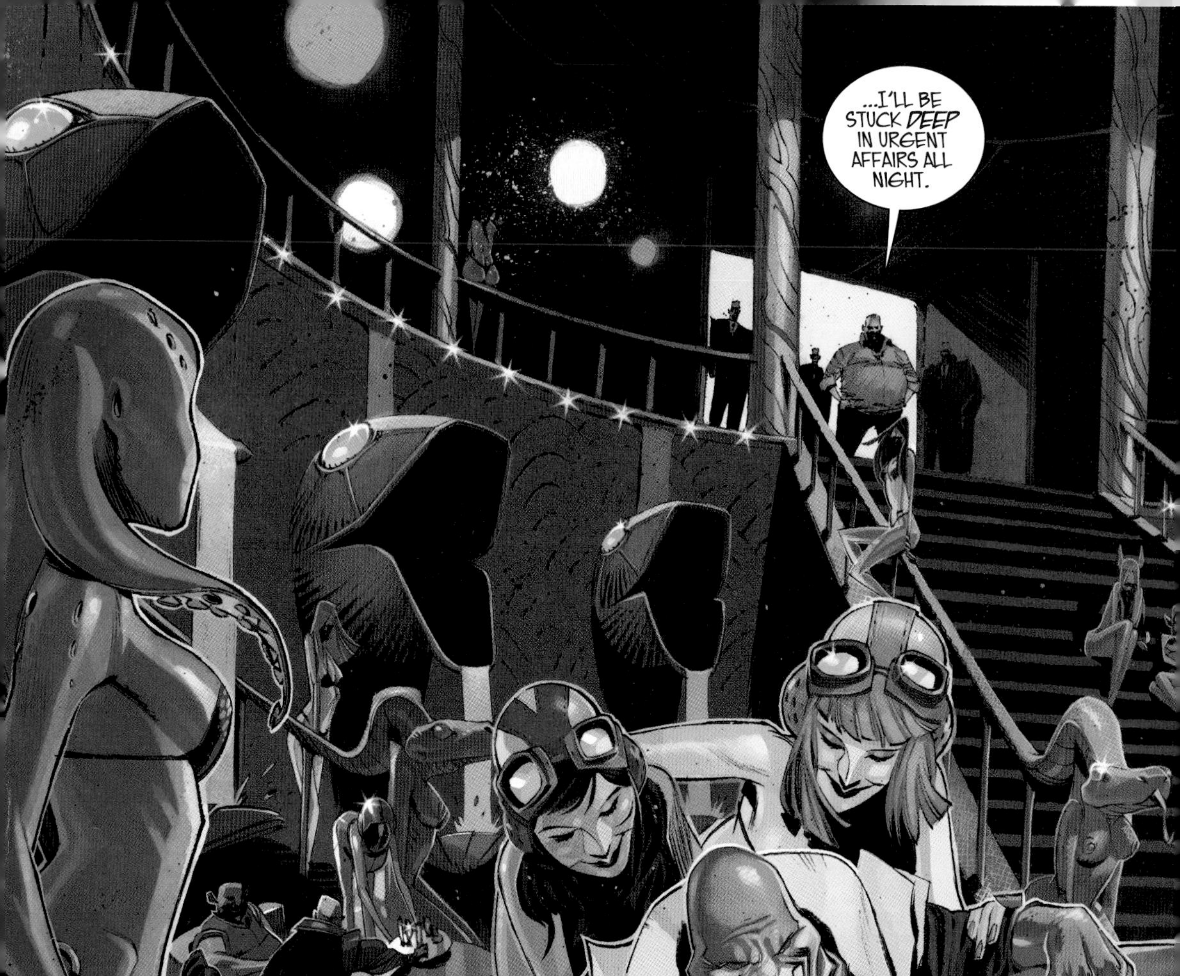
...I'LL BE STUCK DEEP IN URGENT AFFAIRS ALL NIGHT.

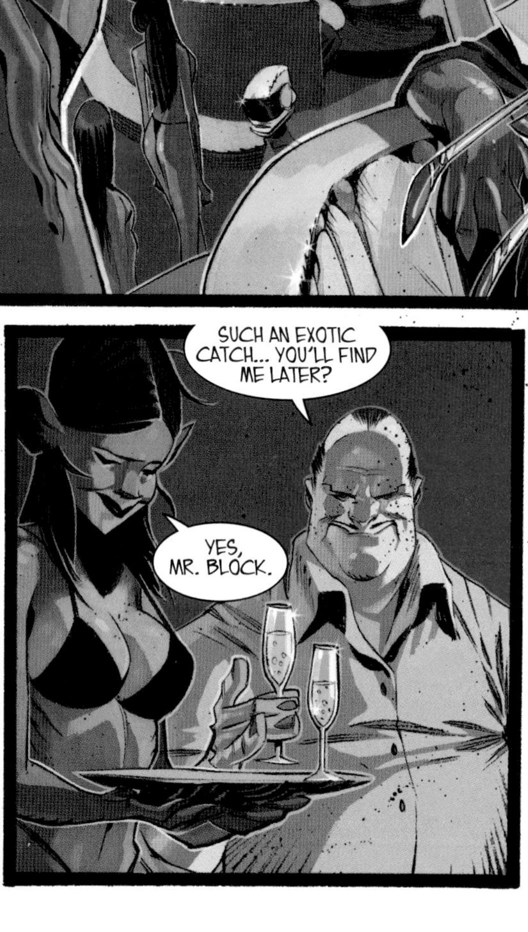
SUCH AN EXOTIC CATCH... YOU'LL FIND ME LATER?
YES, MR. BLOCK.

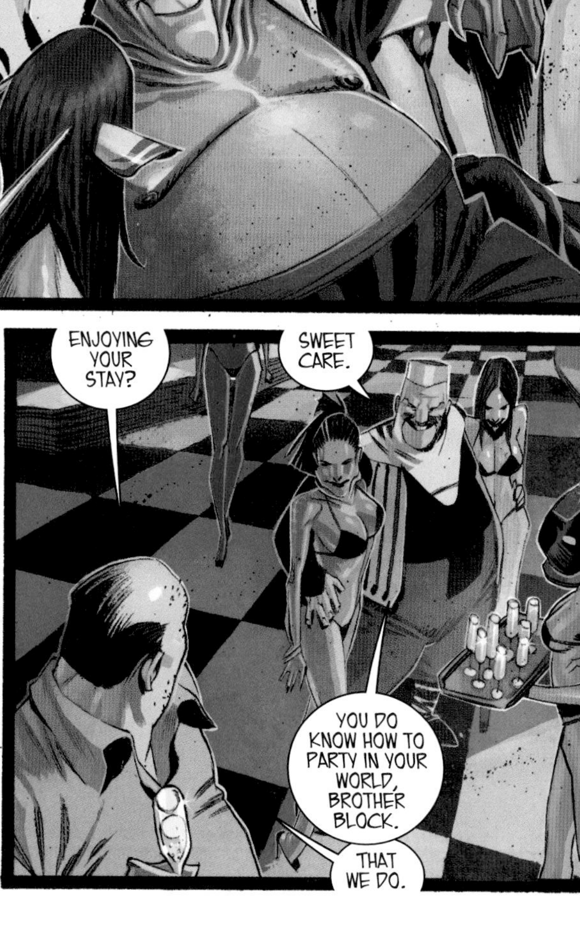
ENJOYING YOUR STAY?
SWEET CARE.
YOU DO KNOW HOW TO PARTY IN YOUR WORLD, BROTHER BLOCK.
THAT WE DO.

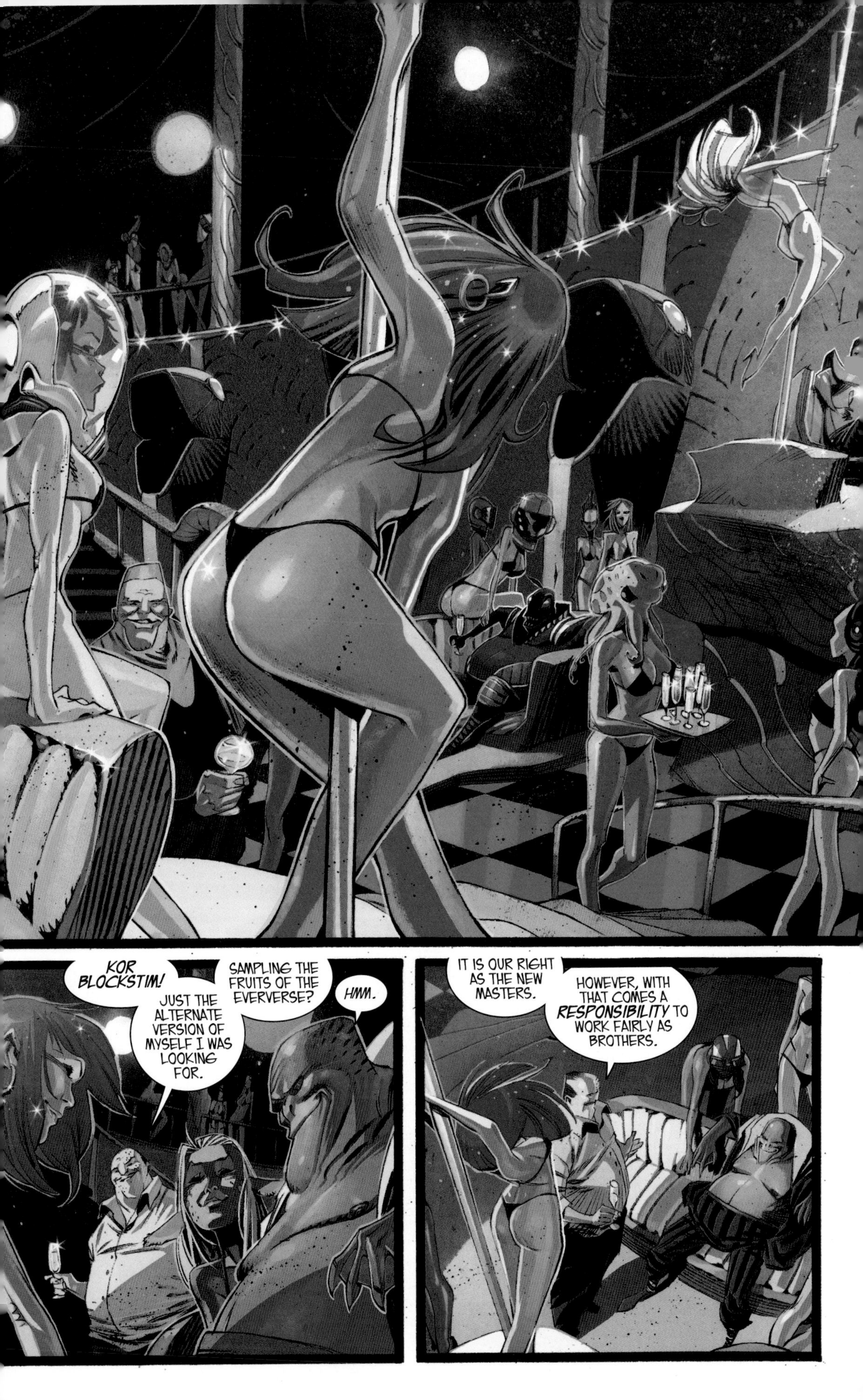
KOR BLOCKSTIM!
SAMPLING THE FRUITS OF THE EVERVERSE?
JUST THE ALTERNATE VERSION OF MYSELF I WAS LOOKING FOR.
HMM.
IT IS OUR RIGHT AS THE NEW MASTERS.
HOWEVER, WITH THAT COMES A *RESPONSIBILITY* TO WORK FAIRLY AS BROTHERS.

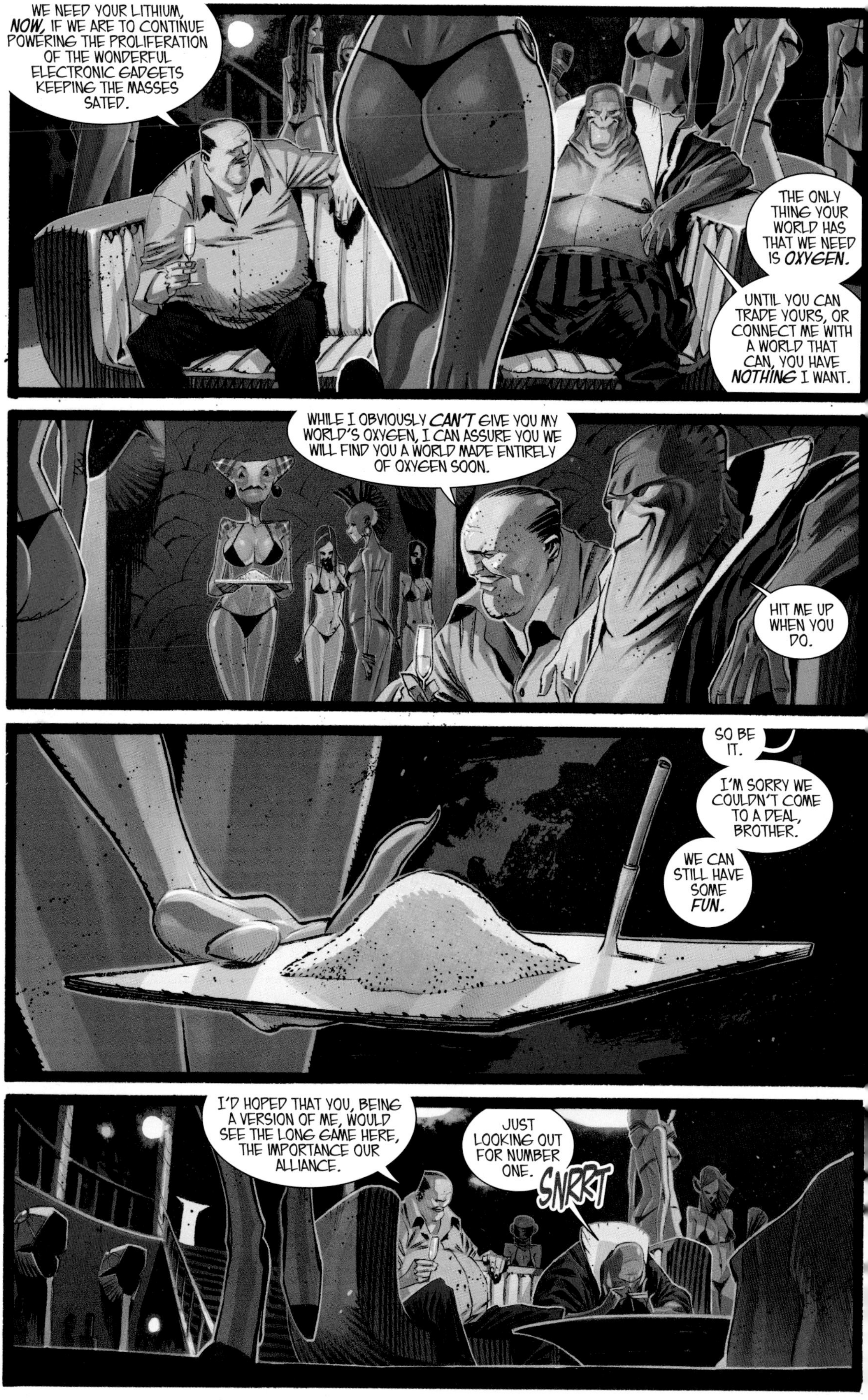

WE NEED YOUR LITHIUM, NOW, IF WE ARE TO CONTINUE POWERING THE PROLIFERATION OF THE WONDERFUL ELECTRONIC GADGETS KEEPING THE MASSES SATED.
THE ONLY THING YOUR WORLD HAS THAT WE NEED IS OXYGEN.
UNTIL YOU CAN TRADE YOURS, OR CONNECT ME WITH A WORLD THAT CAN, YOU HAVE NOTHING I WANT.
WHILE I OBVIOUSLY CAN'T GIVE YOU MY WORLD'S OXYGEN, I CAN ASSURE YOU WE WILL FIND YOU A WORLD MADE ENTIRELY OF OXYGEN SOON.
HIT ME UP WHEN YOU DO.
SO BE IT.
I'M SORRY WE COULDN'T COME TO A DEAL, BROTHER.
WE CAN STILL HAVE SOME FUN.
I'D HOPED THAT YOU, BEING A VERSION OF ME, WOULD SEE THE LONG GAME HERE, THE IMPORTANCE OUR ALLIANCE.
JUST LOOKING OUT FOR NUMBER ONE.
SNRRT

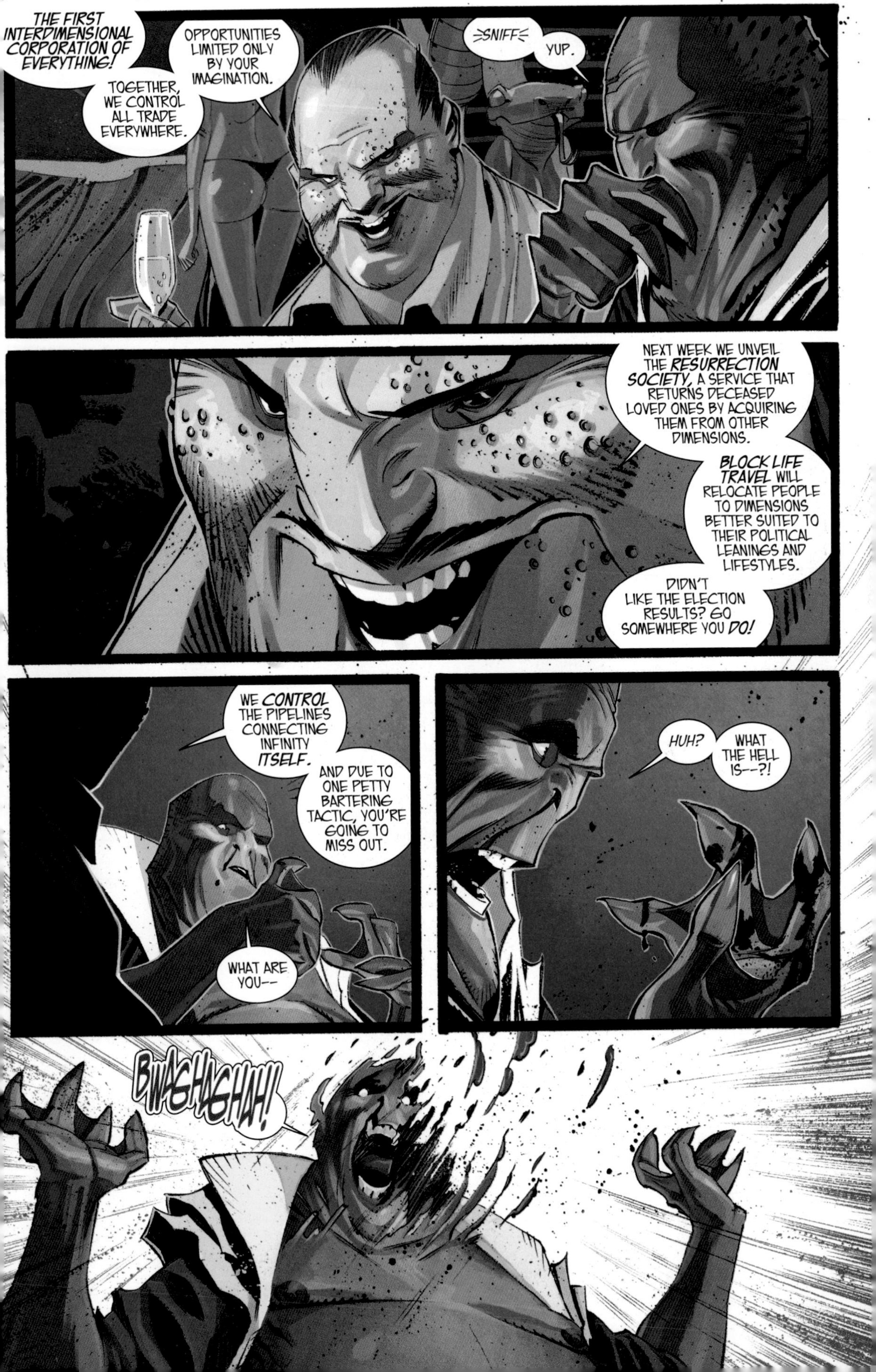
THE FIRST INTERDIMENSIONAL CORPORATION OF EVERYTHING!
TOGETHER, WE CONTROL ALL TRADE EVERYWHERE.
OPPORTUNITIES LIMITED ONLY BY YOUR IMAGINATION.
=SNIFF=
YUP.
NEXT WEEK WE UNVEIL THE RESURRECTION SOCIETY, A SERVICE THAT RETURNS DECEASED LOVED ONES BY ACQUIRING THEM FROM OTHER DIMENSIONS.
BLOCK LIFE TRAVEL WILL RELOCATE PEOPLE TO DIMENSIONS BETTER SUITED TO THEIR POLITICAL LEANINGS AND LIFESTYLES.
DIDN'T LIKE THE ELECTION RESULTS? GO SOMEWHERE YOU DO!
WE CONTROL THE PIPELINES CONNECTING INFINITY ITSELF.
AND DUE TO ONE PETTY BARTERING TACTIC, YOU'RE GOING TO MISS OUT.
WHAT ARE YOU--
HUH?
WHAT THE HELL IS--?!
BWAGHAGHAH!!

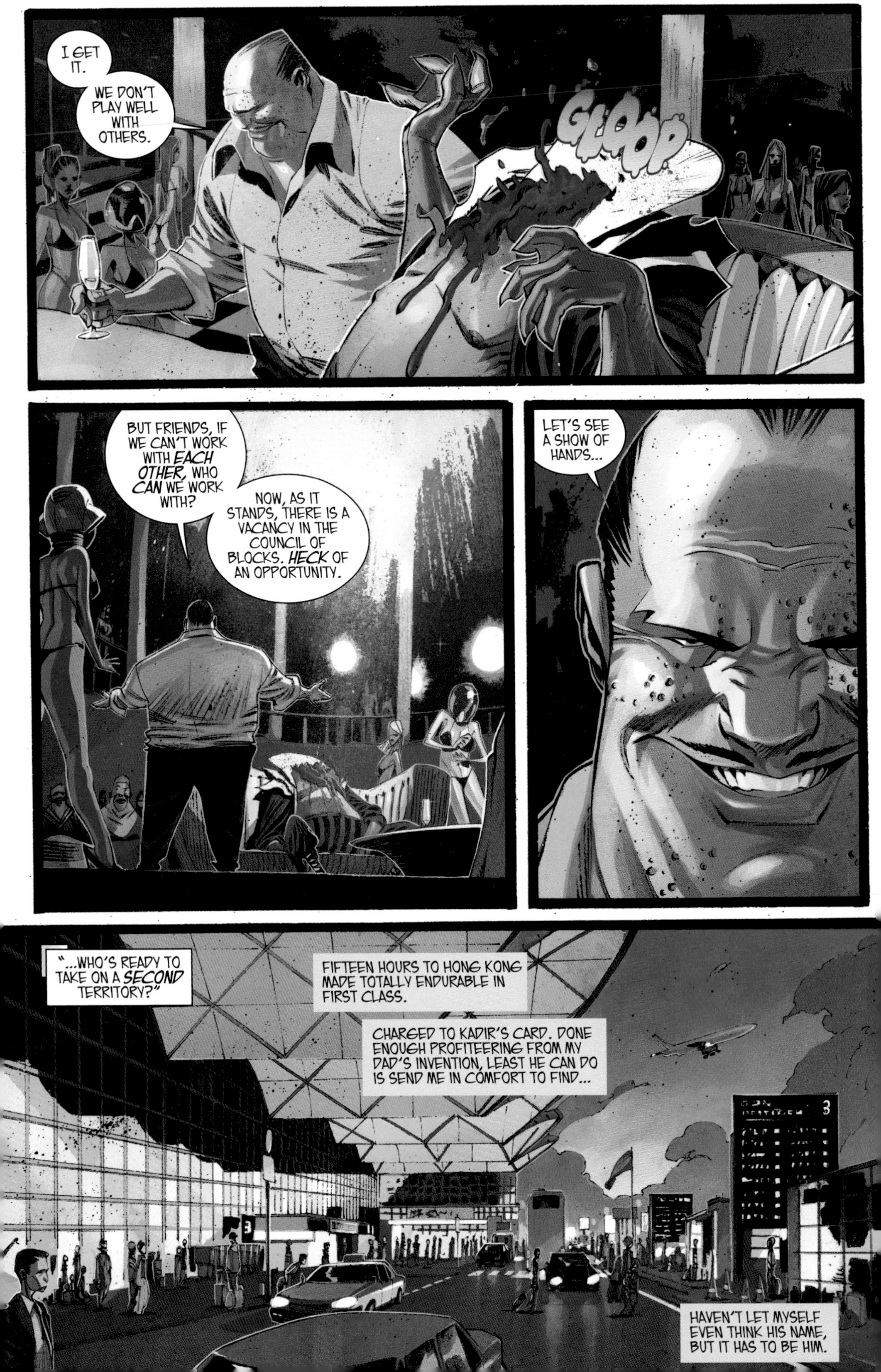
I GET IT.
WE DON'T PLAY WELL WITH OTHERS.
GLOOP
BUT FRIENDS, IF WE CAN'T WORK WITH *EACH OTHER,* WHO *CAN* WE WORK WITH?
NOW, AS IT STANDS, THERE IS A VACANCY IN THE COUNCIL OF BLOCKS. *HECK* OF AN OPPORTUNITY.
LET'S SEE A SHOW OF HANDS...
"...WHO'S READY TO TAKE ON A *SECOND* TERRITORY?"
FIFTEEN HOURS TO HONG KONG MADE TOTALLY ENDURABLE IN FIRST CLASS.
CHARGED TO KADIR'S CARD. DONE ENOUGH PROFITEERING FROM MY DAD'S INVENTION, LEAST HE CAN DO IS SEND ME IN COMFORT TO FIND...
HAVEN'T LET MYSELF EVEN THINK HIS NAME, BUT IT HAS TO BE HIM.

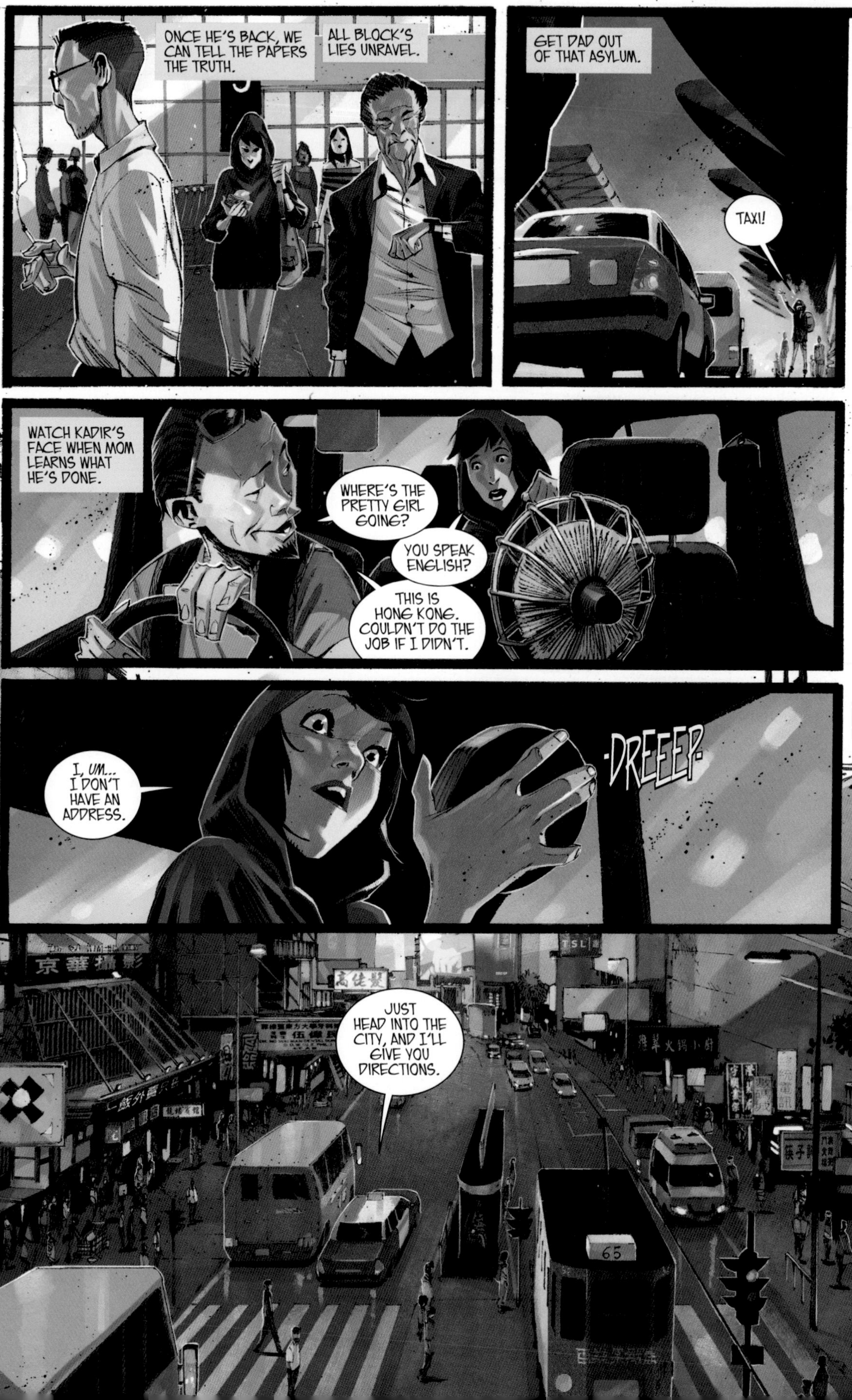

ONCE HE'S BACK, WE CAN TELL THE PAPERS THE TRUTH.
ALL BLOCK'S LIES UNRAVEL.
GET DAD OUT OF THAT ASYLUM.
TAXI!
WATCH KADIR'S FACE WHEN MOM LEARNS WHAT HE'S DONE.
WHERE'S THE PRETTY GIRL GOING?
YOU SPEAK ENGLISH?
THIS IS HONG KONG. COULDN'T DO THE JOB IF I DIDN'T.
I, UM... I DON'T HAVE AN ADDRESS.
-DREEEP-
JUST HEAD INTO THE CITY, AND I'LL GIVE YOU DIRECTIONS.

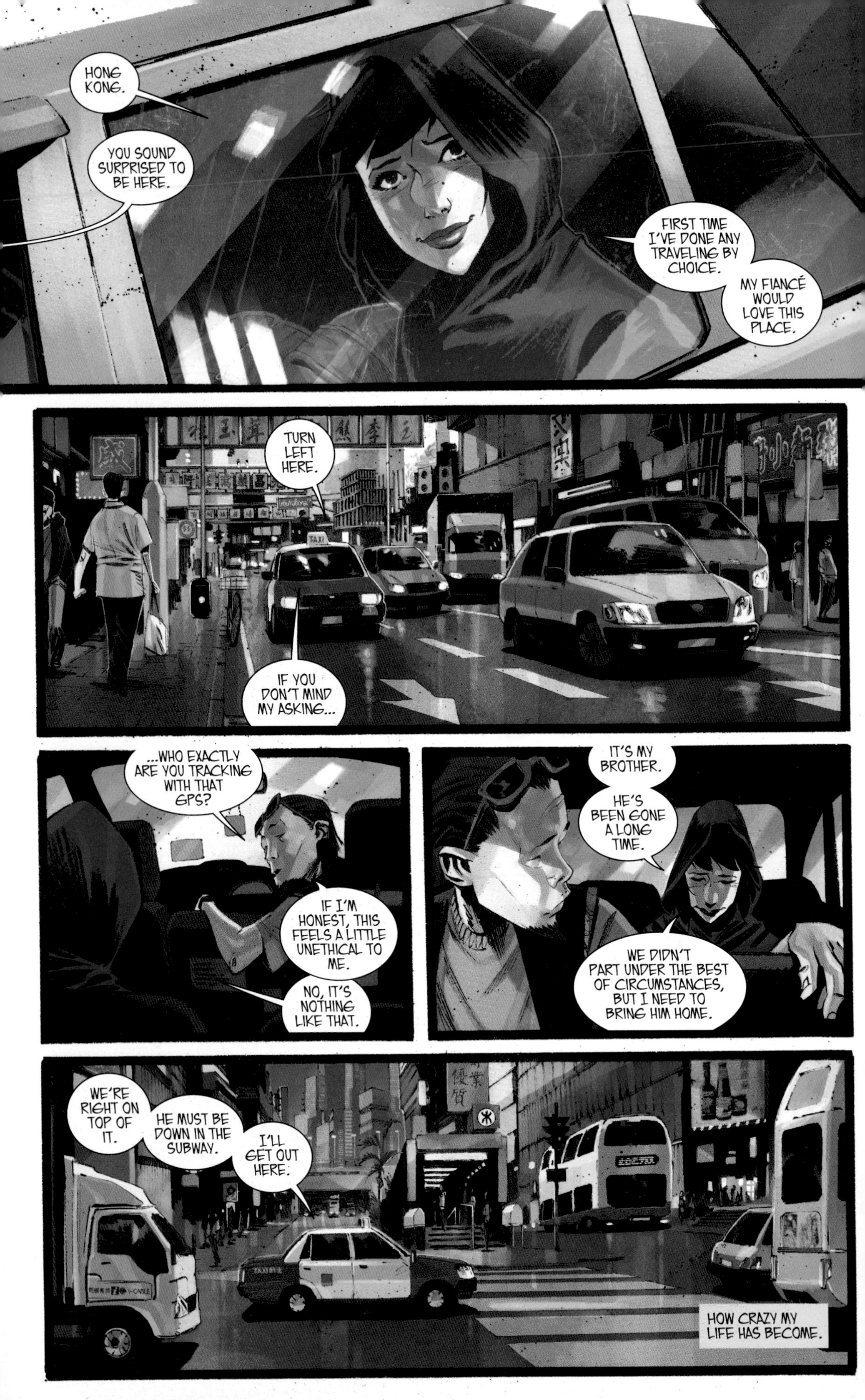
HONG KONG.
YOU SOUND SURPRISED TO BE HERE.
FIRST TIME I'VE DONE ANY TRAVELING BY CHOICE.
MY FIANCÉ WOULD LOVE THIS PLACE.
TURN LEFT HERE.
IF YOU DON'T MIND MY ASKING...
...WHO EXACTLY ARE YOU TRACKING WITH THAT GPS?
IF I'M HONEST, THIS FEELS A LITTLE UNETHICAL TO ME.
NO, IT'S NOTHING LIKE THAT.
IT'S MY BROTHER.
HE'S BEEN GONE A LONG TIME.
WE DIDN'T PART UNDER THE BEST OF CIRCUMSTANCES, BUT I NEED TO BRING HIM HOME.
WE'RE RIGHT ON TOP OF IT.
HE MUST BE DOWN IN THE SUBWAY.
I'LL GET OUT HERE.
HOW CRAZY MY LIFE HAS BECOME.

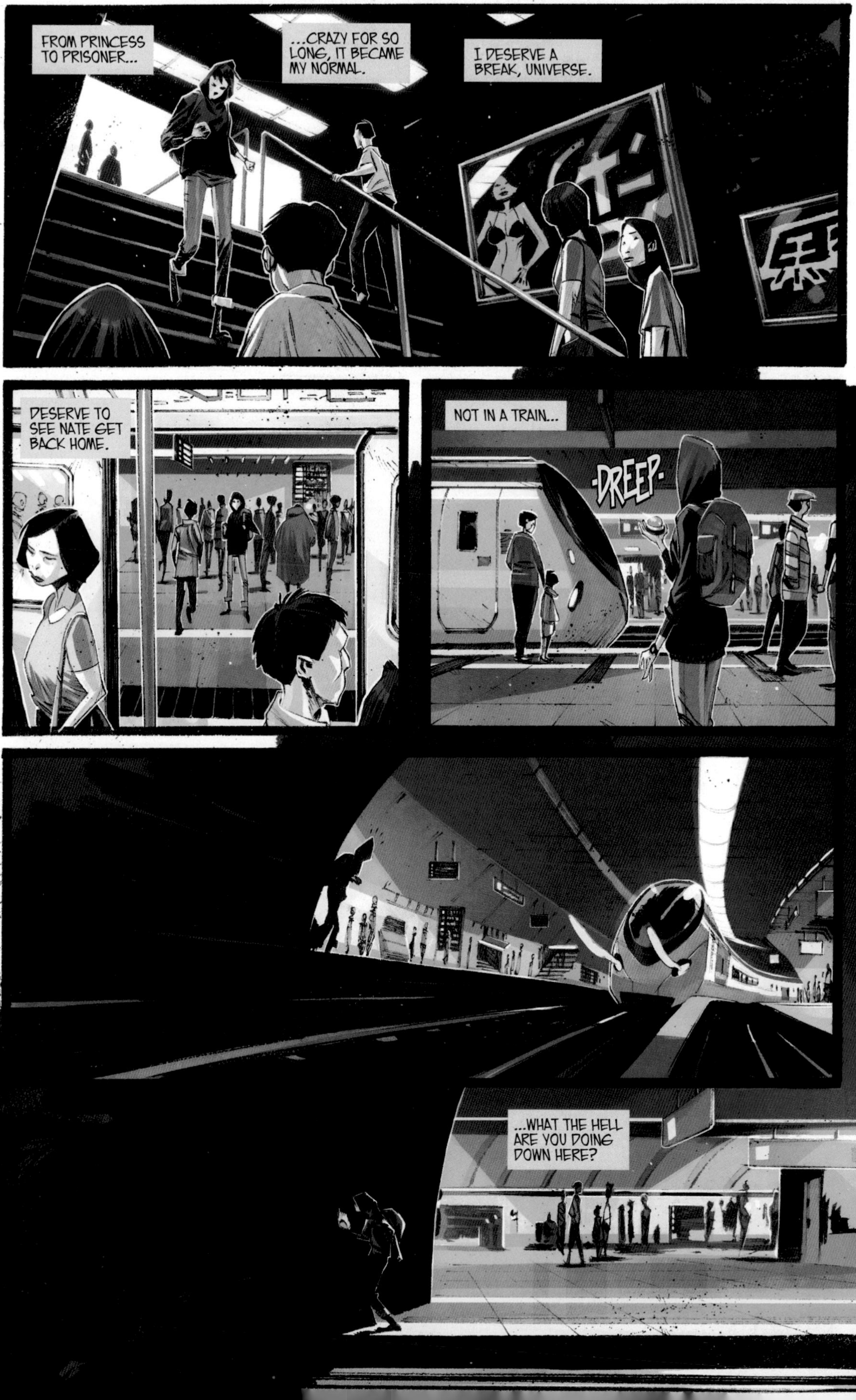
FROM PRINCESS TO PRISONER...
...CRAZY FOR SO LONG, IT BECAME MY NORMAL.
I DESERVE A BREAK, UNIVERSE.
DESERVE TO SEE NATE GET BACK HOME.
NOT IN A TRAIN...
-DREEP-
...WHAT THE HELL ARE YOU DOING DOWN HERE?

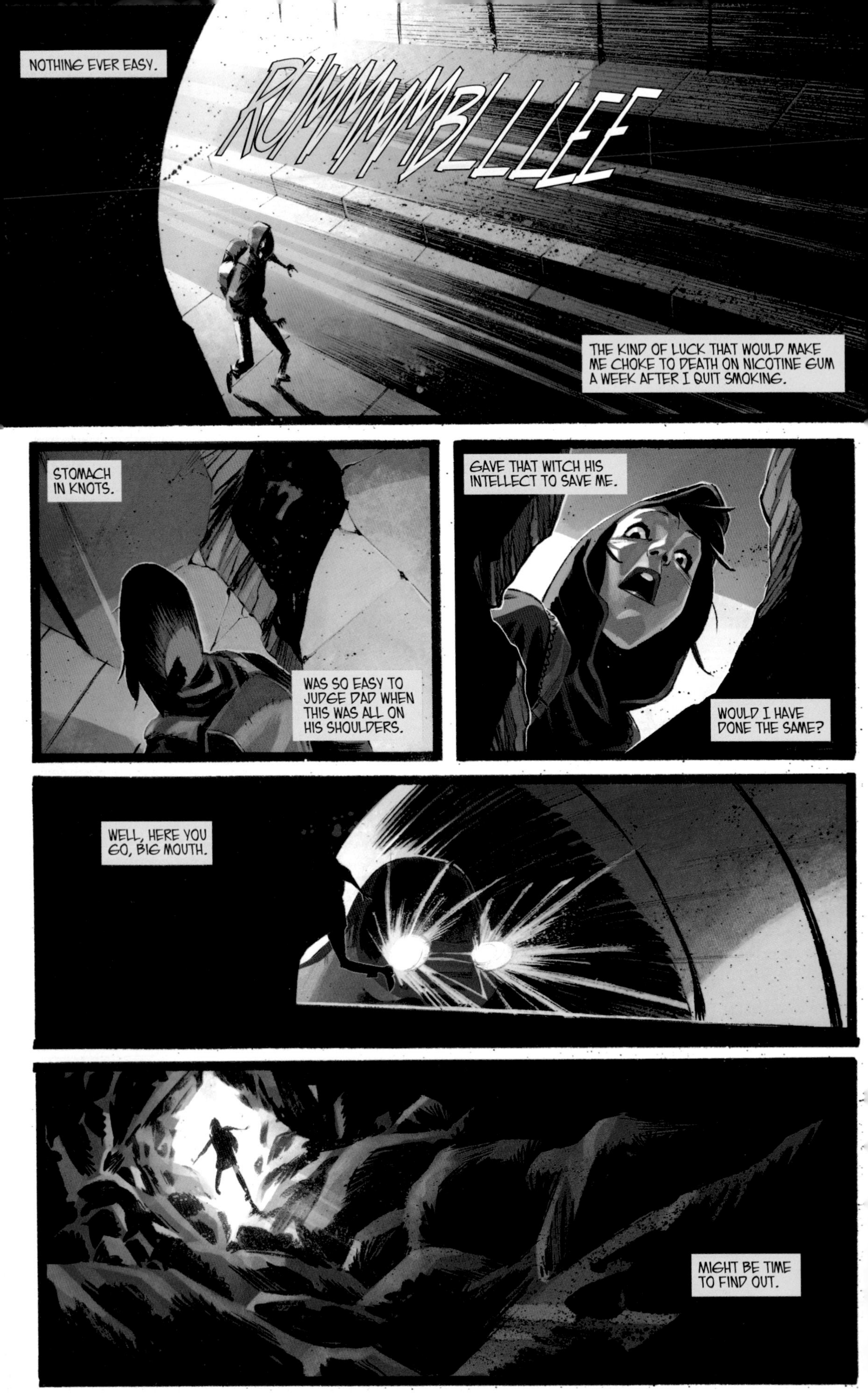
NOTHING EVER EASY.
RUMMMMBLLLEE
THE KIND OF LUCK THAT WOULD MAKE ME CHOKE TO DEATH ON NICOTINE GUM A WEEK AFTER I QUIT SMOKING.
STOMACH IN KNOTS.
WAS SO EASY TO JUDGE DAD WHEN THIS WAS ALL ON HIS SHOULDERS.
GAVE THAT WITCH HIS INTELLECT TO SAVE ME.
WOULD I HAVE DONE THE SAME?
WELL, HERE YOU GO, BIG MOUTH.
MIGHT BE TIME TO FIND OUT.

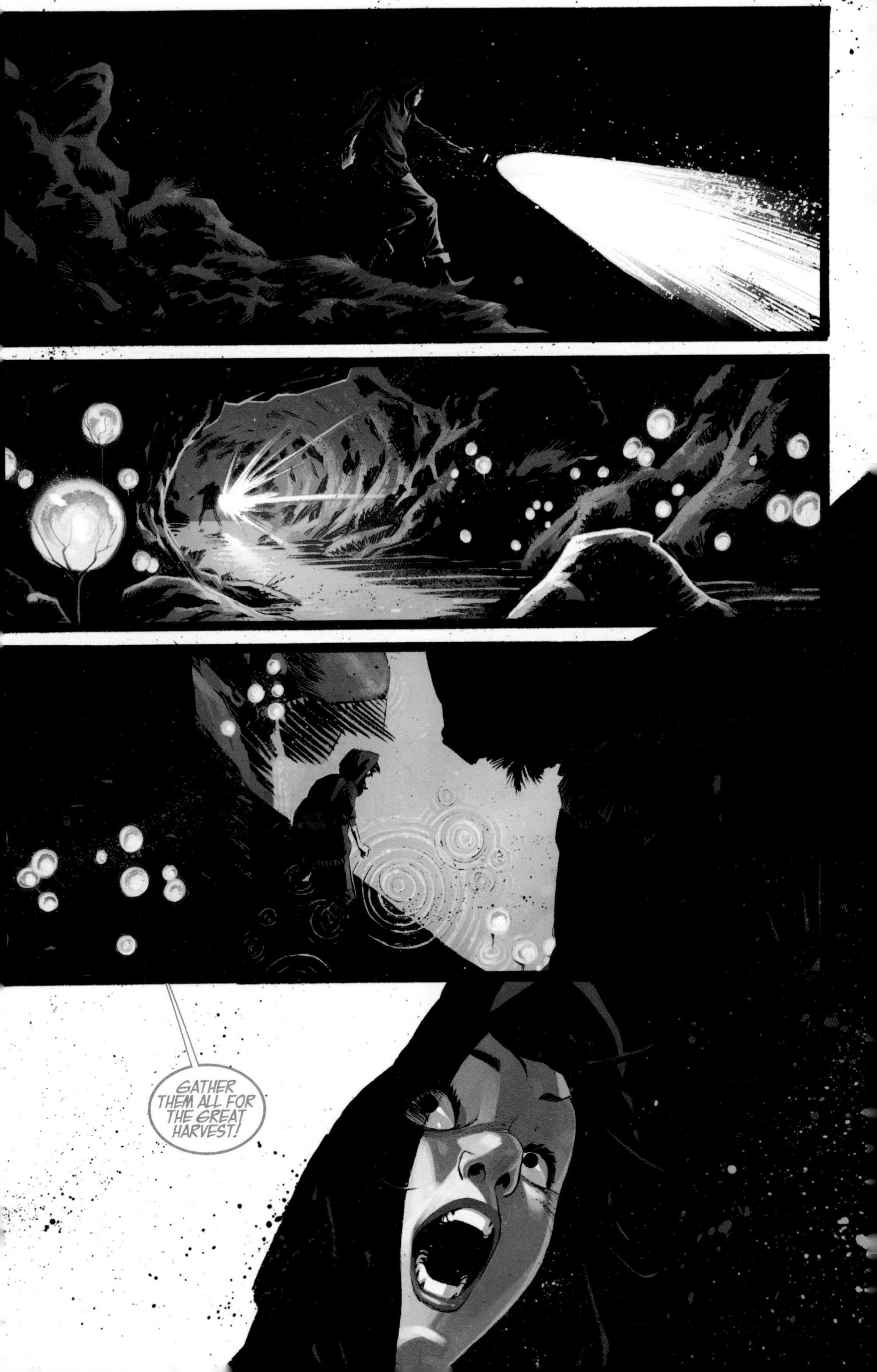
GATHER THEM ALL FOR THE GREAT HARVEST!

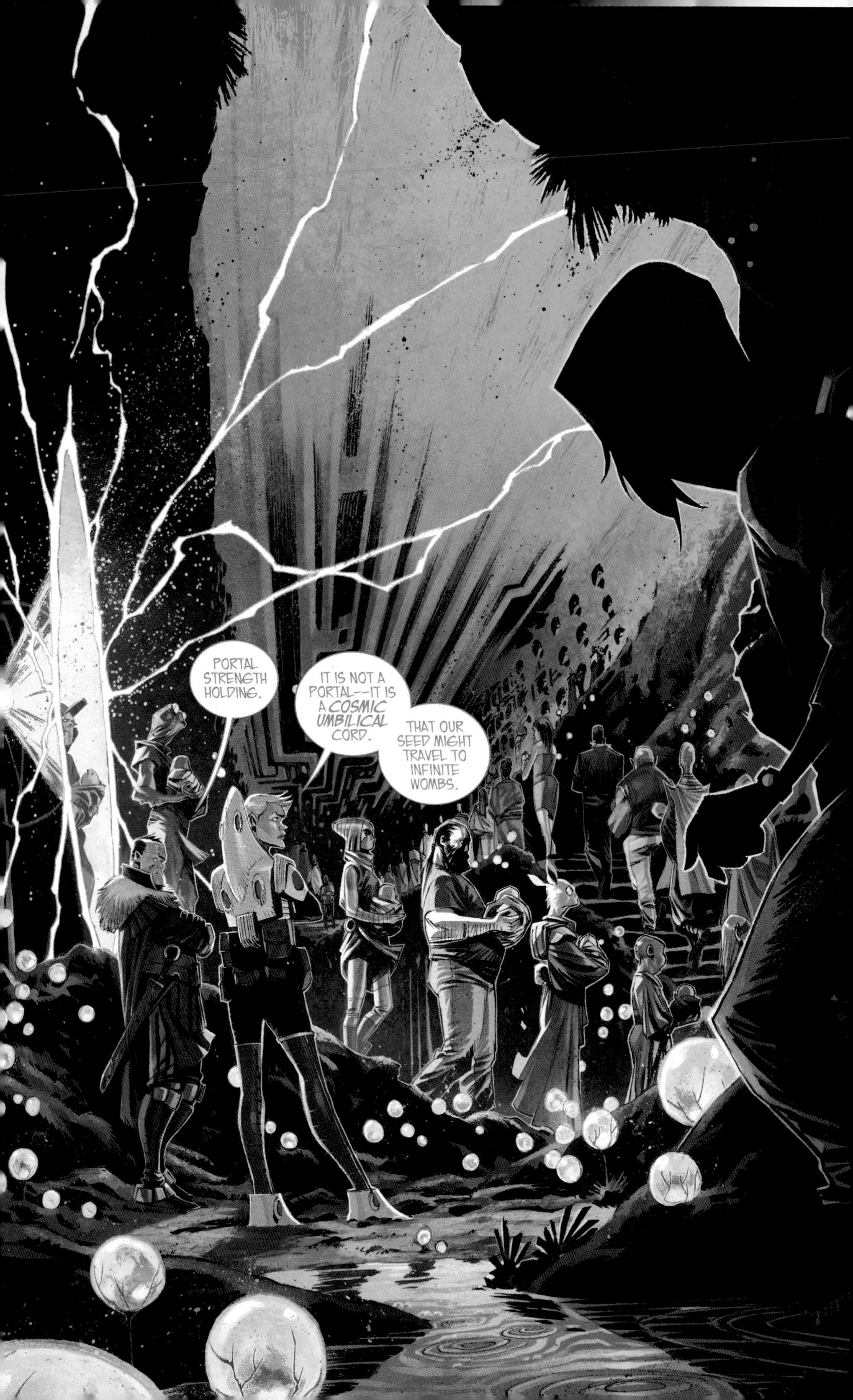
PORTAL STRENGTH HOLDING.
IT IS NOT A PORTAL--IT IS A COSMIC UMBILICAL CORD.
THAT OUR SEED MIGHT TRAVEL TO INFINITE WOMBS.

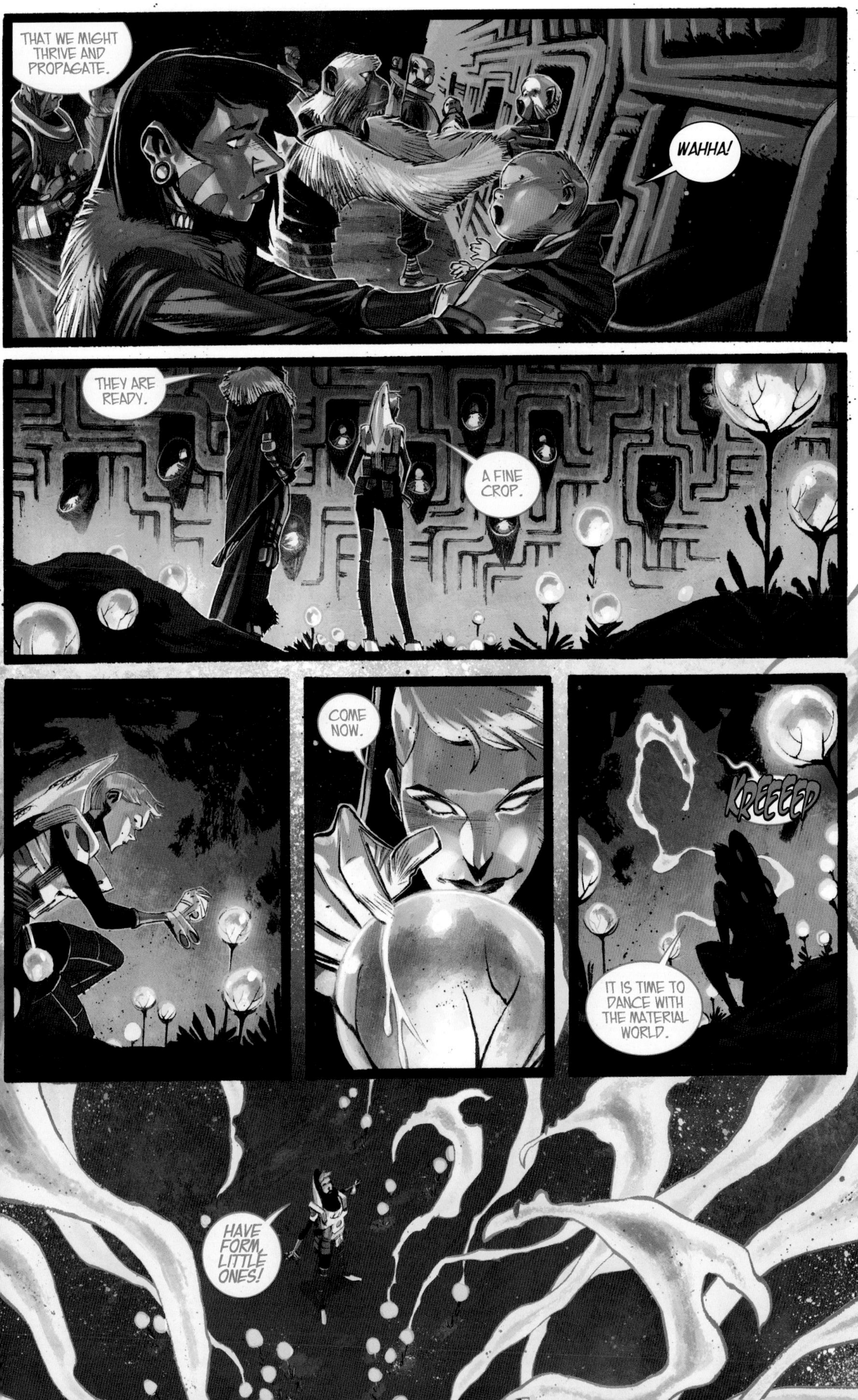
THAT WE MIGHT THRIVE AND PROPAGATE.
WAHHA!
THEY ARE READY.
A FINE CROP.
COME NOW.
KREEEEP
IT IS TIME TO DANCE WITH THE MATERIAL WORLD.
HAVE FORM, LITTLE ONES!

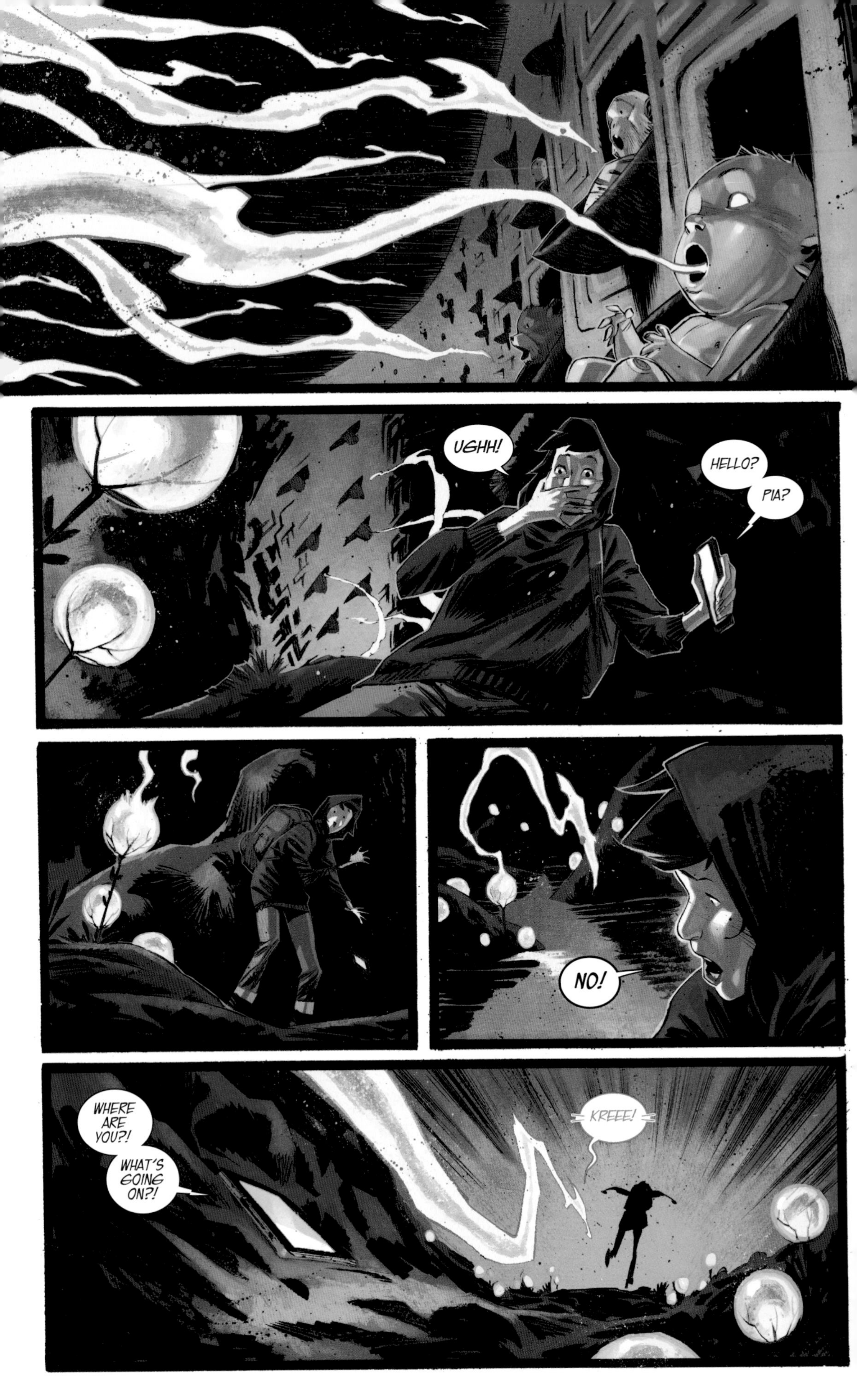
UGHH!
HELLO?
PIA?
NO!
WHERE ARE YOU?!
WHAT'S GOING ON?!
KREEE!

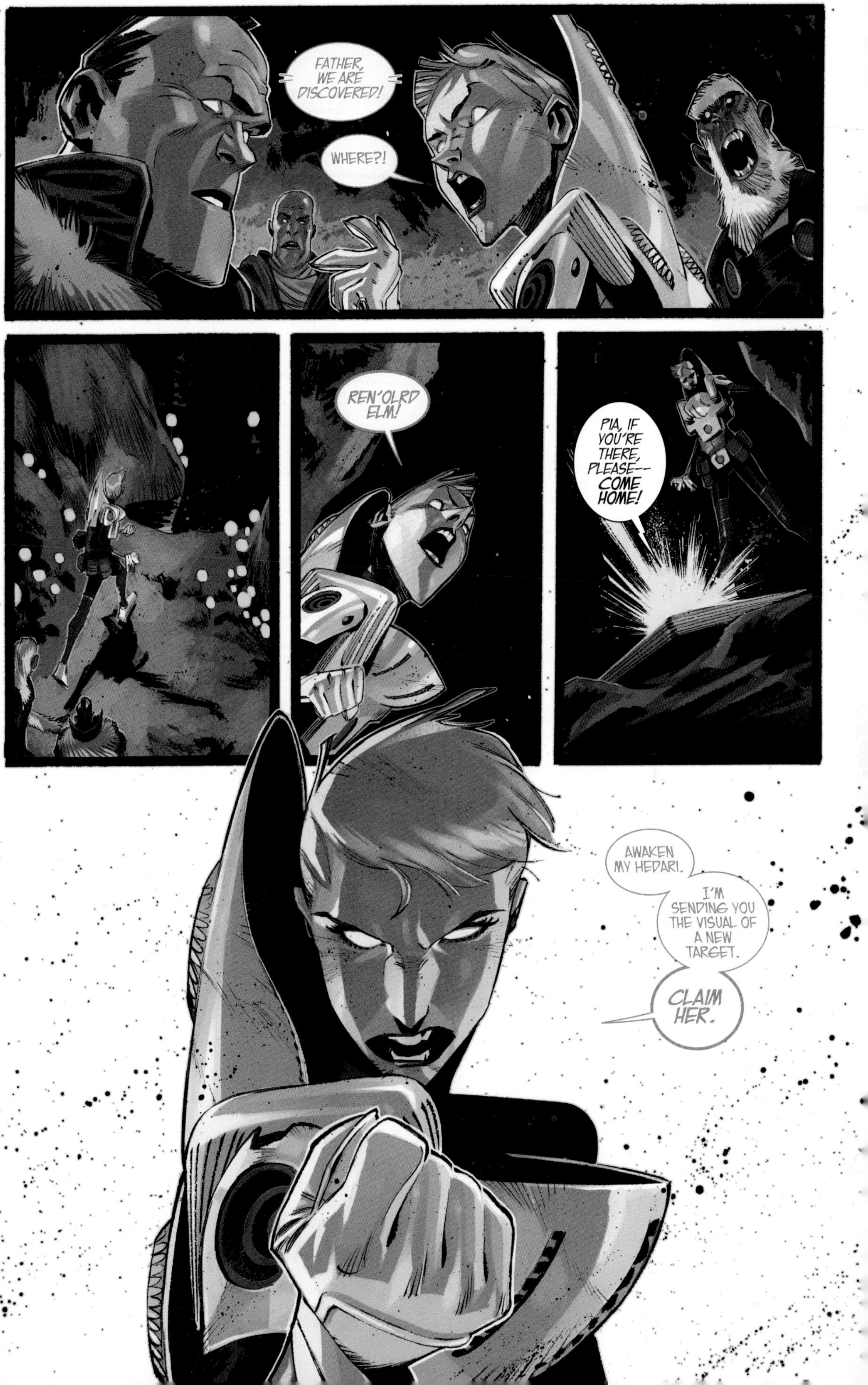
FATHER, WE ARE DISCOVERED!
WHERE?!
REN'OLRD ELM!
PIA, IF YOU'RE THERE, PLEASE-- COME HOME!
AWAKEN MY HEDARI.
I'M SENDING YOU THE VISUAL OF A NEW TARGET.
CLAIM HER.

# 27

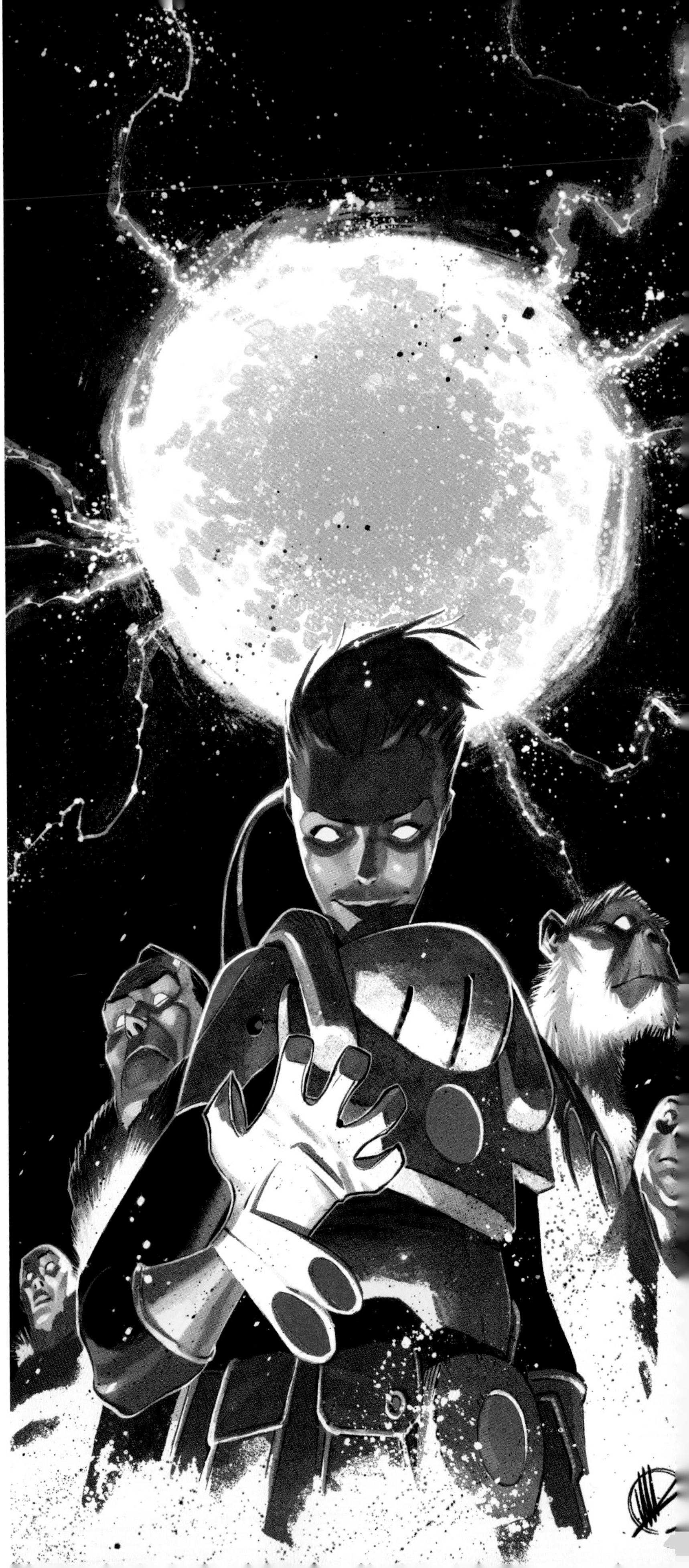

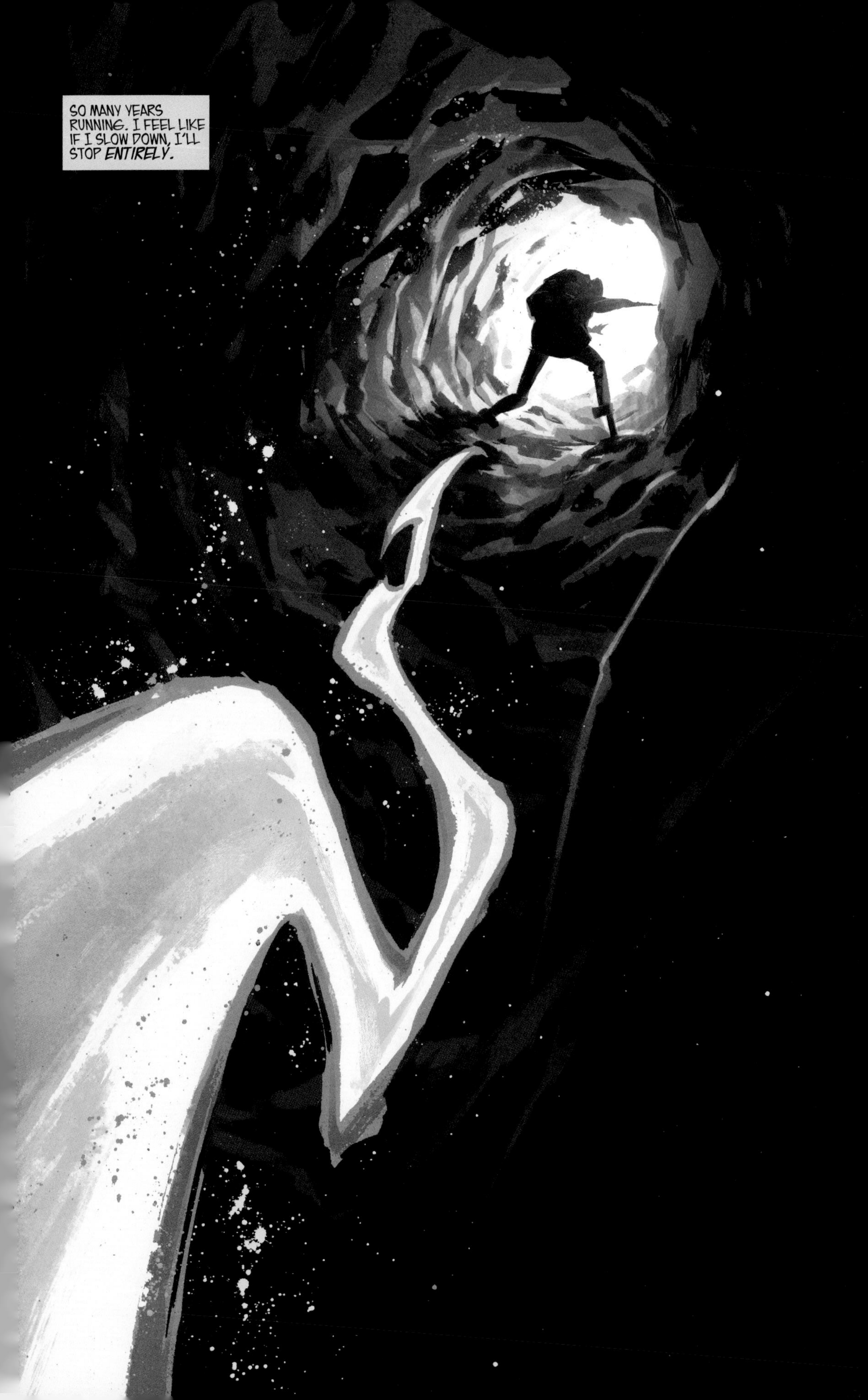
SO MANY YEARS RUNNING. I FEEL LIKE IF I SLOW DOWN, I'LL STOP ENTIRELY.

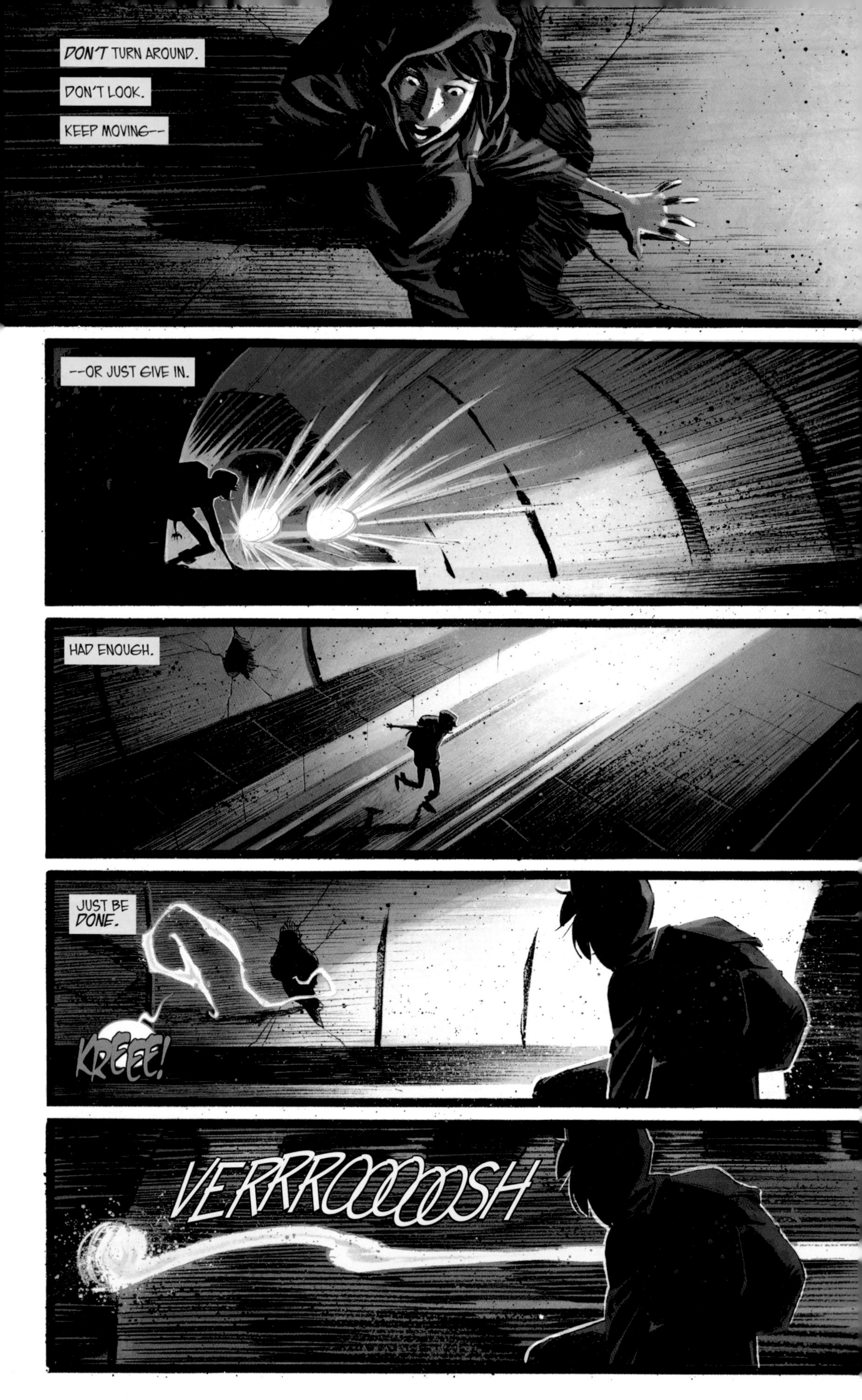
DON'T TURN AROUND.
DON'T LOOK.
KEEP MOVING--
--OR JUST GIVE IN.
HAD ENOUGH.
JUST BE DONE.
KREEE!
VERRRCOOOOOSH

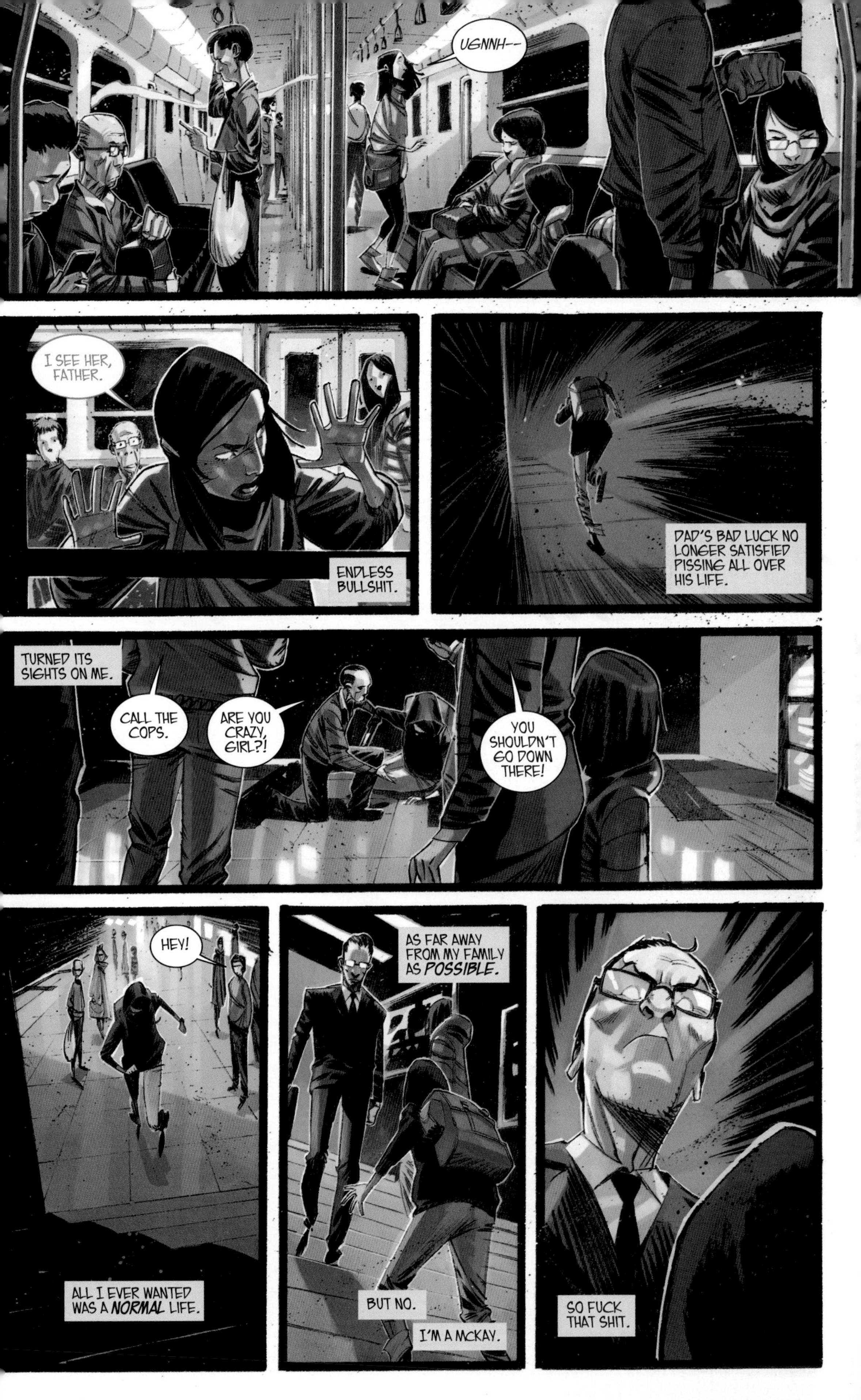
UGNNH--
I SEE HER, FATHER.
ENDLESS BULLSHIT.
DAD'S BAD LUCK NO LONGER SATISFIED PISSING ALL OVER HIS LIFE.
TURNED ITS SIGHTS ON ME.
CALL THE COPS.
ARE YOU CRAZY, GIRL?!
YOU SHOULDN'T GO DOWN THERE!
HEY!
ALL I EVER WANTED WAS A NORMAL LIFE.
AS FAR AWAY FROM MY FAMILY AS POSSIBLE.
BUT NO.
I'M A MCKAY.
SO FUCK THAT SHIT.

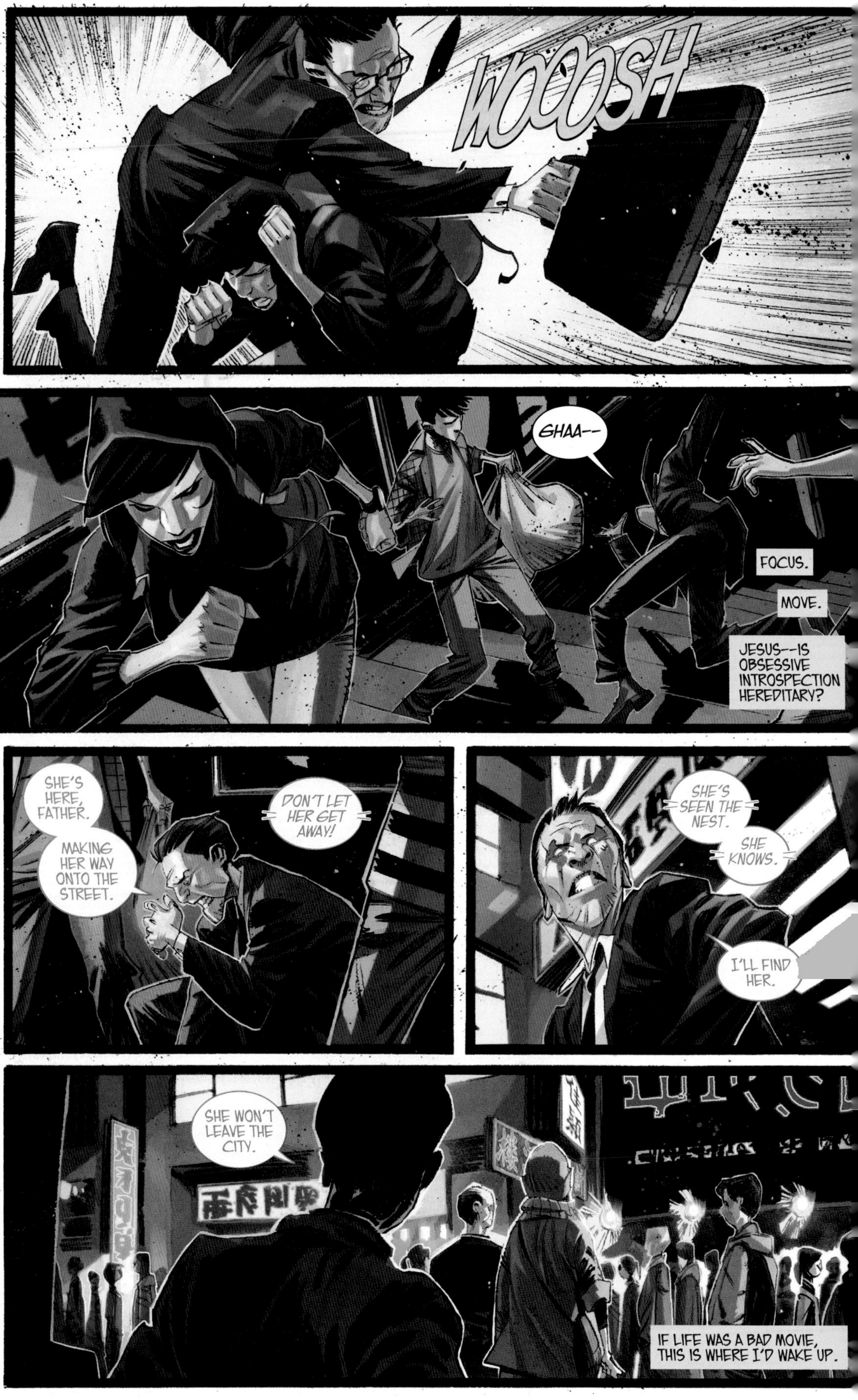
WOOOSH
GHAA--
FOCUS.
MOVE.
JESUS--IS OBSESSIVE INTROSPECTION HEREDITARY?
SHE'S HERE, FATHER.
MAKING HER WAY ONTO THE STREET.
DON'T LET HER GET AWAY!
SHE'S SEEN THE NEST.
SHE KNOWS.
I'LL FIND HER.
SHE WON'T LEAVE THE CITY.
IF LIFE WAS A BAD MOVIE, THIS IS WHERE I'D WAKE UP.

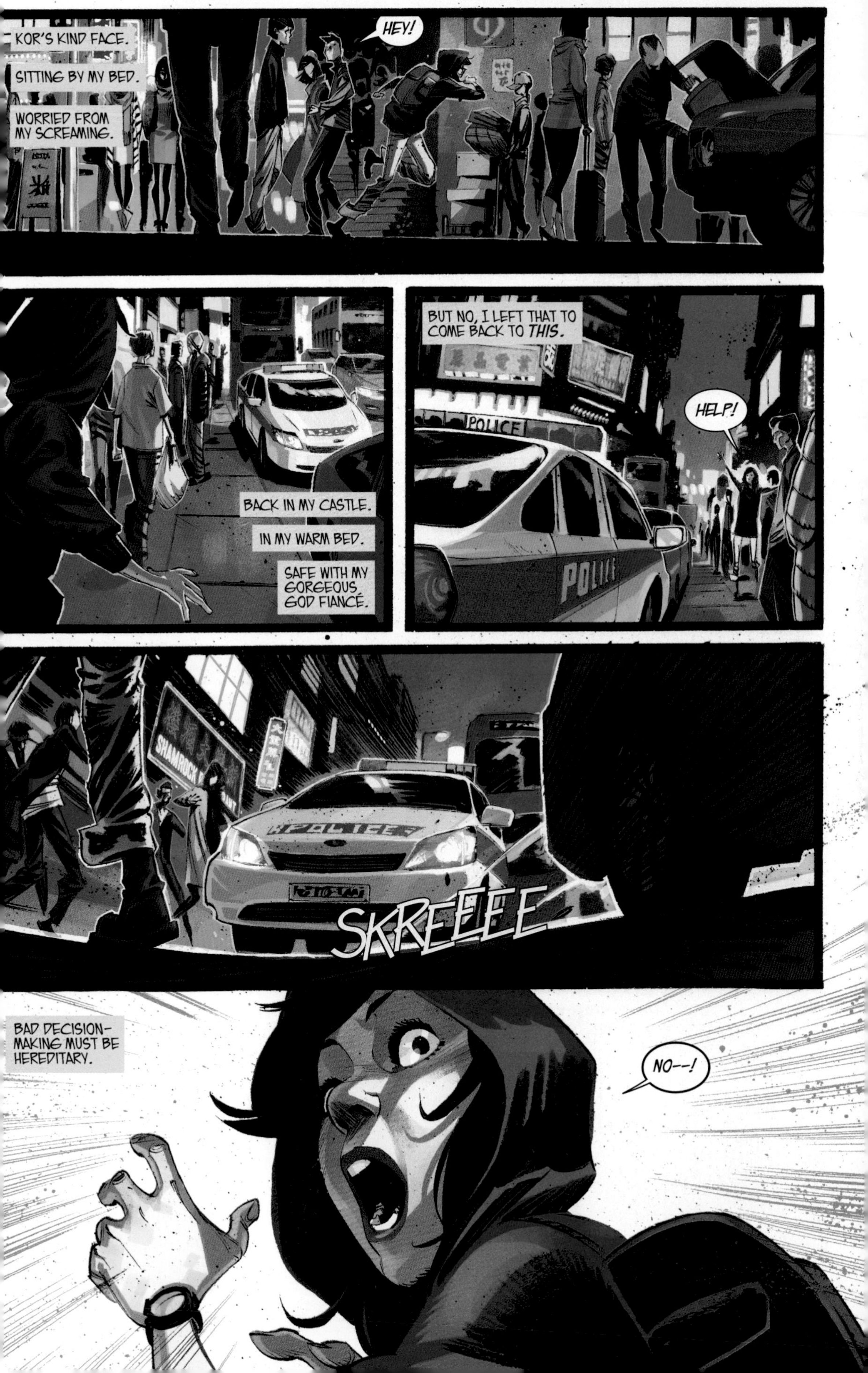
KOR'S KIND FACE.
SITTING BY MY BED.
WORRIED FROM MY SCREAMING.
HEY!
BACK IN MY CASTLE.
IN MY WARM BED.
SAFE WITH MY GORGEOUS GOD FIANCÉ.
BUT NO, I LEFT THAT TO COME BACK TO THIS.
POLICE
HELP!
POLICE
SHAMROCK
POLICE
SKREEEE
BAD DECISION-MAKING MUST BE HEREDITARY.
NO--!

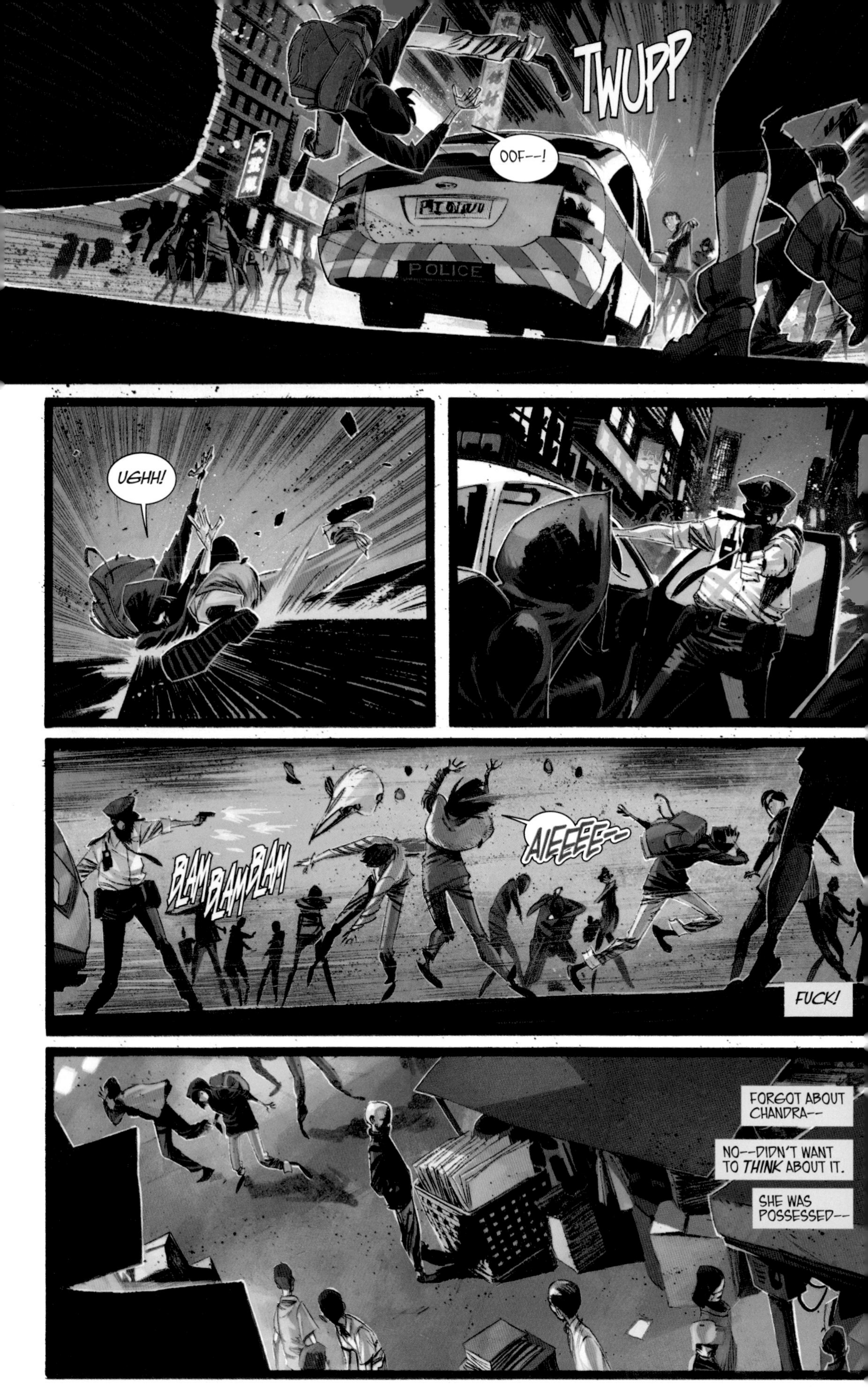
TWUPP
OOF--!
POLICE
UGHH!
BLAM BLAM BLAM
AIEEEEE--
FUCK!
FORGOT ABOUT CHANDRA--
NO--DIDN'T WANT TO *THINK* ABOUT IT.
SHE WAS POSSESSED--

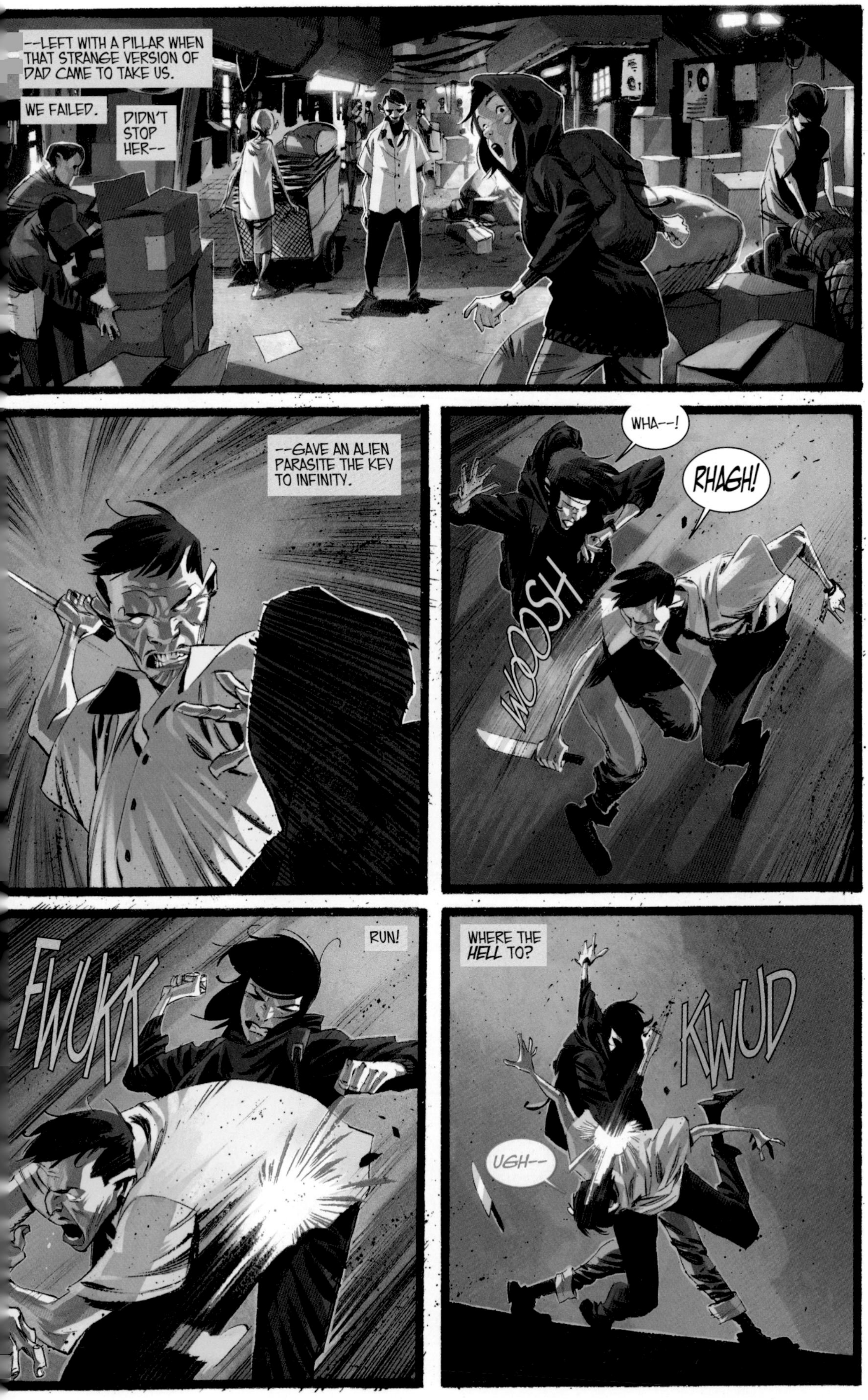
--LEFT WITH A PILLAR WHEN THAT STRANGE VERSION OF DAD CAME TO TAKE US.
WE FAILED.
DIDN'T STOP HER--
--GAVE AN ALIEN PARASITE THE KEY TO INFINITY.
WHA--!
RHAGH!
WOOSH
FWUKK
RUN!
WHERE THE HELL TO?
KWUD
UGH--

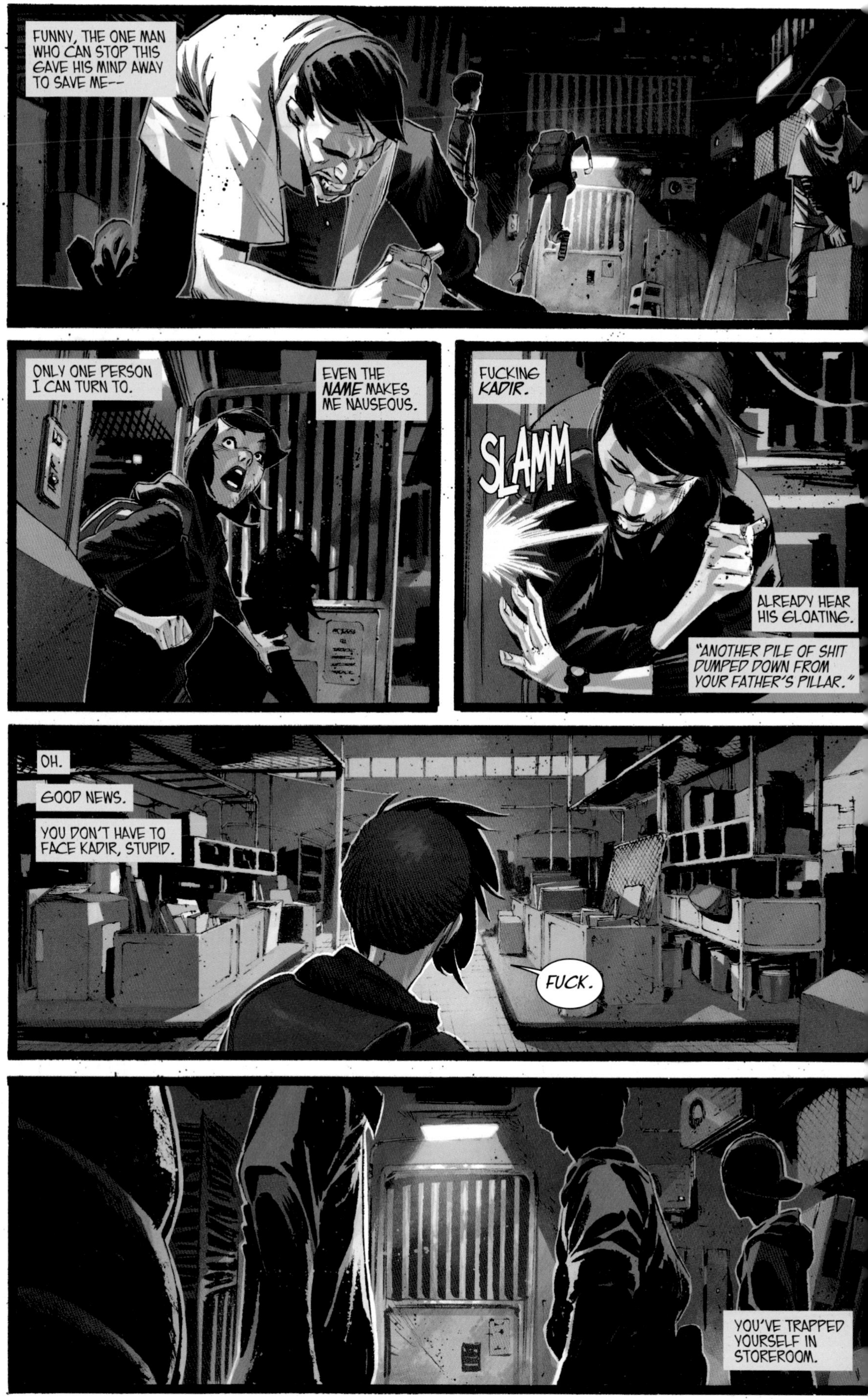
FUNNY, THE ONE MAN WHO CAN STOP THIS GAVE HIS MIND AWAY TO SAVE ME--
ONLY ONE PERSON I CAN TURN TO.
EVEN THE NAME MAKES ME NAUSEOUS.
FUCKING KADIR.
SLAMM
ALREADY HEAR HIS GLOATING.
"ANOTHER PILE OF SHIT DUMPED DOWN FROM YOUR FATHER'S PILLAR."
OH.
GOOD NEWS.
YOU DON'T HAVE TO FACE KADIR, STUPID.
FUCK.
YOU'VE TRAPPED YOURSELF IN STOREROOM.

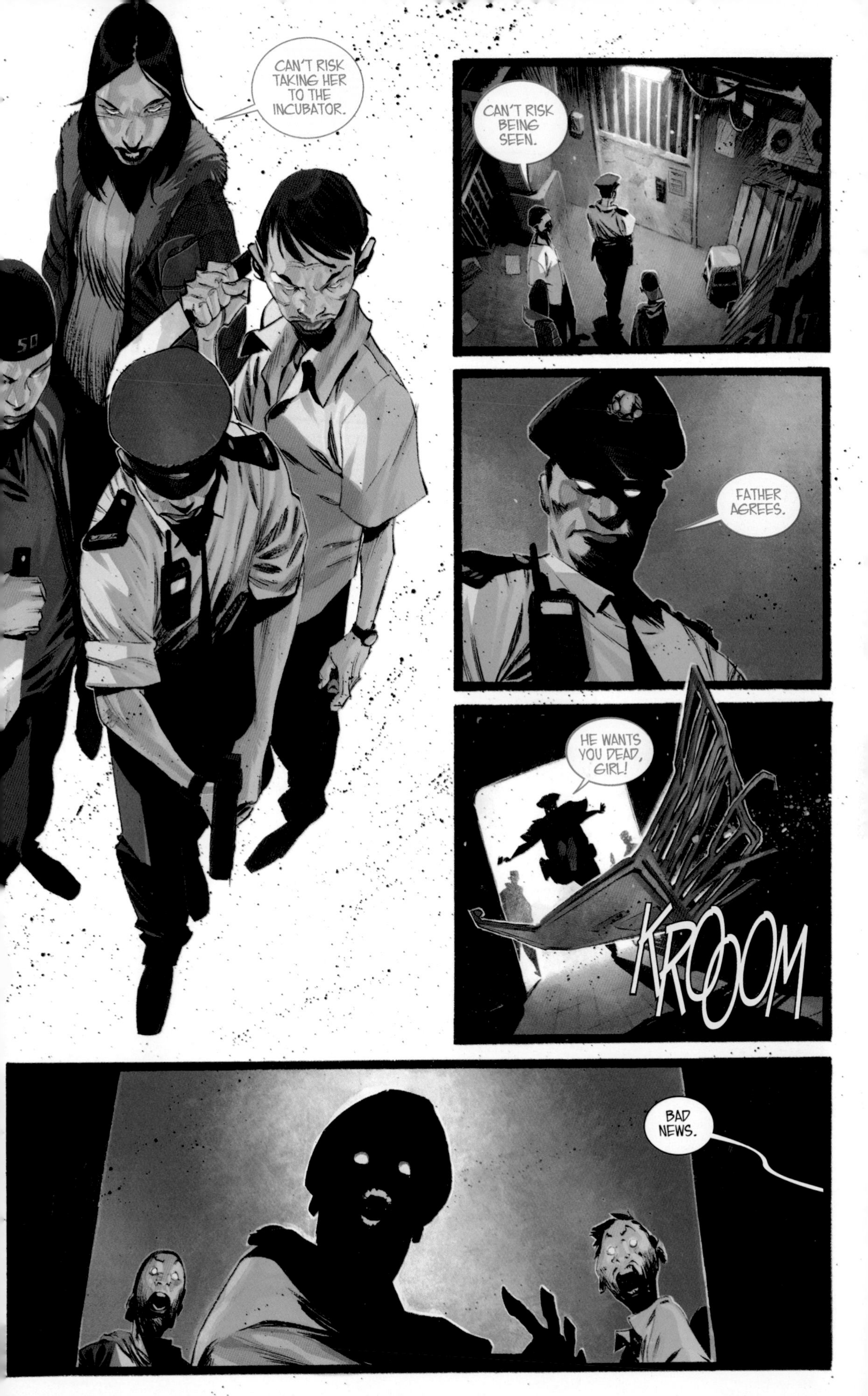
CAN'T RISK TAKING HER TO THE INCUBATOR.
CAN'T RISK BEING SEEN.
FATHER AGREES.
HE WANTS YOU DEAD, GIRL!
KROOOM
BAD NEWS.

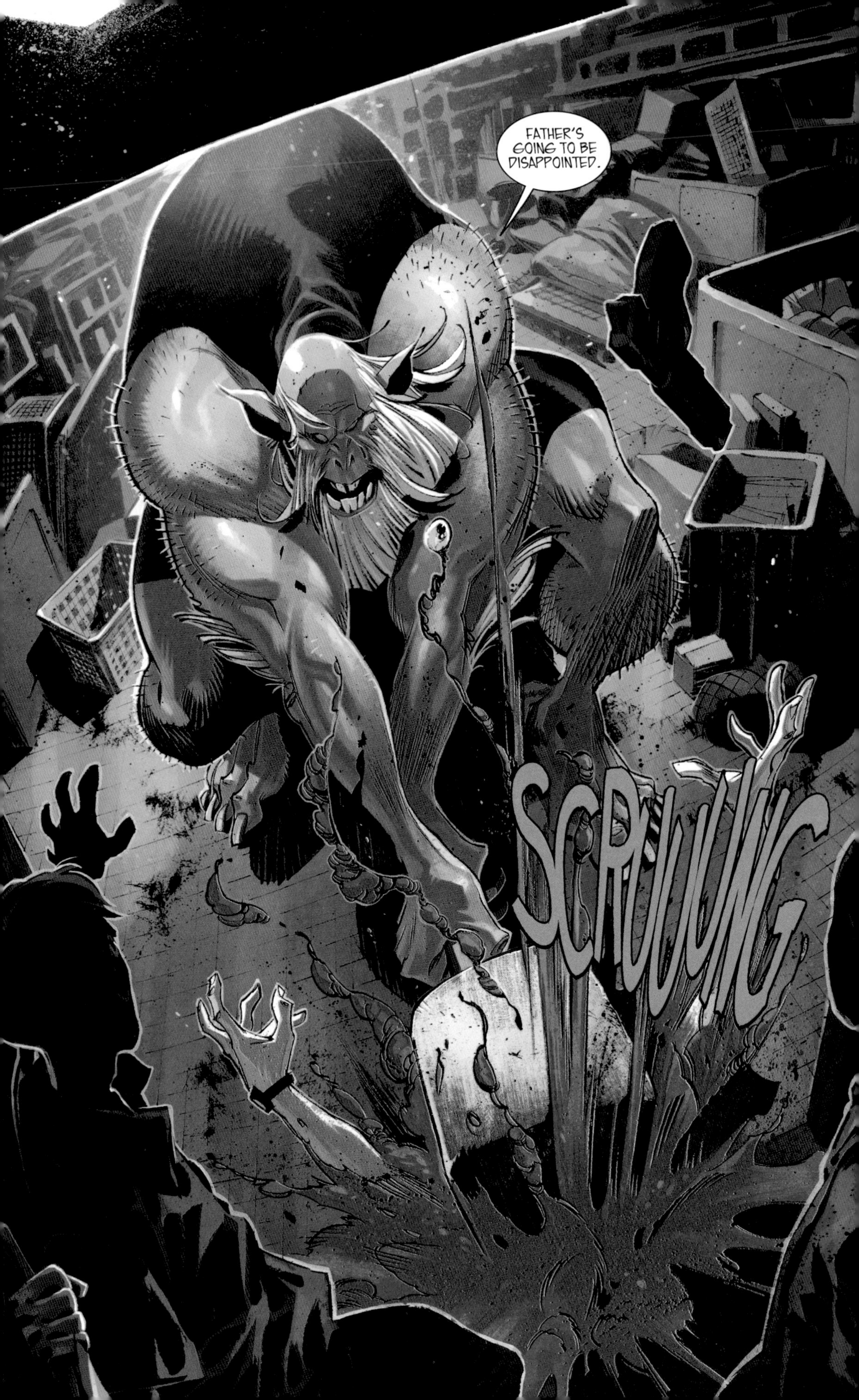
FATHER'S GOING TO BE DISAPPOINTED.
SCRUUNG

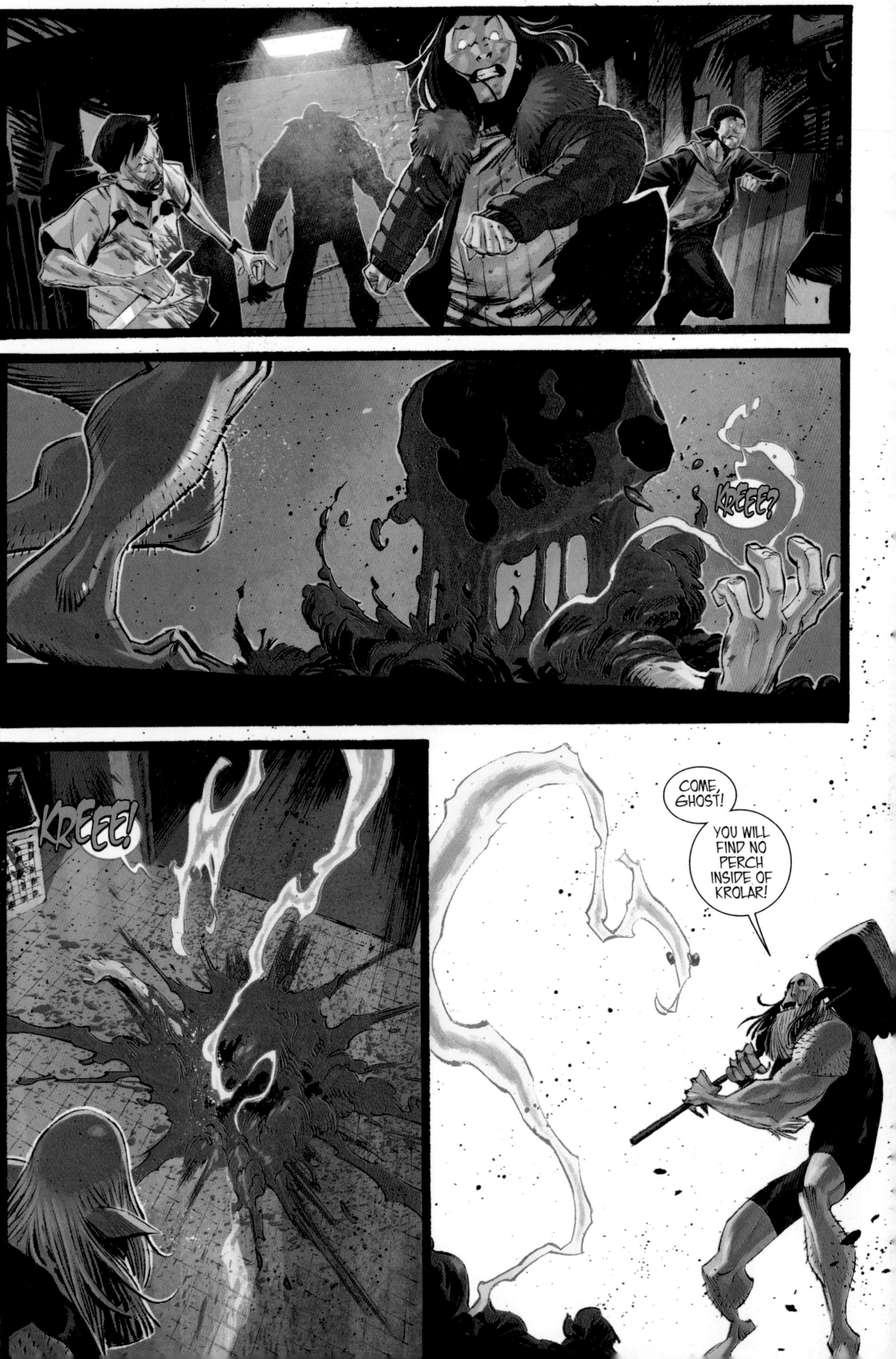
KREEE?
KREEE!
COME, GHOST!
YOU WILL FIND NO PERCH INSIDE OF KROLAR!

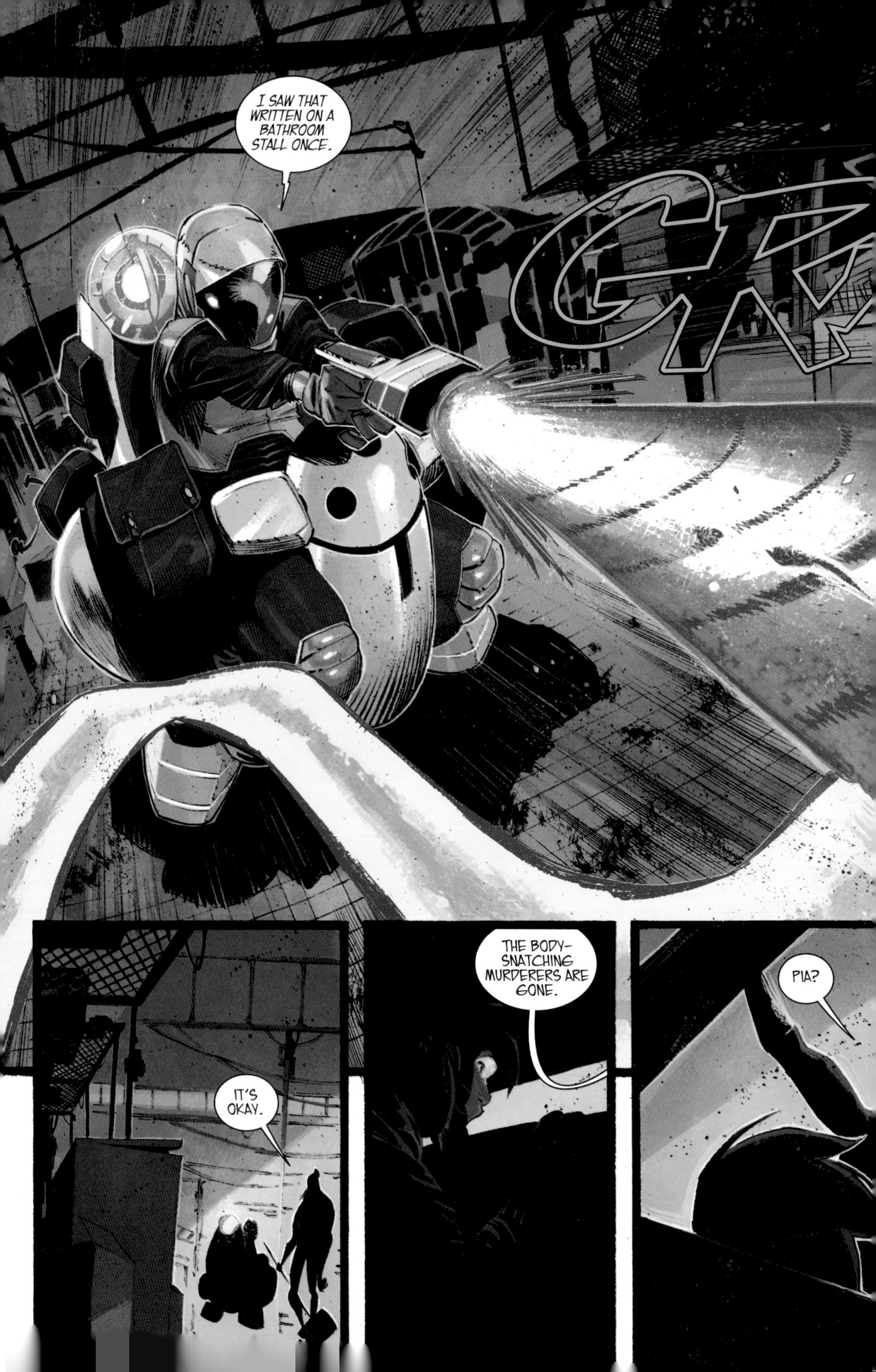
I SAW THAT WRITTEN ON A BATHROOM STALL ONCE.
CR
IT'S OKAY.
THE BODY-SNATCHING MURDERERS ARE GONE.
PIA?

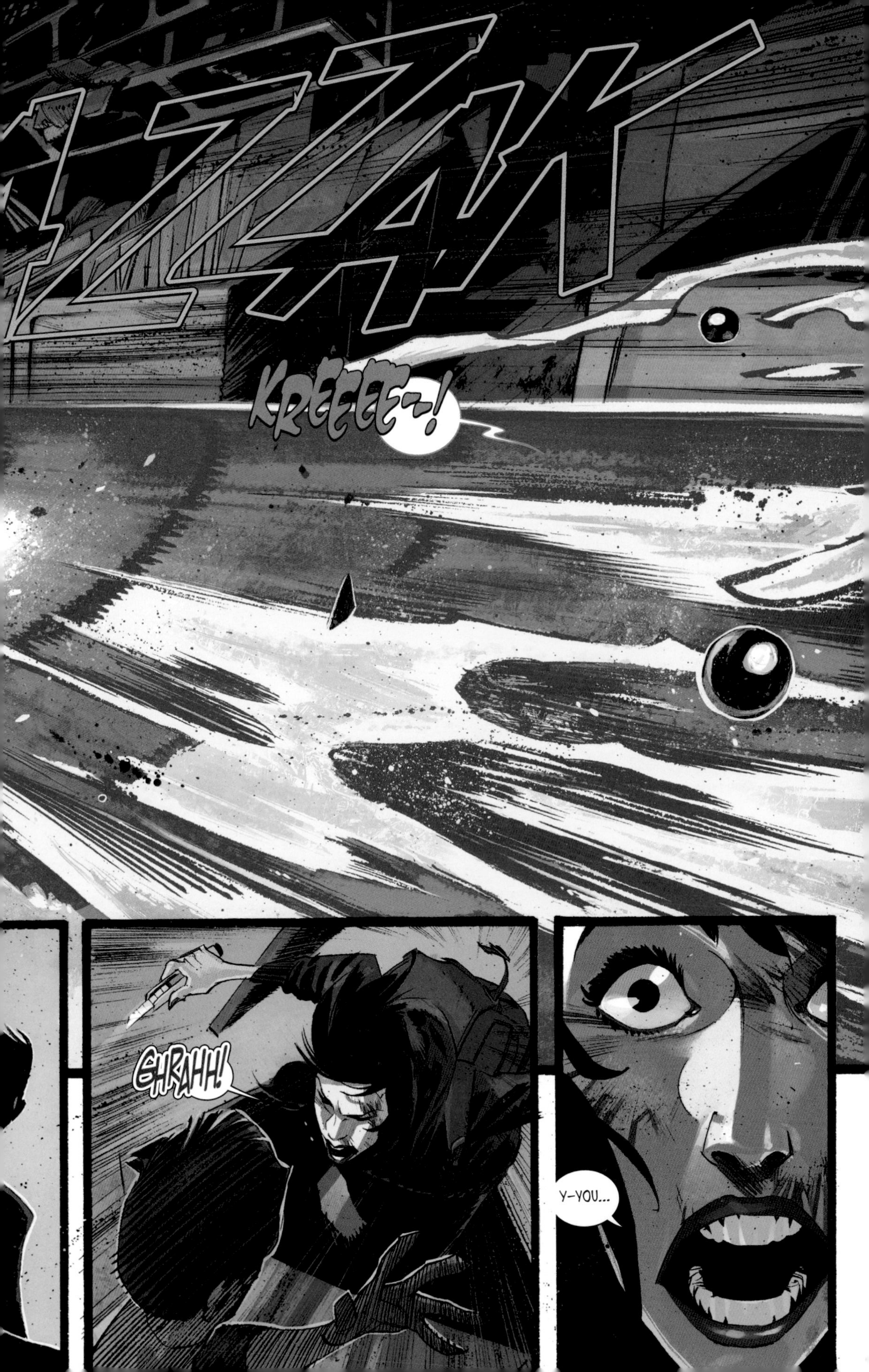
ZZAK
KREEEE--!
GHRAHH!
Y-YOU...

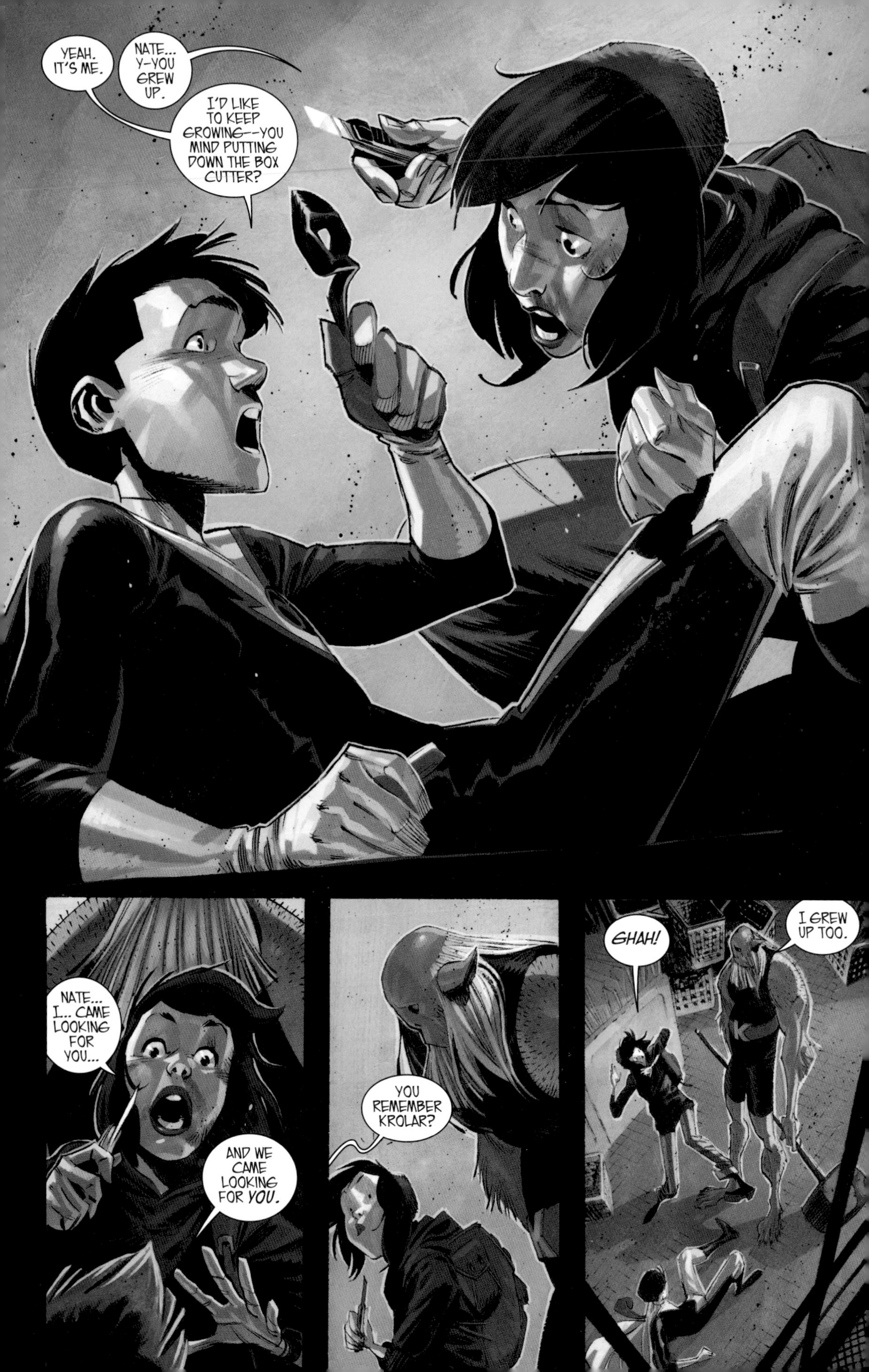
NATE... Y-YOU GREW UP.
YEAH. IT'S ME.
I'D LIKE TO KEEP GROWING--YOU MIND PUTTING DOWN THE BOX CUTTER?
NATE... I... CAME LOOKING FOR YOU...
AND WE CAME LOOKING FOR YOU.
YOU REMEMBER KROLAR?
GHAH!
I GREW UP TOO.

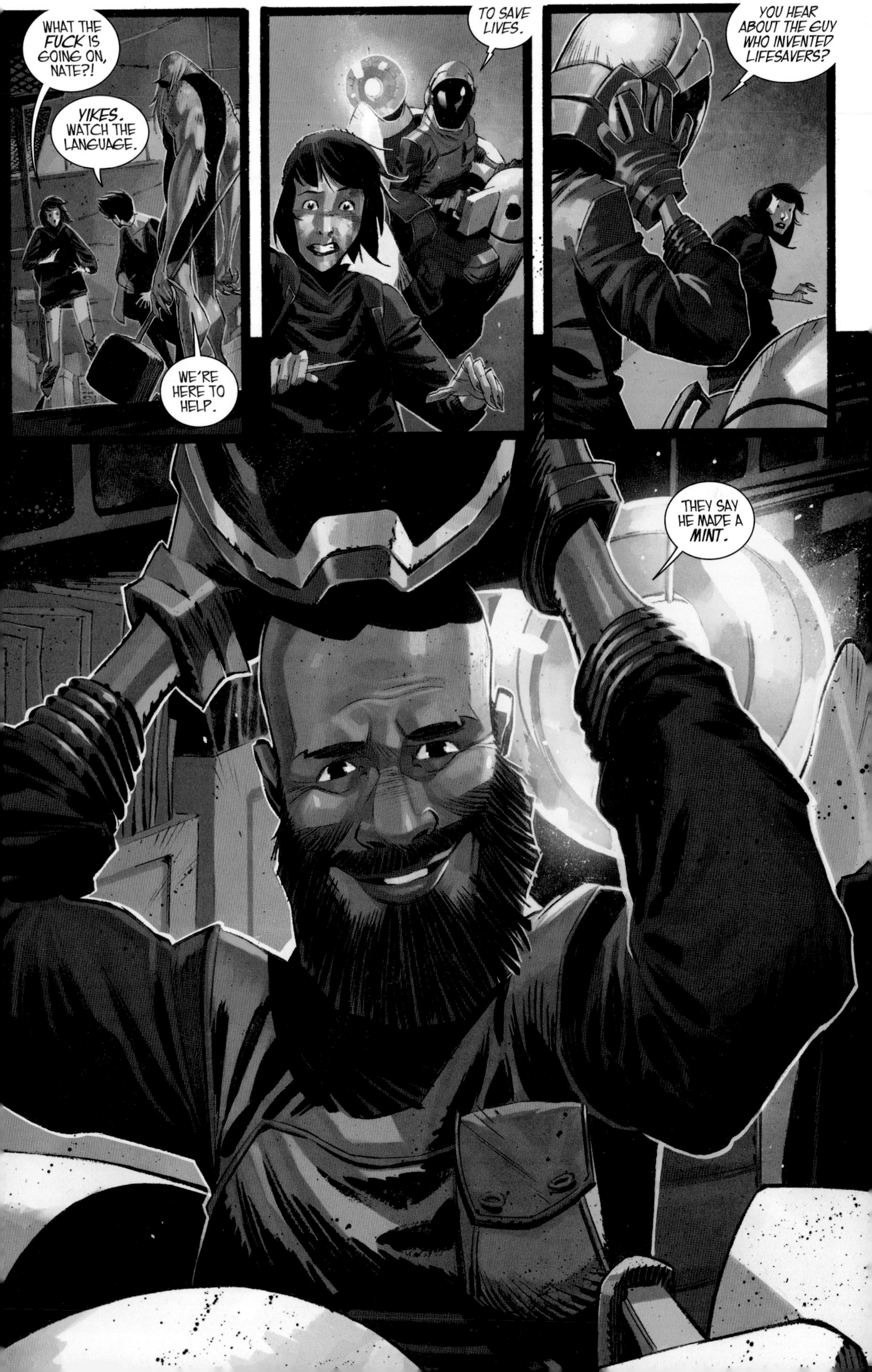
WHAT THE FUCK IS GOING ON, NATE?!
YIKES. WATCH THE LANGUAGE.
WE'RE HERE TO HELP.
TO SAVE LIVES.
YOU HEAR ABOUT THE GUY WHO INVENTED LIFESAVERS?
THEY SAY HE MADE A MINT.

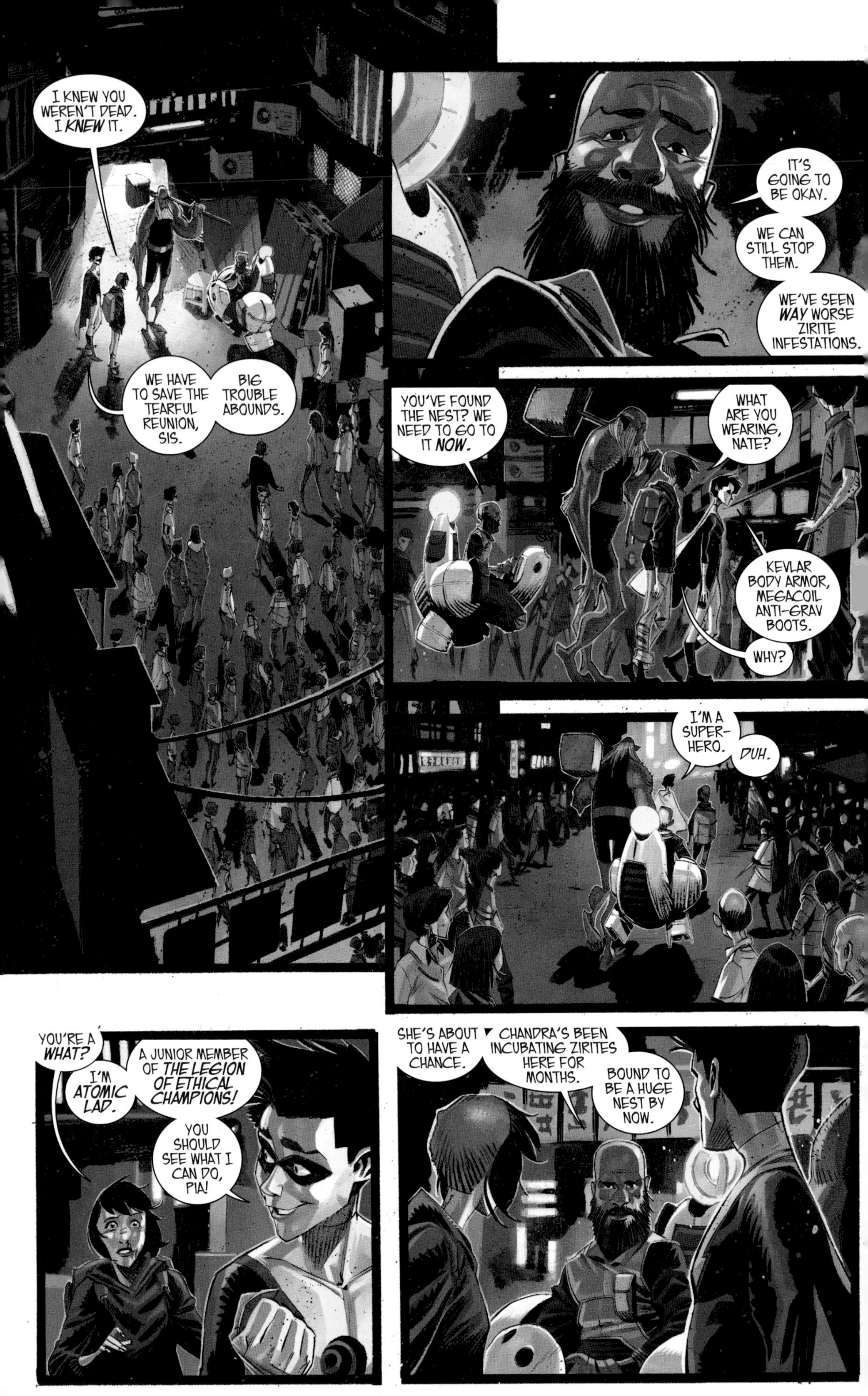
I KNEW YOU WEREN'T DEAD. I KNEW IT.
IT'S GOING TO BE OKAY.
WE CAN STILL STOP THEM.
WE'VE SEEN WAY WORSE ZIRITE INFESTATIONS.
WE HAVE TO SAVE THE TEARFUL REUNION, SIS.
BIG TROUBLE ABOUNDS.
YOU'VE FOUND THE NEST? WE NEED TO GO TO IT NOW.
WHAT ARE YOU WEARING, NATE?
KEVLAR BODY ARMOR, MEGACOIL ANTI-GRAV BOOTS.
WHY?
I'M A SUPER-HERO.
DUH.
YOU'RE A WHAT?
I'M ATOMIC LAD.
A JUNIOR MEMBER OF THE LEGION OF ETHICAL CHAMPIONS!
YOU SHOULD SEE WHAT I CAN DO, PIA!
SHE'S ABOUT TO HAVE A CHANCE.
CHANDRA'S BEEN INCUBATING ZIRITES HERE FOR MONTHS.
BOUND TO BE A HUGE NEST BY NOW.

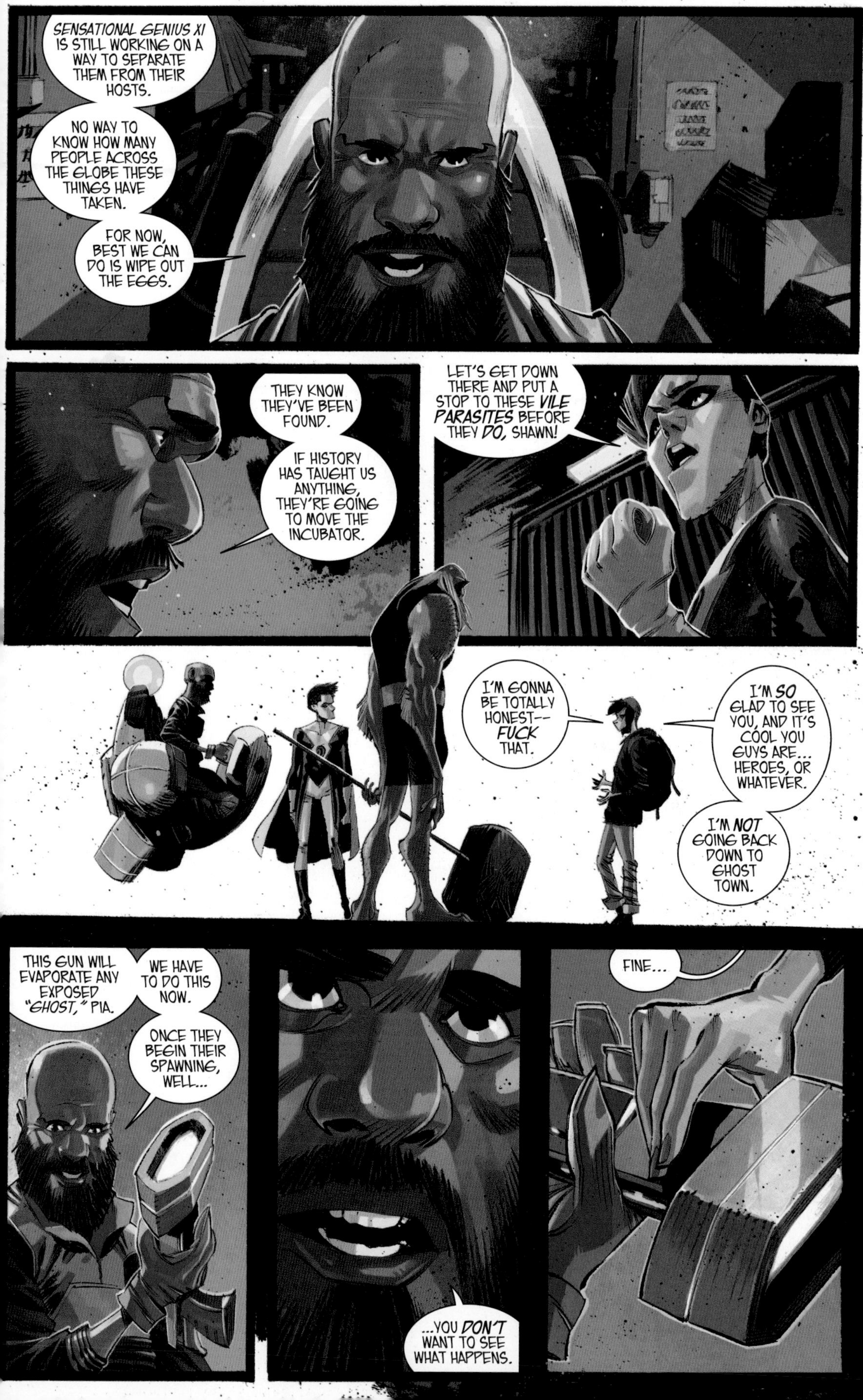
SENSATIONAL GENIUS XI IS STILL WORKING ON A WAY TO SEPARATE THEM FROM THEIR HOSTS.
NO WAY TO KNOW HOW MANY PEOPLE ACROSS THE GLOBE THESE THINGS HAVE TAKEN.
FOR NOW, BEST WE CAN DO IS WIPE OUT THE EGGS.
THEY KNOW THEY'VE BEEN FOUND.
IF HISTORY HAS TAUGHT US ANYTHING, THEY'RE GOING TO MOVE THE INCUBATOR.
LET'S GET DOWN THERE AND PUT A STOP TO THESE VILE PARASITES BEFORE THEY DO, SHAWN!
I'M SO GLAD TO SEE YOU, AND IT'S COOL YOU GUYS ARE... HEROES, OR WHATEVER.
I'M NOT GOING BACK DOWN TO GHOST TOWN.
I'M GONNA BE TOTALLY HONEST-- FUCK THAT.
THIS GUN WILL EVAPORATE ANY EXPOSED "GHOST," PIA.
WE HAVE TO DO THIS NOW.
ONCE THEY BEGIN THEIR SPAWNING, WELL...
...YOU DON'T WANT TO SEE WHAT HAPPENS.
FINE...

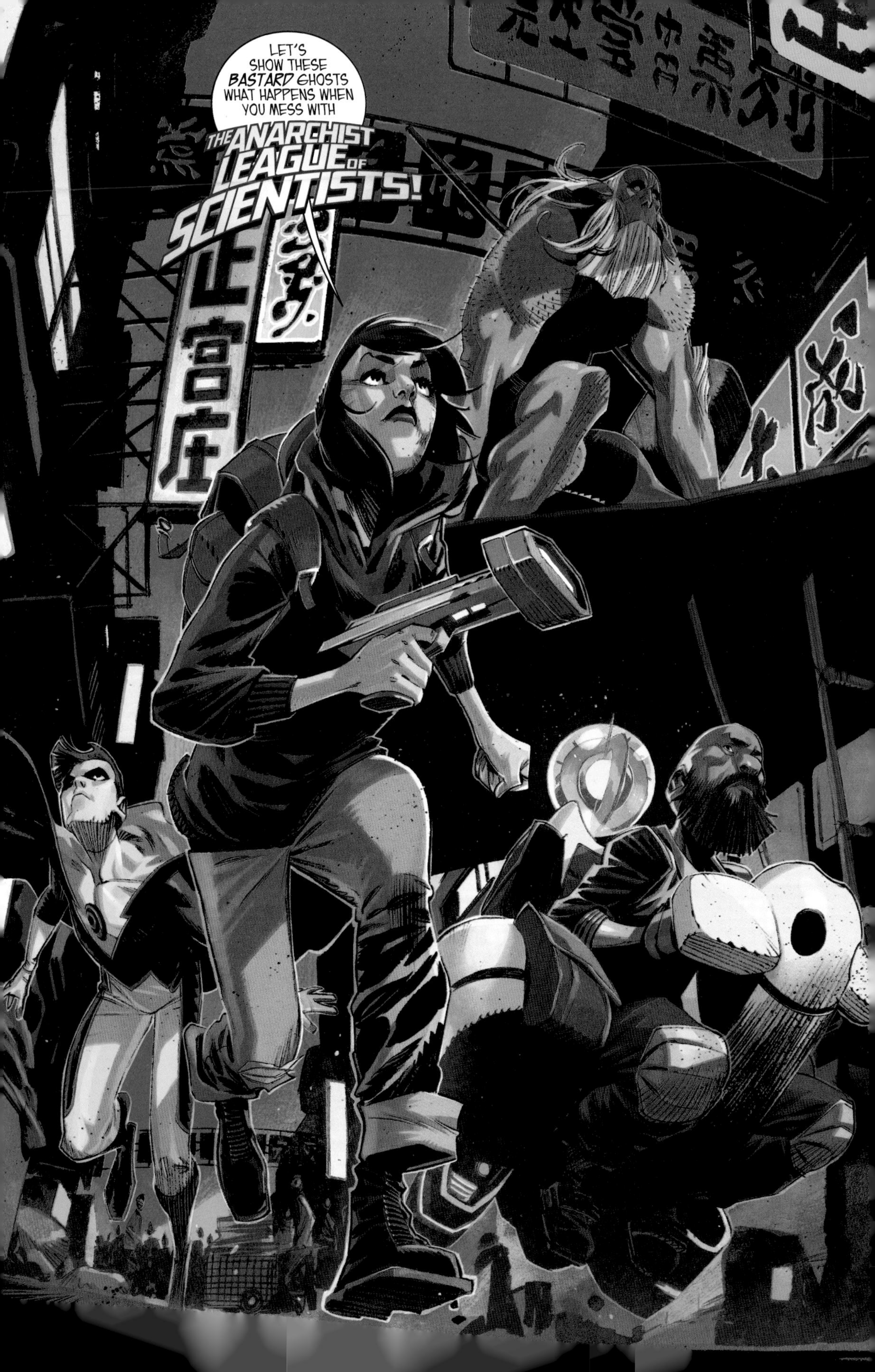
LET'S SHOW THESE BASTARD GHOSTS WHAT HAPPENS WHEN YOU MESS WITH THE ANARCHIST LEAGUE OF SCIENTISTS!

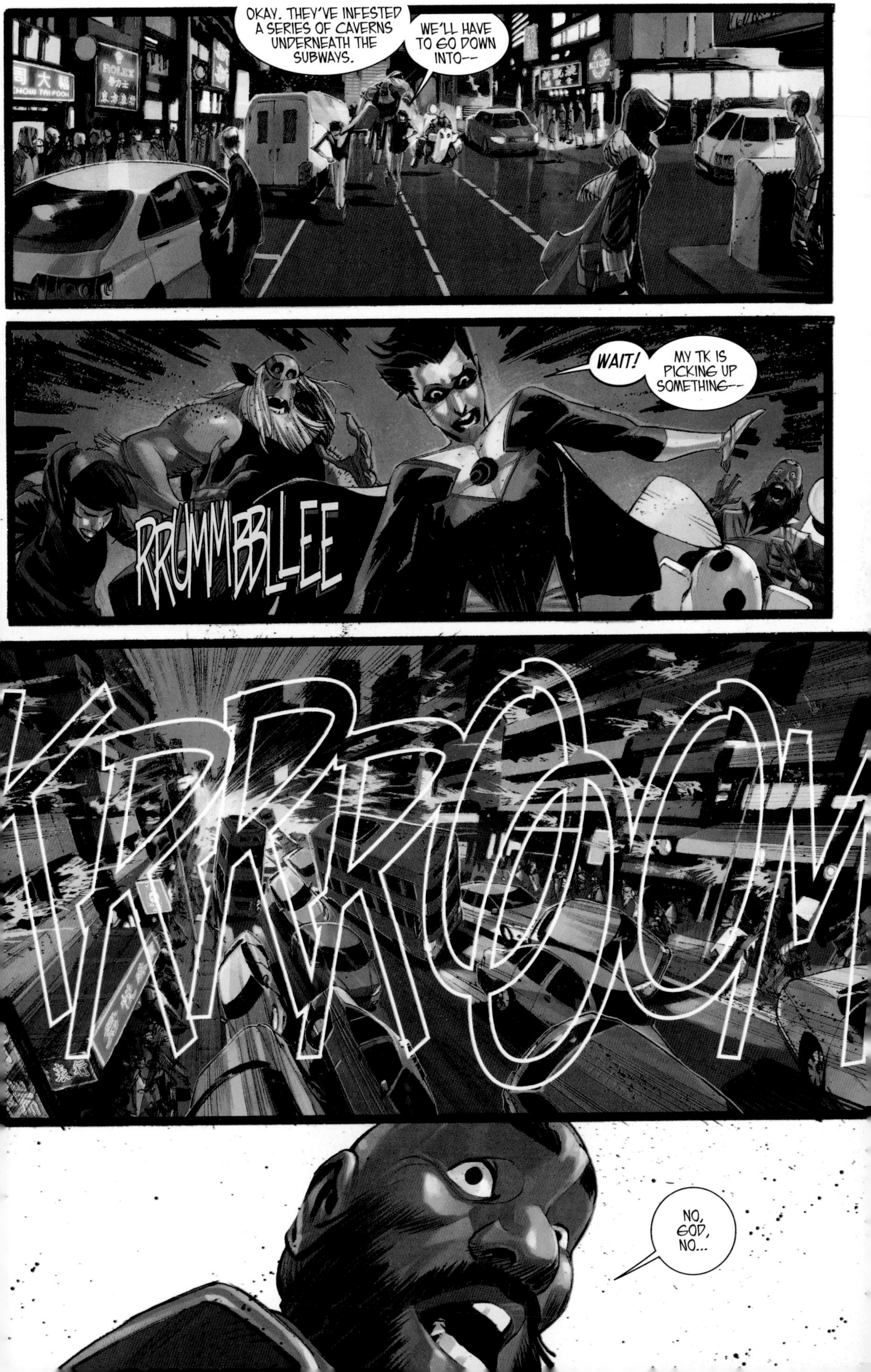

CHOW TAI FOOK
ROLEX
OKAY. THEY'VE INFESTED A SERIES OF CAVERNS UNDERNEATH THE SUBWAYS.
WE'LL HAVE TO GO DOWN INTO--
WAIT!
MY TK IS PICKING UP SOMETHING--
RRUMMBBLLEE
KRRROOOM
NO, GOD, NO...

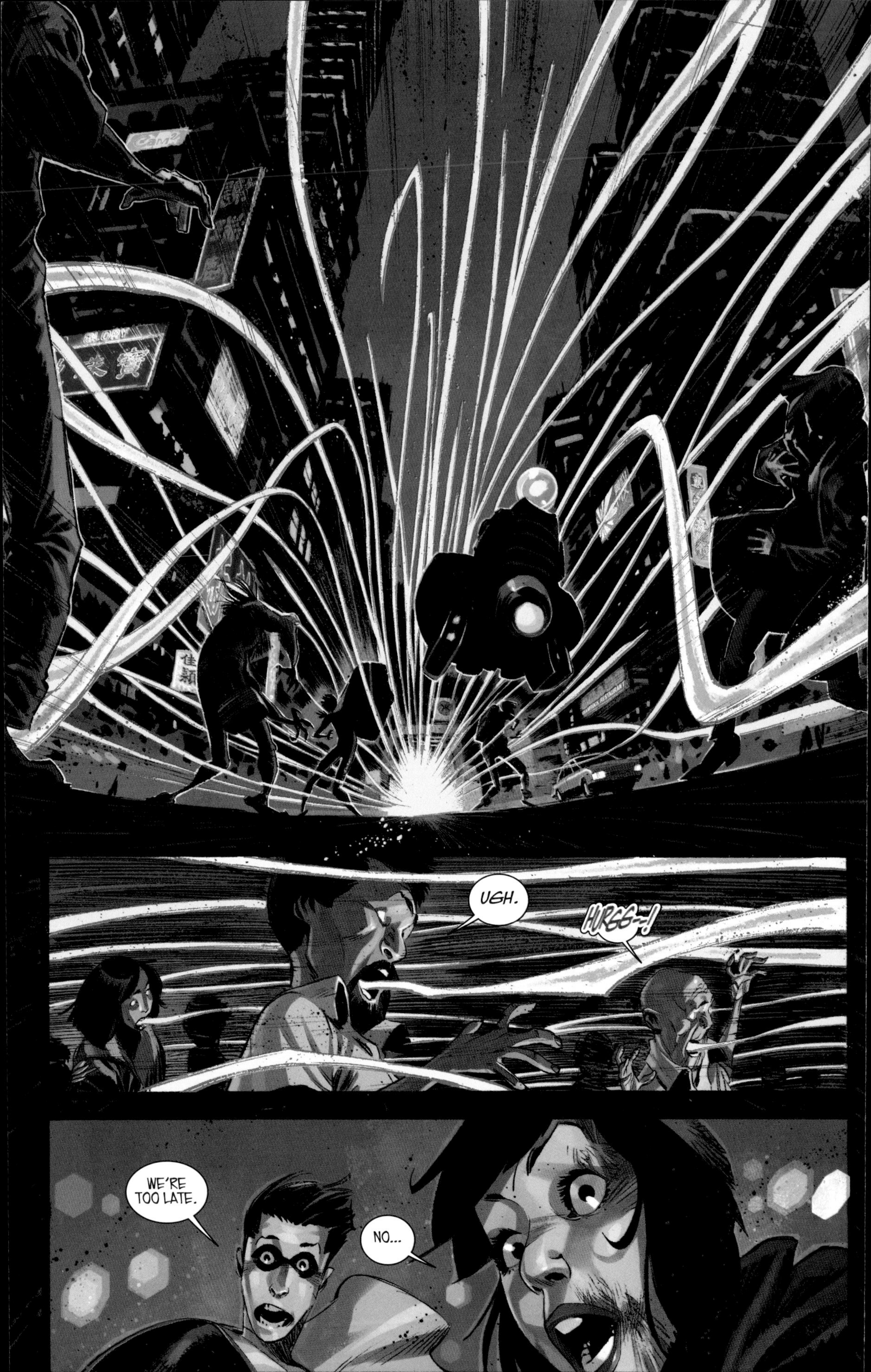
UGH.
HURGG--!
WE'RE TOO LATE.
NO...

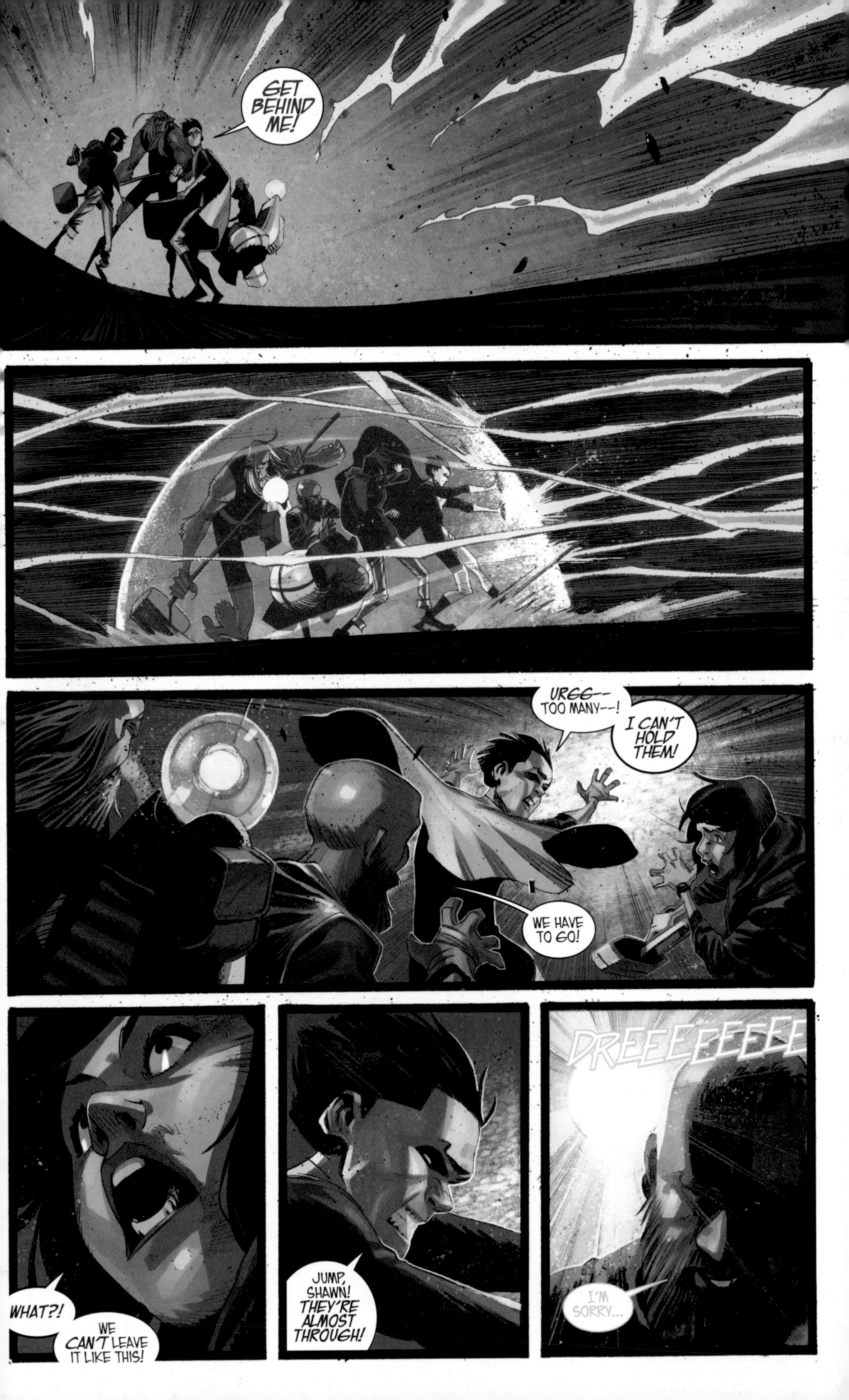
GET BEHIND ME!
URGG-- TOO MANY--!
I CAN'T HOLD THEM!
WE HAVE TO GO!
WHAT?!
WE CAN'T LEAVE IT LIKE THIS!
JUMP, SHAWN! THEY'RE ALMOST THROUGH!
DREEEEEEEE
I'M SORRY...

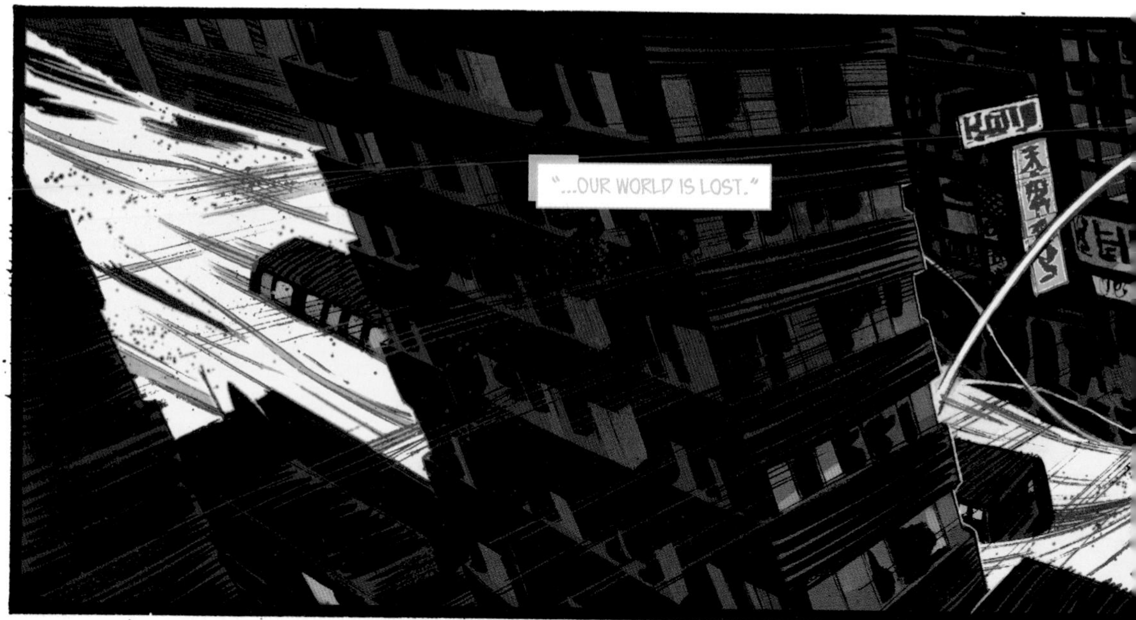
"...OUR WORLD IS LOST."

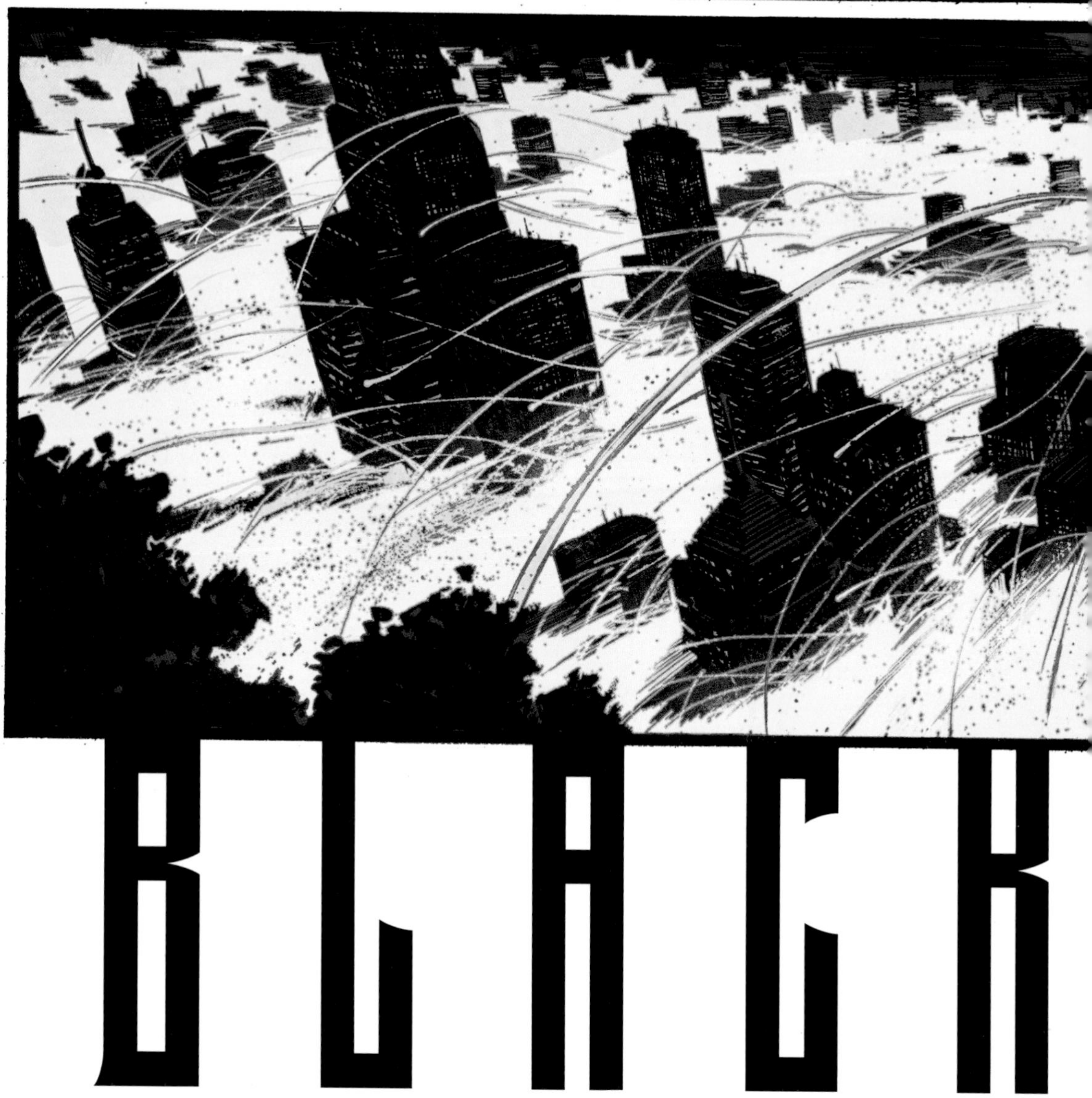

# BLACK

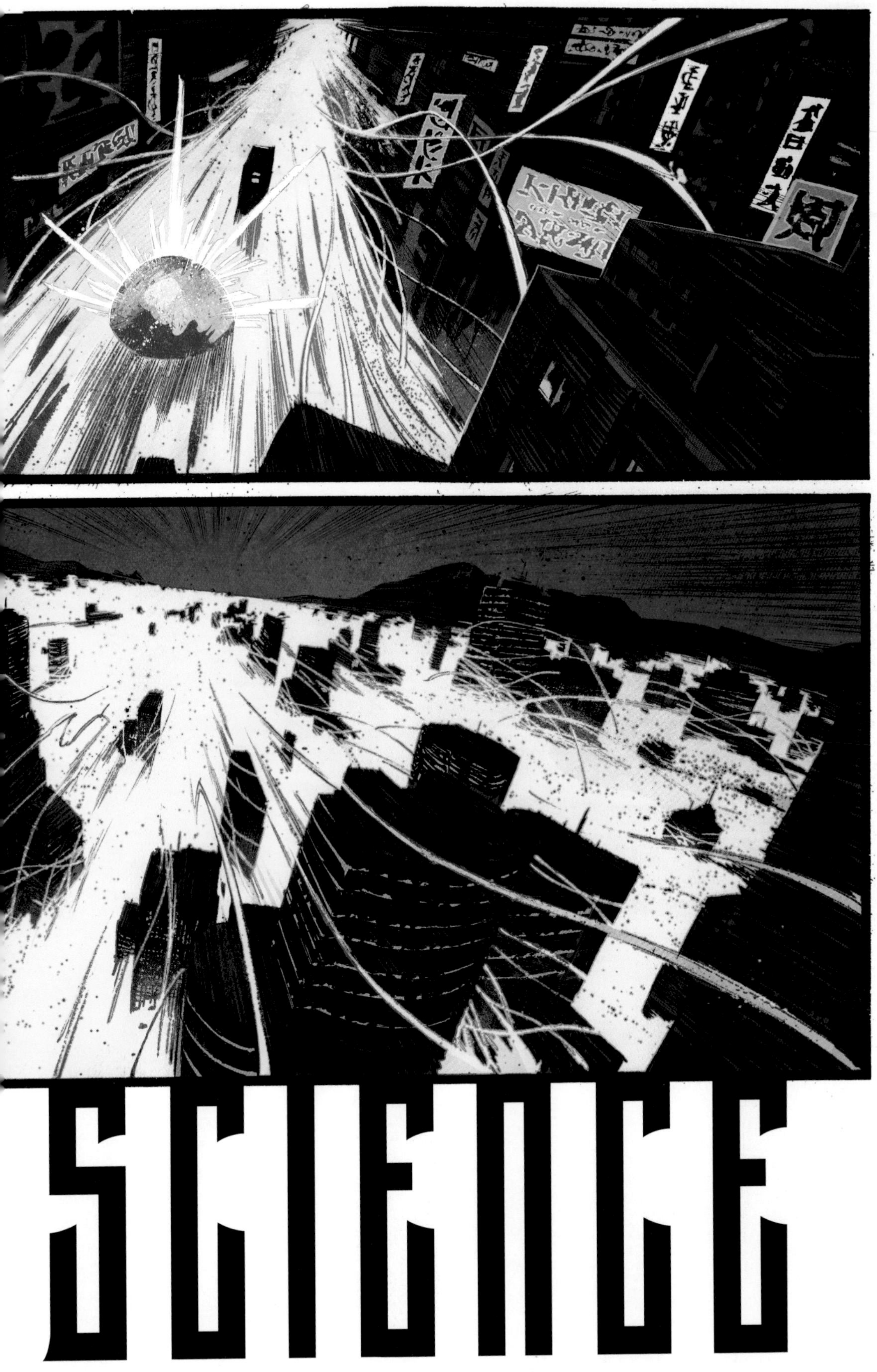

# SCIENCE

# 28

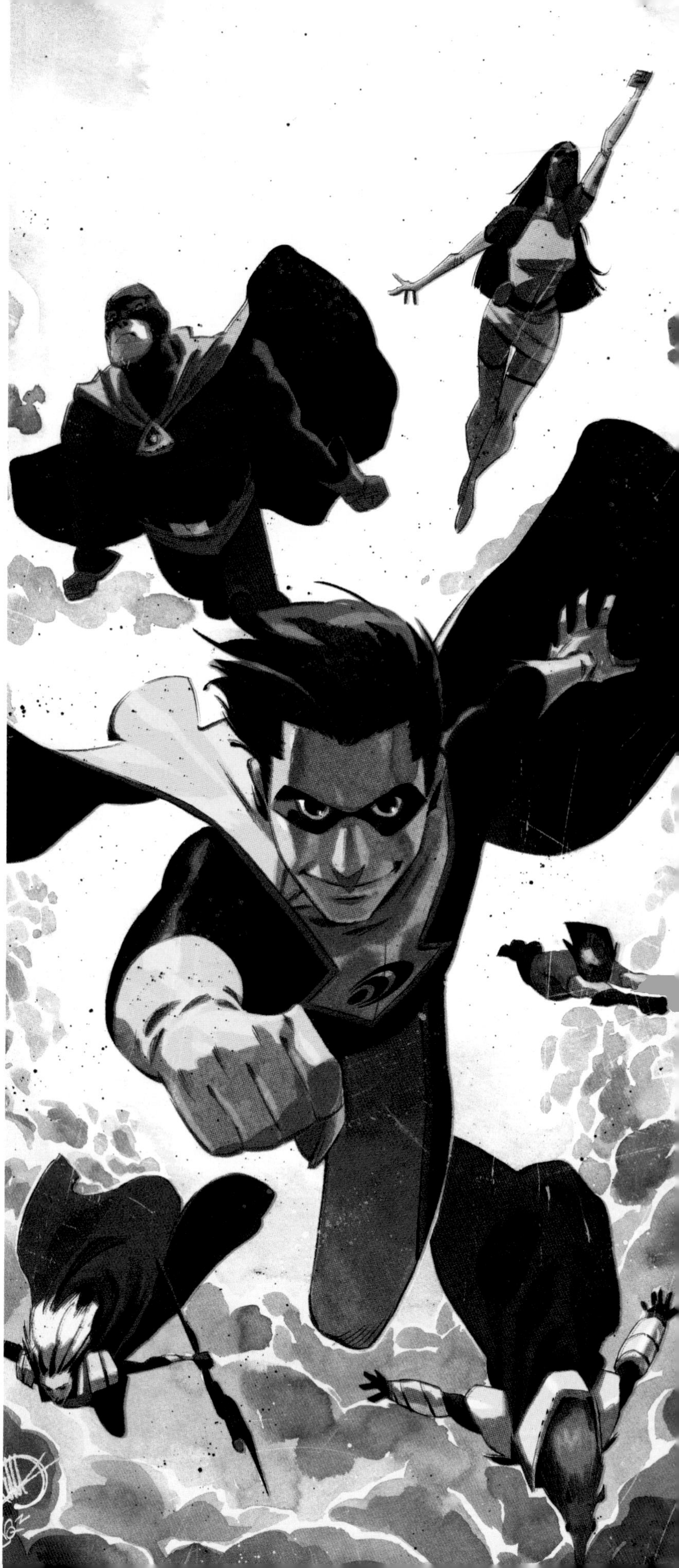

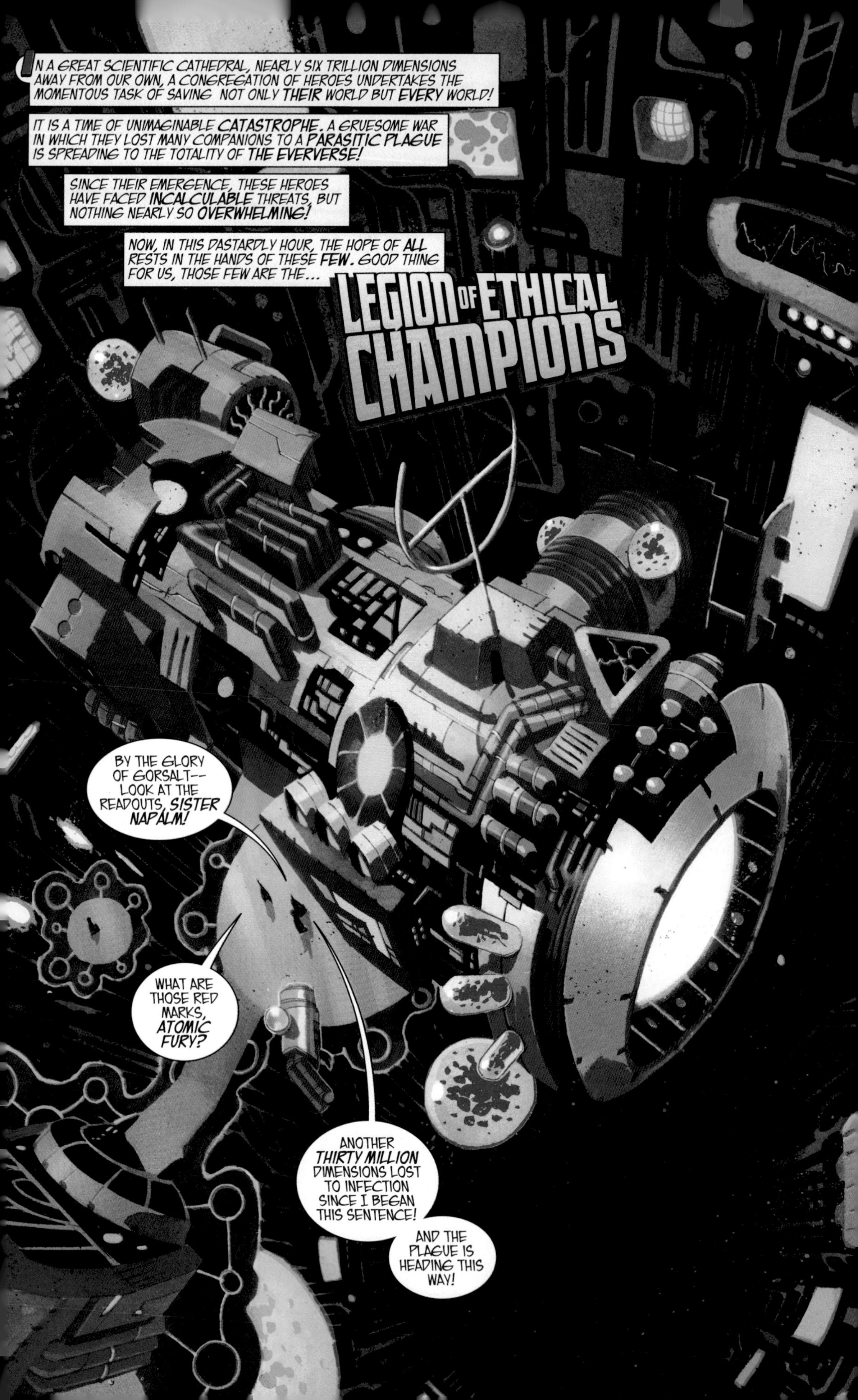
IN A GREAT SCIENTIFIC CATHEDRAL, NEARLY SIX TRILLION DIMENSIONS AWAY FROM OUR OWN, A CONGREGATION OF HEROES UNDERTAKES THE MOMENTOUS TASK OF SAVING NOT ONLY THEIR WORLD BUT EVERY WORLD!
IT IS A TIME OF UNIMAGINABLE CATASTROPHE. A GRUESOME WAR IN WHICH THEY LOST MANY COMPANIONS TO A PARASITIC PLAGUE IS SPREADING TO THE TOTALITY OF THE EVERVERSE!
SINCE THEIR EMERGENCE, THESE HEROES HAVE FACED INCALCULABLE THREATS, BUT NOTHING NEARLY SO OVERWHELMING!
NOW, IN THIS DASTARDLY HOUR, THE HOPE OF ALL RESTS IN THE HANDS OF THESE FEW. GOOD THING FOR US, THOSE FEW ARE THE...
LEGION OF ETHICAL CHAMPIONS
BY THE GLORY OF GORSALT-- LOOK AT THE READOUTS, SISTER NAPALM!
WHAT ARE THOSE RED MARKS, ATOMIC FURY?
ANOTHER THIRTY MILLION DIMENSIONS LOST TO INFECTION SINCE I BEGAN THIS SENTENCE!
AND THE PLAGUE IS HEADING THIS WAY!

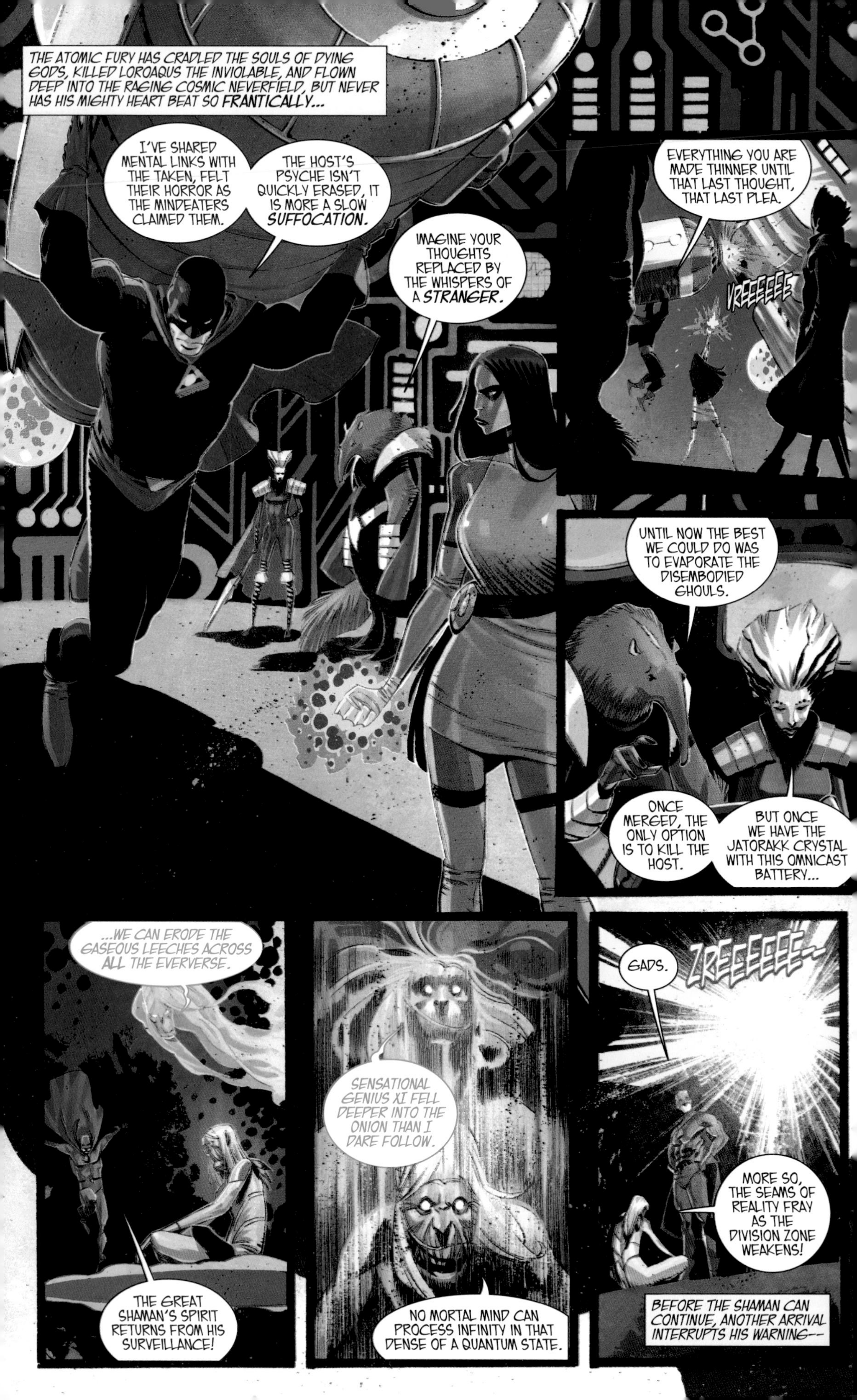
THE ATOMIC FURY HAS CRADLED THE SOULS OF DYING GODS, KILLED LOROAQUS THE INVIOLABLE, AND FLOWN DEEP INTO THE RAGING COSMIC NEVERFIELD, BUT NEVER HAS HIS MIGHTY HEART BEAT SO FRANTICALLY...
I'VE SHARED MENTAL LINKS WITH THE TAKEN, FELT THEIR HORROR AS THE MINDEATERS CLAIMED THEM.
THE HOST'S PSYCHE ISN'T QUICKLY ERASED, IT IS MORE A SLOW SUFFOCATION.
IMAGINE YOUR THOUGHTS REPLACED BY THE WHISPERS OF A STRANGER.
EVERYTHING YOU ARE MADE THINNER UNTIL THAT LAST THOUGHT, THAT LAST PLEA.
VREEEEEE
UNTIL NOW THE BEST WE COULD DO WAS TO EVAPORATE THE DISEMBODIED GHOULS.
ONCE MERGED, THE ONLY OPTION IS TO KILL THE HOST.
BUT ONCE WE HAVE THE JATORAKK CRYSTAL WITH THIS OMNICAST BATTERY...
...WE CAN ERODE THE GASEOUS LEECHES ACROSS ALL THE EVERVERSE.
THE GREAT SHAMAN'S SPIRIT RETURNS FROM HIS SURVEILLANCE!
SENSATIONAL GENIUS XI FELL DEEPER INTO THE ONION THAN I DARE FOLLOW.
NO MORTAL MIND CAN PROCESS INFINITY IN THAT DENSE OF A QUANTUM STATE.
GADS.
ZREEEEEE--
MORE SO, THE SEAMS OF REALITY FRAY AS THE DIVISION ZONE WEAKENS!
BEFORE THE SHAMAN CAN CONTINUE, ANOTHER ARRIVAL INTERRUPTS HIS WARNING--

THE AIR *SHATTERS,* A *DEAFENING* BUZZ OF ATOMS UNRAVELING AND SHIFTING MATTER INTO *IMPOSSIBILITY!*

THE SOUND OF THE LAWS OF NATURE BEING *BROKEN*--

THE SOUND OF DIMENSIONAUTS RETURNING!

NATHAN, MY BOY, I'M SO *GLAD* TO SEE YOU MAKE IT BACK SAFELY.

I-I WASN'T FAST ENOUGH!

*MY* PARENTS--

CLINT, THE GHOSTS TOOK OVER EARTH, *MY* EARTH! I *HAVE TO GO* BACK--

WE CAN'T RISK INFECTION, BUT WE'RE CLOSE TO COMPLETING THE SOLUTION.

THERE'S HOPE.

HOPE?

WE JUST WATCHED MILLIONS OF THOSE THINGS *INVADE* OUR *HOME!*

AND YOU MUST BE PIA.

JUST AS NATHAN-- I SENSE IN YOU A *MIGHTY* SPIRIT.

I'M THE ATOMIC FURY, BUT THAT MUST SOUND SILLY TO YOU. JUST CALL ME CLINT.

YOU TOOK CARE OF NATE?

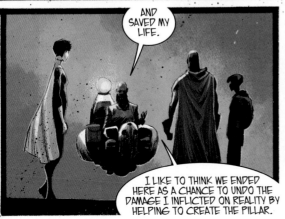

AND SAVED MY LIFE.

I LIKE TO THINK WE ENDED HERE AS A CHANCE TO UNDO THE DAMAGE I INFLICTED ON REALITY BY HELPING TO CREATE THE PILLAR.

AND I MEAN TO EARN IT.

SOON, SHAWN.

I TRUST SENSATIONAL GENIUS XI WITH HIS TASK. HE *WILL* RETURN WITH THE CRYSTAL.

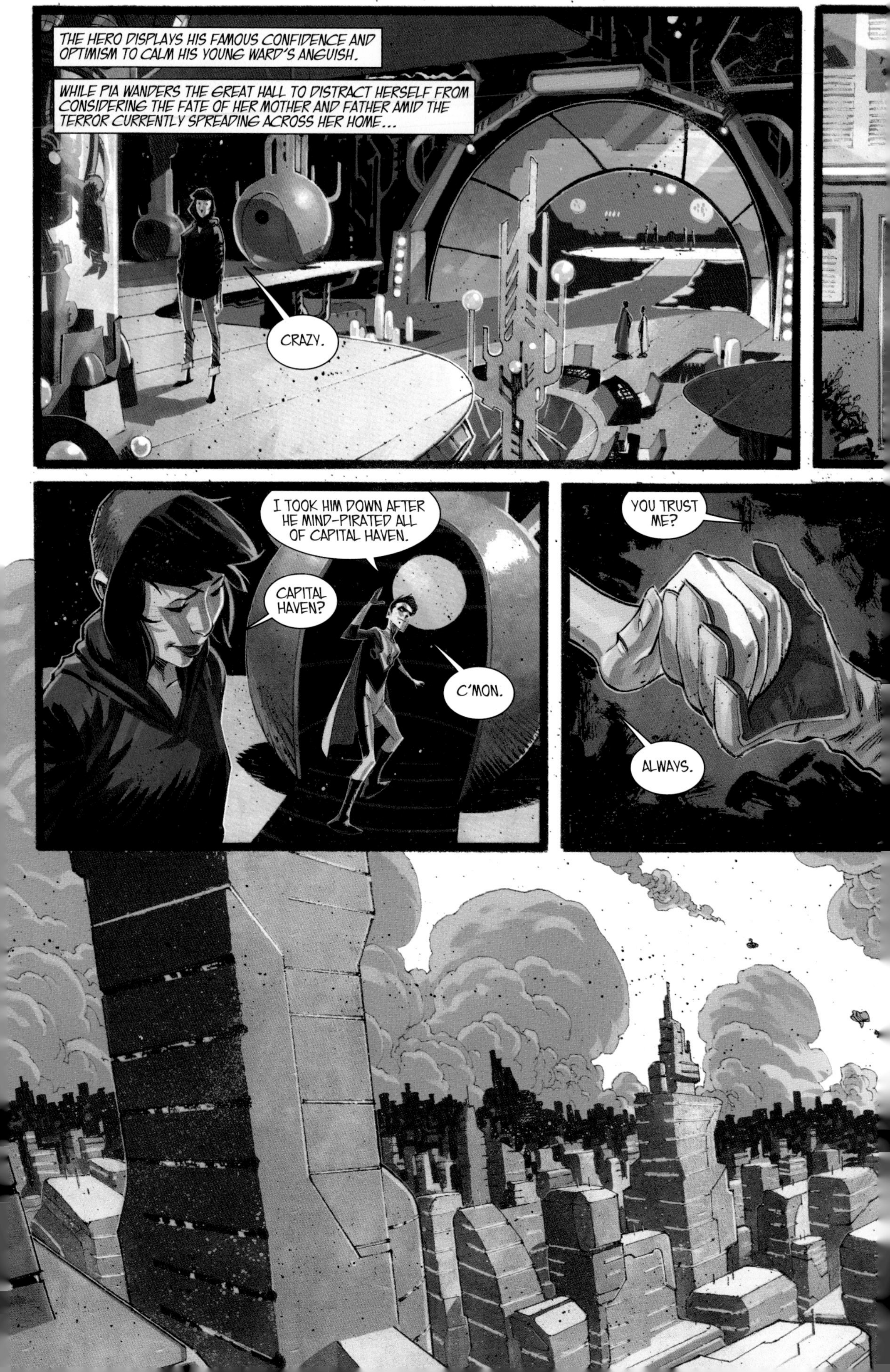

THE HERO DISPLAYS HIS FAMOUS CONFIDENCE AND OPTIMISM TO CALM HIS YOUNG WARD'S ANGUISH.
WHILE PIA WANDERS THE GREAT HALL TO DISTRACT HERSELF FROM CONSIDERING THE FATE OF HER MOTHER AND FATHER AMID THE TERROR CURRENTLY SPREADING ACROSS HER HOME...
CRAZY.
I TOOK HIM DOWN AFTER HE MIND-PIRATED ALL OF CAPITAL HAVEN.
CAPITAL HAVEN?
C'MON.
YOU TRUST ME?
ALWAYS.

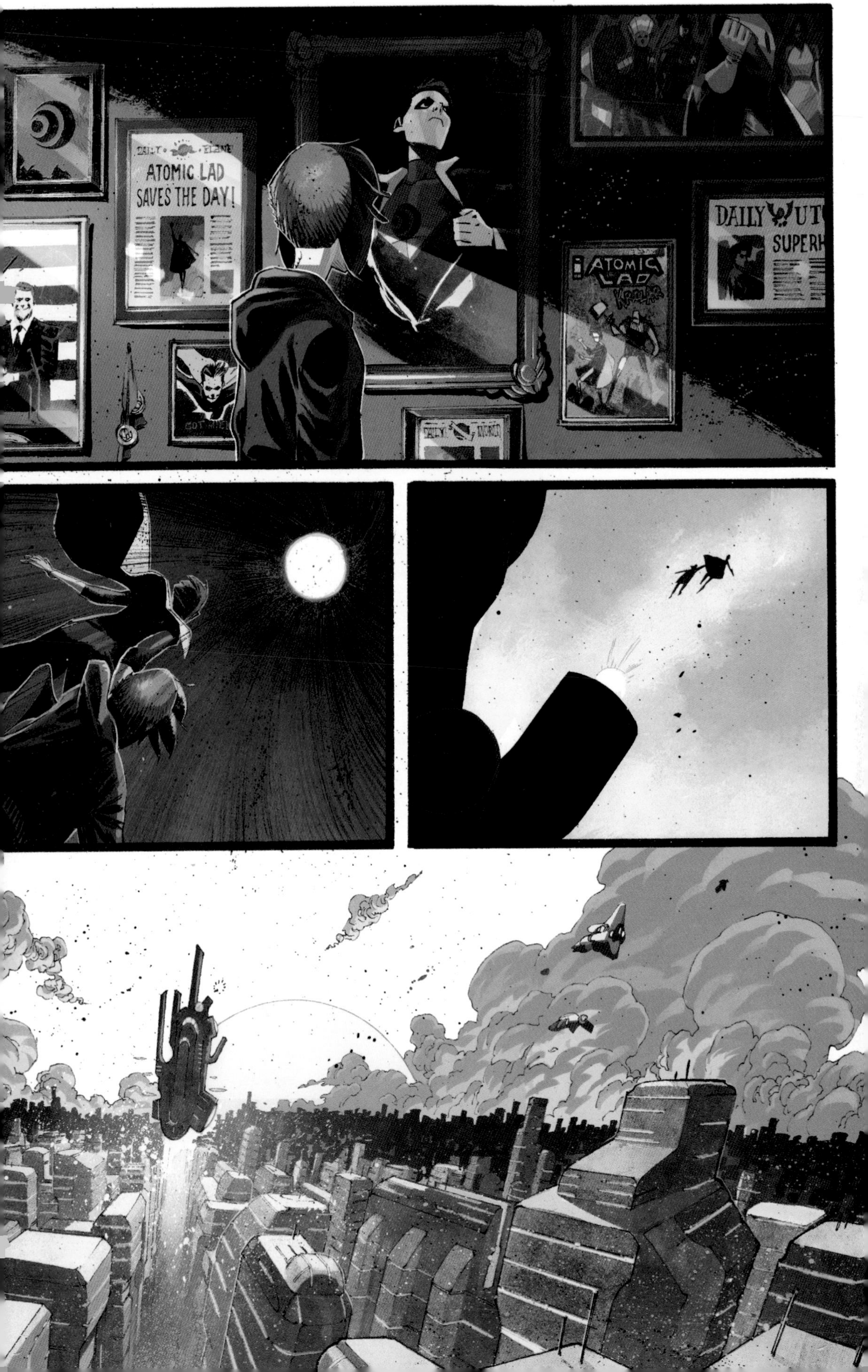
ATOMIC LAD
SAVES THE DAY!
DAILY
ATOMIC
LAD

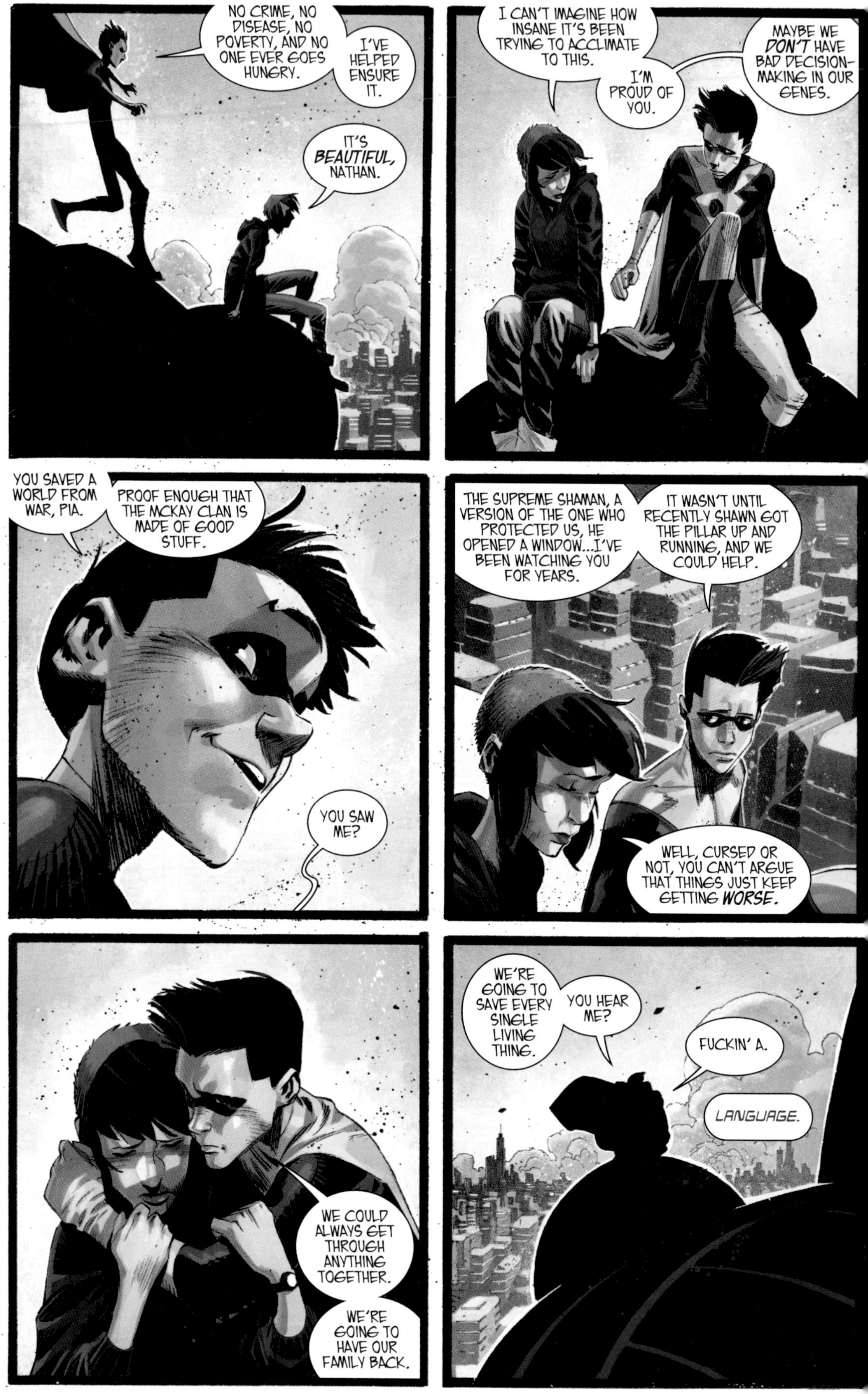
NO CRIME, NO DISEASE, NO POVERTY, AND NO ONE EVER GOES HUNGRY.
I'VE HELPED ENSURE IT.
IT'S BEAUTIFUL, NATHAN.
I CAN'T IMAGINE HOW INSANE IT'S BEEN TRYING TO ACCLIMATE TO THIS.
I'M PROUD OF YOU.
MAYBE WE DON'T HAVE BAD DECISION-MAKING IN OUR GENES.
YOU SAVED A WORLD FROM WAR, PIA.
PROOF ENOUGH THAT THE MCKAY CLAN IS MADE OF GOOD STUFF.
YOU SAW ME?
THE SUPREME SHAMAN, A VERSION OF THE ONE WHO PROTECTED US, HE OPENED A WINDOW...I'VE BEEN WATCHING YOU FOR YEARS.
IT WASN'T UNTIL RECENTLY SHAWN GOT THE PILLAR UP AND RUNNING, AND WE COULD HELP.
WELL, CURSED OR NOT, YOU CAN'T ARGUE THAT THINGS JUST KEEP GETTING WORSE.
WE COULD ALWAYS GET THROUGH ANYTHING TOGETHER.
WE'RE GOING TO HAVE OUR FAMILY BACK.
WE'RE GOING TO SAVE EVERY SINGLE LIVING THING.
YOU HEAR ME?
FUCKIN' A.
LANGUAGE.

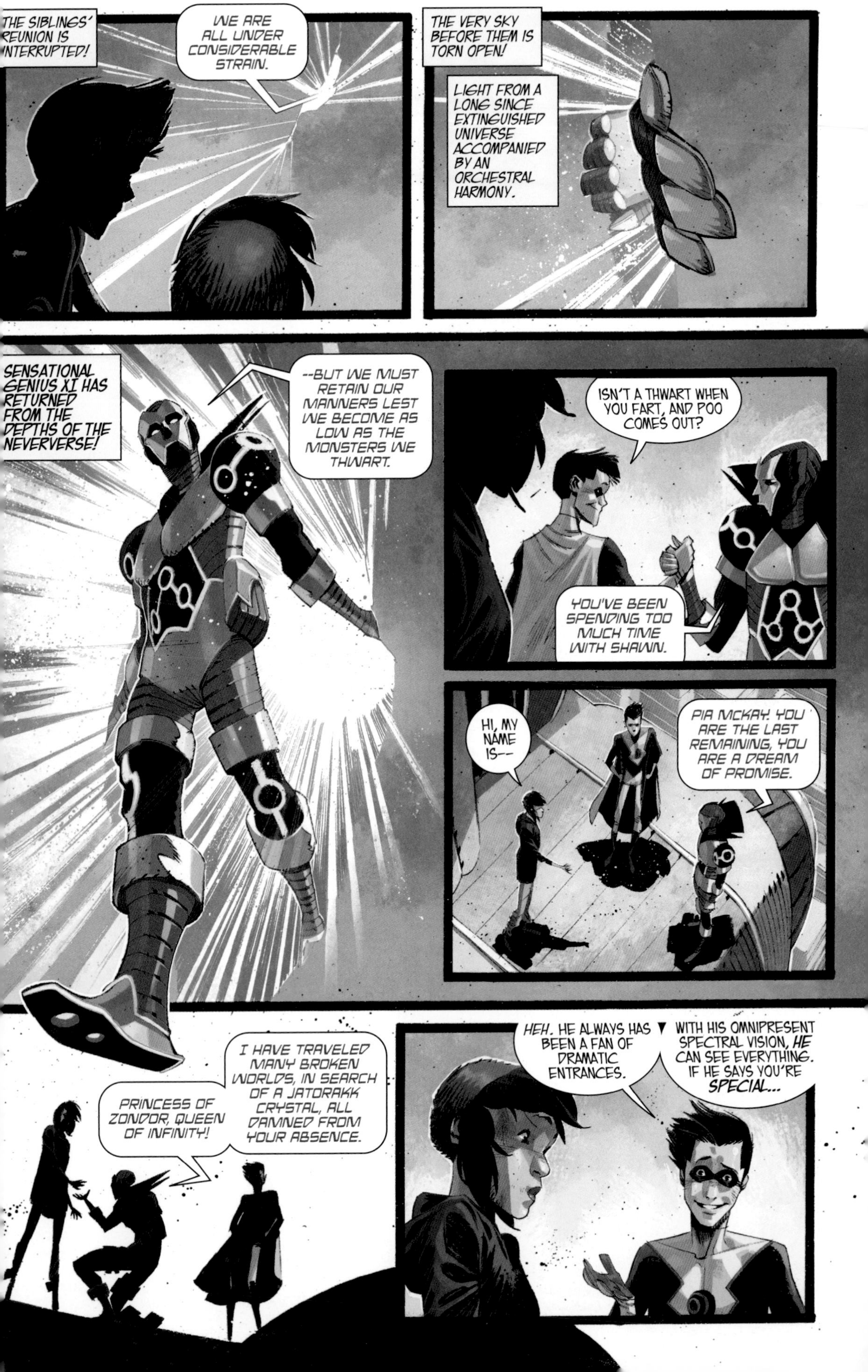
THE SIBLINGS' REUNION IS INTERRUPTED!
WE ARE ALL UNDER CONSIDERABLE STRAIN.
THE VERY SKY BEFORE THEM IS TORN OPEN!
LIGHT FROM A LONG SINCE EXTINGUISHED UNIVERSE ACCOMPANIED BY AN ORCHESTRAL HARMONY.
SENSATIONAL GENIUS XI HAS RETURNED FROM THE DEPTHS OF THE NEVERVERSE!
--BUT WE MUST RETAIN OUR MANNERS LEST WE BECOME AS LOW AS THE MONSTERS WE THWART.
ISN'T A THWART WHEN YOU FART, AND POO COMES OUT?
YOU'VE BEEN SPENDING TOO MUCH TIME WITH SHAWN.
HI, MY NAME IS--
PIA MCKAY. YOU ARE THE LAST REMAINING, YOU ARE A DREAM OF PROMISE.
PRINCESS OF ZONDOR, QUEEN OF INFINITY!
I HAVE TRAVELED MANY BROKEN WORLDS, IN SEARCH OF A JATORAKK CRYSTAL, ALL DAMNED FROM YOUR ABSENCE.
HEH. HE ALWAYS HAS BEEN A FAN OF DRAMATIC ENTRANCES.
WITH HIS OMNIPRESENT SPECTRAL VISION, HE CAN SEE EVERYTHING. IF HE SAYS YOU'RE SPECIAL...

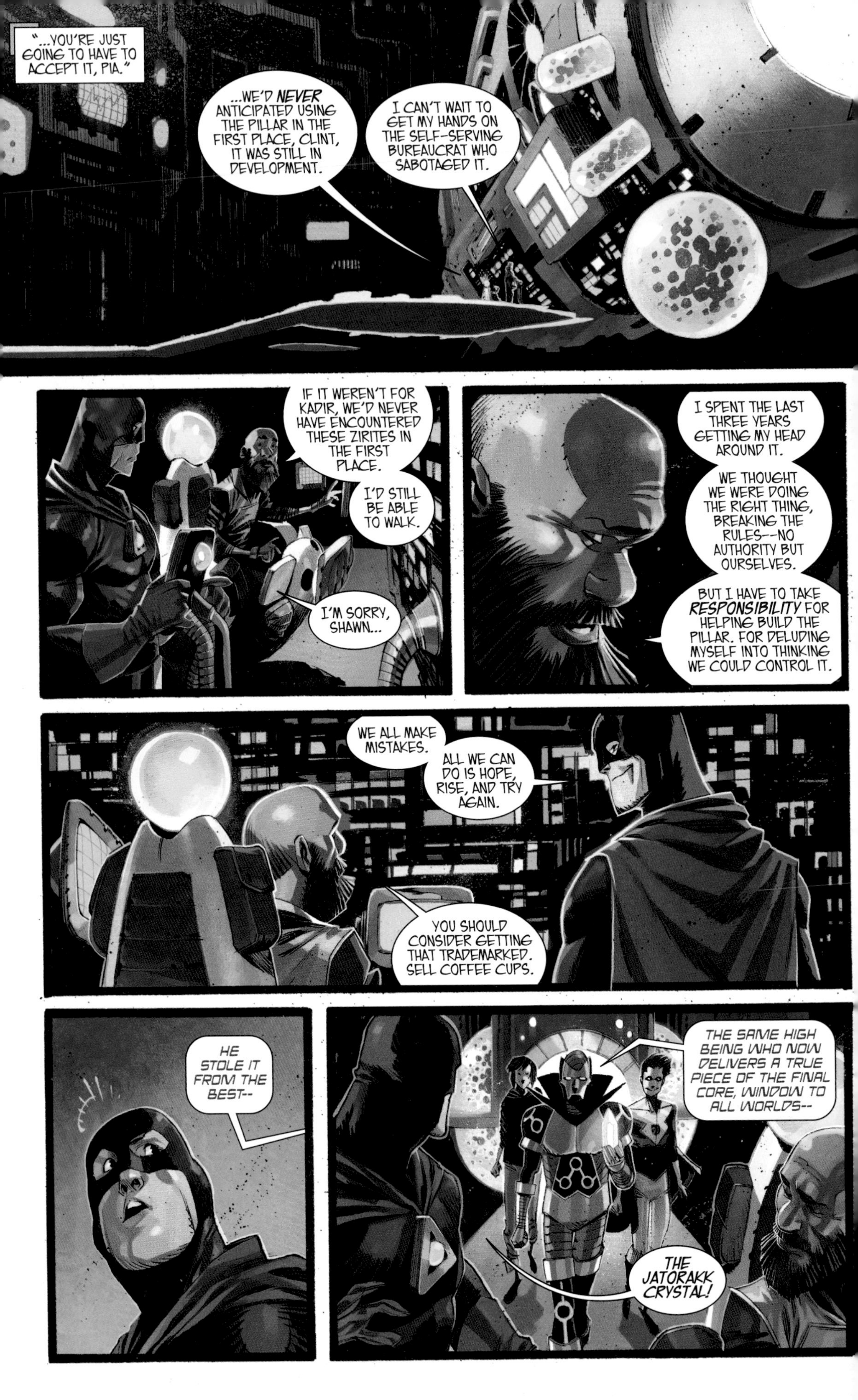
"...YOU'RE JUST GOING TO HAVE TO ACCEPT IT, PIA."
...WE'D NEVER ANTICIPATED USING THE PILLAR IN THE FIRST PLACE, CLINT, IT WAS STILL IN DEVELOPMENT.
I CAN'T WAIT TO GET MY HANDS ON THE SELF-SERVING BUREAUCRAT WHO SABOTAGED IT.
IF IT WEREN'T FOR KADIR, WE'D NEVER HAVE ENCOUNTERED THESE ZIRITES IN THE FIRST PLACE.
I'D STILL BE ABLE TO WALK.
I'M SORRY, SHAWN...
I SPENT THE LAST THREE YEARS GETTING MY HEAD AROUND IT.
WE THOUGHT WE WERE DOING THE RIGHT THING, BREAKING THE RULES--NO AUTHORITY BUT OURSELVES.
BUT I HAVE TO TAKE RESPONSIBILITY FOR HELPING BUILD THE PILLAR. FOR DELUDING MYSELF INTO THINKING WE COULD CONTROL IT.
WE ALL MAKE MISTAKES.
ALL WE CAN DO IS HOPE, RISE, AND TRY AGAIN.
YOU SHOULD CONSIDER GETTING THAT TRADEMARKED. SELL COFFEE CUPS.
HE STOLE IT FROM THE BEST--
THE SAME HIGH BEING WHO NOW DELIVERS A TRUE PIECE OF THE FINAL CORE, WINDOW TO ALL WORLDS--
THE JATORAKK CRYSTAL!

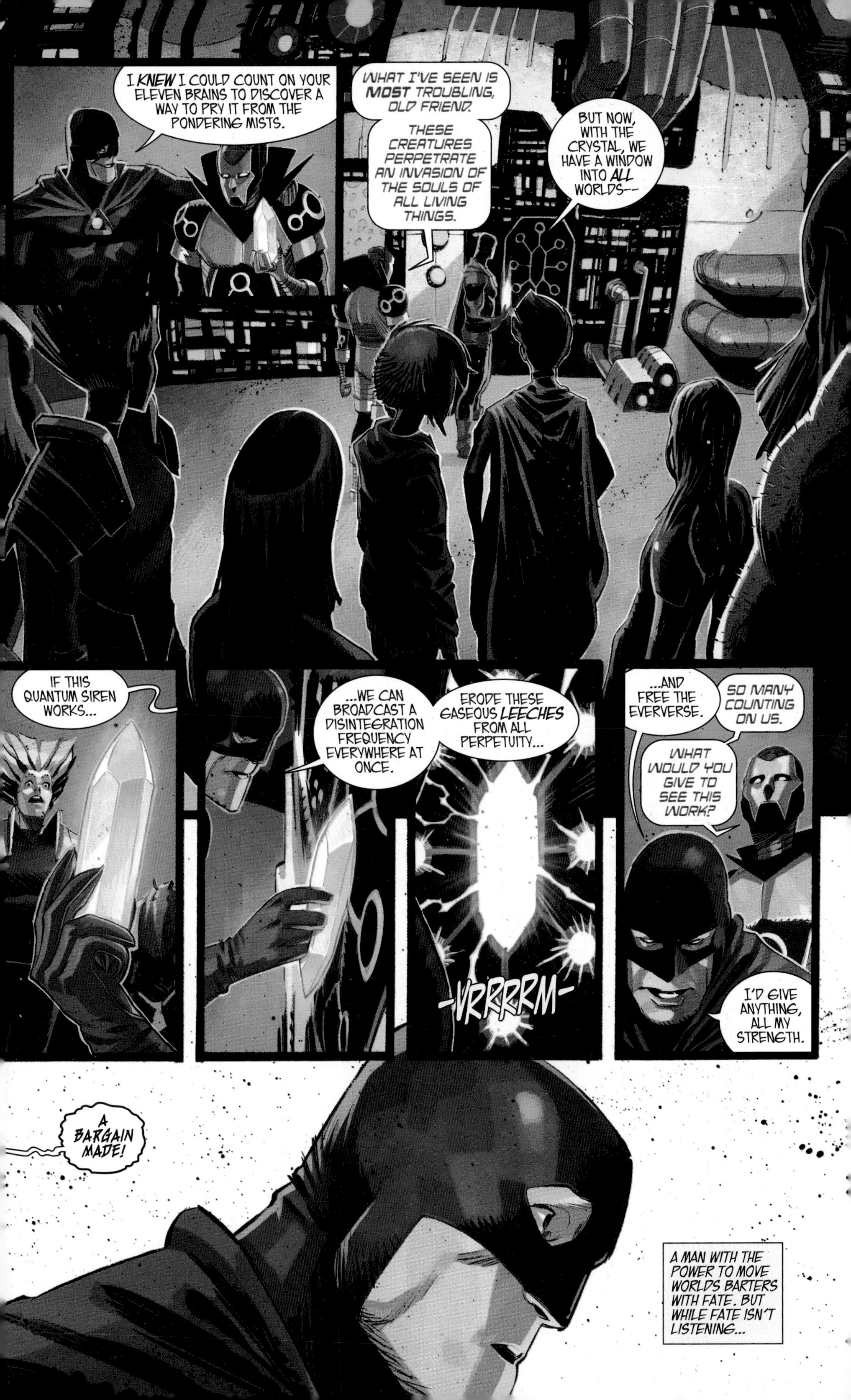
I KNEW I COULD COUNT ON YOUR ELEVEN BRAINS TO DISCOVER A WAY TO PRY IT FROM THE PONDERING MISTS.
WHAT I'VE SEEN IS MOST TROUBLING, OLD FRIEND.
THESE CREATURES PERPETRATE AN INVASION OF THE SOULS OF ALL LIVING THINGS.
BUT NOW, WITH THE CRYSTAL, WE HAVE A WINDOW INTO ALL WORLDS--
IF THIS QUANTUM SIREN WORKS...
...WE CAN BROADCAST A DISINTEGRATION FREQUENCY EVERYWHERE AT ONCE.
ERODE THESE GASEOUS LEECHES FROM ALL PERPETUITY...
-VRRRRM-
...AND FREE THE EVERVERSE.
SO MANY COUNTING ON US.
WHAT WOULD YOU GIVE TO SEE THIS WORK?
I'D GIVE ANYTHING, ALL MY STRENGTH.
A BARGAIN MADE!
A MAN WITH THE POWER TO MOVE WORLDS BARTERS WITH FATE. BUT WHILE FATE ISN'T LISTENING...

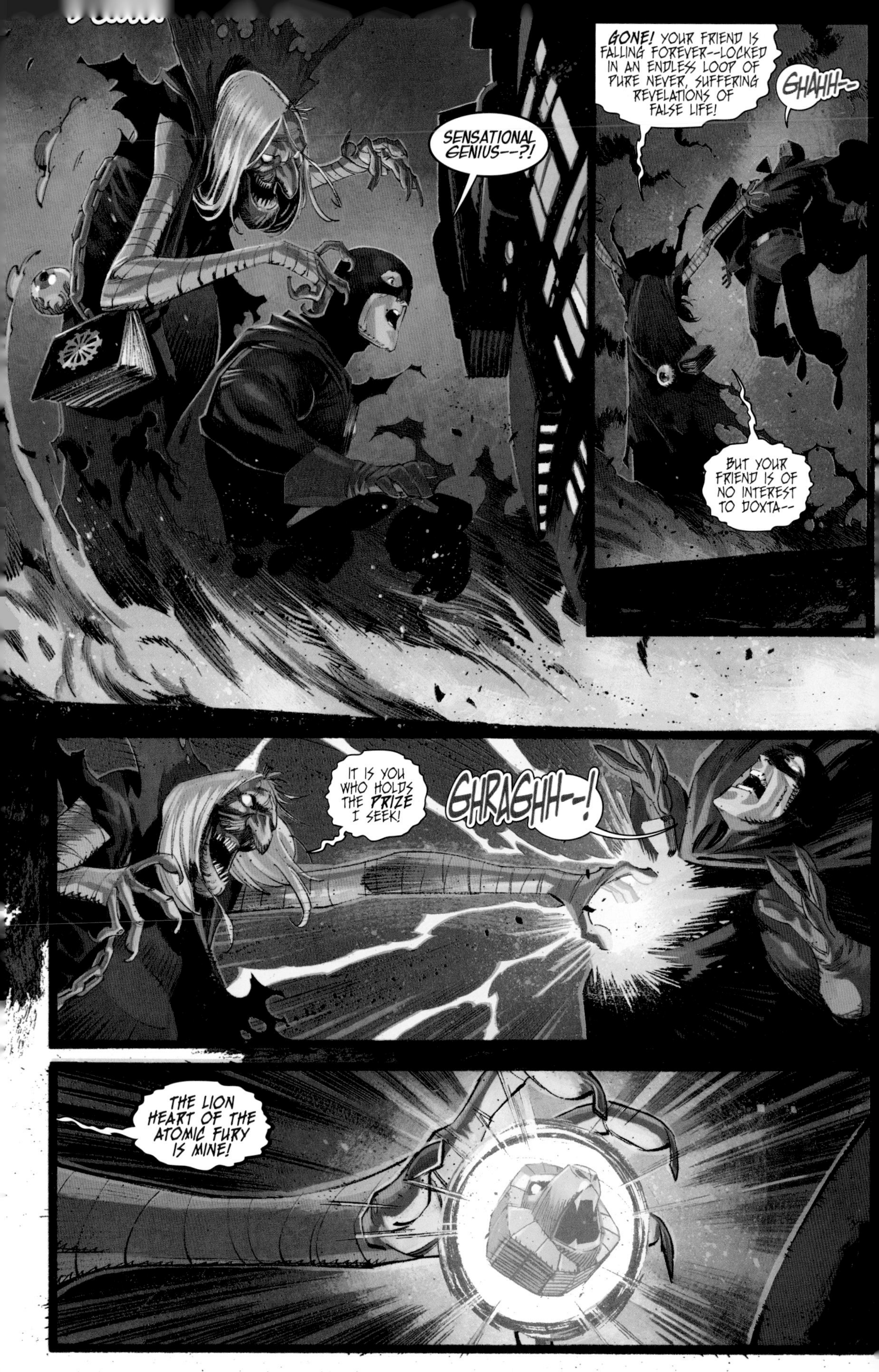
SENSATIONAL GENIUS--?!
GONE! YOUR FRIEND IS FALLING FOREVER--LOCKED IN AN ENDLESS LOOP OF PURE NEVER, SUFFERING REVELATIONS OF FALSE LIFE!
GHAHH--
BUT YOUR FRIEND IS OF NO INTEREST TO DOXTA--
IT IS YOU WHO HOLDS THE PRIZE I SEEK!
GHRAGHH--!
THE LION HEART OF THE ATOMIC FURY IS MINE!

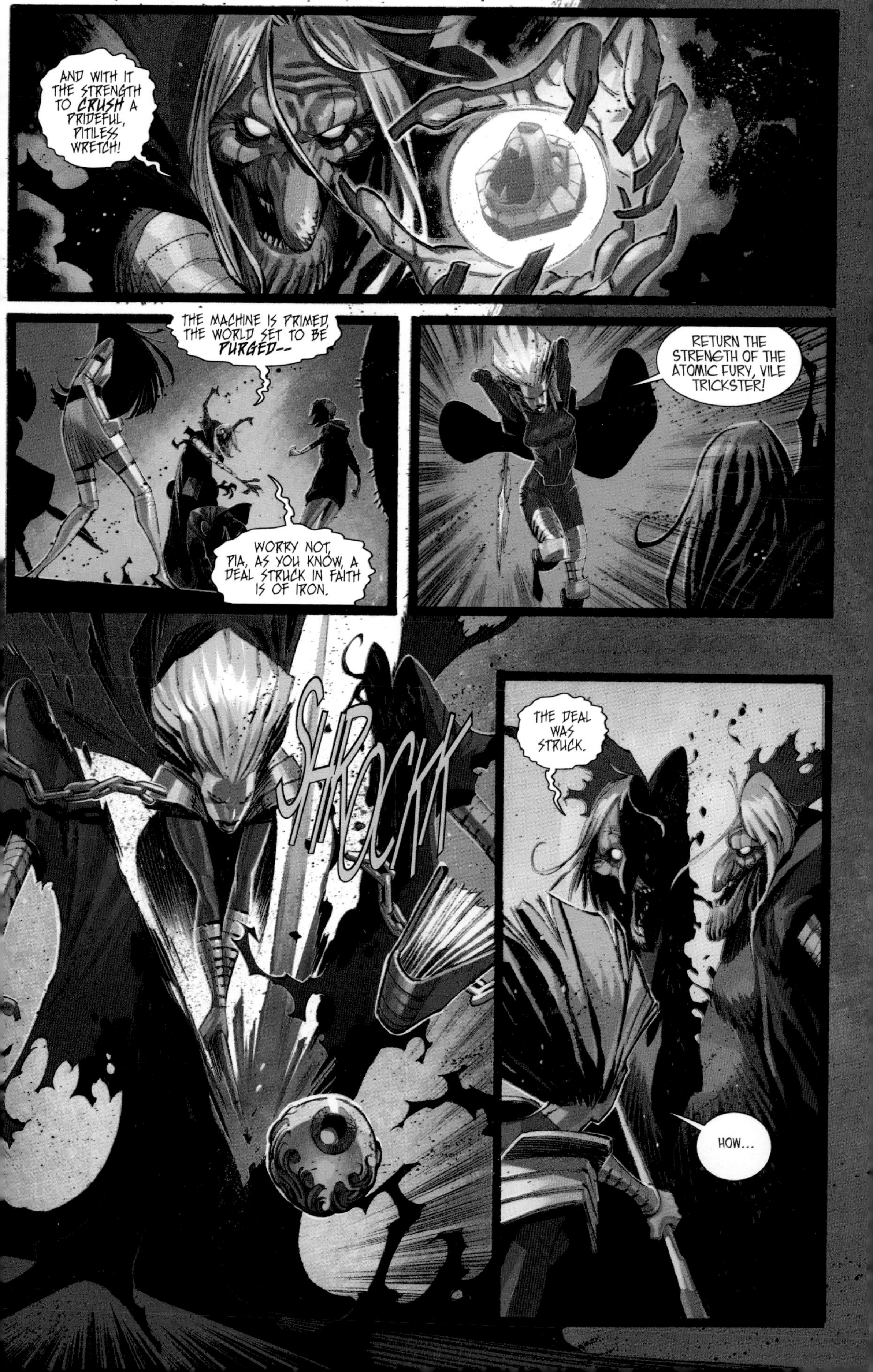
AND WITH IT THE STRENGTH TO CRUSH A PRIDEFUL, PITILESS WRETCH!
THE MACHINE IS PRIMED, THE WORLD SET TO BE PURGED--
WORRY NOT, PIA, AS YOU KNOW, A DEAL STRUCK IN FAITH IS OF IRON.
RETURN THE STRENGTH OF THE ATOMIC FURY, VILE TRICKSTER!
SHROCK
THE DEAL WAS STRUCK.
HOW...

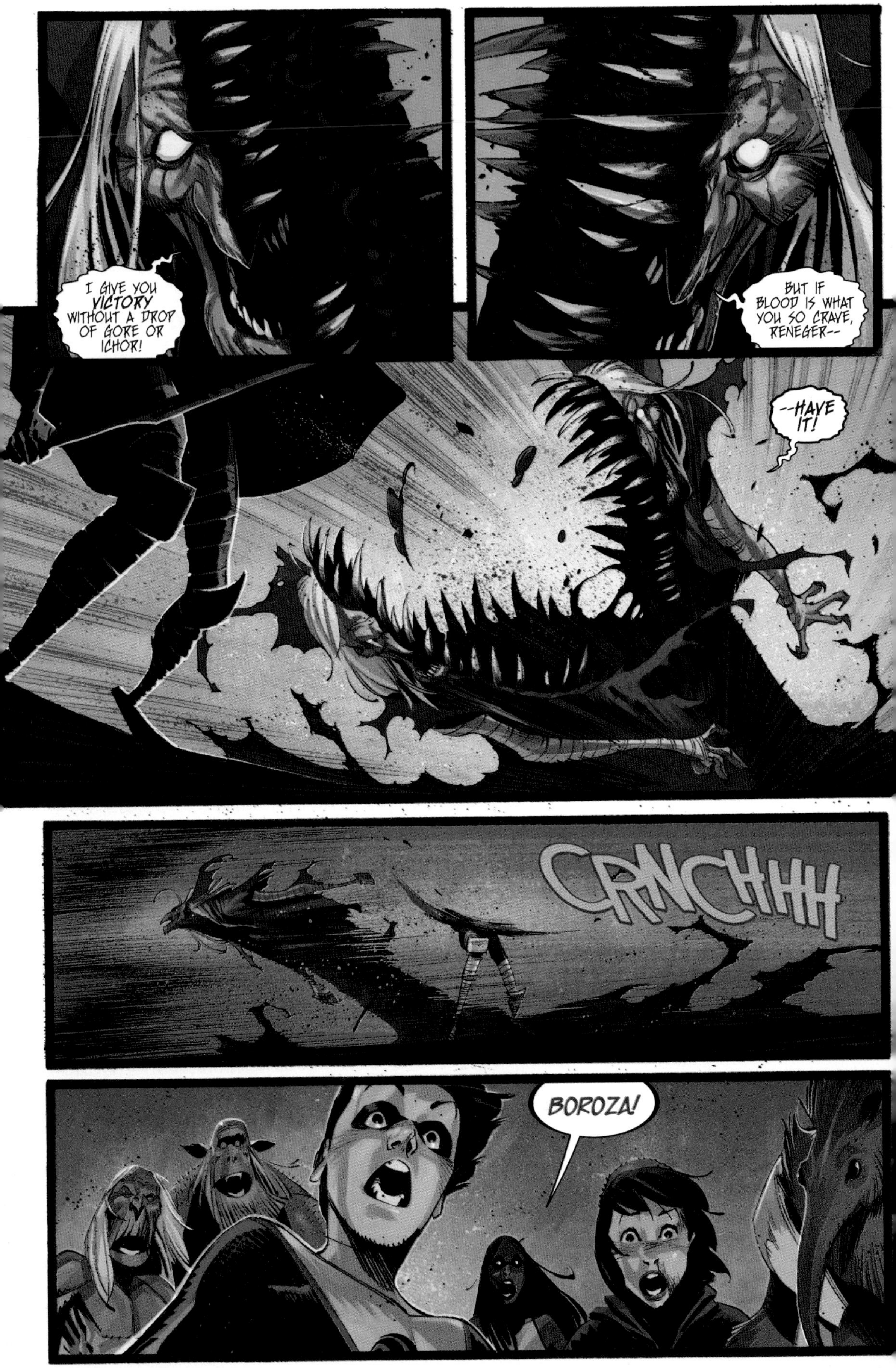
I GIVE YOU VICTORY WITHOUT A DROP OF GORE OR ICHOR!
BUT IF BLOOD IS WHAT YOU SO CRAVE, RENEGER--
--HAVE IT!
CRNCHHH
BOROZA!

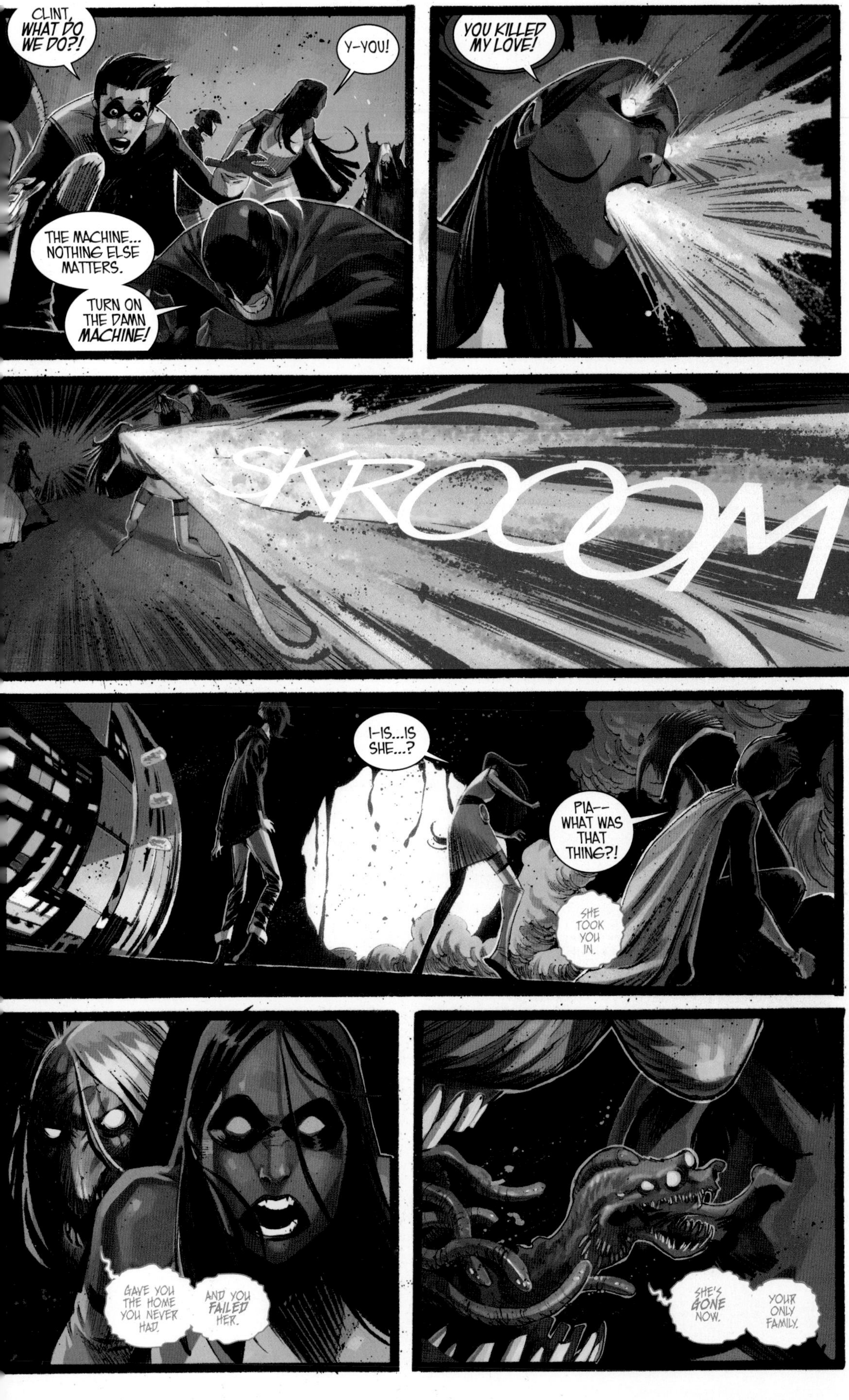
CLINT, WHAT DO WE DO?!
Y-YOU!
THE MACHINE... NOTHING ELSE MATTERS.
TURN ON THE DAMN MACHINE!
YOU KILLED MY LOVE!
SKROOOOM
I-IS...IS SHE...?
PIA-- WHAT WAS THAT THING?!
SHE TOOK YOU IN.
GAVE YOU THE HOME YOU NEVER HAD.
AND YOU FAILED HER.
SHE'S GONE NOW.
YOUR ONLY FAMILY.

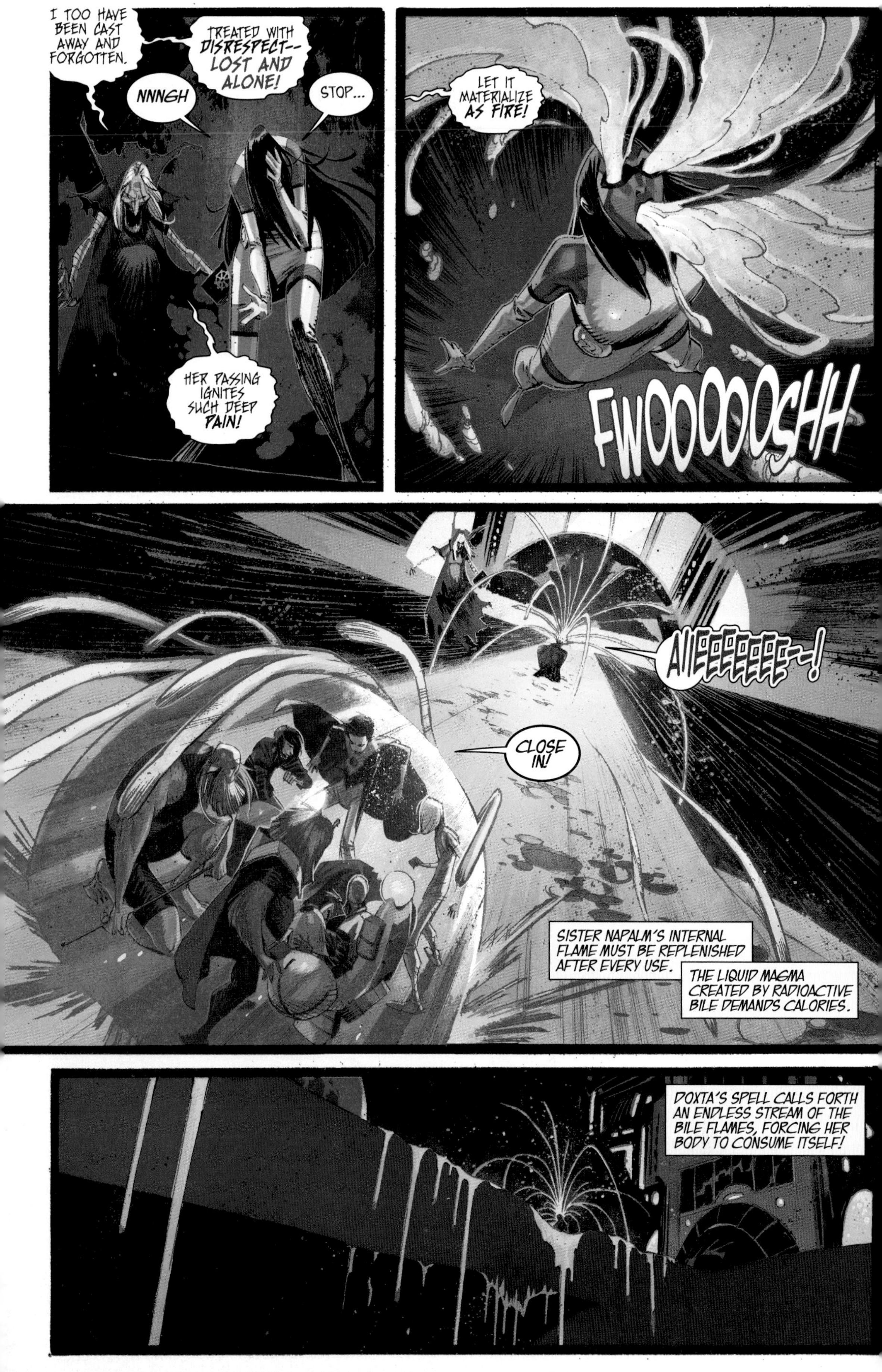

I TOO HAVE BEEN CAST AWAY AND FORGOTTEN.
TREATED WITH DISRESPECT-- LOST AND ALONE!
NNNGH
STOP...
HER PASSING IGNITES SUCH DEEP PAIN!
LET IT MATERIALIZE AS FIRE!
FWOOOOOOSHH
AIIEEEEEEEE--!
CLOSE IN!
SISTER NAPALM'S INTERNAL FLAME MUST BE REPLENISHED AFTER EVERY USE.
THE LIQUID MAGMA CREATED BY RADIOACTIVE BILE DEMANDS CALORIES.
DOXTA'S SPELL CALLS FORTH AN ENDLESS STREAM OF THE BILE FLAMES, FORCING HER BODY TO CONSUME ITSELF!

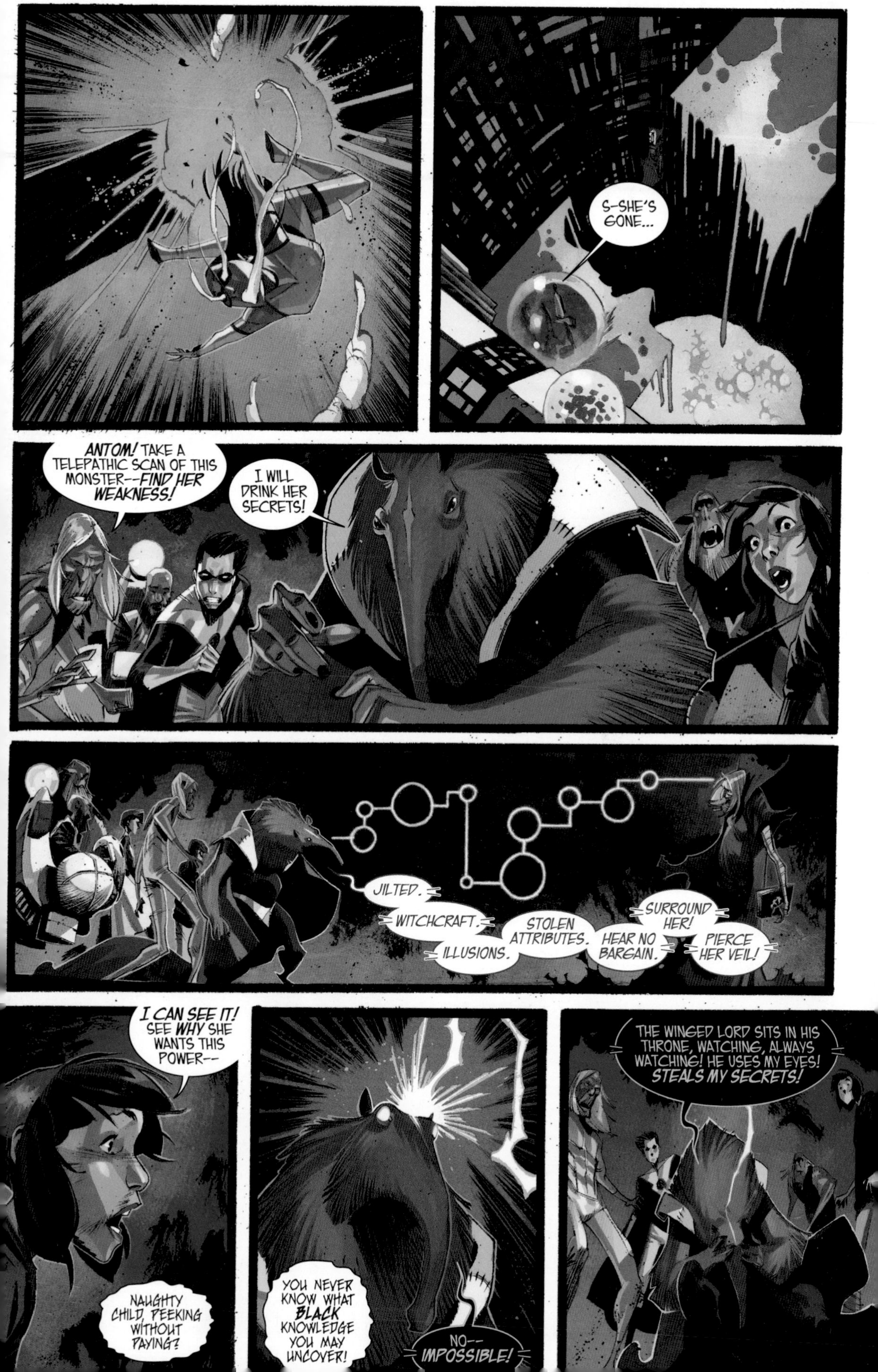
S-SHE'S GONE...
ANTOM! TAKE A TELEPATHIC SCAN OF THIS MONSTER--FIND HER WEAKNESS!
I WILL DRINK HER SECRETS!
JILTED.
WITCHCRAFT.
ILLUSIONS.
STOLEN ATTRIBUTES.
HEAR NO BARGAIN.
SURROUND HER!
PIERCE HER VEIL!
I CAN SEE IT! SEE WHY SHE WANTS THIS POWER--
NAUGHTY CHILD, PEEKING WITHOUT PAYING?
YOU NEVER KNOW WHAT BLACK KNOWLEDGE YOU MAY UNCOVER!
NO-- IMPOSSIBLE!
THE WINGED LORD SITS IN HIS THRONE, WATCHING, ALWAYS WATCHING! HE USES MY EYES! STEALS MY SECRETS!

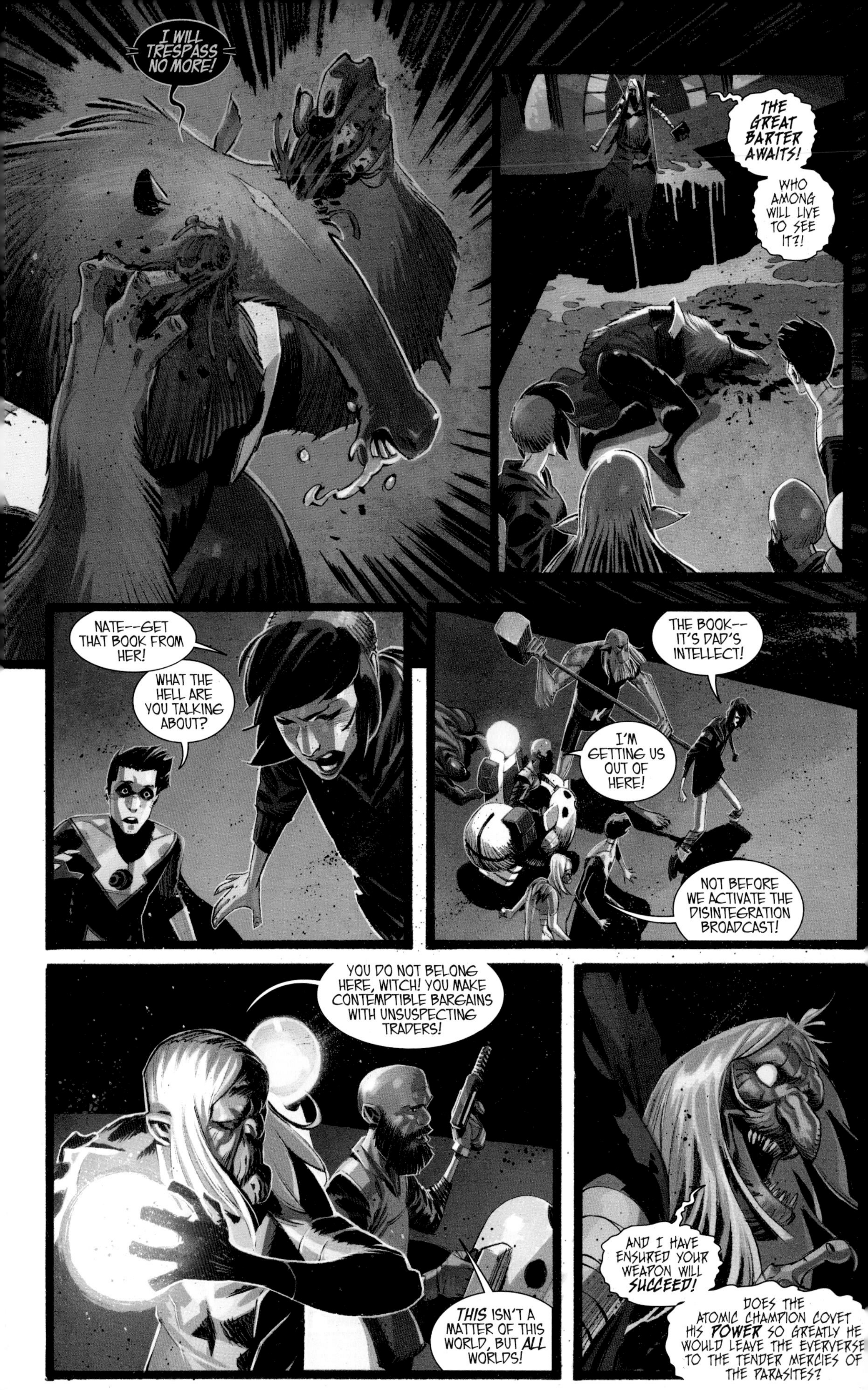
I WILL TRESPASS NO MORE!
THE GREAT BARTER AWAITS!
WHO AMONG WILL LIVE TO SEE IT?!
NATE--GET THAT BOOK FROM HER!
WHAT THE HELL ARE YOU TALKING ABOUT?
THE BOOK-- IT'S DAD'S INTELLECT!
I'M GETTING US OUT OF HERE!
NOT BEFORE WE ACTIVATE THE DISINTEGRATION BROADCAST!
YOU DO NOT BELONG HERE, WITCH! YOU MAKE CONTEMPTIBLE BARGAINS WITH UNSUSPECTING TRADERS!
THIS ISN'T A MATTER OF THIS WORLD, BUT ALL WORLDS!
AND I HAVE ENSURED YOUR WEAPON WILL SUCCEED!
DOES THE ATOMIC CHAMPION COVET HIS POWER SO GREATLY HE WOULD LEAVE THE EVERVERSE TO THE TENDER MERCIES OF THE PARASITES?

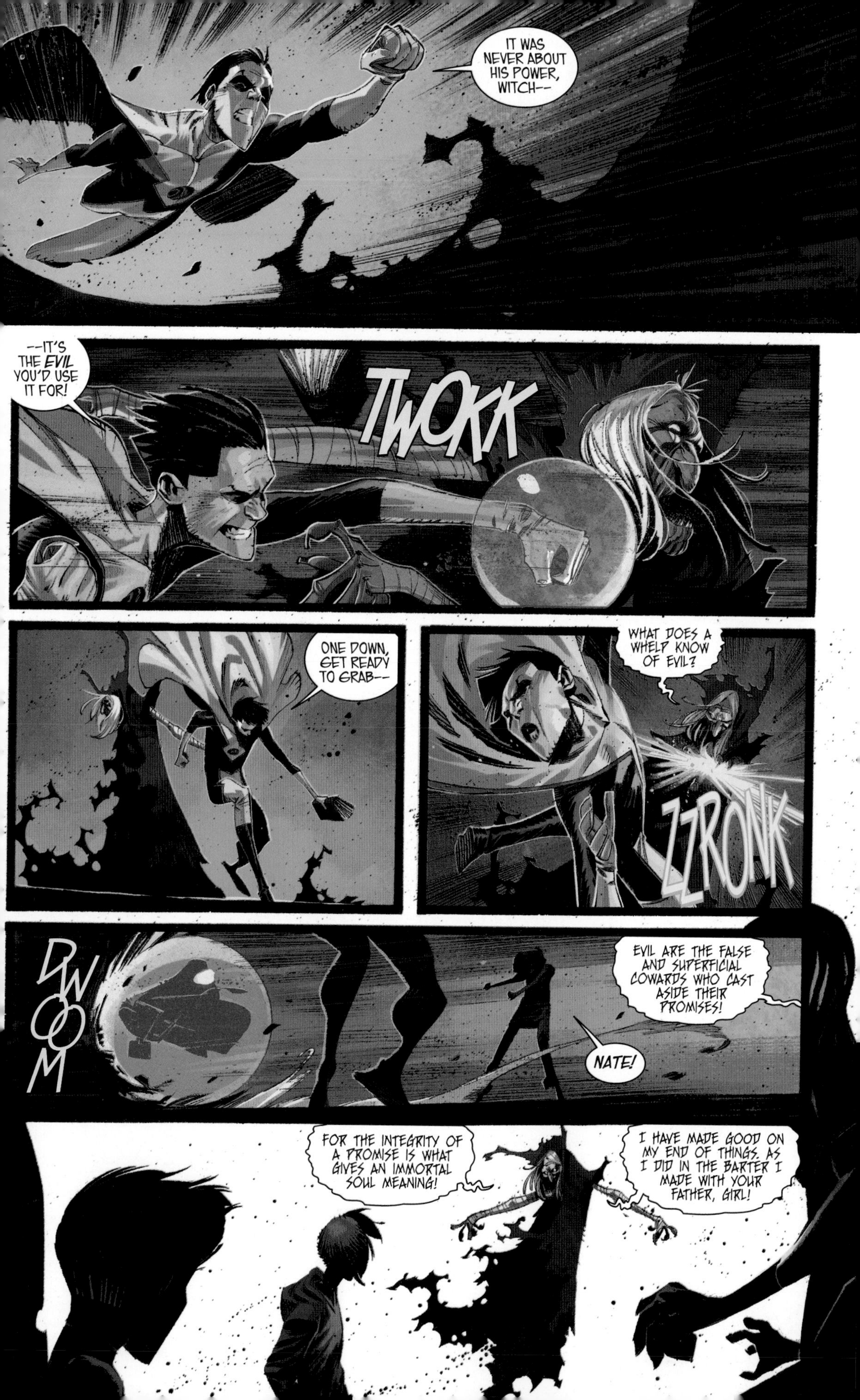
IT WAS NEVER ABOUT HIS POWER, WITCH--
--IT'S THE EVIL YOU'D USE IT FOR!
TWOKK
ONE DOWN, GET READY TO GRAB--
WHAT DOES A WHELP KNOW OF EVIL?
ZZRONK
DWOOM
EVIL ARE THE FALSE AND SUPERFICIAL COWARDS WHO CAST ASIDE THEIR PROMISES!
NATE!
FOR THE INTEGRITY OF A PROMISE IS WHAT GIVES AN IMMORTAL SOUL MEANING!
I HAVE MADE GOOD ON MY END OF THINGS. AS I DID IN THE BARTER I MADE WITH YOUR FATHER, GIRL!

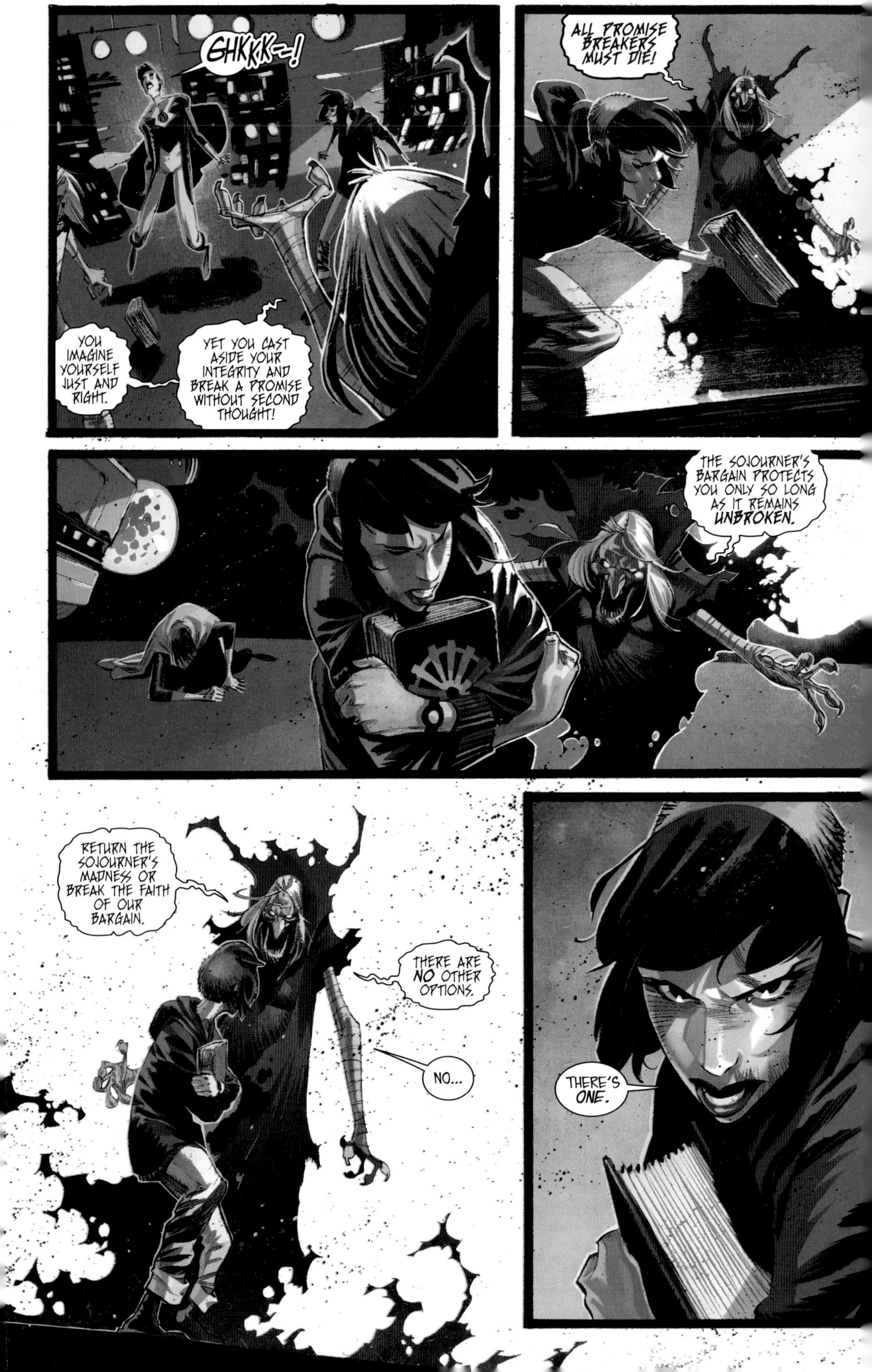
GHKKK--!
YOU IMAGINE YOURSELF JUST AND RIGHT.
YET YOU CAST ASIDE YOUR INTEGRITY AND BREAK A PROMISE WITHOUT SECOND THOUGHT!
ALL PROMISE BREAKERS MUST DIE!
THE SOJOURNER'S BARGAIN PROTECTS YOU ONLY SO LONG AS IT REMAINS UNBROKEN.
RETURN THE SOJOURNER'S MADNESS OR BREAK THE FAITH OF OUR BARGAIN.
THERE ARE NO OTHER OPTIONS.
NO...
THERE'S ONE.

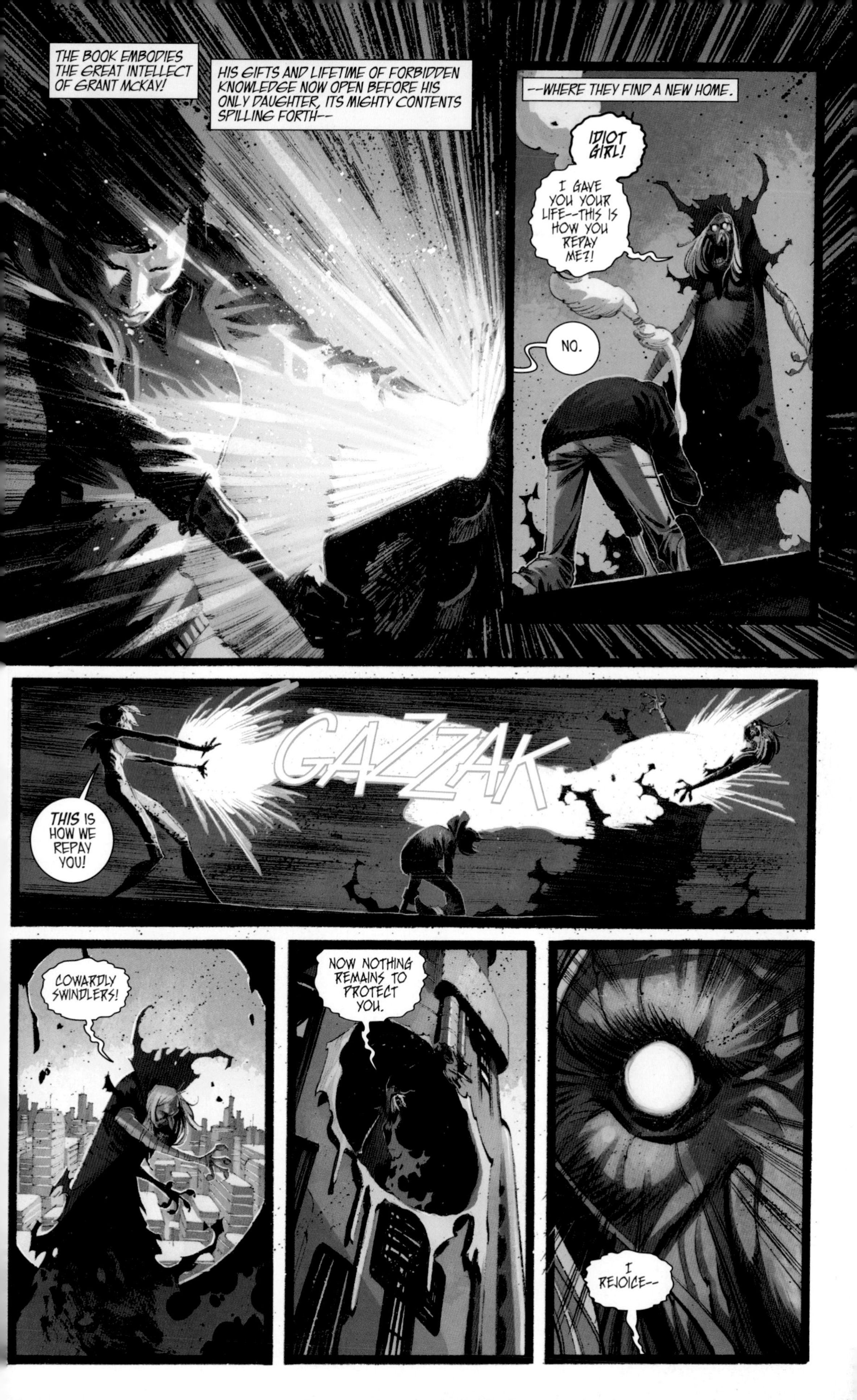
THE BOOK EMBODIES THE GREAT INTELLECT OF GRANT MCKAY!
HIS GIFTS AND LIFETIME OF FORBIDDEN KNOWLEDGE NOW OPEN BEFORE HIS ONLY DAUGHTER, ITS MIGHTY CONTENTS SPILLING FORTH--
--WHERE THEY FIND A NEW HOME.
IDIOT GIRL!
I GAVE YOU YOUR LIFE--THIS IS HOW YOU REPAY ME?!
NO.
GAZZAK
THIS IS HOW WE REPAY YOU!
COWARDLY SWINDLERS!
NOW NOTHING REMAINS TO PROTECT YOU.
I REJOICE--

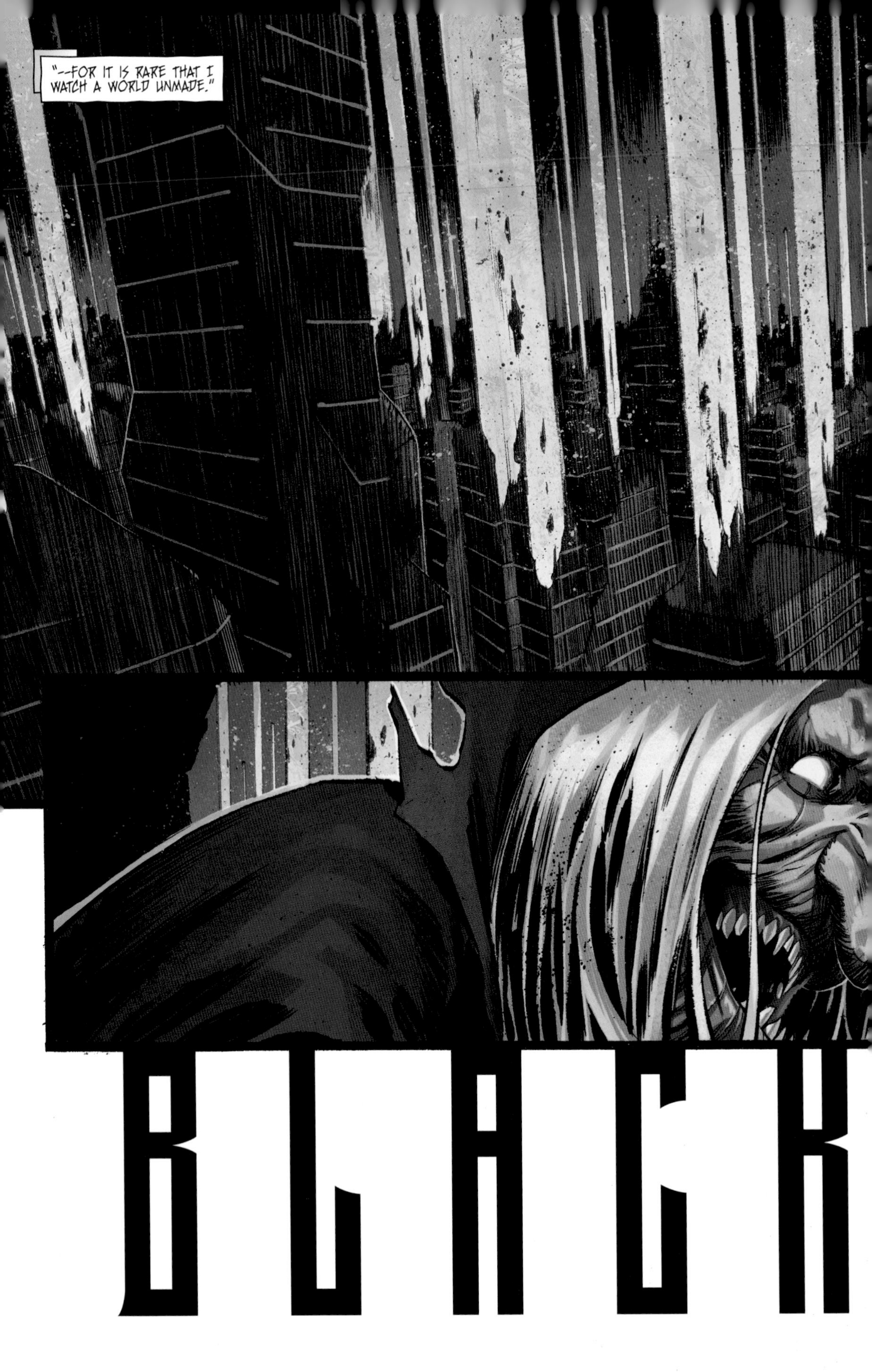
"--FOR IT IS RARE THAT I WATCH A WORLD UNMADE."
BLACK

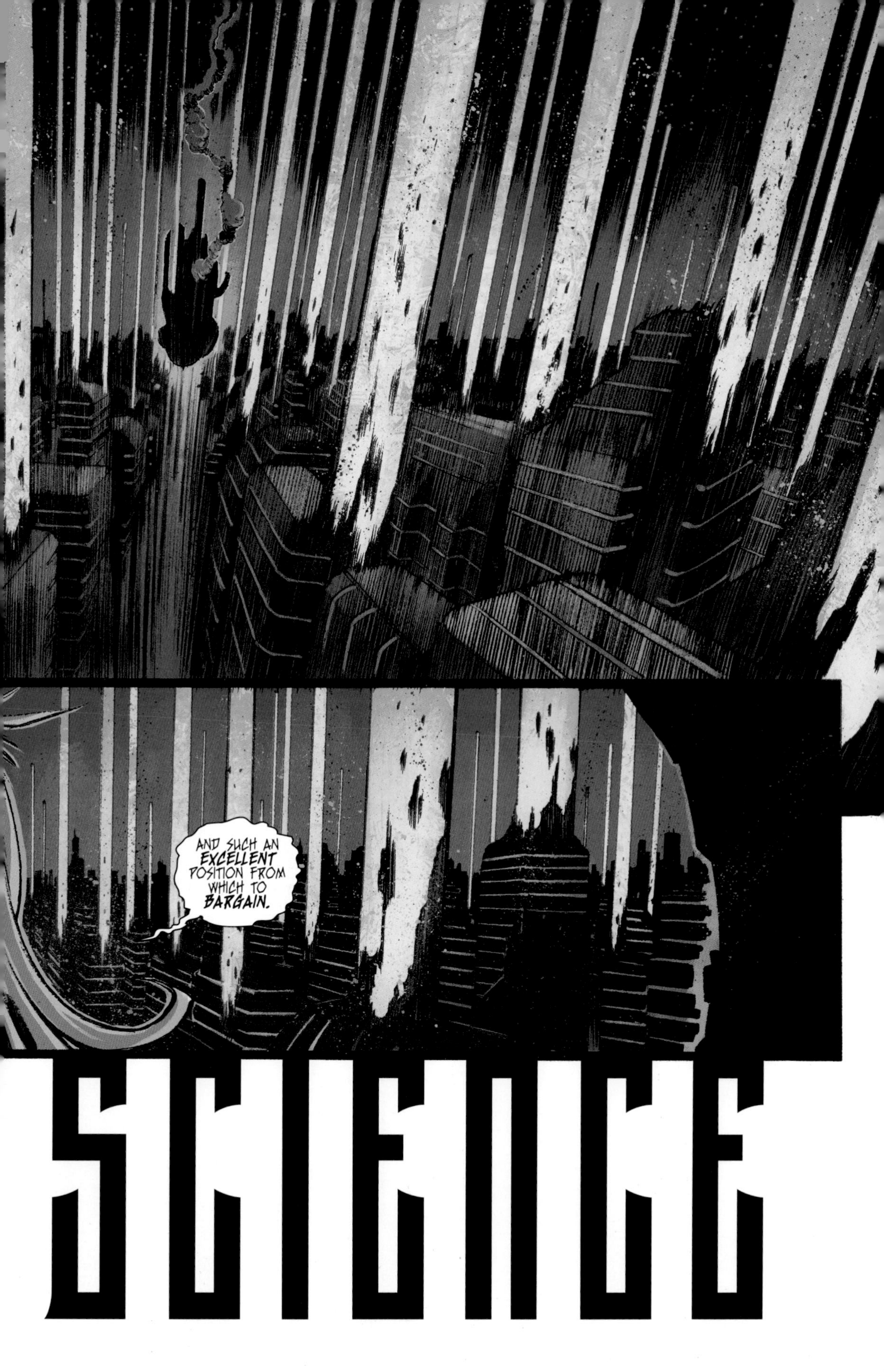
AND SUCH AN EXCELLENT POSITION FROM WHICH TO BARGAIN.
SCIENCE

# 29

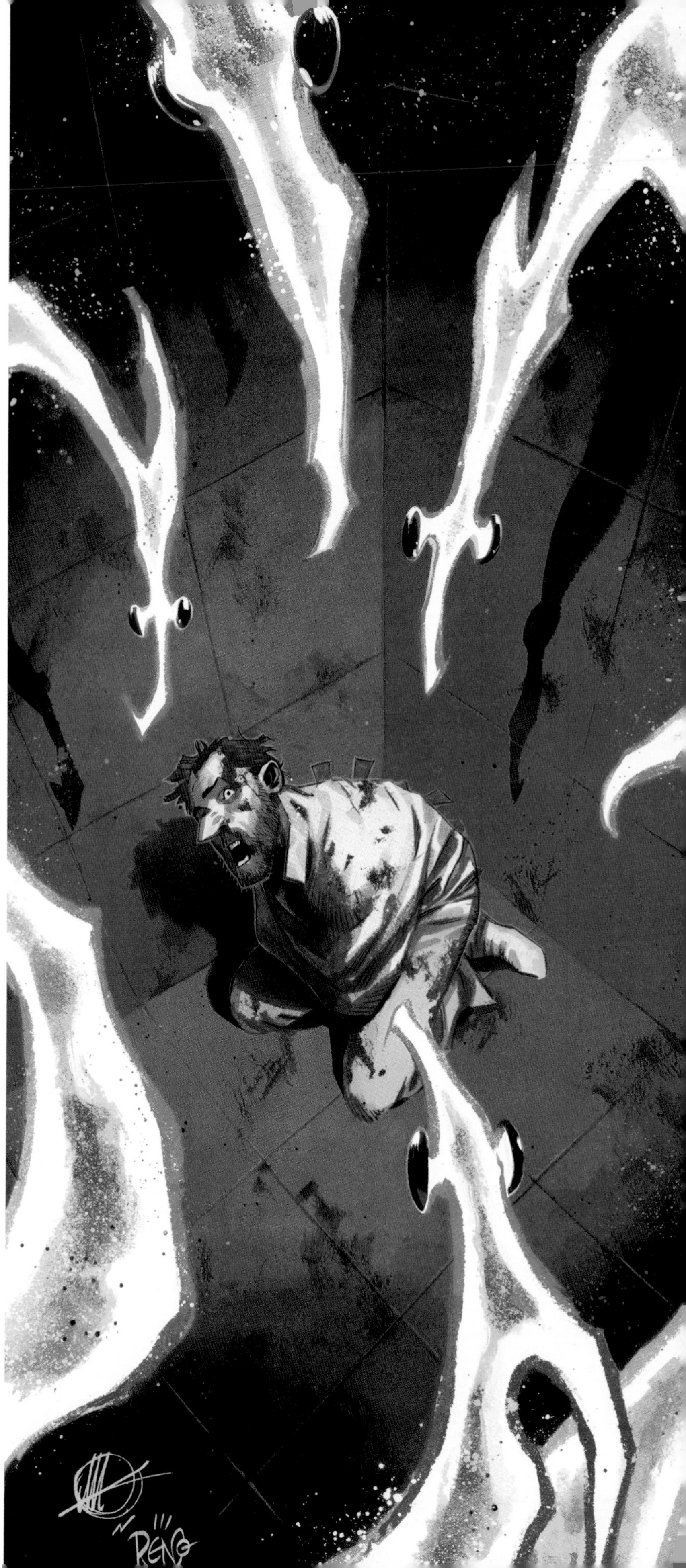

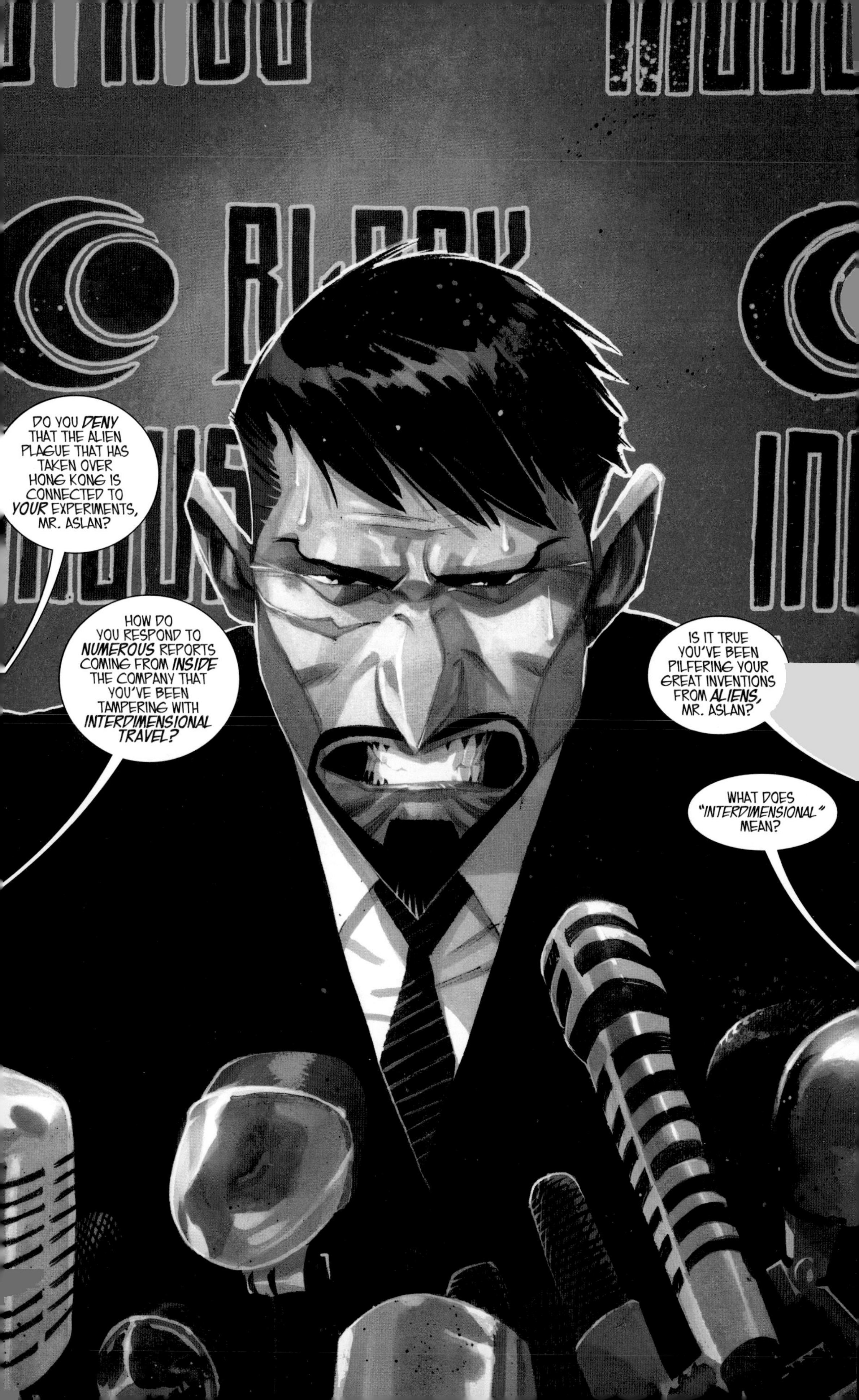
DO YOU *DENY* THAT THE ALIEN PLAGUE THAT HAS TAKEN OVER HONG KONG IS CONNECTED TO *YOUR* EXPERIMENTS, MR. ASLAN?
HOW DO YOU RESPOND TO *NUMEROUS* REPORTS COMING FROM *INSIDE* THE COMPANY THAT YOU'VE BEEN TAMPERING WITH *INTERDIMENSIONAL TRAVEL?*
IS IT TRUE YOU'VE BEEN PILFERING YOUR GREAT INVENTIONS FROM *ALIENS,* MR. ASLAN?
WHAT DOES "*INTERDIMENSIONAL*" MEAN?

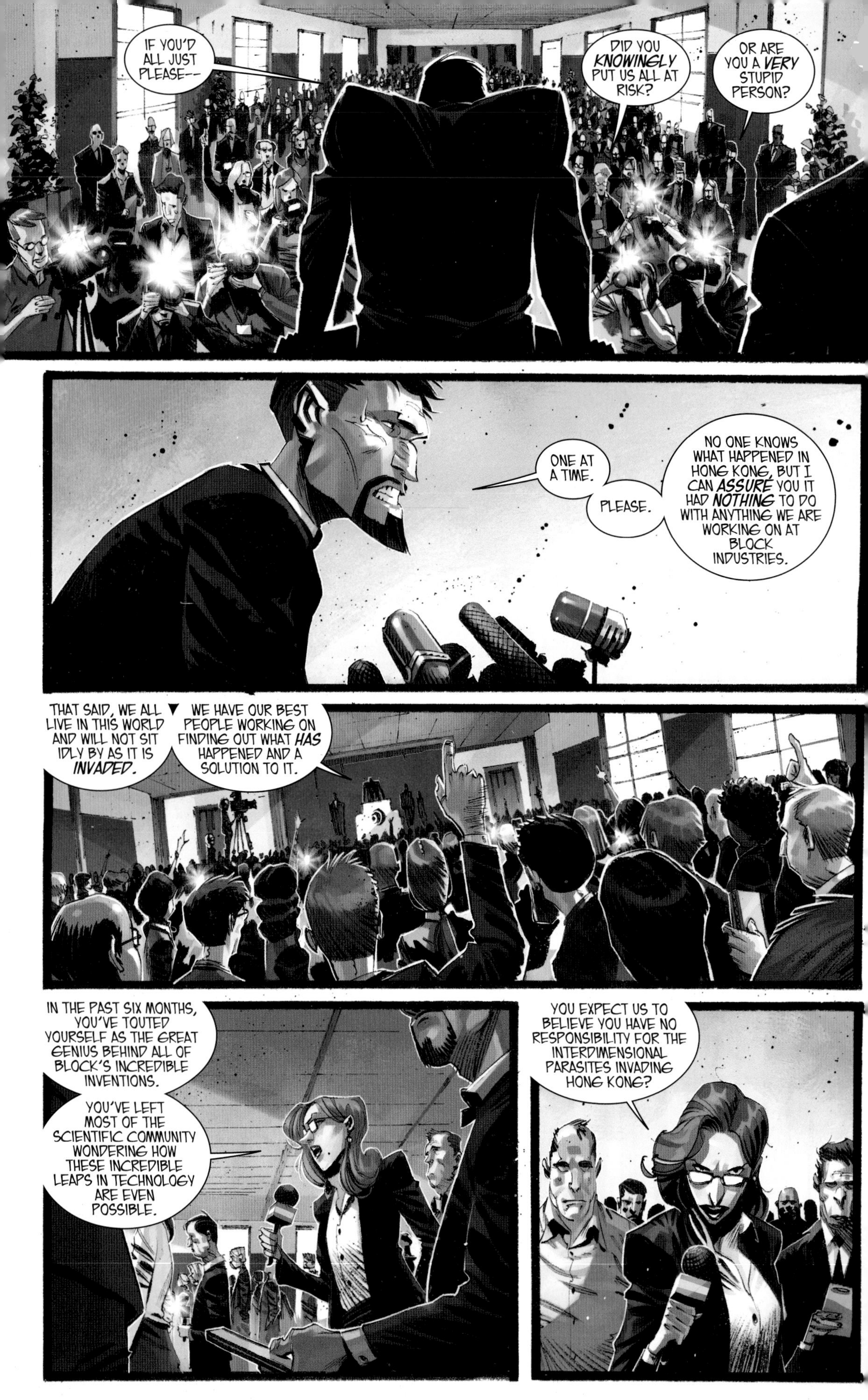
IF YOU'D ALL JUST PLEASE--
DID YOU KNOWINGLY PUT US ALL AT RISK?
OR ARE YOU A VERY STUPID PERSON?
ONE AT A TIME.
PLEASE.
NO ONE KNOWS WHAT HAPPENED IN HONG KONG, BUT I CAN ASSURE YOU IT HAD NOTHING TO DO WITH ANYTHING WE ARE WORKING ON AT BLOCK INDUSTRIES.
THAT SAID, WE ALL LIVE IN THIS WORLD AND WILL NOT SIT IDLY BY AS IT IS INVADED.
WE HAVE OUR BEST PEOPLE WORKING ON FINDING OUT WHAT HAS HAPPENED AND A SOLUTION TO IT.
IN THE PAST SIX MONTHS, YOU'VE TOUTED YOURSELF AS THE GREAT GENIUS BEHIND ALL OF BLOCK'S INCREDIBLE INVENTIONS.
YOU'VE LEFT MOST OF THE SCIENTIFIC COMMUNITY WONDERING HOW THESE INCREDIBLE LEAPS IN TECHNOLOGY ARE EVEN POSSIBLE.
YOU EXPECT US TO BELIEVE YOU HAVE NO RESPONSIBILITY FOR THE INTERDIMENSIONAL PARASITES INVADING HONG KONG?

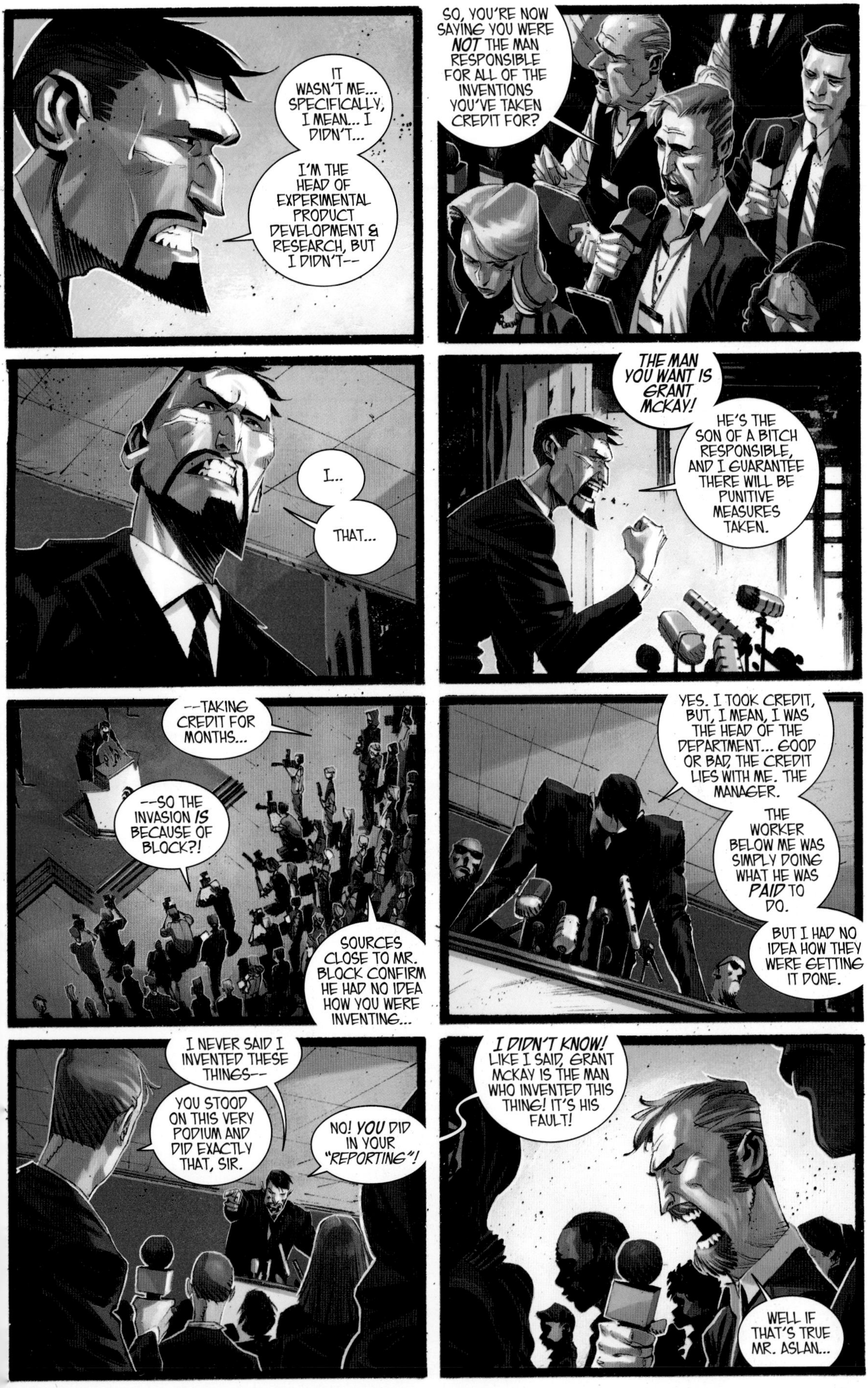
IT WASN'T ME... SPECIFICALLY, I MEAN... I DIDN'T...
I'M THE HEAD OF EXPERIMENTAL PRODUCT DEVELOPMENT & RESEARCH, BUT I DIDN'T--
SO, YOU'RE NOW SAYING YOU WERE NOT THE MAN RESPONSIBLE FOR ALL OF THE INVENTIONS YOU'VE TAKEN CREDIT FOR?
I...
THAT...
THE MAN YOU WANT IS GRANT MCKAY!
HE'S THE SON OF A BITCH RESPONSIBLE, AND I GUARANTEE THERE WILL BE PUNITIVE MEASURES TAKEN.
--TAKING CREDIT FOR MONTHS...
--SO THE INVASION IS BECAUSE OF BLOCK?!
SOURCES CLOSE TO MR. BLOCK CONFIRM HE HAD NO IDEA HOW YOU WERE INVENTING...
YES. I TOOK CREDIT, BUT, I MEAN, I WAS THE HEAD OF THE DEPARTMENT... GOOD OR BAD, THE CREDIT LIES WITH ME. THE MANAGER.
THE WORKER BELOW ME WAS SIMPLY DOING WHAT HE WAS PAID TO DO.
BUT I HAD NO IDEA HOW THEY WERE GETTING IT DONE.
I NEVER SAID I INVENTED THESE THINGS--
YOU STOOD ON THIS VERY PODIUM AND DID EXACTLY THAT, SIR.
NO! YOU DID IN YOUR "REPORTING"!
I DIDN'T KNOW! LIKE I SAID, GRANT MCKAY IS THE MAN WHO INVENTED THIS THING! IT'S HIS FAULT!
WELL IF THAT'S TRUE MR. ASLAN...

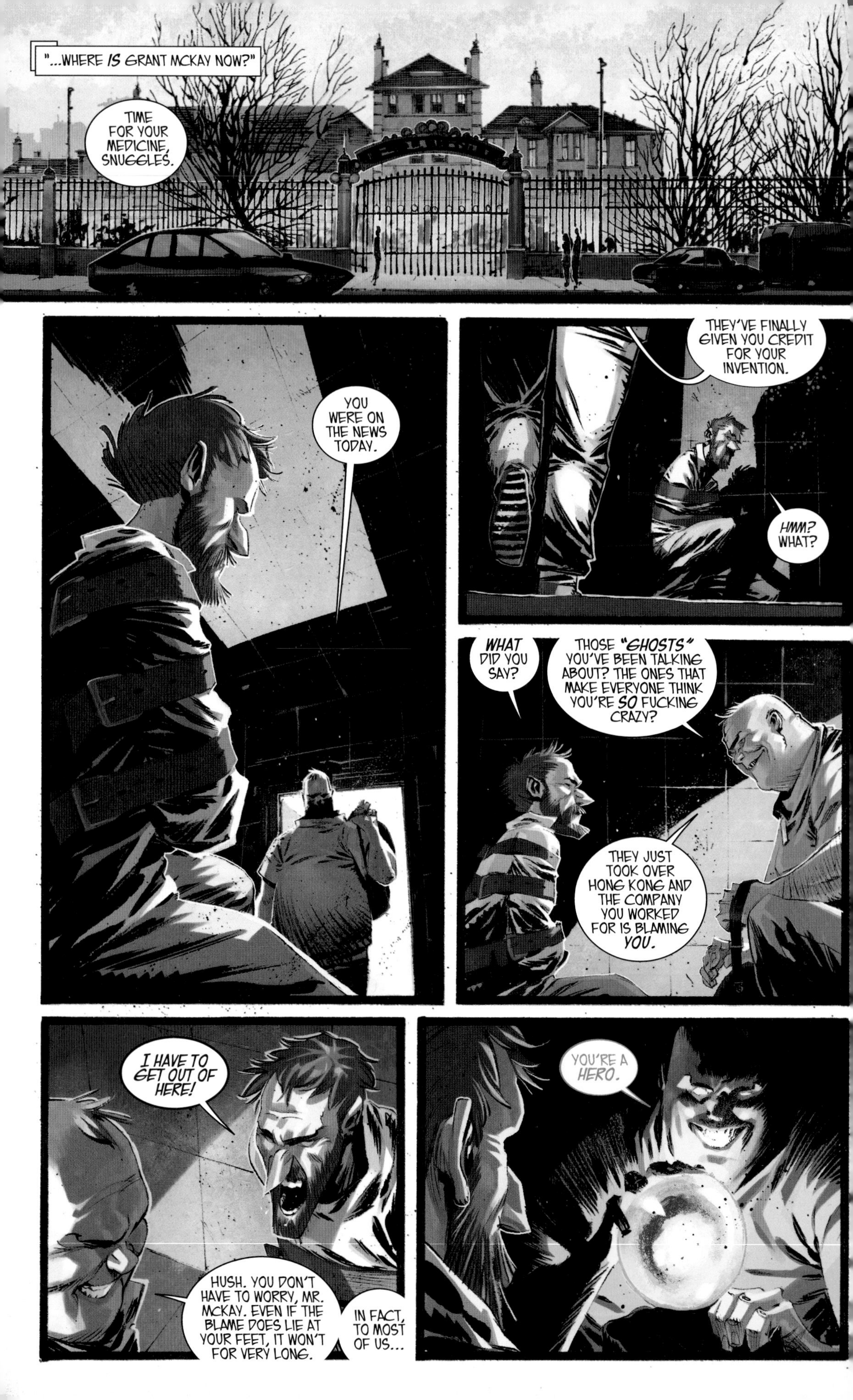
"...WHERE IS GRANT MCKAY NOW?"
TIME FOR YOUR MEDICINE, SNUGGLES.
YOU WERE ON THE NEWS TODAY.
THEY'VE FINALLY GIVEN YOU CREDIT FOR YOUR INVENTION.
HMM? WHAT?
WHAT DID YOU SAY?
THOSE "GHOSTS" YOU'VE BEEN TALKING ABOUT? THE ONES THAT MAKE EVERYONE THINK YOU'RE SO FUCKING CRAZY?
THEY JUST TOOK OVER HONG KONG AND THE COMPANY YOU WORKED FOR IS BLAMING YOU.
I HAVE TO GET OUT OF HERE!
HUSH. YOU DON'T HAVE TO WORRY, MR. MCKAY. EVEN IF THE BLAME DOES LIE AT YOUR FEET, IT WON'T FOR VERY LONG.
IN FACT, TO MOST OF US...
YOU'RE A HERO.

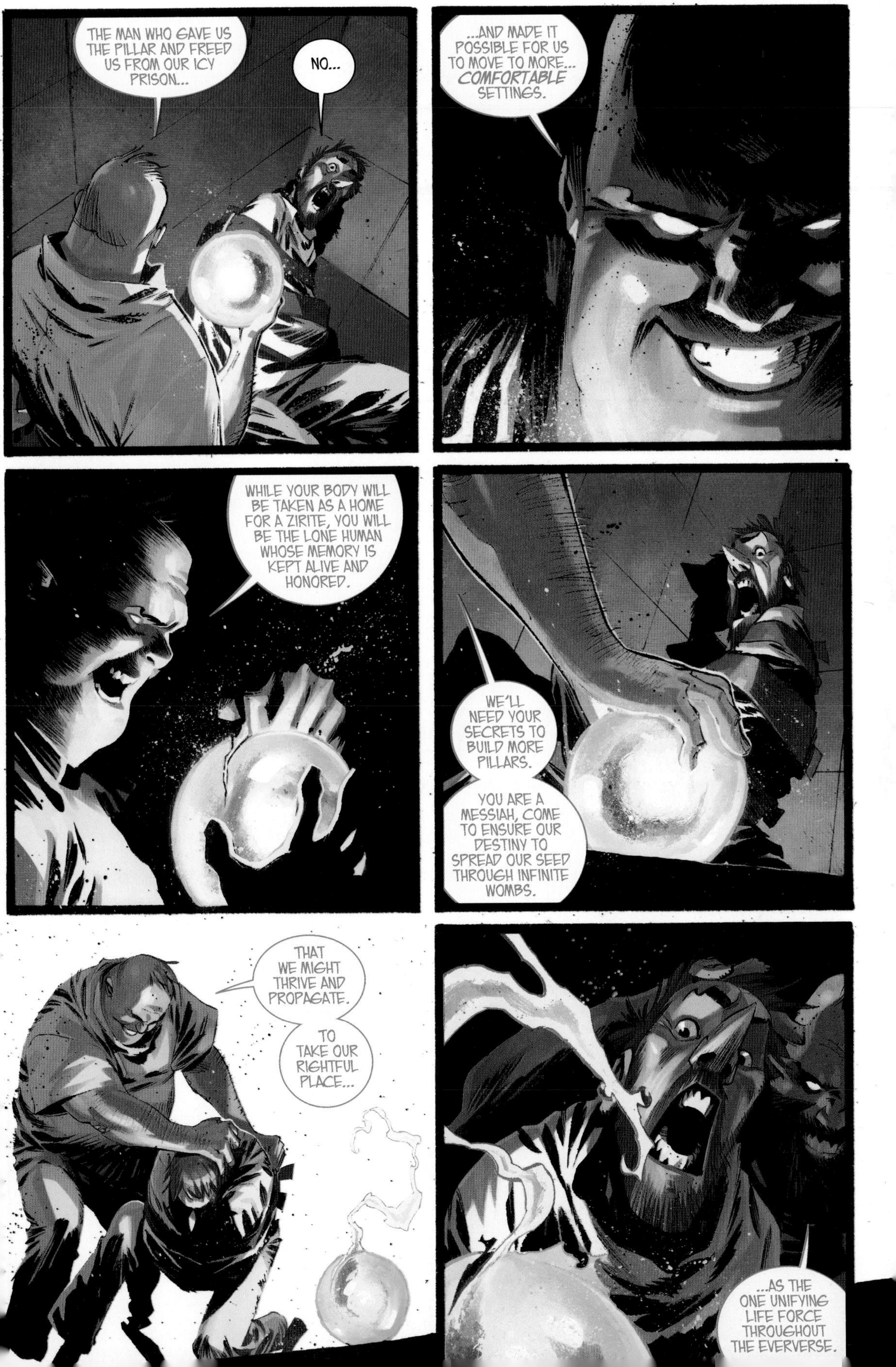
THE MAN WHO GAVE US THE PILLAR AND FREED US FROM OUR ICY PRISON...
NO...
...AND MADE IT POSSIBLE FOR US TO MOVE TO MORE... *COMFORTABLE* SETTINGS.
WHILE YOUR BODY WILL BE TAKEN AS A HOME FOR A ZIRITE, YOU WILL BE THE LONE HUMAN WHOSE MEMORY IS KEPT ALIVE AND HONORED.
WE'LL NEED YOUR SECRETS TO BUILD MORE PILLARS.
YOU ARE A MESSIAH, COME TO ENSURE OUR DESTINY TO SPREAD OUR SEED THROUGH INFINITE WOMBS.
THAT WE MIGHT THRIVE AND PROPAGATE.
TO TAKE OUR RIGHTFUL PLACE...
...AS THE ONE UNIFYING LIFE FORCE THROUGHOUT THE EVERVERSE.

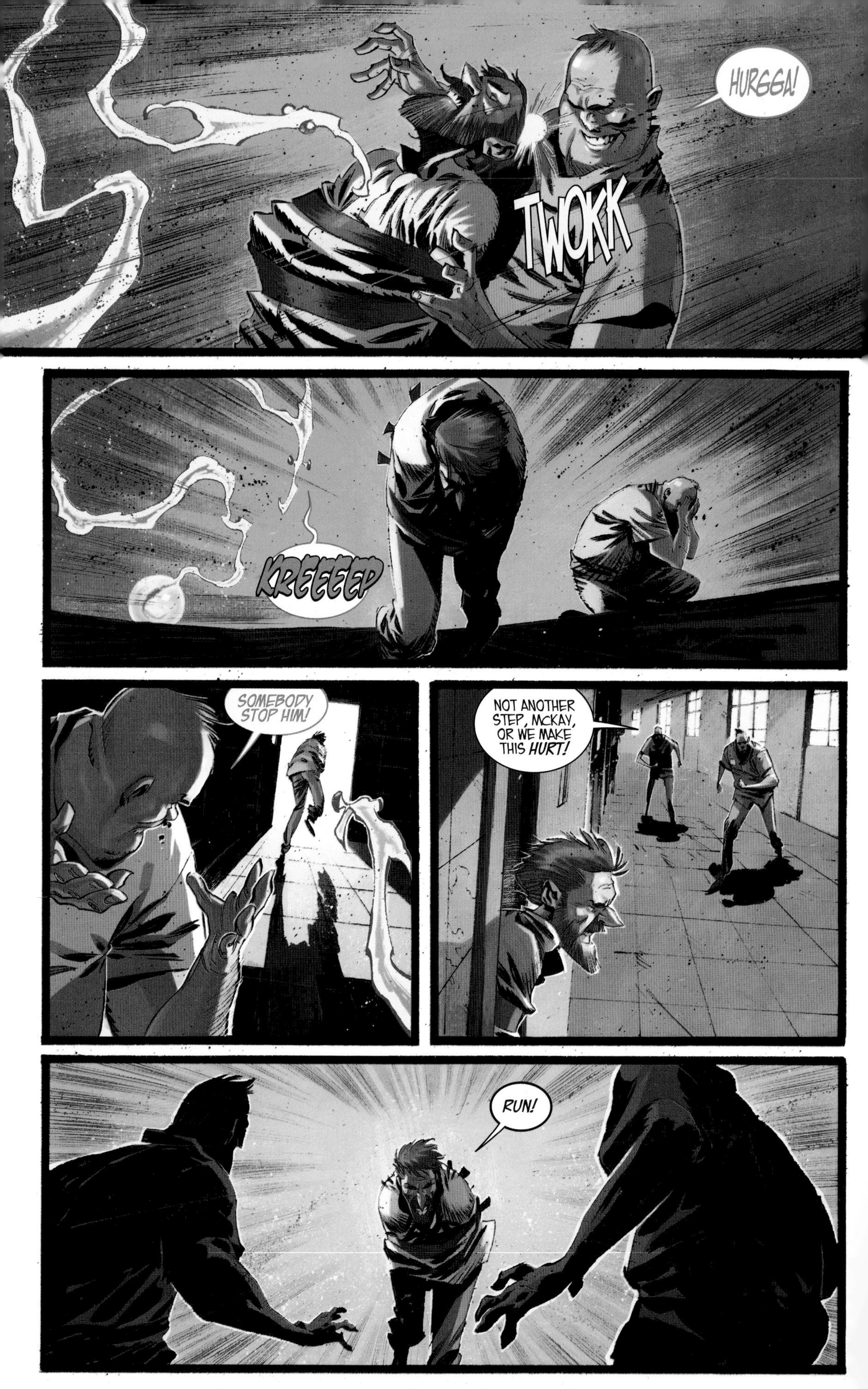
HURGGA!
TWOKK
KREEEEP
SOMEBODY STOP HIM!
NOT ANOTHER STEP, MCKAY, OR WE MAKE THIS HURT!
RUN!

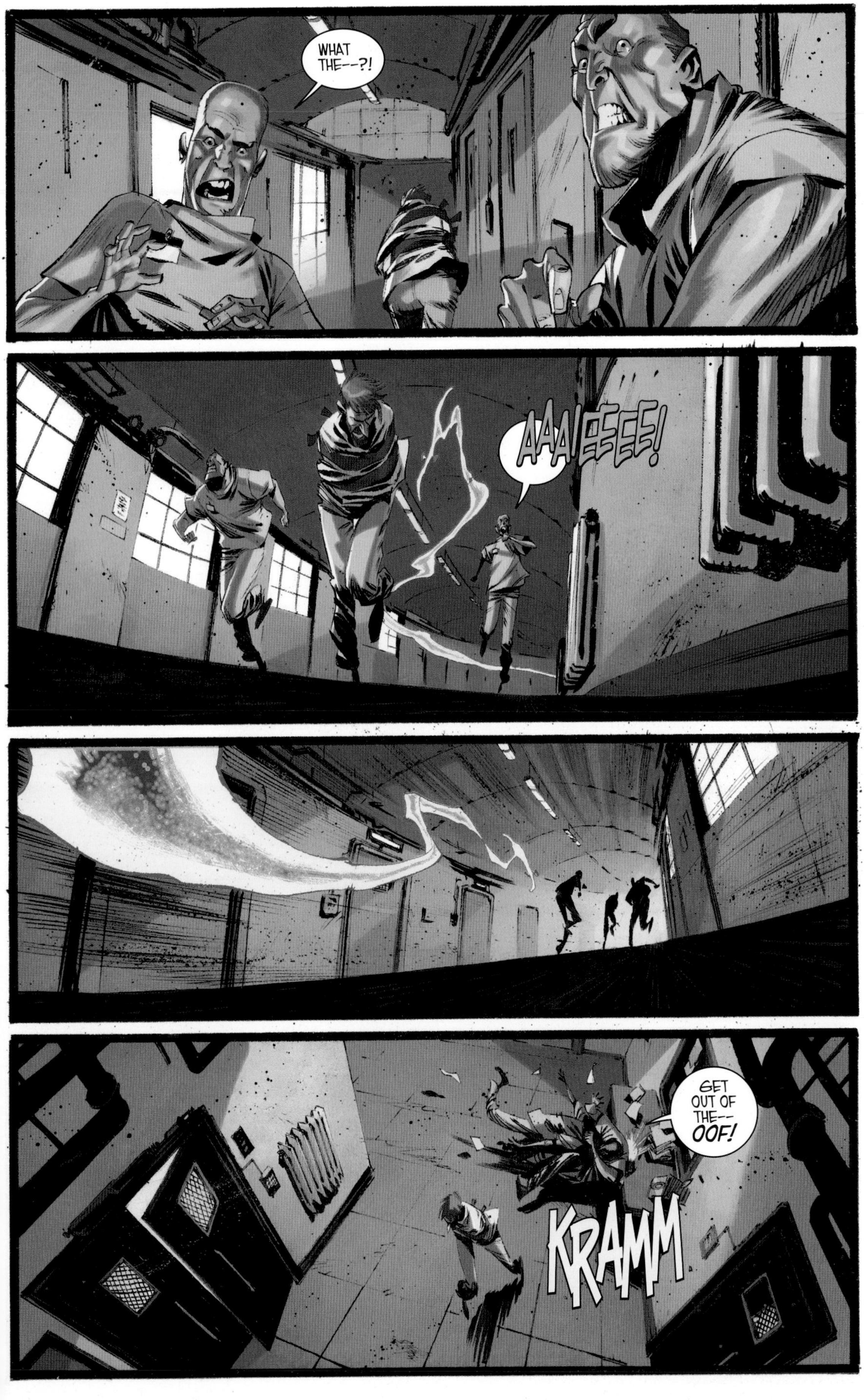
WHAT THE--?!
AAAIEEEEE!
GET OUT OF THE-- OOF!
KRAMM

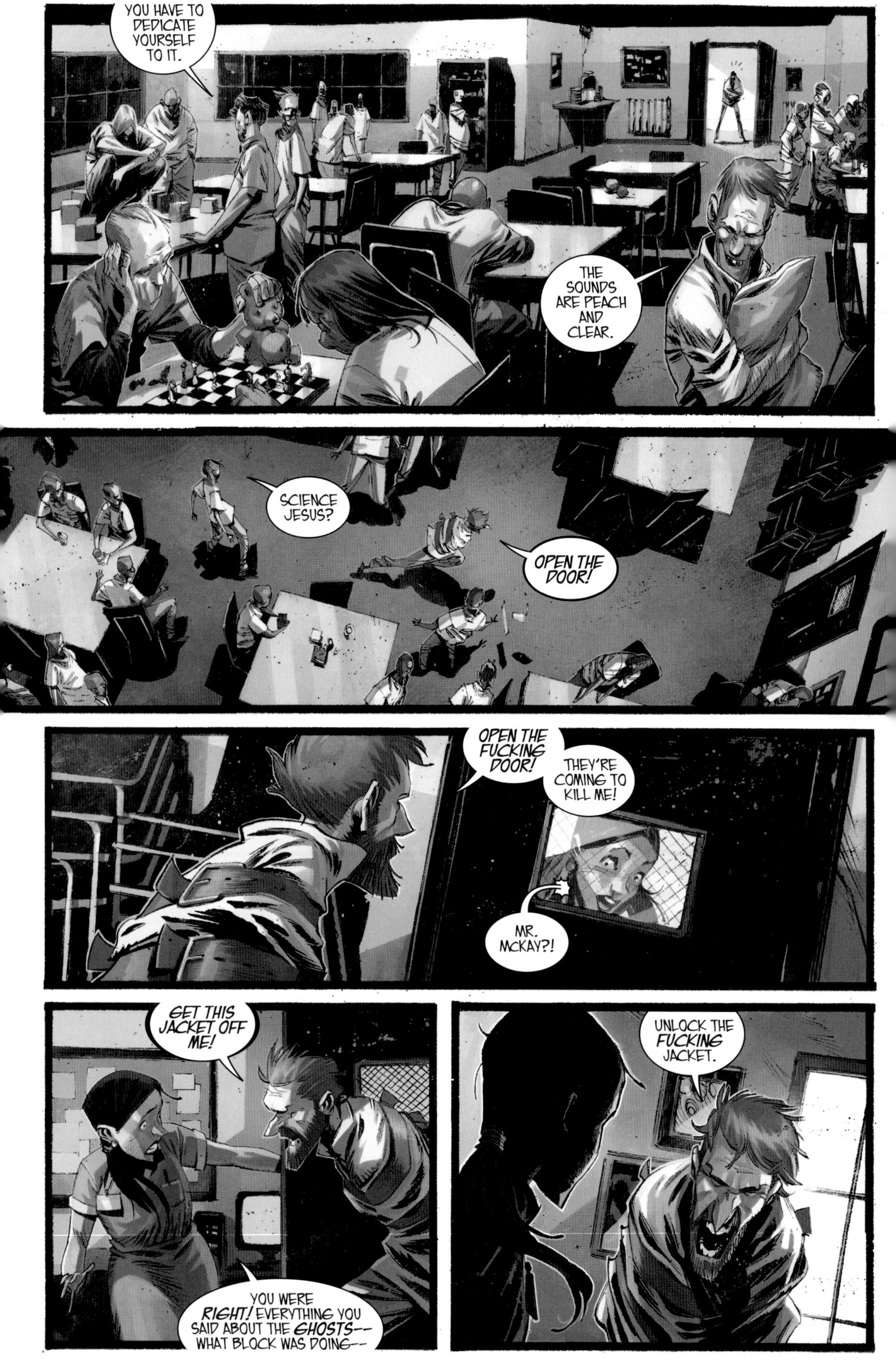
YOU HAVE TO DEDICATE YOURSELF TO IT.
THE SOUNDS ARE PEACH AND CLEAR.
SCIENCE JESUS?
OPEN THE DOOR!
OPEN THE FUCKING DOOR!
THEY'RE COMING TO KILL ME!
MR. MCKAY?!
GET THIS JACKET OFF ME!
YOU WERE RIGHT! EVERYTHING YOU SAID ABOUT THE GHOSTS-- WHAT BLOCK WAS DOING--
UNLOCK THE FUCKING JACKET.

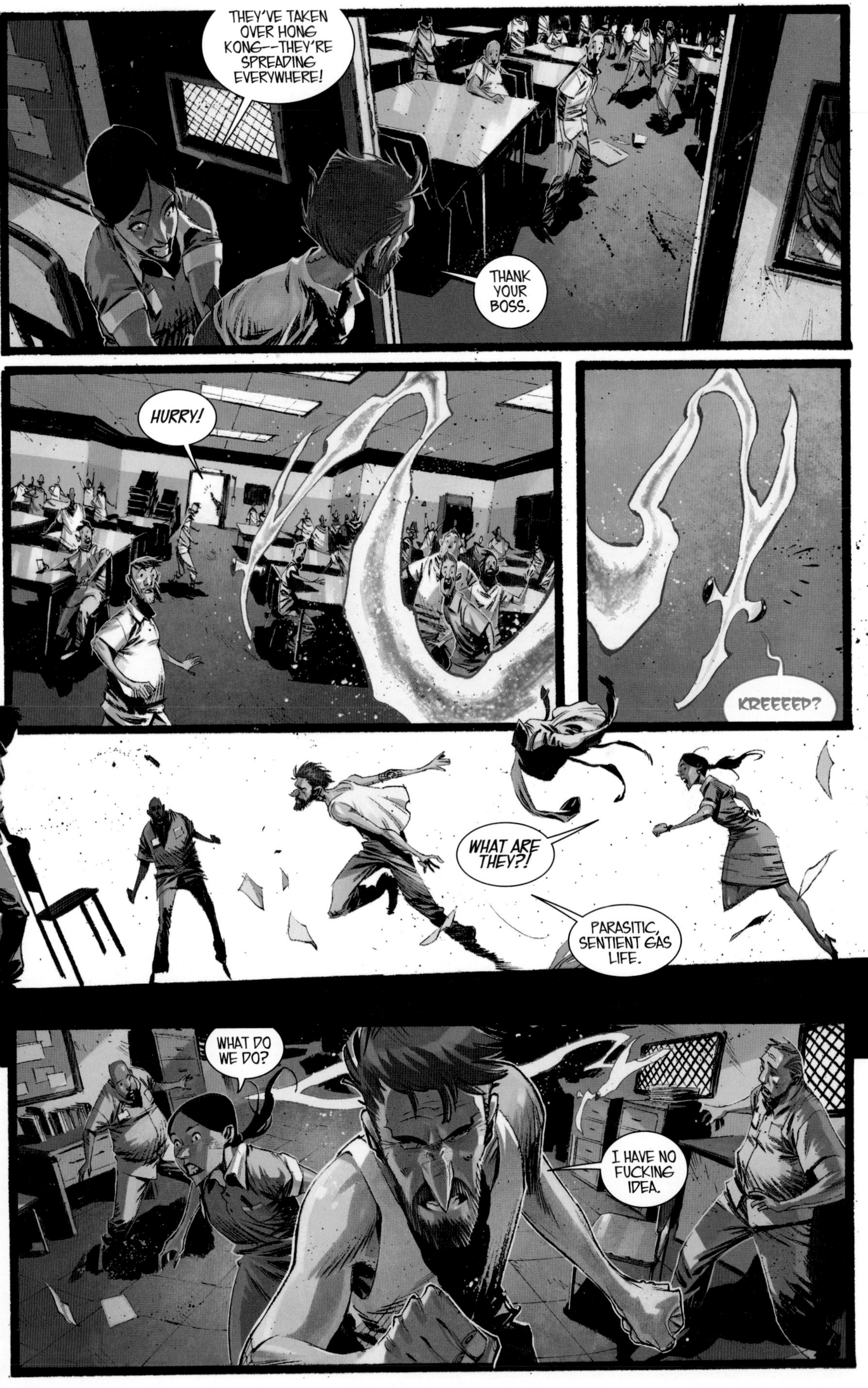
THEY'VE TAKEN OVER HONG KONG--THEY'RE SPREADING EVERYWHERE!
THANK YOUR BOSS.
HURRY!
KREEEEP?
WHAT ARE THEY?!
PARASITIC, SENTIENT GAS LIFE.
WHAT DO WE DO?
I HAVE NO FUCKING IDEA.

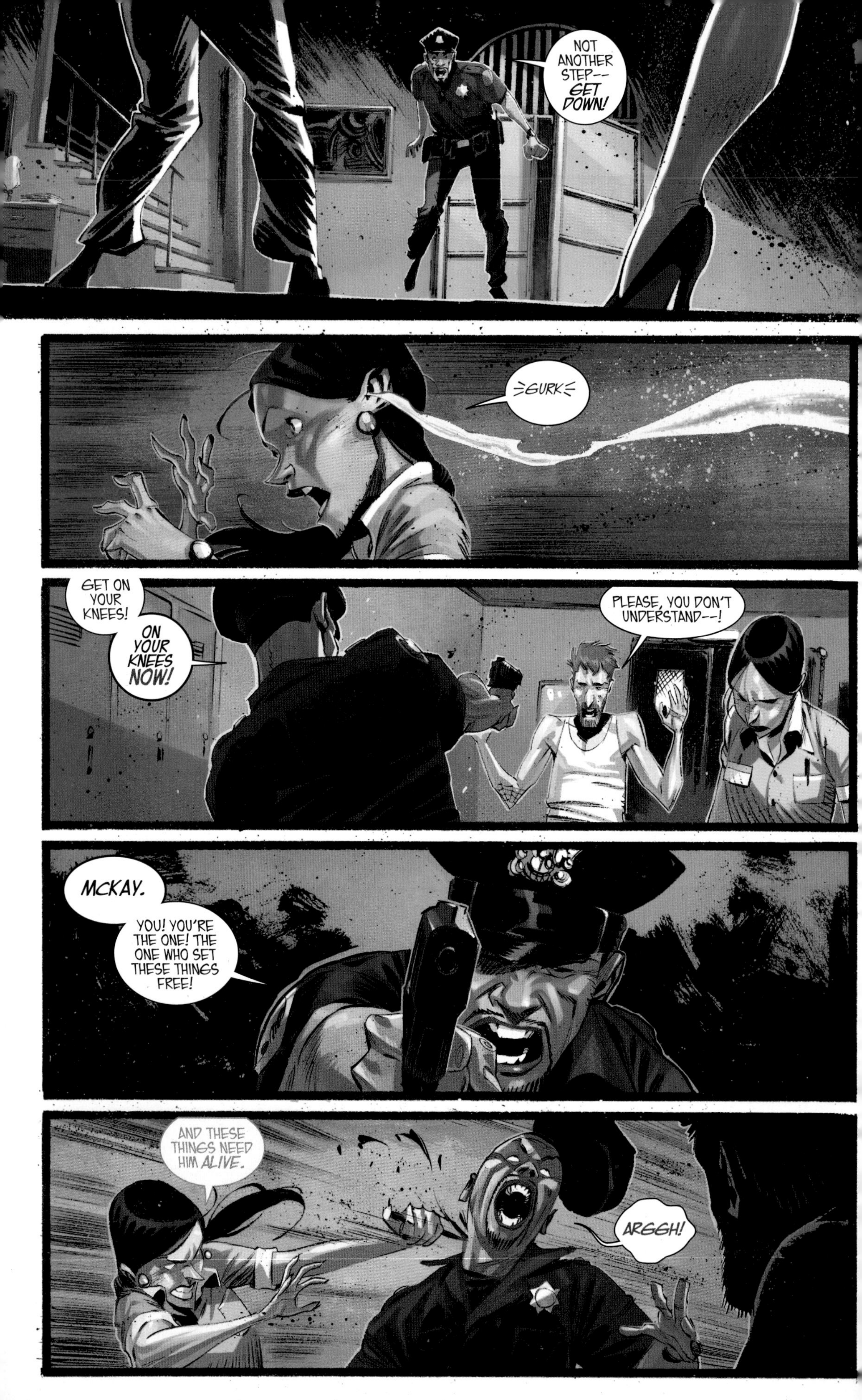
NOT ANOTHER STEP-- GET DOWN!
GURK
GET ON YOUR KNEES!
ON YOUR KNEES NOW!
PLEASE, YOU DON'T UNDERSTAND--!
MCKAY.
YOU! YOU'RE THE ONE! THE ONE WHO SET THESE THINGS FREE!
AND THESE THINGS NEED HIM ALIVE.
ARGGH!

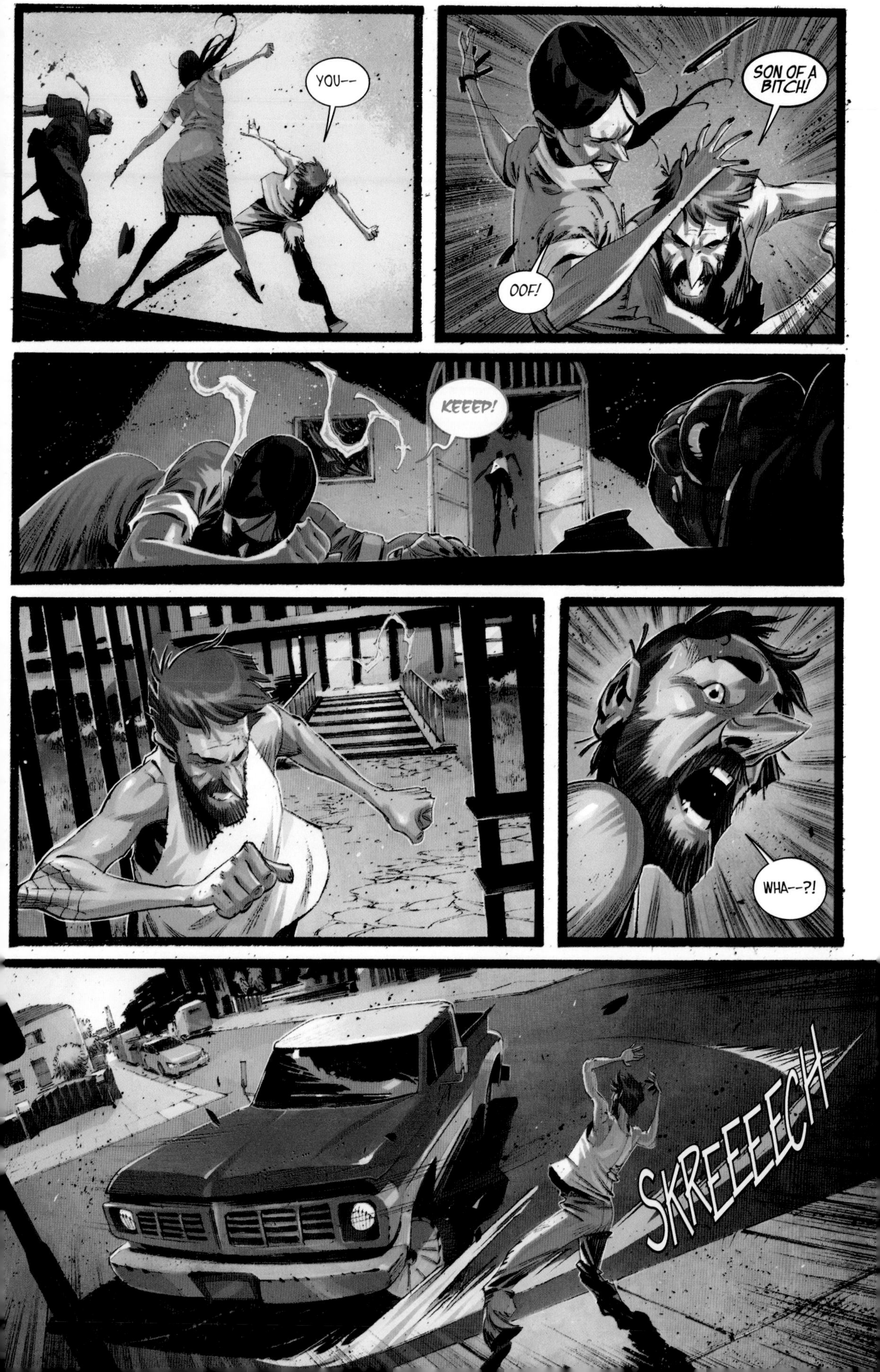
YOU--
SON OF A BITCH!
OOF!
KEEEP!
WHA--?!
SKREEEECH

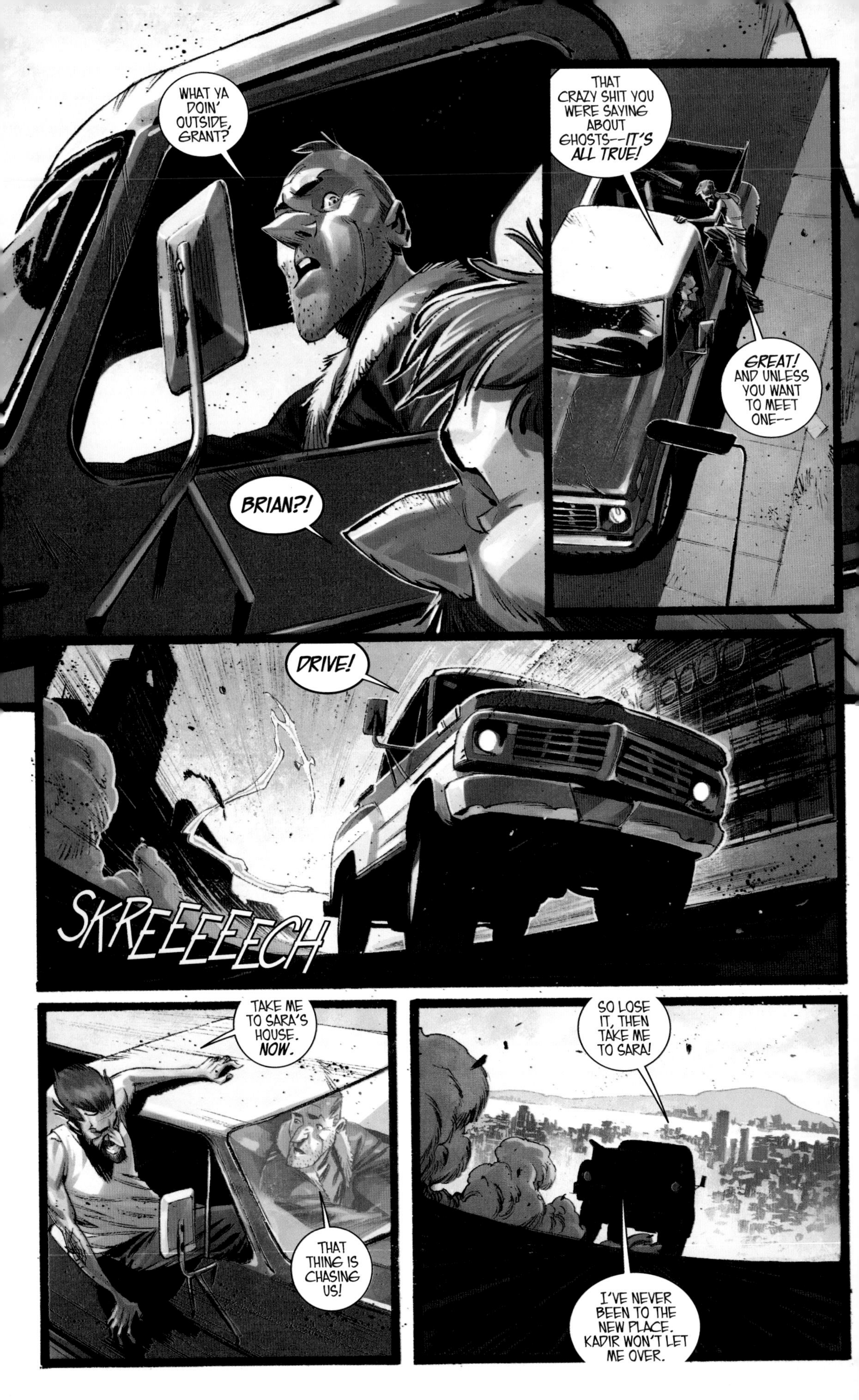
WHAT YA DOIN' OUTSIDE, GRANT?
BRIAN?!
THAT CRAZY SHIT YOU WERE SAYING ABOUT GHOSTS--IT'S ALL TRUE!
GREAT! AND UNLESS YOU WANT TO MEET ONE--
DRIVE!
SKREEEEEECH
TAKE ME TO SARA'S HOUSE. NOW.
THAT THING IS CHASING US!
SO LOSE IT, THEN TAKE ME TO SARA!
I'VE NEVER BEEN TO THE NEW PLACE. KADIR WON'T LET ME OVER.

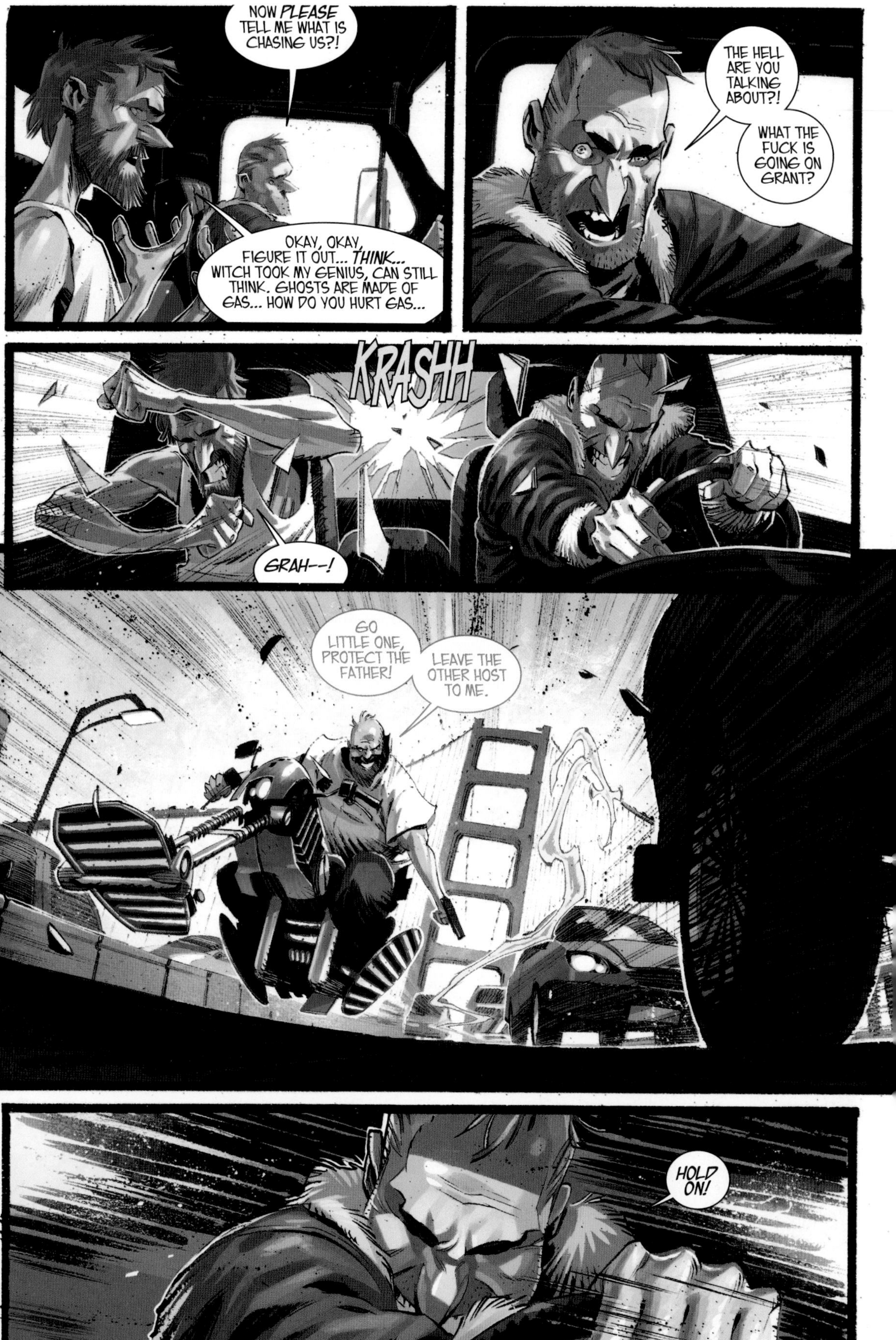
NOW PLEASE TELL ME WHAT IS CHASING US?!
OKAY, OKAY, FIGURE IT OUT... THINK... WITCH TOOK MY GENIUS, CAN STILL THINK. GHOSTS ARE MADE OF GAS... HOW DO YOU HURT GAS...
THE HELL ARE YOU TALKING ABOUT?!
WHAT THE FUCK IS GOING ON GRANT?
KRASHH
GRAH--!
GO LITTLE ONE, PROTECT THE FATHER!
LEAVE THE OTHER HOST TO ME.
HOLD ON!

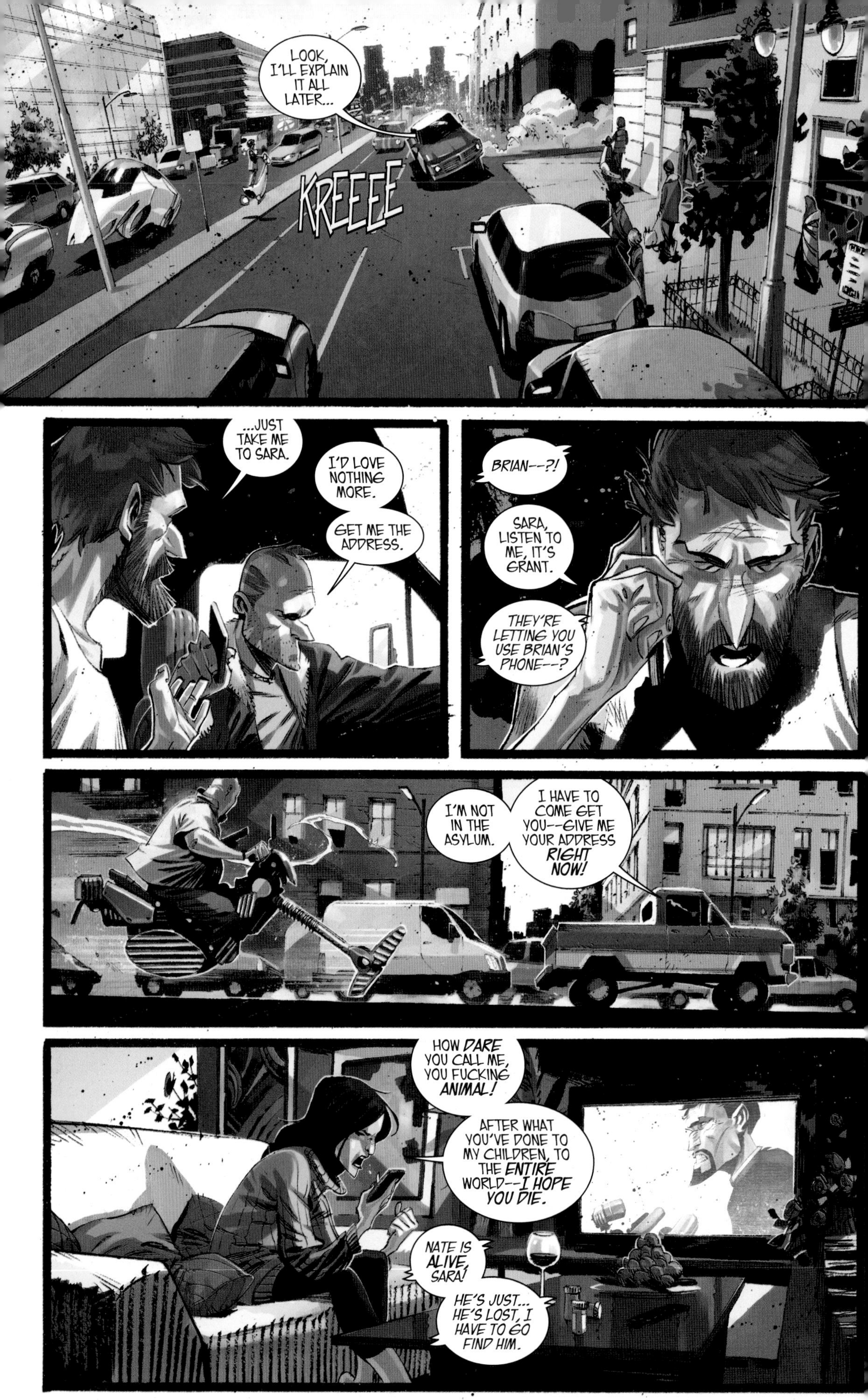
LOOK, I'LL EXPLAIN IT ALL LATER...
KREEEE
...JUST TAKE ME TO SARA.
I'D LOVE NOTHING MORE.
GET ME THE ADDRESS.
BRIAN--?!
SARA, LISTEN TO ME, IT'S GRANT.
THEY'RE LETTING YOU USE BRIAN'S PHONE--?
I'M NOT IN THE ASYLUM.
I HAVE TO COME GET YOU--GIVE ME YOUR ADDRESS RIGHT NOW!
HOW DARE YOU CALL ME, YOU FUCKING ANIMAL!
AFTER WHAT YOU'VE DONE TO MY CHILDREN, TO THE ENTIRE WORLD--I HOPE YOU DIE.
NATE IS ALIVE, SARA!
HE'S JUST... HE'S LOST, I HAVE TO GO FIND HIM.

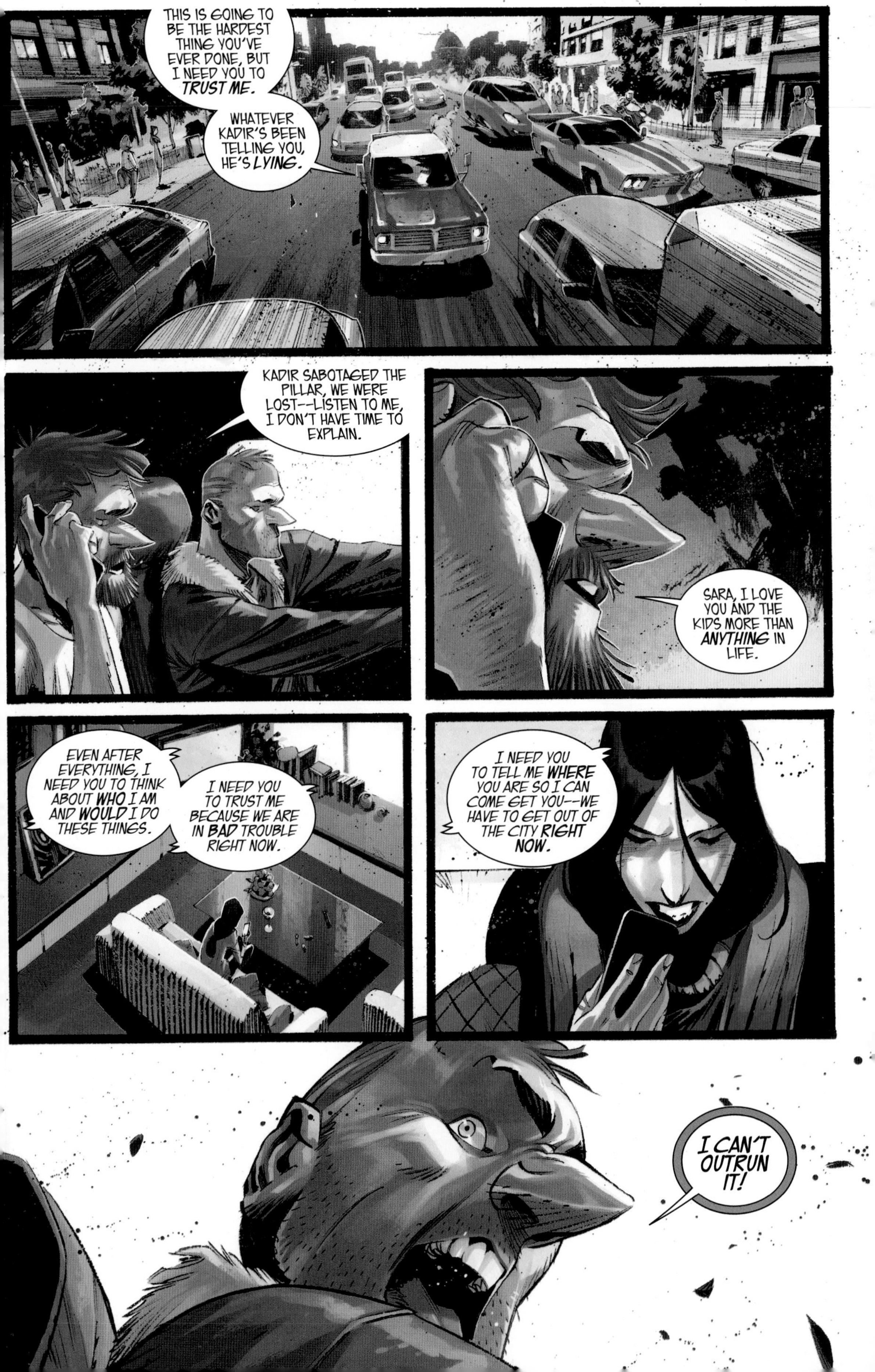
THIS IS GOING TO BE THE HARDEST THING YOU'VE EVER DONE, BUT I NEED YOU TO TRUST ME.
WHATEVER KADIR'S BEEN TELLING YOU, HE'S LYING.
KADIR SABOTAGED THE PILLAR, WE WERE LOST--LISTEN TO ME, I DON'T HAVE TIME TO EXPLAIN.
SARA, I LOVE YOU AND THE KIDS MORE THAN ANYTHING IN LIFE.
EVEN AFTER EVERYTHING, I NEED YOU TO THINK ABOUT WHO I AM AND WOULD I DO THESE THINGS.
I NEED YOU TO TRUST ME BECAUSE WE ARE IN BAD TROUBLE RIGHT NOW.
I NEED YOU TO TELL ME WHERE YOU ARE SO I CAN COME GET YOU--WE HAVE TO GET OUT OF THE CITY RIGHT NOW.
I CAN'T OUTRUN IT!

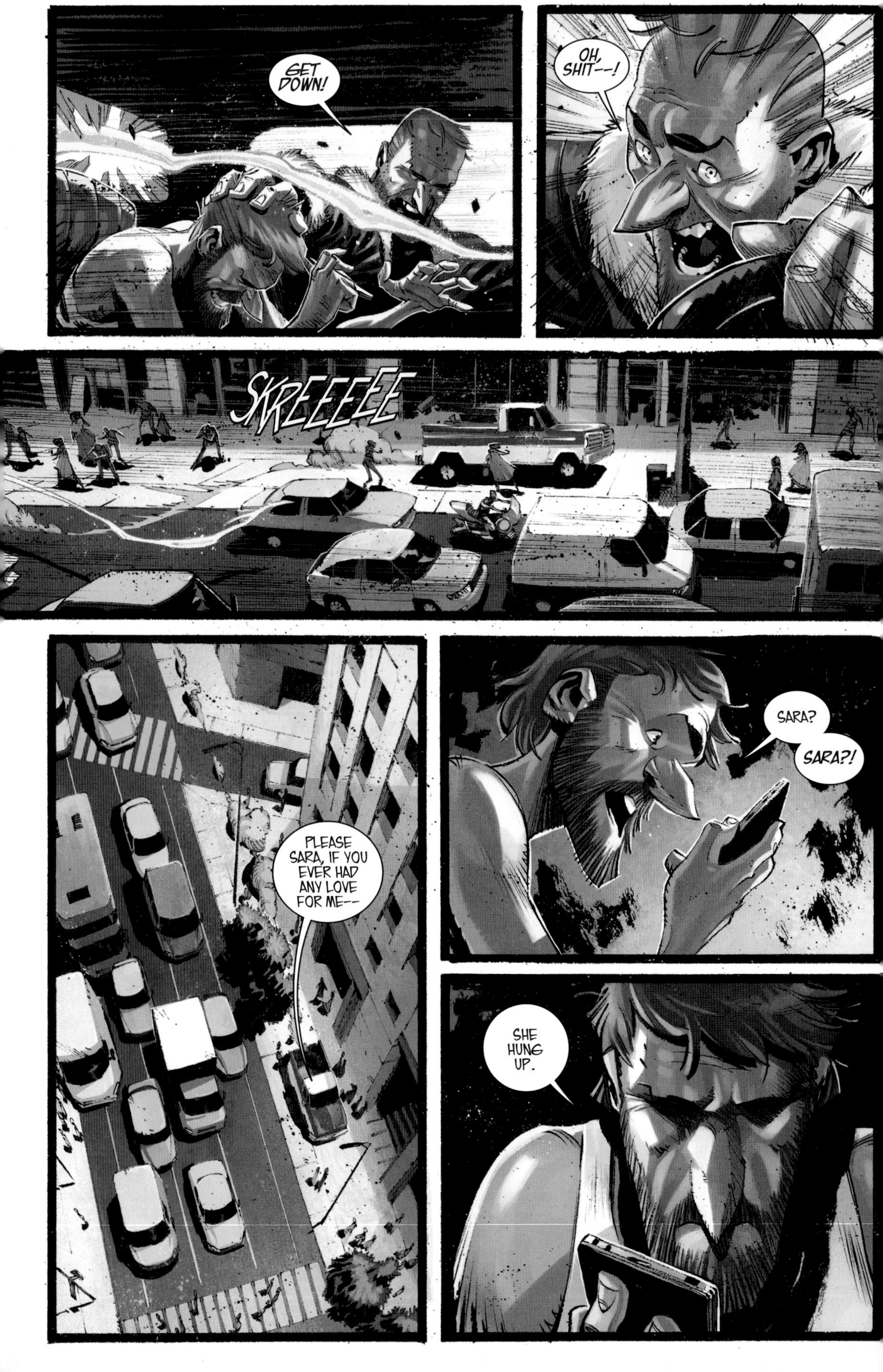
GET DOWN!
OH, SHIT--!
SKREEEEEE
PLEASE SARA, IF YOU EVER HAD ANY LOVE FOR ME--
SARA?
SARA?!
SHE HUNG UP.

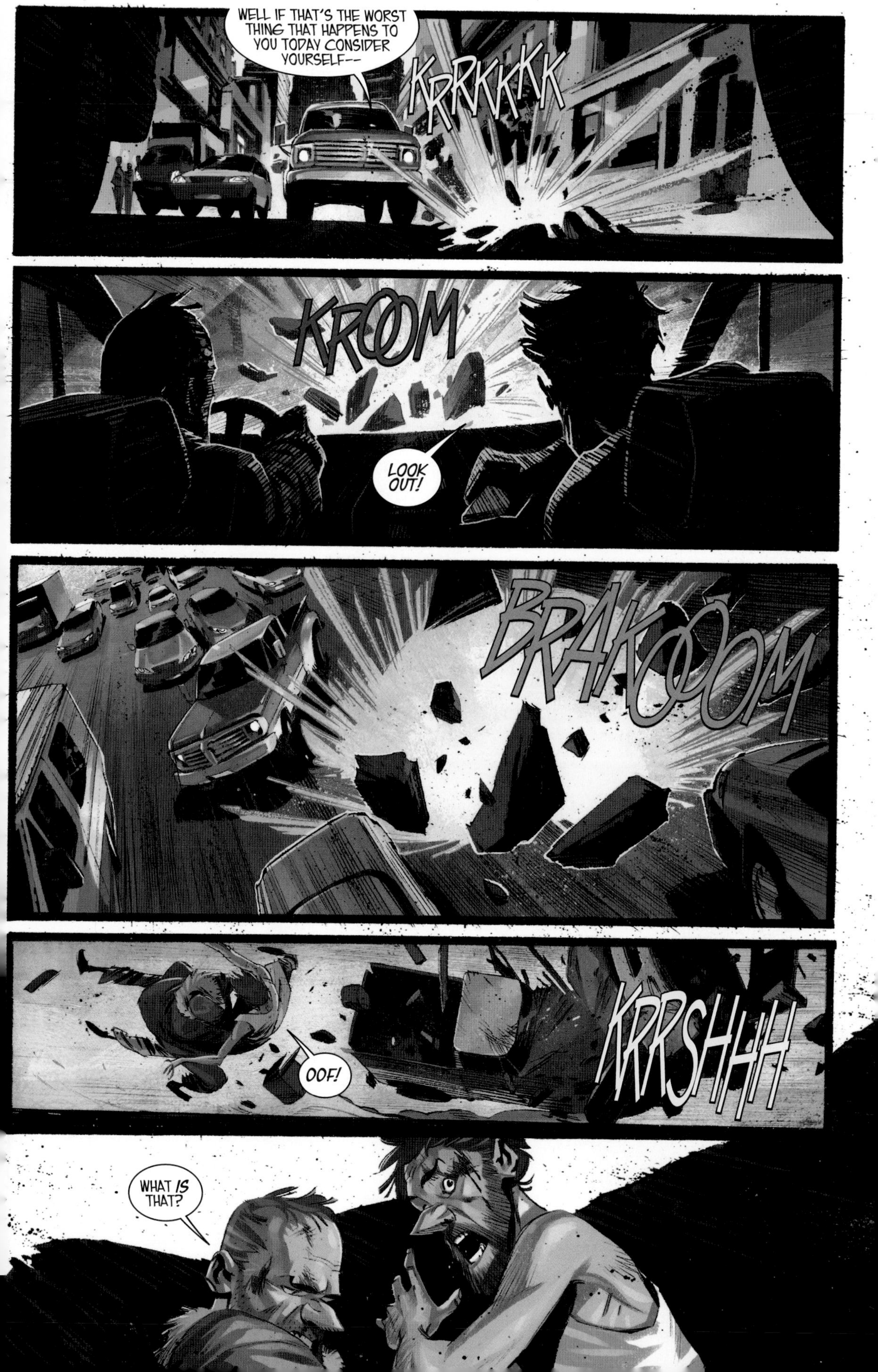
WELL IF THAT'S THE WORST THING THAT HAPPENS TO YOU TODAY CONSIDER YOURSELF--
KRRKKKK
KROOM
LOOK OUT!
BRAKOOOM
OOF!
KRRSHHH
WHAT IS THAT?

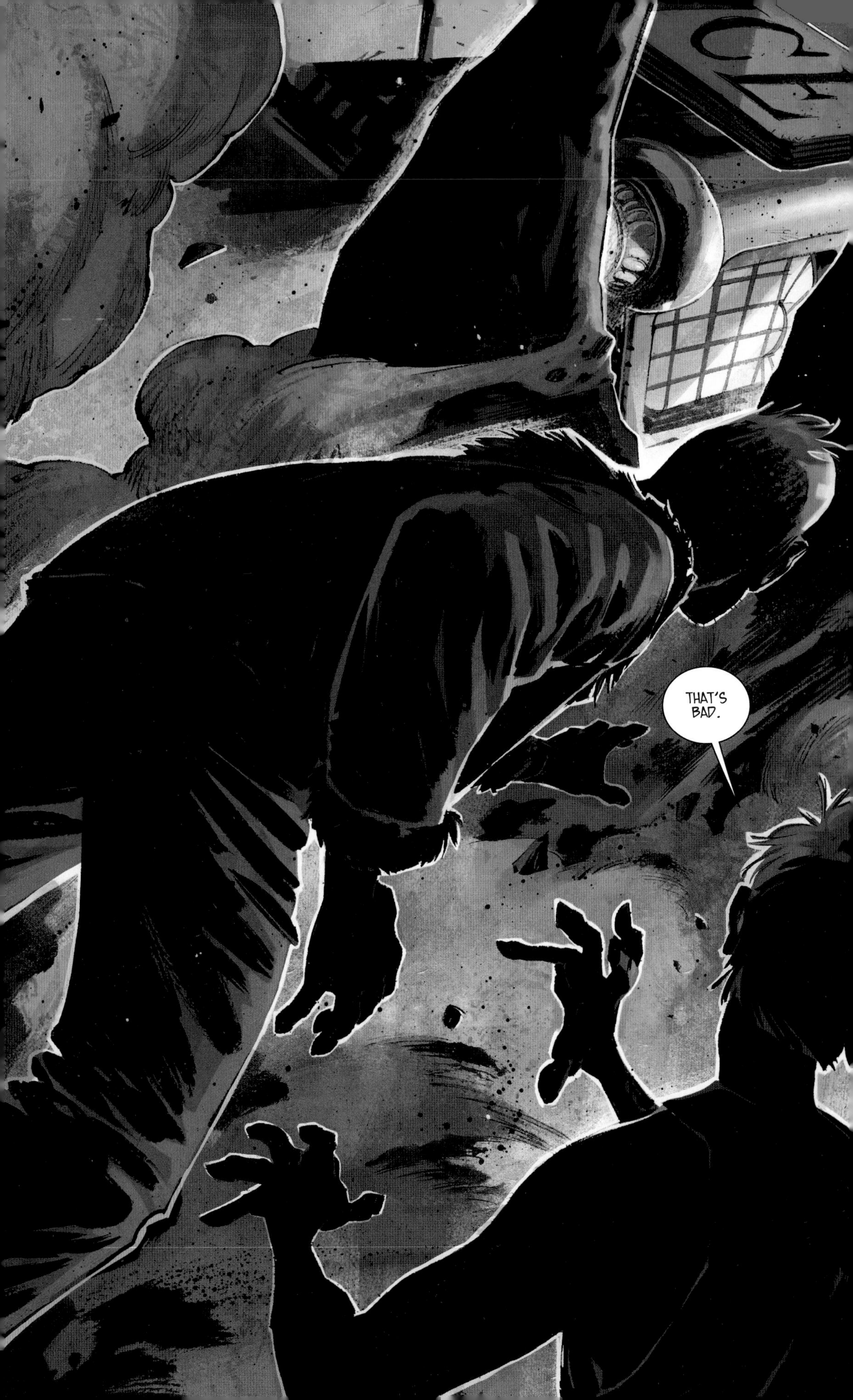
THAT'S BAD.

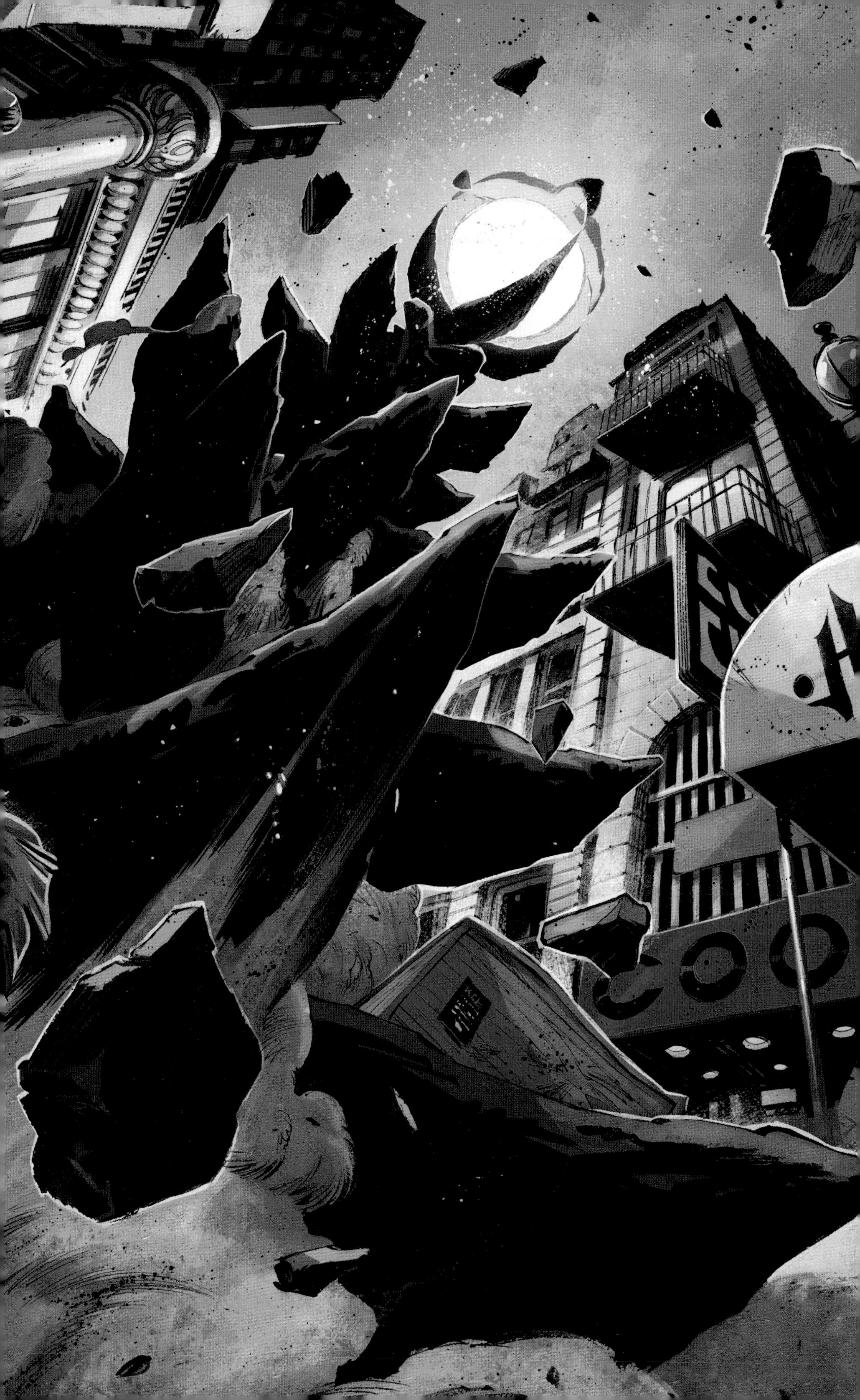

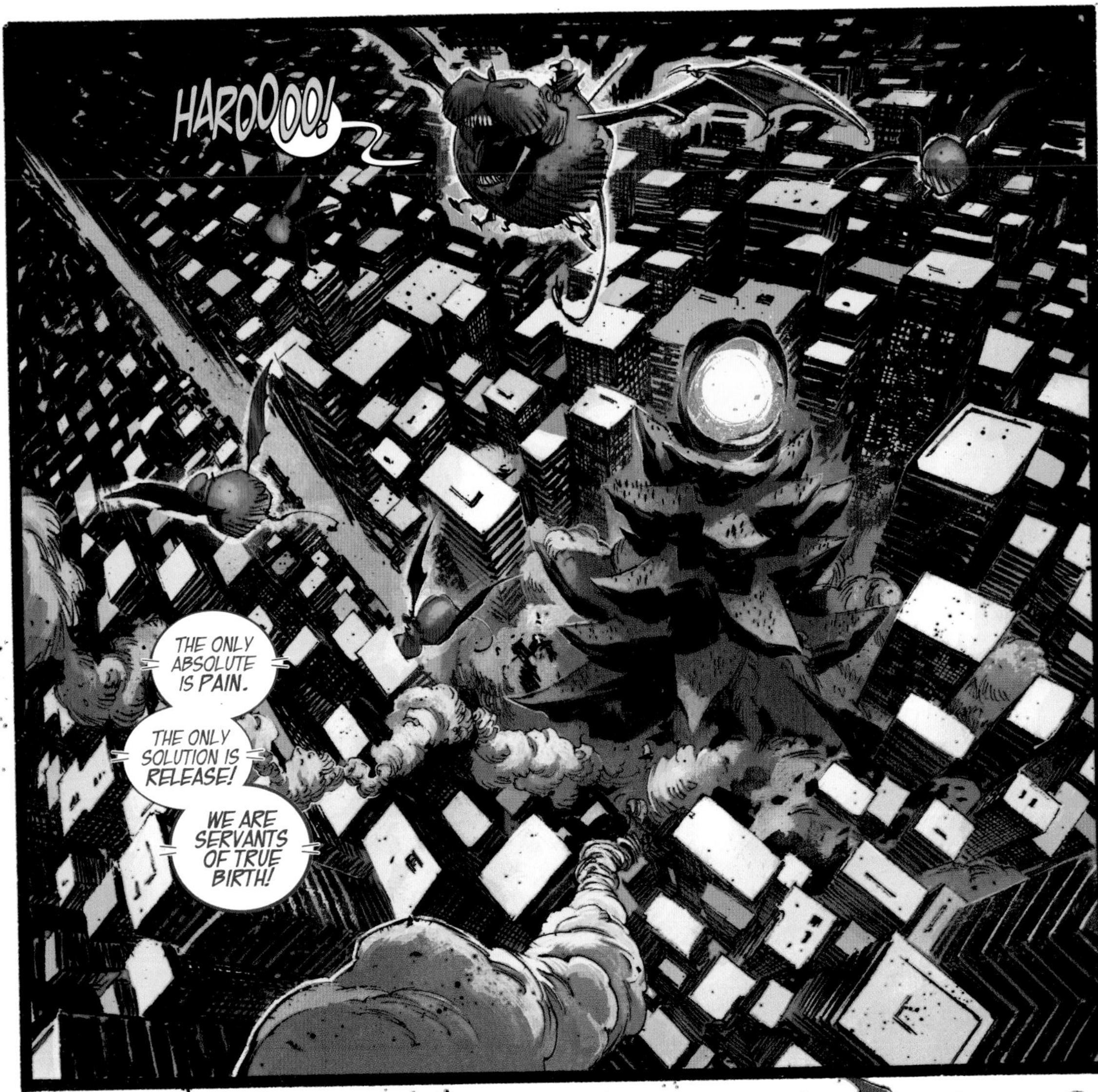
HAROOOOO!
THE ONLY ABSOLUTE IS PAIN.
THE ONLY SOLUTION IS RELEASE!
WE ARE SERVANTS OF TRUE BIRTH!

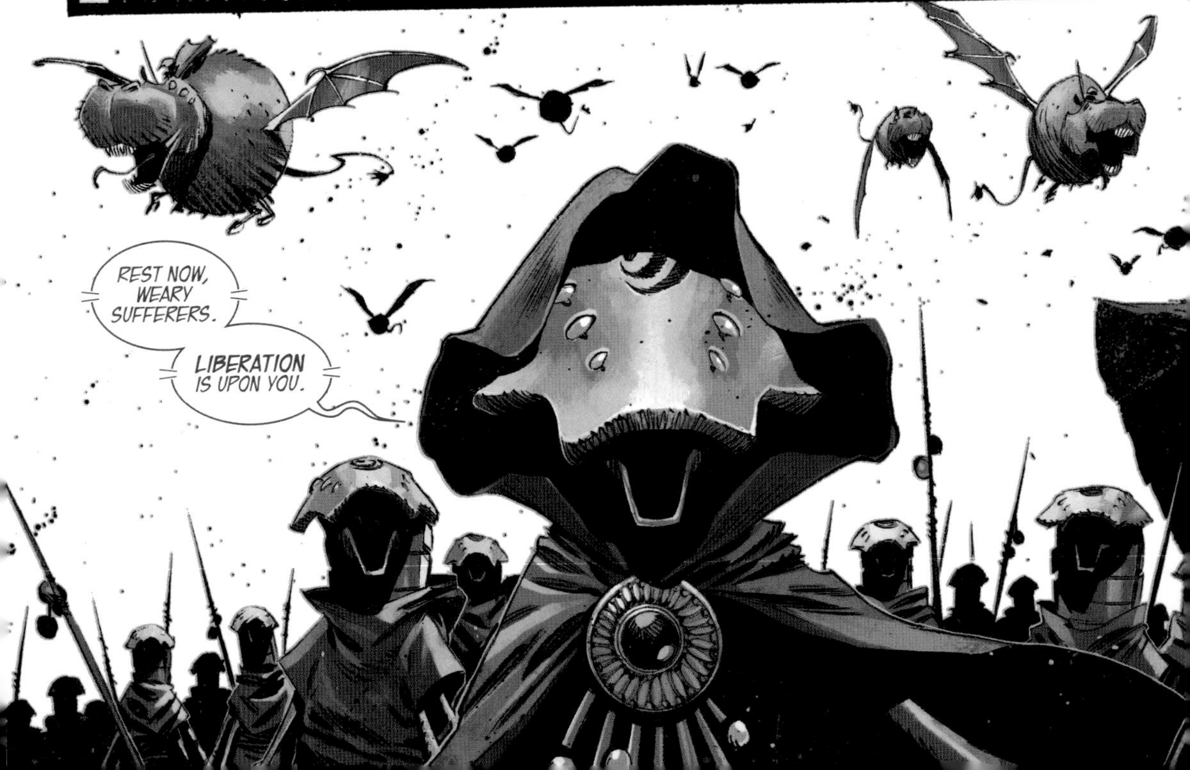
REST NOW, WEARY SUFFERERS.
LIBERATION IS UPON YOU.

# 30

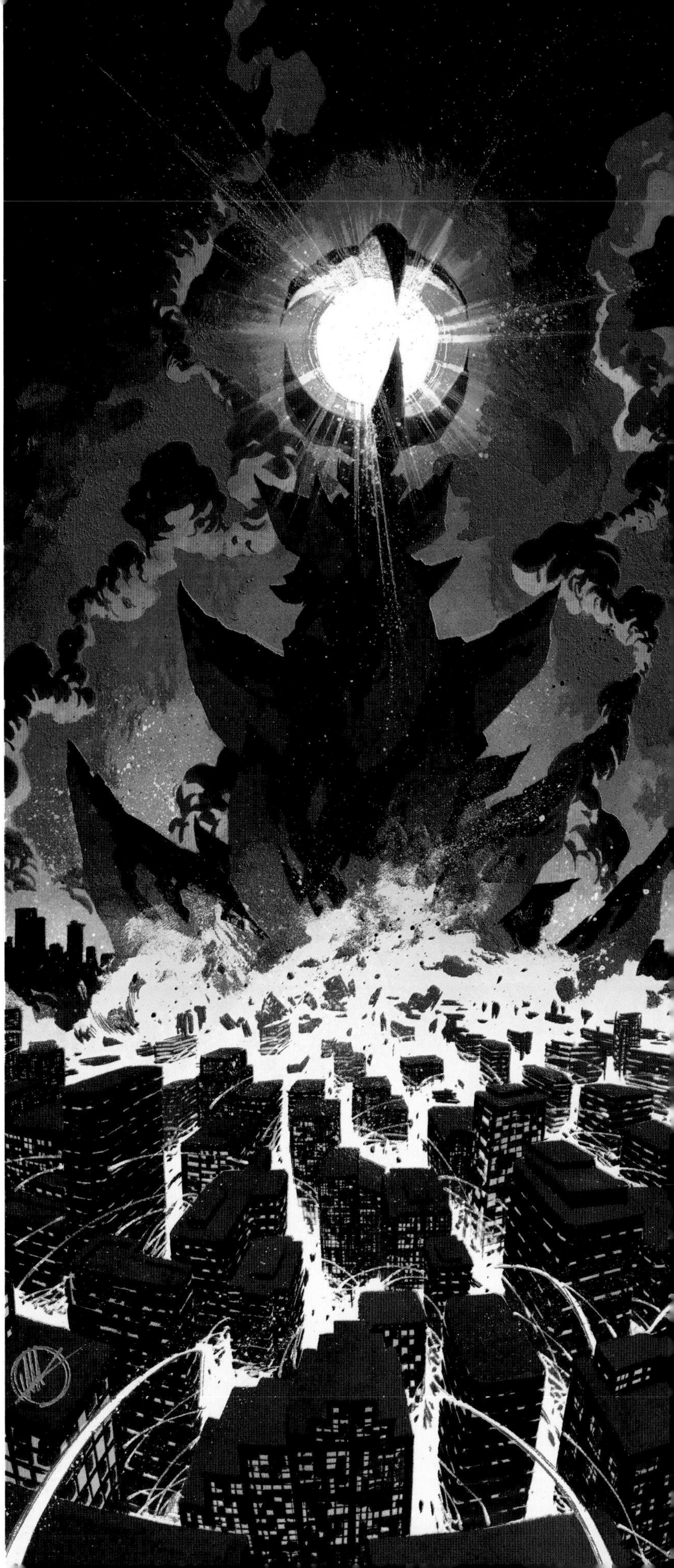

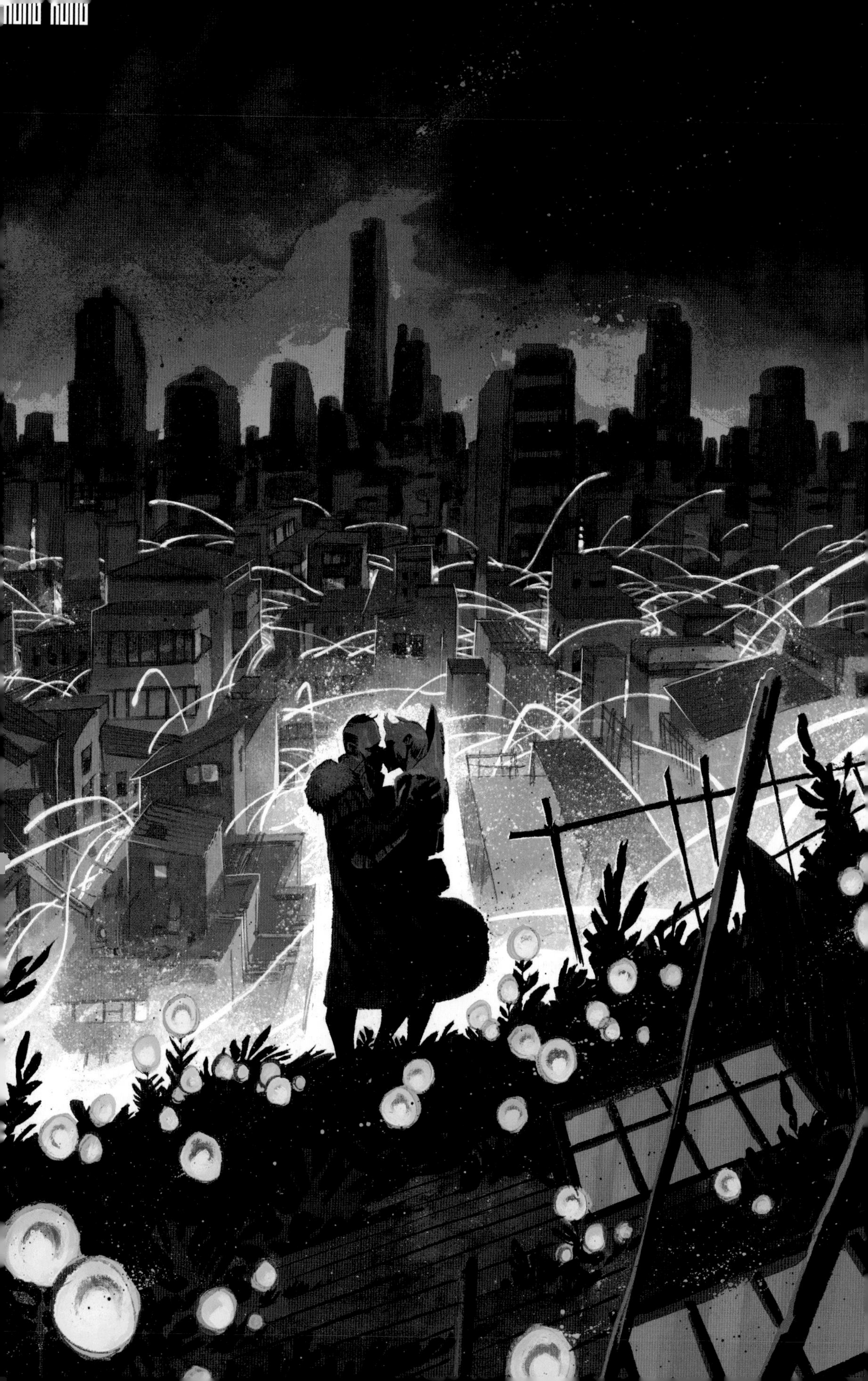

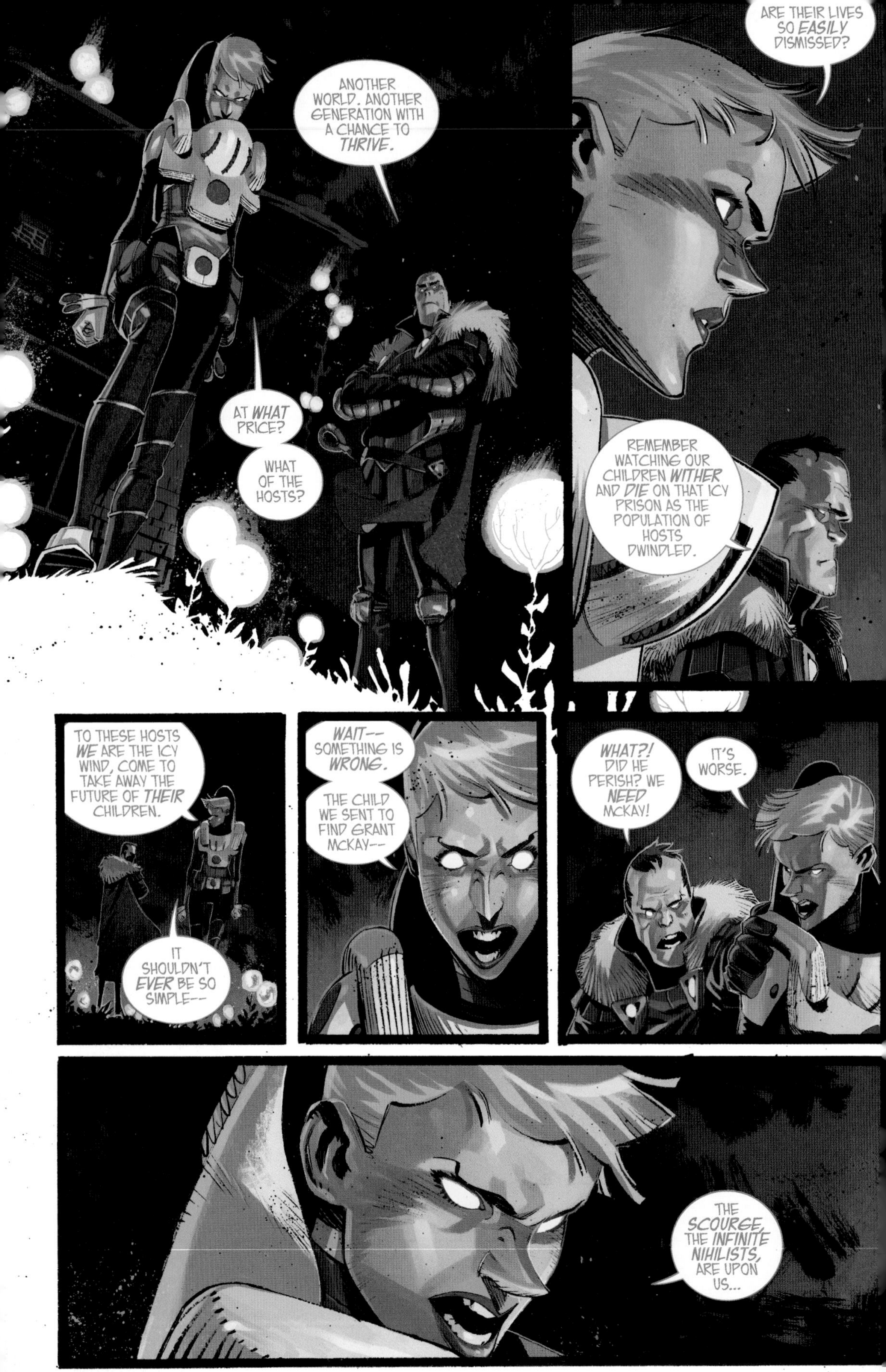
ANOTHER WORLD. ANOTHER GENERATION WITH A CHANCE TO THRIVE.
AT WHAT PRICE?
WHAT OF THE HOSTS?
ARE THEIR LIVES SO EASILY DISMISSED?
REMEMBER WATCHING OUR CHILDREN WITHER AND DIE ON THAT ICY PRISON AS THE POPULATION OF HOSTS DWINDLED.
TO THESE HOSTS WE ARE THE ICY WIND, COME TO TAKE AWAY THE FUTURE OF THEIR CHILDREN.
IT SHOULDN'T EVER BE SO SIMPLE--
WAIT-- SOMETHING IS WRONG.
THE CHILD WE SENT TO FIND GRANT MCKAY--
WHAT?! DID HE PERISH? WE NEED MCKAY!
IT'S WORSE.
THE SCOURGE, THE INFINITE NIHILISTS, ARE UPON US...

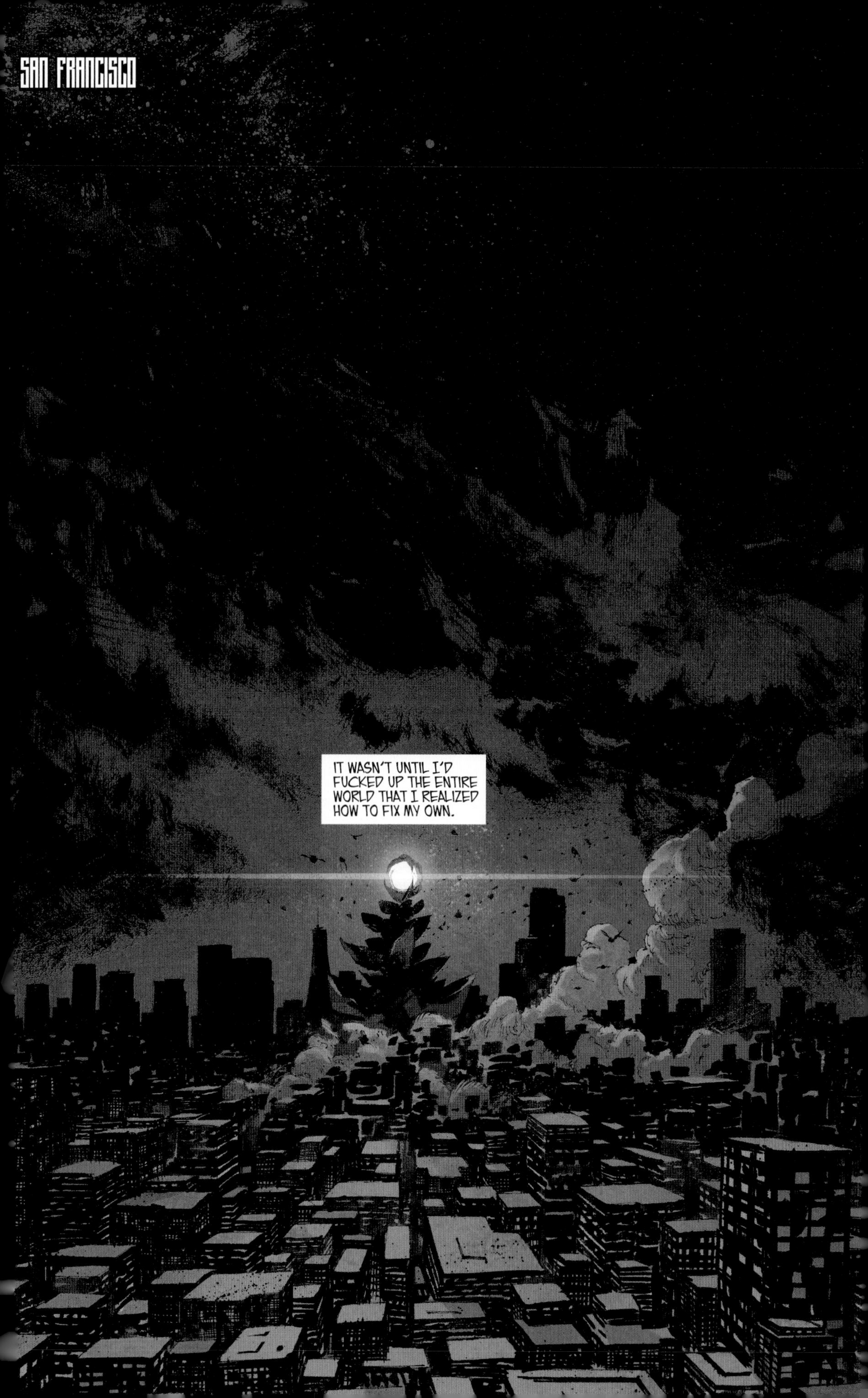
SAN FRANCISCO
IT WASN'T UNTIL I'D FUCKED UP THE ENTIRE WORLD THAT I REALIZED HOW TO FIX MY OWN.

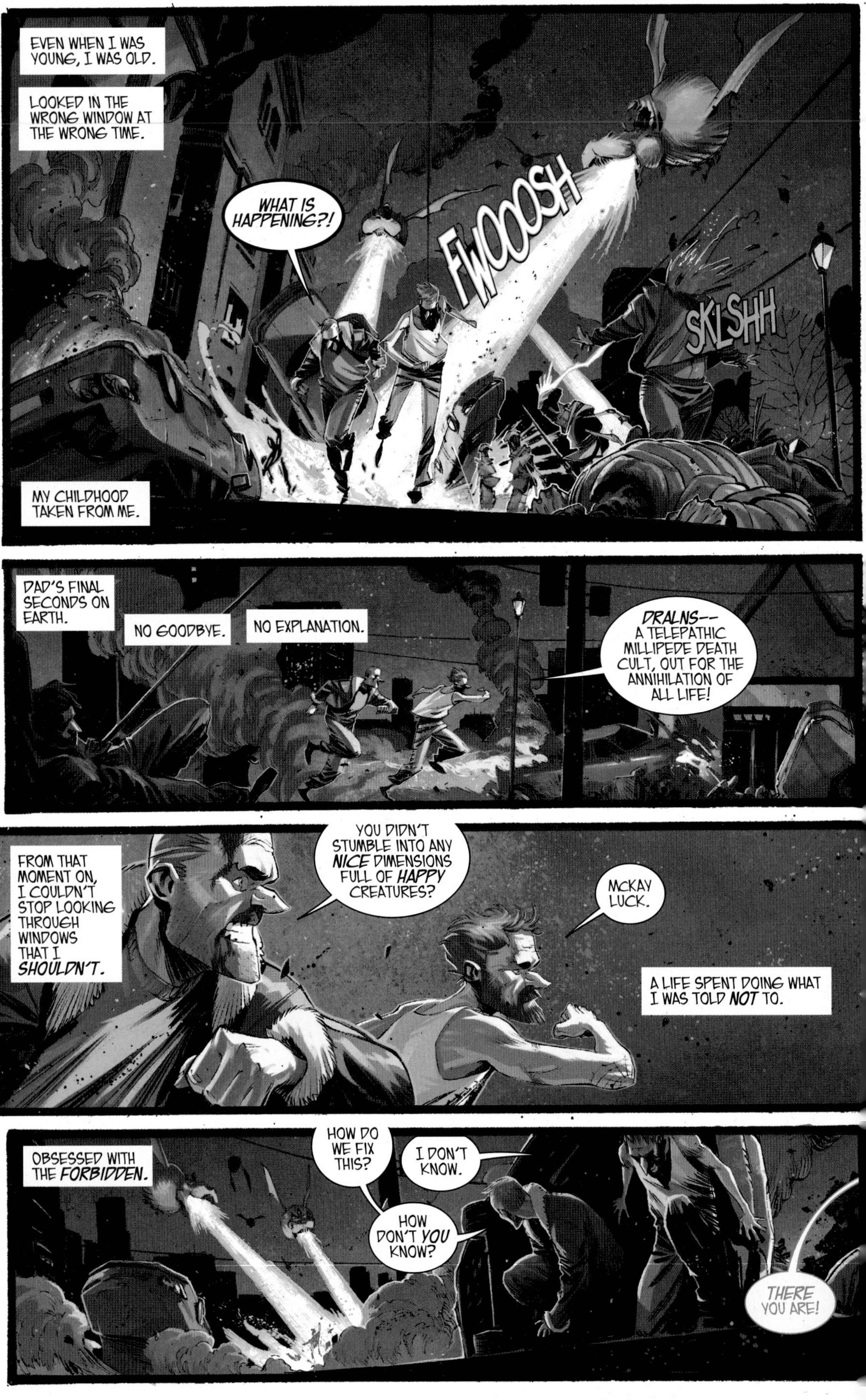
EVEN WHEN I WAS YOUNG, I WAS OLD.
LOOKED IN THE WRONG WINDOW AT THE WRONG TIME.
WHAT IS HAPPENING?!
FWOOOSH
SKLSHH
MY CHILDHOOD TAKEN FROM ME.
DAD'S FINAL SECONDS ON EARTH.
NO GOODBYE.
NO EXPLANATION.
DRALNS-- A TELEPATHIC MILLIPEDE DEATH CULT, OUT FOR THE ANNIHILATION OF ALL LIFE!
FROM THAT MOMENT ON, I COULDN'T STOP LOOKING THROUGH WINDOWS THAT I SHOULDN'T.
YOU DIDN'T STUMBLE INTO ANY NICE DIMENSIONS FULL OF HAPPY CREATURES?
MCKAY LUCK.
A LIFE SPENT DOING WHAT I WAS TOLD NOT TO.
OBSESSED WITH THE FORBIDDEN.
HOW DO WE FIX THIS?
I DON'T KNOW.
HOW DON'T YOU KNOW?
THERE YOU ARE!

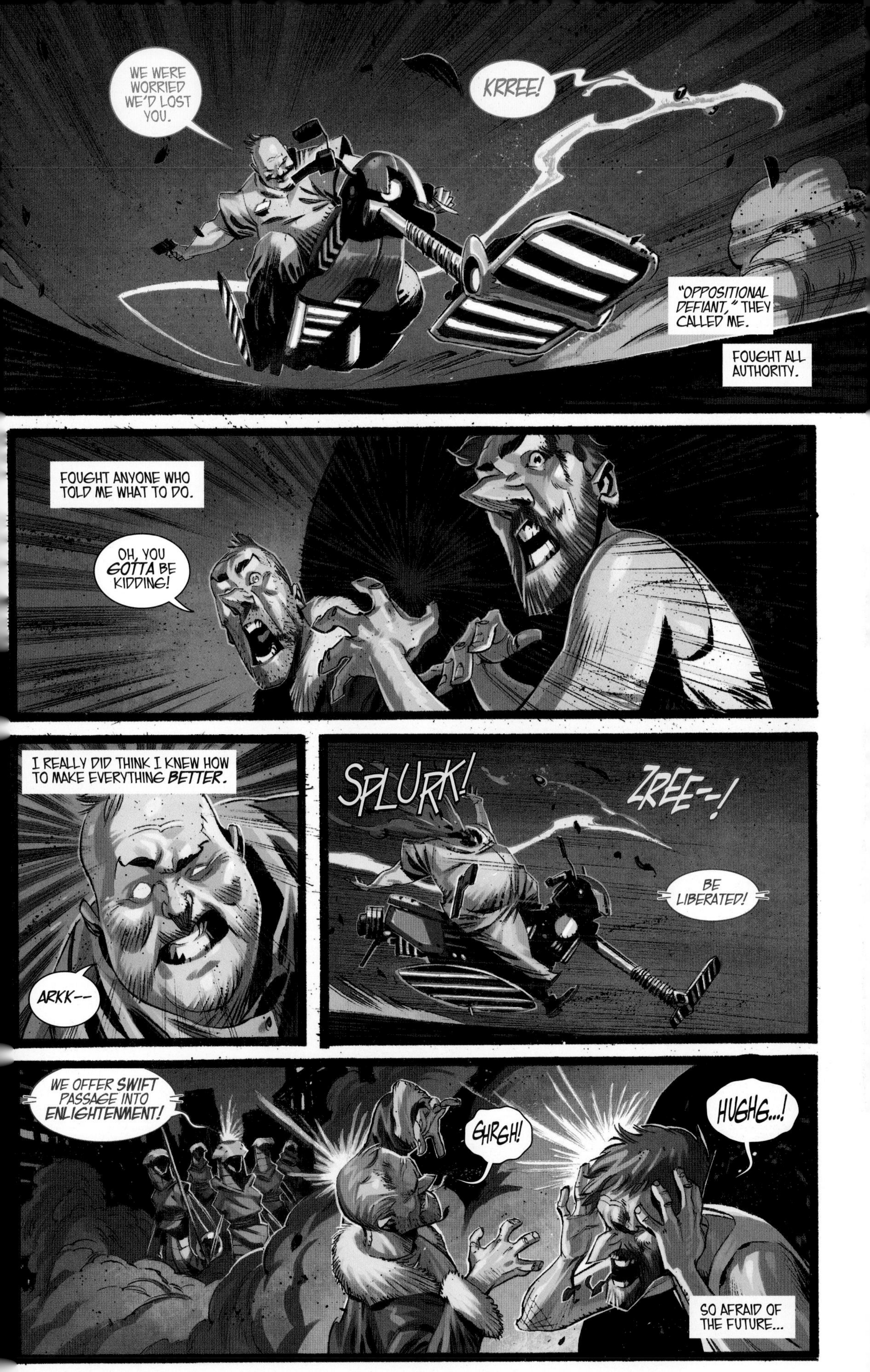
WE WERE WORRIED WE'D LOST YOU.
KRREE!
"OPPOSITIONAL DEFIANT," THEY CALLED ME.
FOUGHT ALL AUTHORITY.
FOUGHT ANYONE WHO TOLD ME WHAT TO DO.
OH, YOU GOTTA BE KIDDING!
I REALLY DID THINK I KNEW HOW TO MAKE EVERYTHING BETTER.
ARKK--
SPLURK!
ZREE--!
BE LIBERATED!
WE OFFER SWIFT PASSAGE INTO ENLIGHTENMENT!
GHRGH!
HUGHG...!
SO AFRAID OF THE FUTURE...

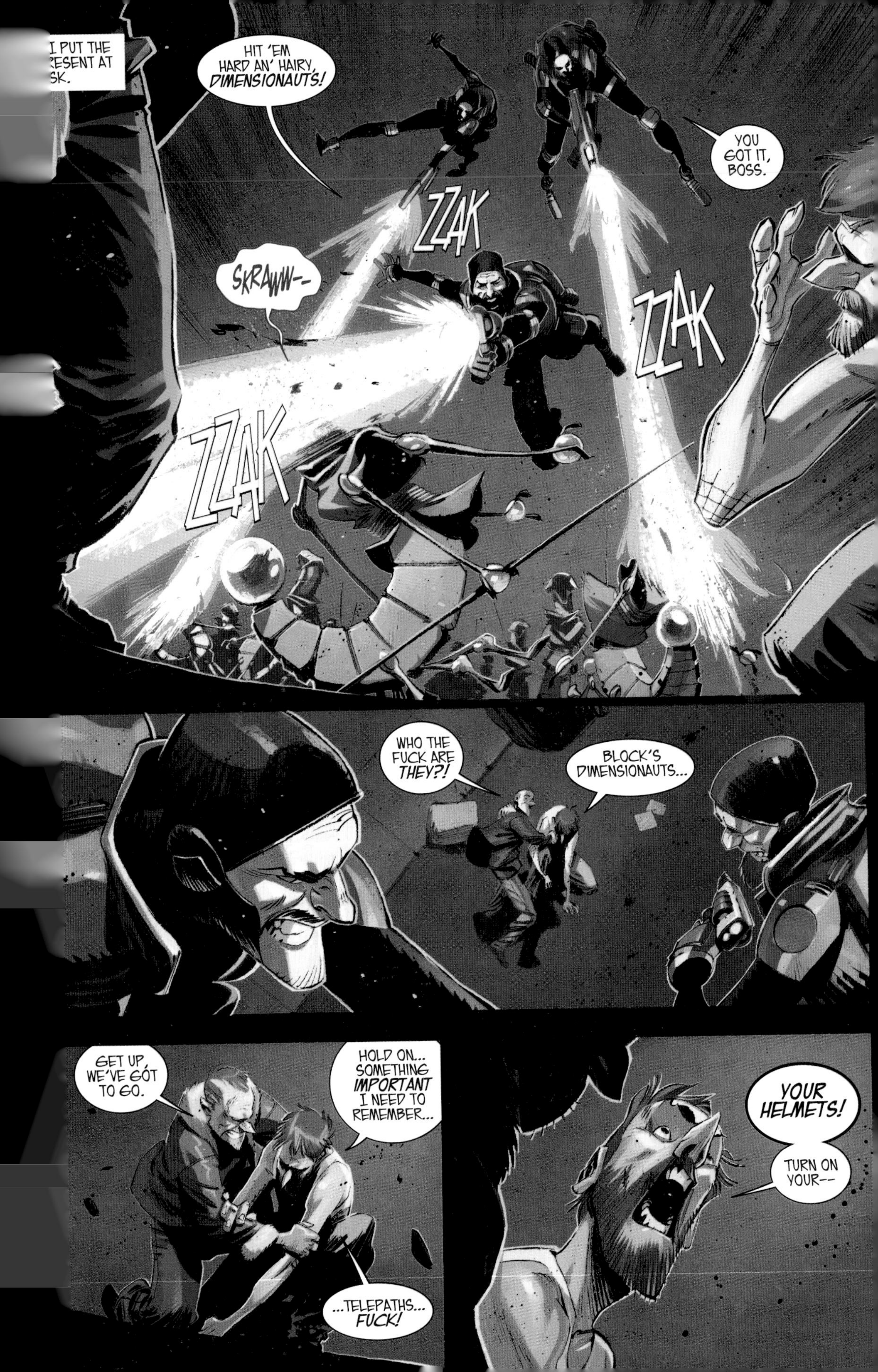
I PUT THE RESENT AT SK.
HIT 'EM HARD AN' HAIRY, DIMENSIONAUTS!
YOU GOT IT, BOSS.
ZZAK
SKRAWW--
ZZAK
ZZAK
WHO THE FUCK ARE THEY?!
BLOCK'S DIMENSIONAUTS...
GET UP, WE'VE GOT TO GO.
HOLD ON... SOMETHING IMPORTANT I NEED TO REMEMBER...
...TELEPATHS... FUCK!
YOUR HELMETS!
TURN ON YOUR--

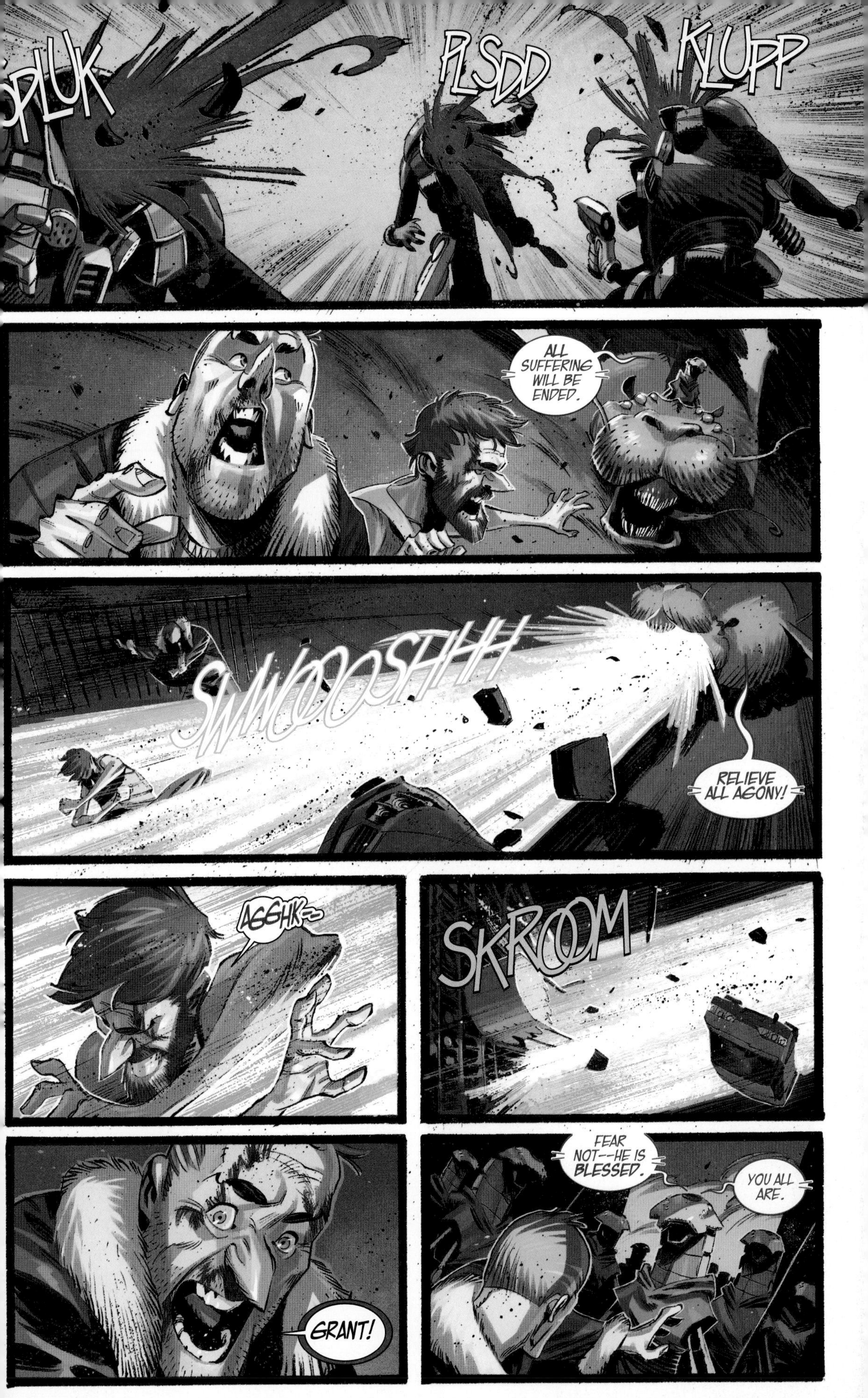
PLUK
PLSDD
KLUPP
ALL SUFFERING WILL BE ENDED.
SWWOOOSHHH
RELIEVE ALL AGONY!
AGGHK--
SKROOM
GRANT!
FEAR NOT--HE IS BLESSED.
YOU ALL ARE.

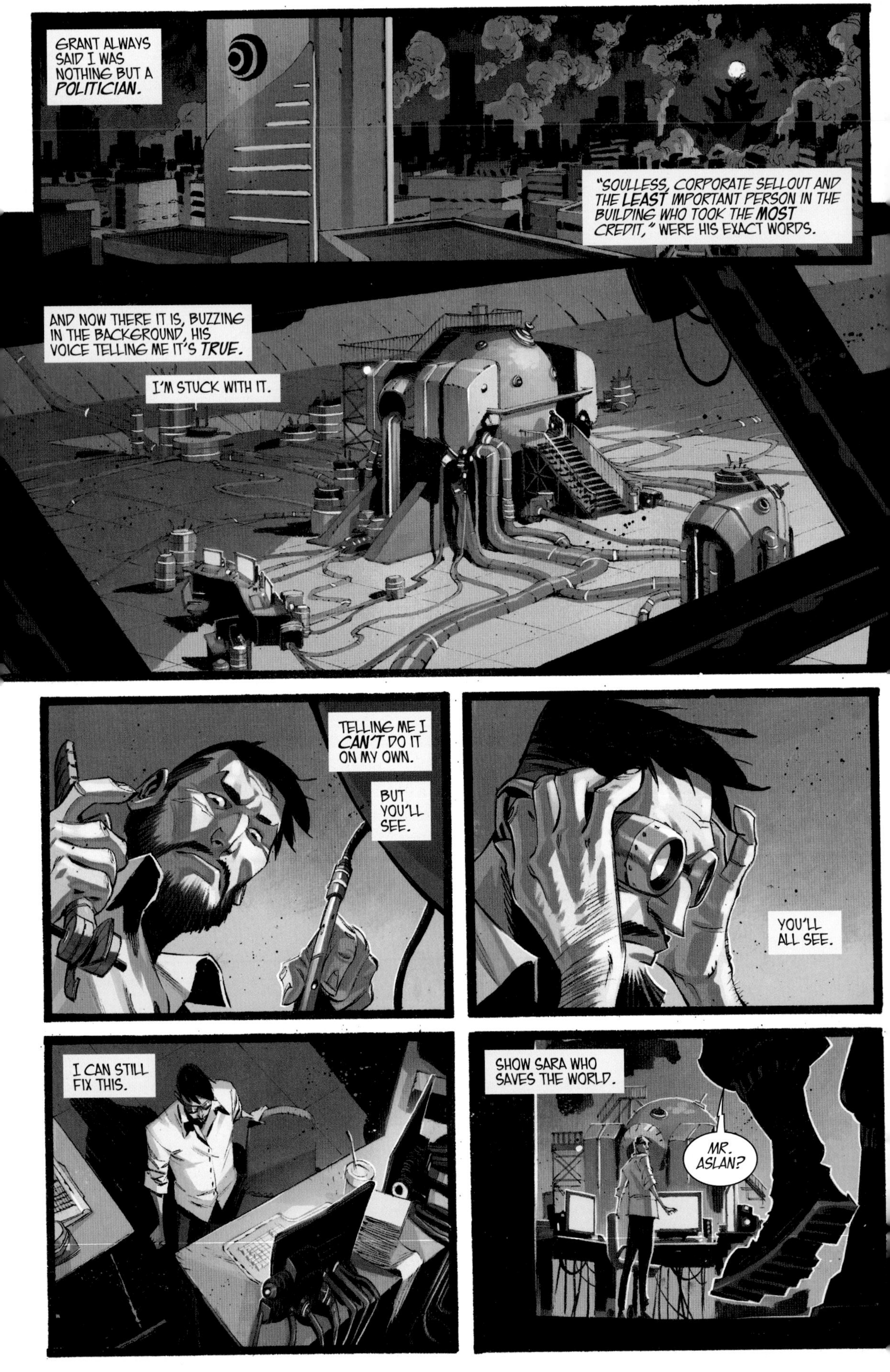
GRANT ALWAYS SAID I WAS NOTHING BUT A POLITICIAN.
"SOULLESS, CORPORATE SELLOUT AND THE LEAST IMPORTANT PERSON IN THE BUILDING WHO TOOK THE MOST CREDIT," WERE HIS EXACT WORDS.
AND NOW THERE IT IS, BUZZING IN THE BACKGROUND, HIS VOICE TELLING ME IT'S TRUE.
I'M STUCK WITH IT.
TELLING ME I CAN'T DO IT ON MY OWN.
BUT YOU'LL SEE.
YOU'LL ALL SEE.
I CAN STILL FIX THIS.
SHOW SARA WHO SAVES THE WORLD.
MR. ASLAN?

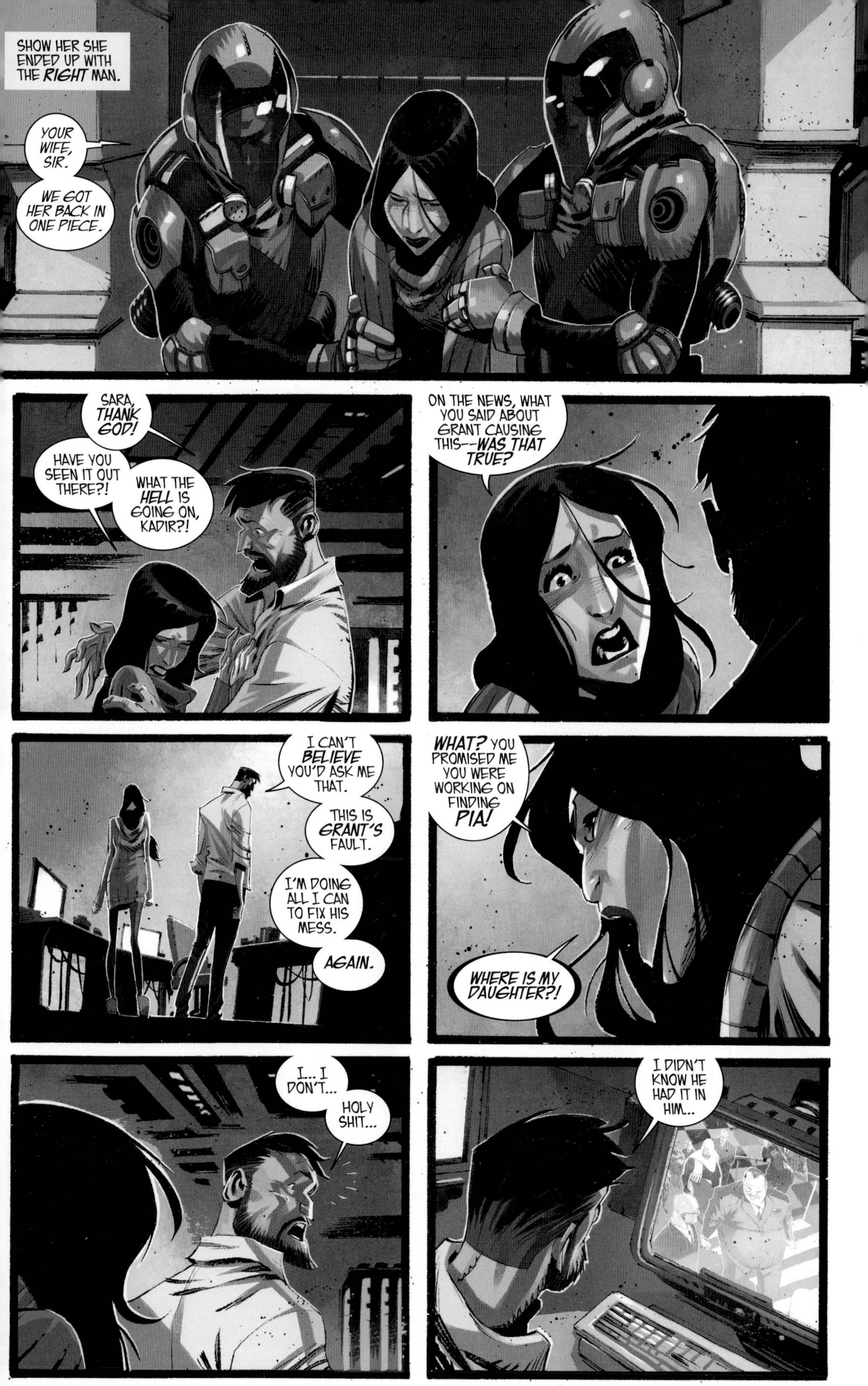
SHOW HER SHE ENDED UP WITH THE RIGHT MAN.
YOUR WIFE, SIR.
WE GOT HER BACK IN ONE PIECE.
SARA, THANK GOD!
HAVE YOU SEEN IT OUT THERE?!
WHAT THE HELL IS GOING ON, KADIR?!
ON THE NEWS, WHAT YOU SAID ABOUT GRANT CAUSING THIS--WAS THAT TRUE?
I CAN'T BELIEVE YOU'D ASK ME THAT.
THIS IS GRANT'S FAULT.
I'M DOING ALL I CAN TO FIX HIS MESS.
AGAIN.
WHAT? YOU PROMISED ME YOU WERE WORKING ON FINDING PIA!
WHERE IS MY DAUGHTER?!
I... I DON'T...
HOLY SHIT...
I DIDN'T KNOW HE HAD IT IN HIM...

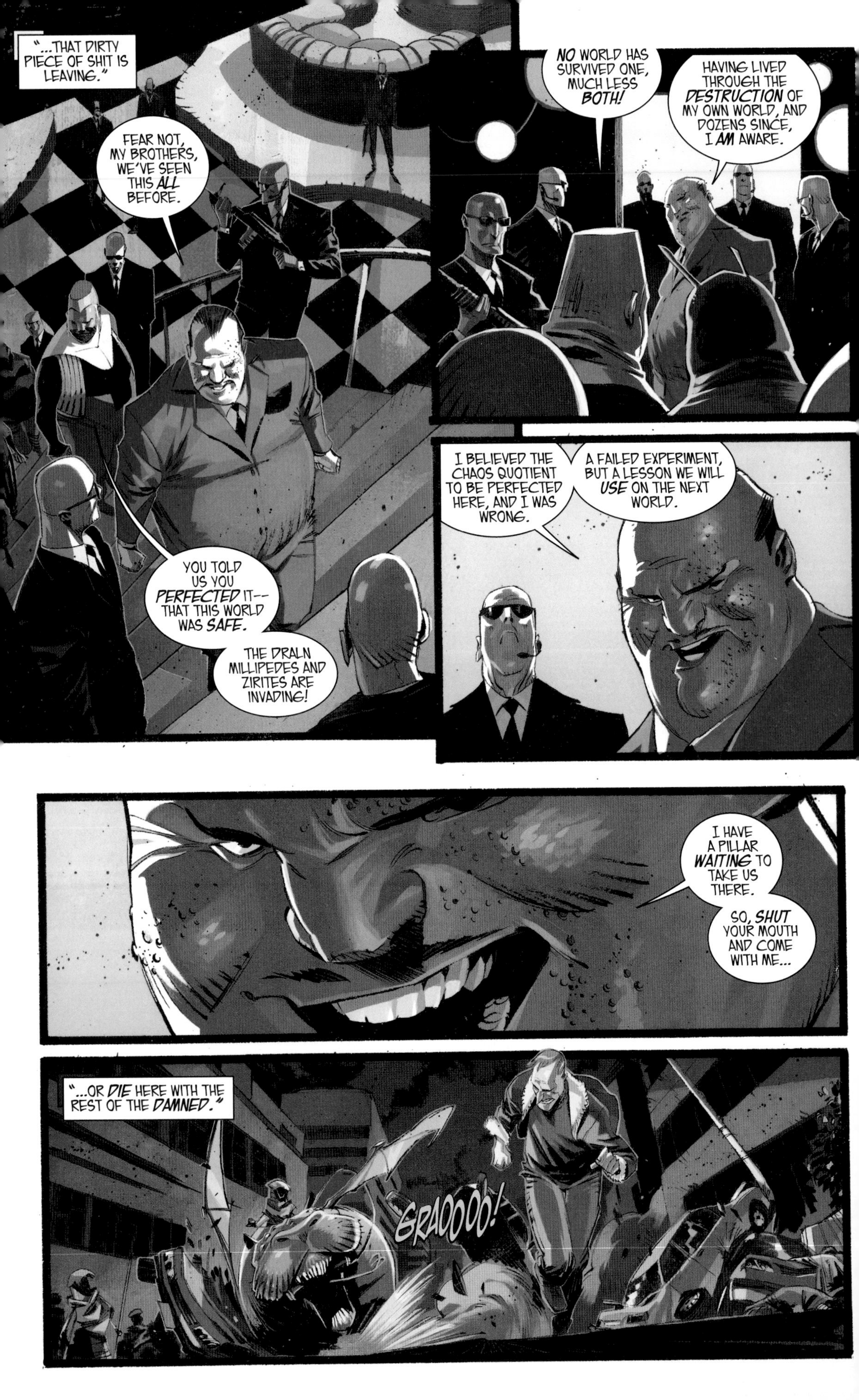
"...THAT DIRTY PIECE OF SHIT IS LEAVING."
FEAR NOT, MY BROTHERS, WE'VE SEEN THIS ALL BEFORE.
YOU TOLD US YOU PERFECTED IT-- THAT THIS WORLD WAS SAFE.
THE DRALN MILLIPEDES AND ZIRITES ARE INVADING!
NO WORLD HAS SURVIVED ONE, MUCH LESS BOTH!
HAVING LIVED THROUGH THE DESTRUCTION OF MY OWN WORLD, AND DOZENS SINCE, I AM AWARE.
I BELIEVED THE CHAOS QUOTIENT TO BE PERFECTED HERE, AND I WAS WRONG.
A FAILED EXPERIMENT, BUT A LESSON WE WILL USE ON THE NEXT WORLD.
I HAVE A PILLAR WAITING TO TAKE US THERE.
SO, SHUT YOUR MOUTH AND COME WITH ME...
"...OR DIE HERE WITH THE REST OF THE DAMNED."
GRAOOOO!

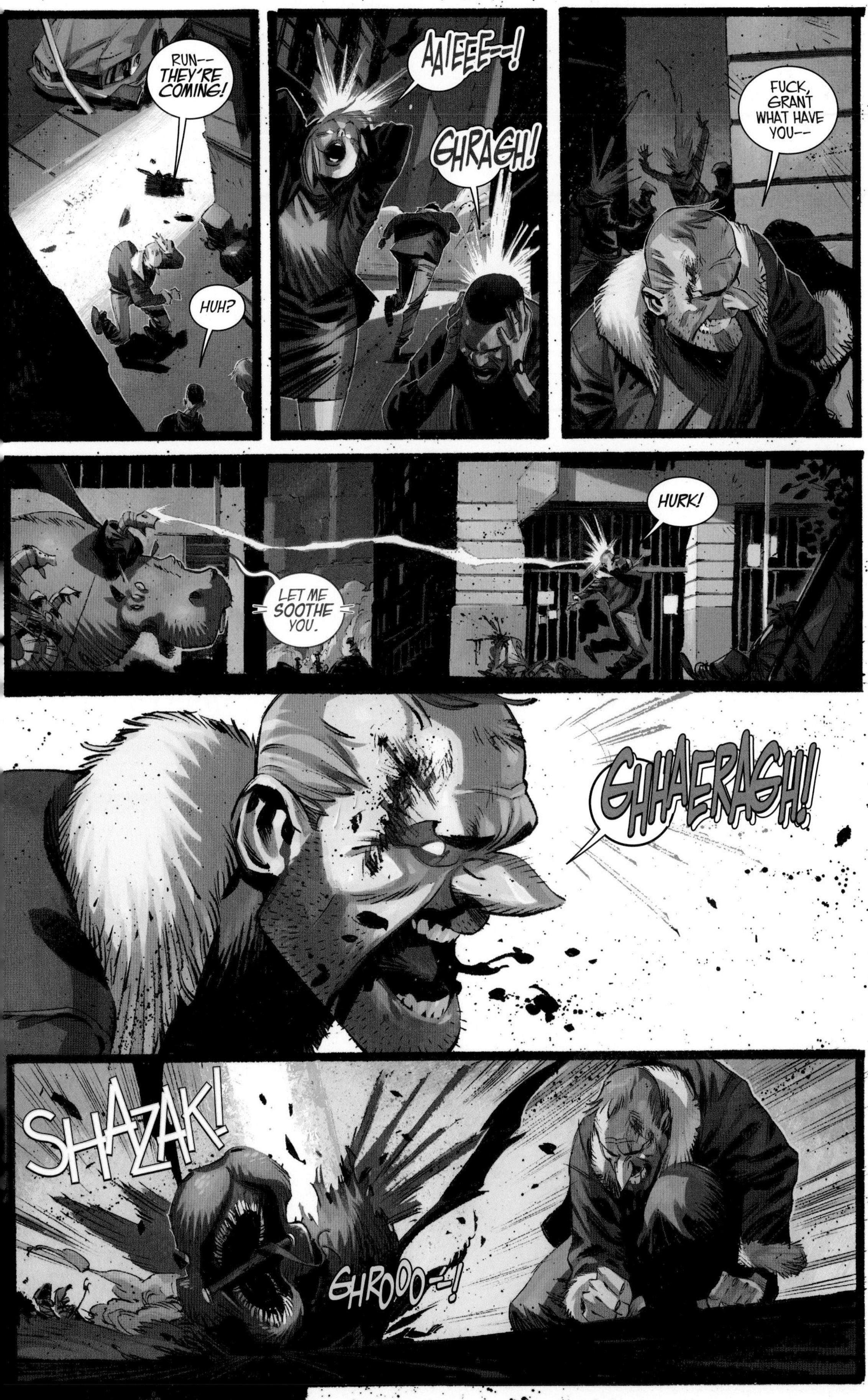
RUN-- THEY'RE COMING!
HUH?
AAIEEEE--!
GHRAGH!
FUCK, GRANT WHAT HAVE YOU--
LET ME SOOTHE YOU.
HURK!
GHHAERAGH!
SHAZAK!
GHROOOO--!

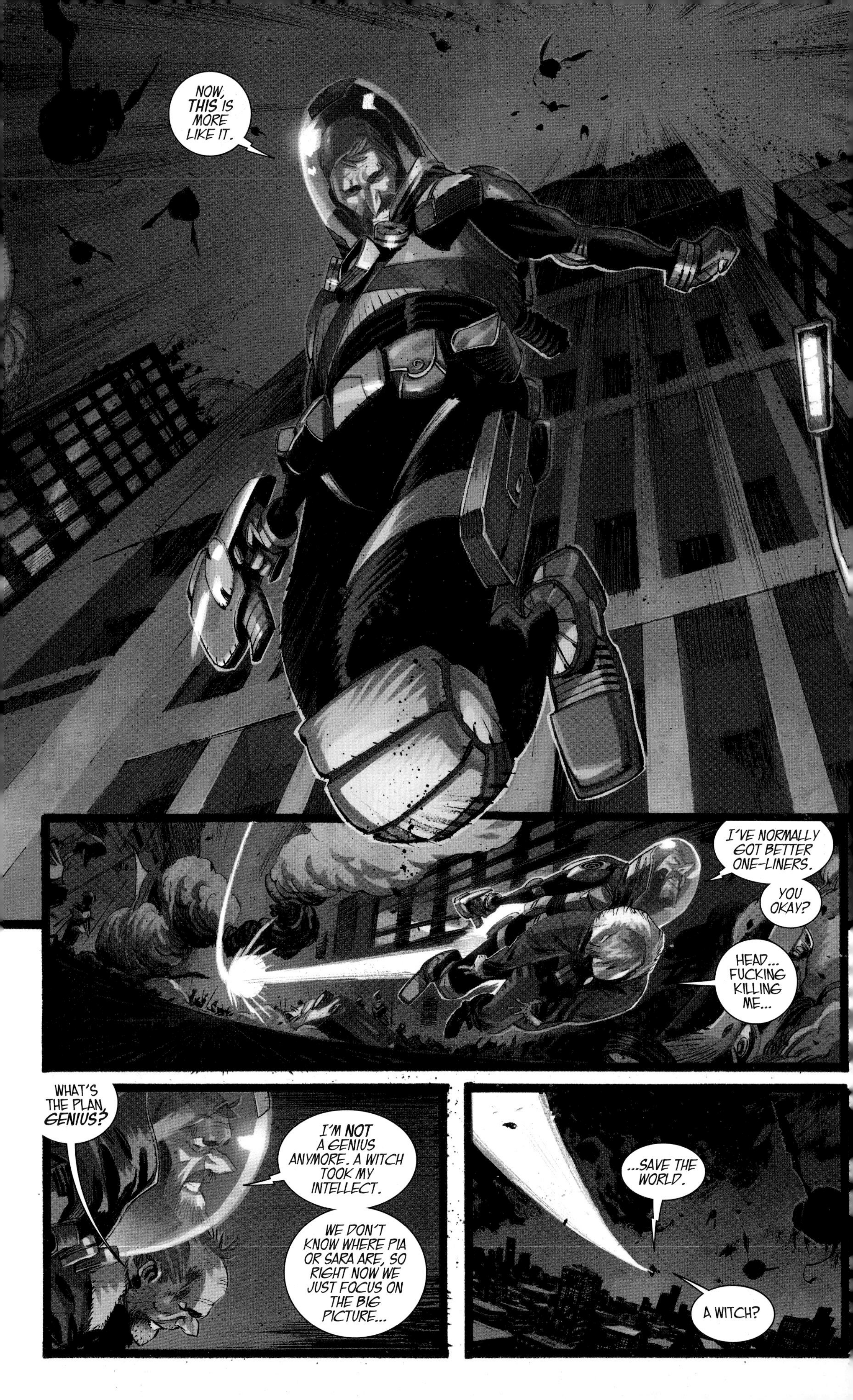
NOW, THIS IS MORE LIKE IT.
I'VE NORMALLY GOT BETTER ONE-LINERS.
YOU OKAY?
HEAD... FUCKING KILLING ME...
WHAT'S THE PLAN, GENIUS?
I'M NOT A GENIUS ANYMORE. A WITCH TOOK MY INTELLECT.
WE DON'T KNOW WHERE PIA OR SARA ARE, SO RIGHT NOW WE JUST FOCUS ON THE BIG PICTURE...
...SAVE THE WORLD.
A WITCH?

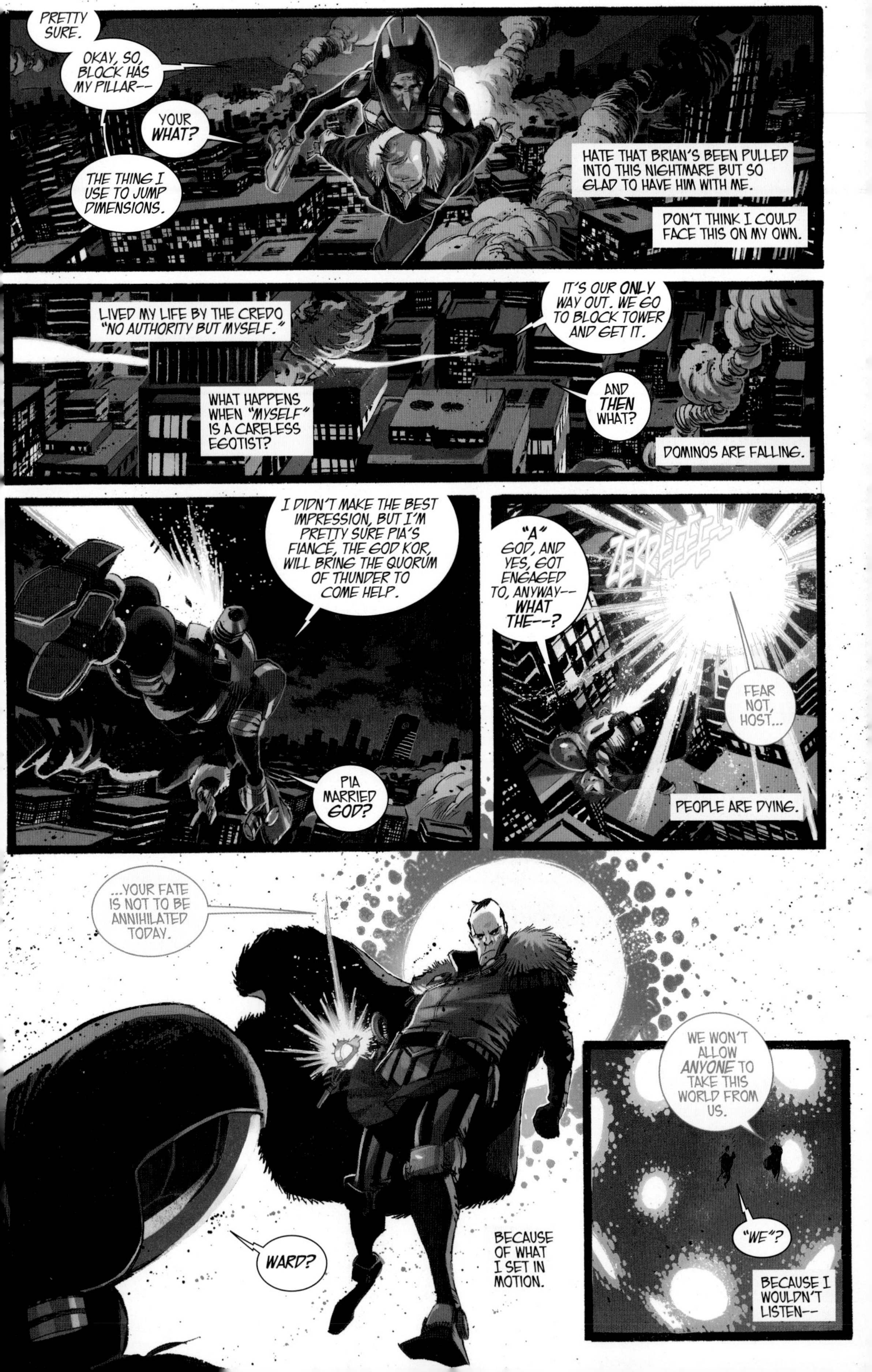
PRETTY SURE.
OKAY, SO, BLOCK HAS MY PILLAR--
YOUR WHAT?
THE THING I USE TO JUMP DIMENSIONS.
HATE THAT BRIAN'S BEEN PULLED INTO THIS NIGHTMARE BUT SO GLAD TO HAVE HIM WITH ME.
DON'T THINK I COULD FACE THIS ON MY OWN.
LIVED MY LIFE BY THE CREDO "NO AUTHORITY BUT MYSELF."
WHAT HAPPENS WHEN "MYSELF" IS A CARELESS EGOTIST?
IT'S OUR ONLY WAY OUT. WE GO TO BLOCK TOWER AND GET IT.
AND THEN WHAT?
DOMINOS ARE FALLING.
I DIDN'T MAKE THE BEST IMPRESSION, BUT I'M PRETTY SURE PIA'S FIANCÉ, THE GOD KOR, WILL BRING THE QUORÚM OF THUNDER TO COME HELP.
PIA MARRIED GOD?
"A" GOD, AND YES, GOT ENGAGED TO, ANYWAY-- WHAT THE--?
ZERREEEEE--
FEAR NOT, HOST...
PEOPLE ARE DYING.
...YOUR FATE IS NOT TO BE ANNIHILATED TODAY.
WARD?
BECAUSE OF WHAT I SET IN MOTION.
WE WON'T ALLOW ANYONE TO TAKE THIS WORLD FROM US.
"WE"?
BECAUSE I WOULDN'T LISTEN--

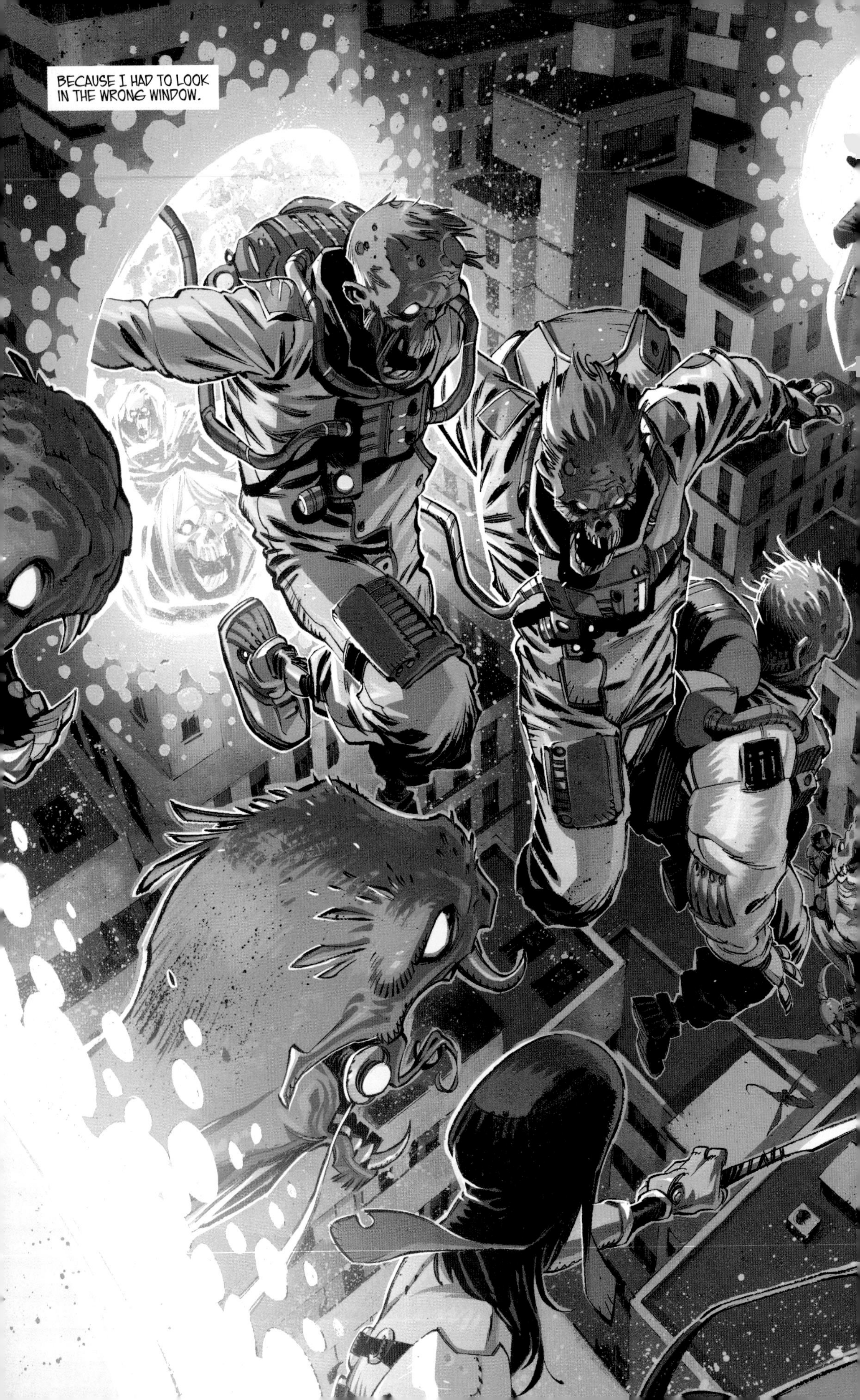
BECAUSE I HAD TO LOOK IN THE WRONG WINDOW.

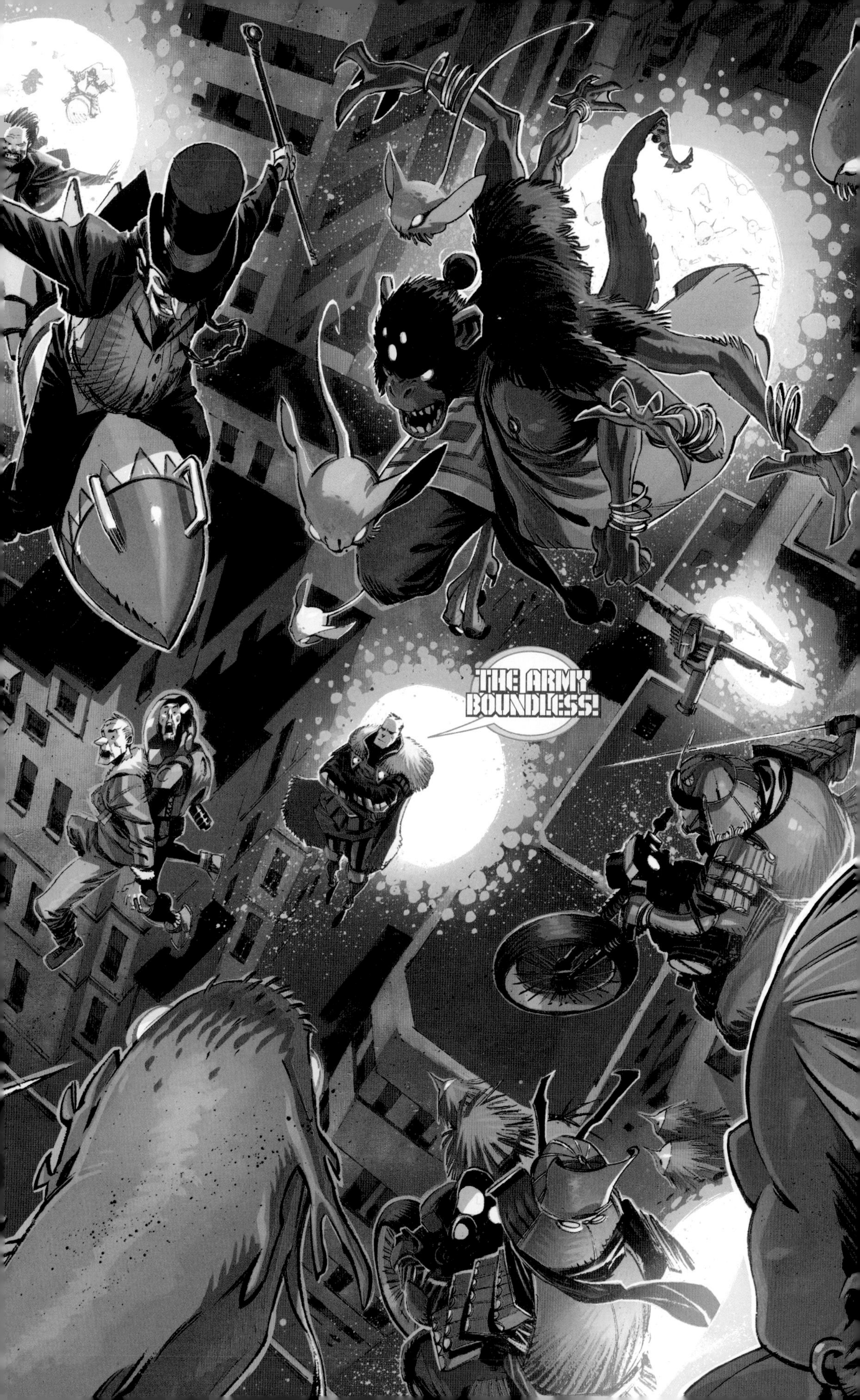
THE ARMY BOUNDLESS!

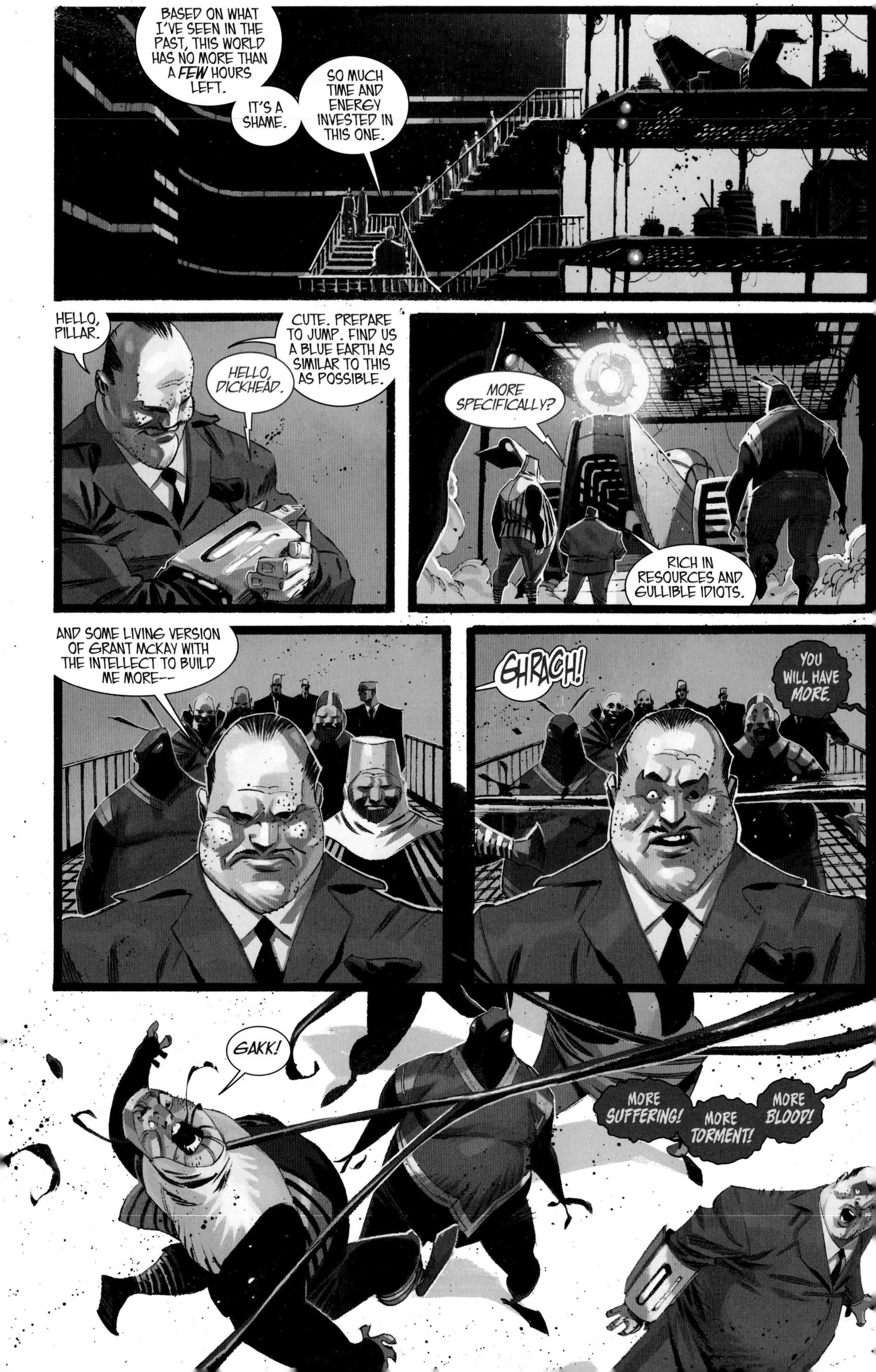
BASED ON WHAT I'VE SEEN IN THE PAST, THIS WORLD HAS NO MORE THAN A FEW HOURS LEFT.
IT'S A SHAME.
SO MUCH TIME AND ENERGY INVESTED IN THIS ONE.
HELLO, PILLAR.
HELLO, DICKHEAD.
CUTE. PREPARE TO JUMP. FIND US A BLUE EARTH AS SIMILAR TO THIS AS POSSIBLE.
MORE SPECIFICALLY?
RICH IN RESOURCES AND GULLIBLE IDIOTS.
AND SOME LIVING VERSION OF GRANT McKAY WITH THE INTELLECT TO BUILD ME MORE--
GHRACH!
YOU WILL HAVE MORE.
GAKK!
MORE SUFFERING!
MORE TORMENT!
MORE BLOOD!

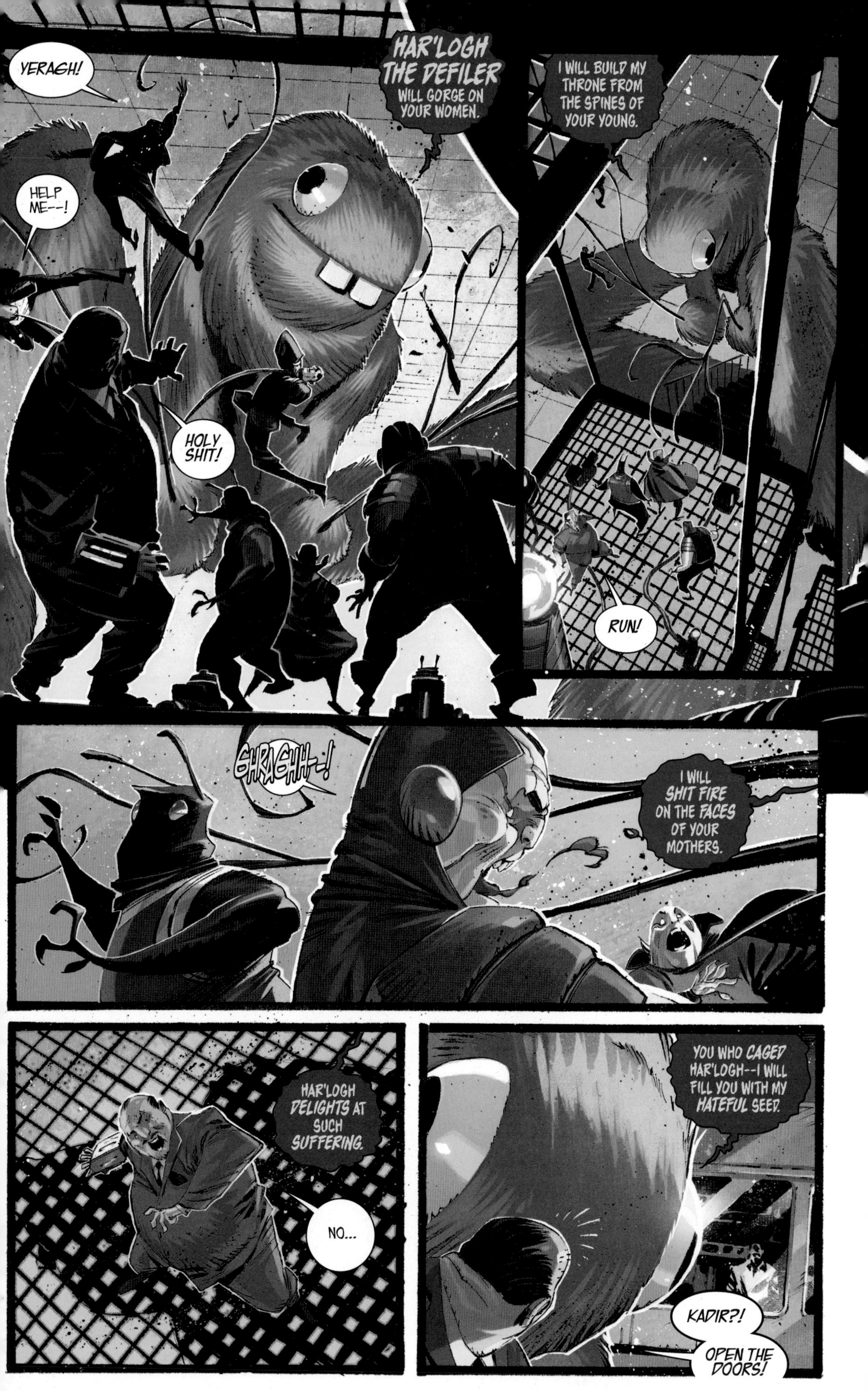
YERAGH!
HAR'LOGH THE DEFILER WILL GORGE ON YOUR WOMEN.
HELP ME--!
HOLY SHIT!
I WILL BUILD MY THRONE FROM THE SPINES OF YOUR YOUNG.
RUN!
GHRAGHH--!
I WILL SHIT FIRE ON THE FACES OF YOUR MOTHERS.
HAR'LOGH DELIGHTS AT SUCH SUFFERING.
NO...
YOU WHO CAGED HAR'LOGH--I WILL FILL YOU WITH MY HATEFUL SEED.
KADIR?!
OPEN THE DOORS!

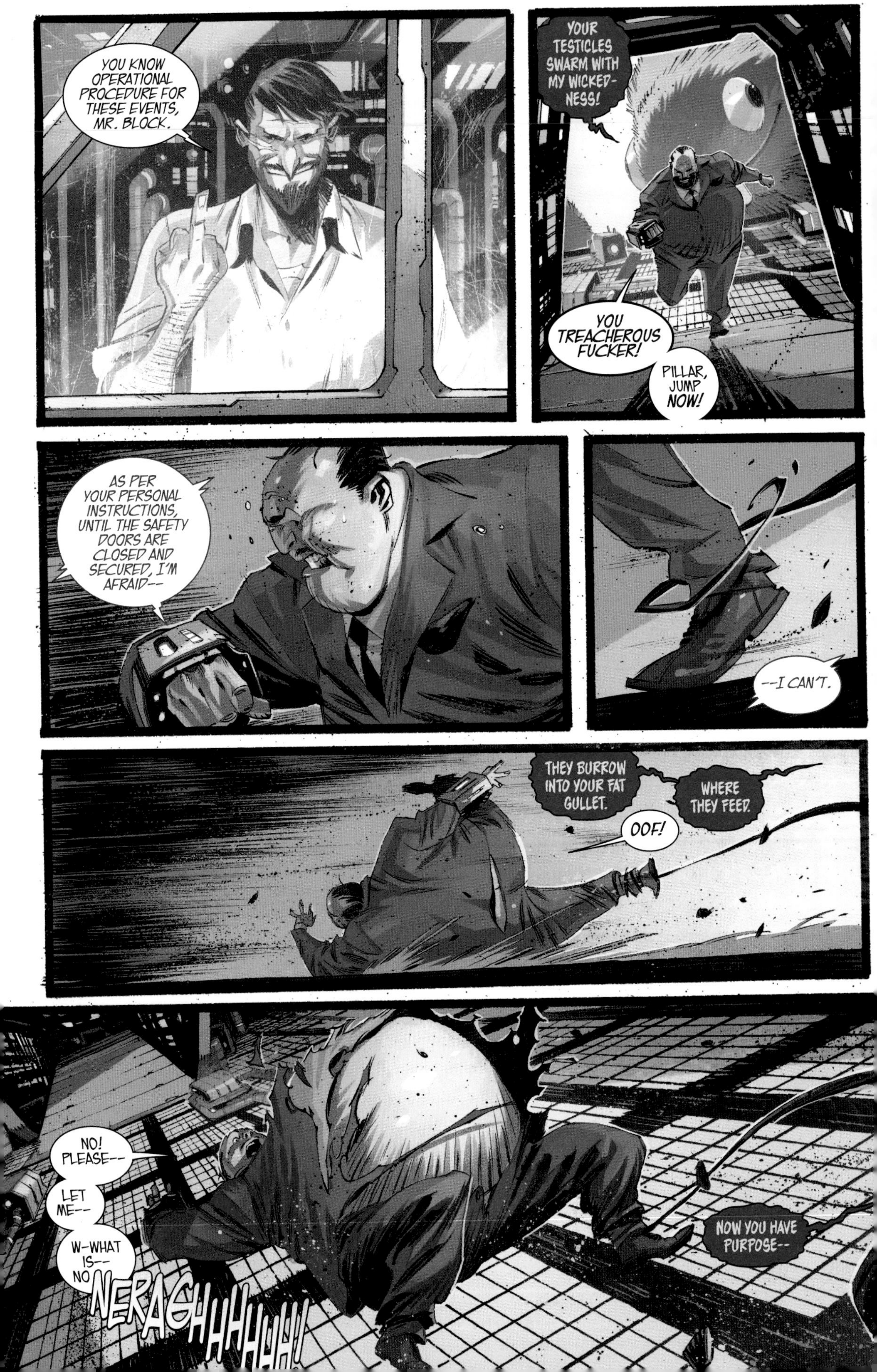
YOU KNOW OPERATIONAL PROCEDURE FOR THESE EVENTS, MR. BLOCK.
YOUR TESTICLES SWARM WITH MY WICKED-NESS!
YOU TREACHEROUS FUCKER!
PILLAR, JUMP NOW!
AS PER YOUR PERSONAL INSTRUCTIONS, UNTIL THE SAFETY DOORS ARE CLOSED AND SECURED, I'M AFRAID--
--I CAN'T.
THEY BURROW INTO YOUR FAT GULLET.
WHERE THEY FEED.
OOF!
NO! PLEASE--
LET ME--
W-WHAT IS--
NO
NERAGHHHHUH!
NOW YOU HAVE PURPOSE--

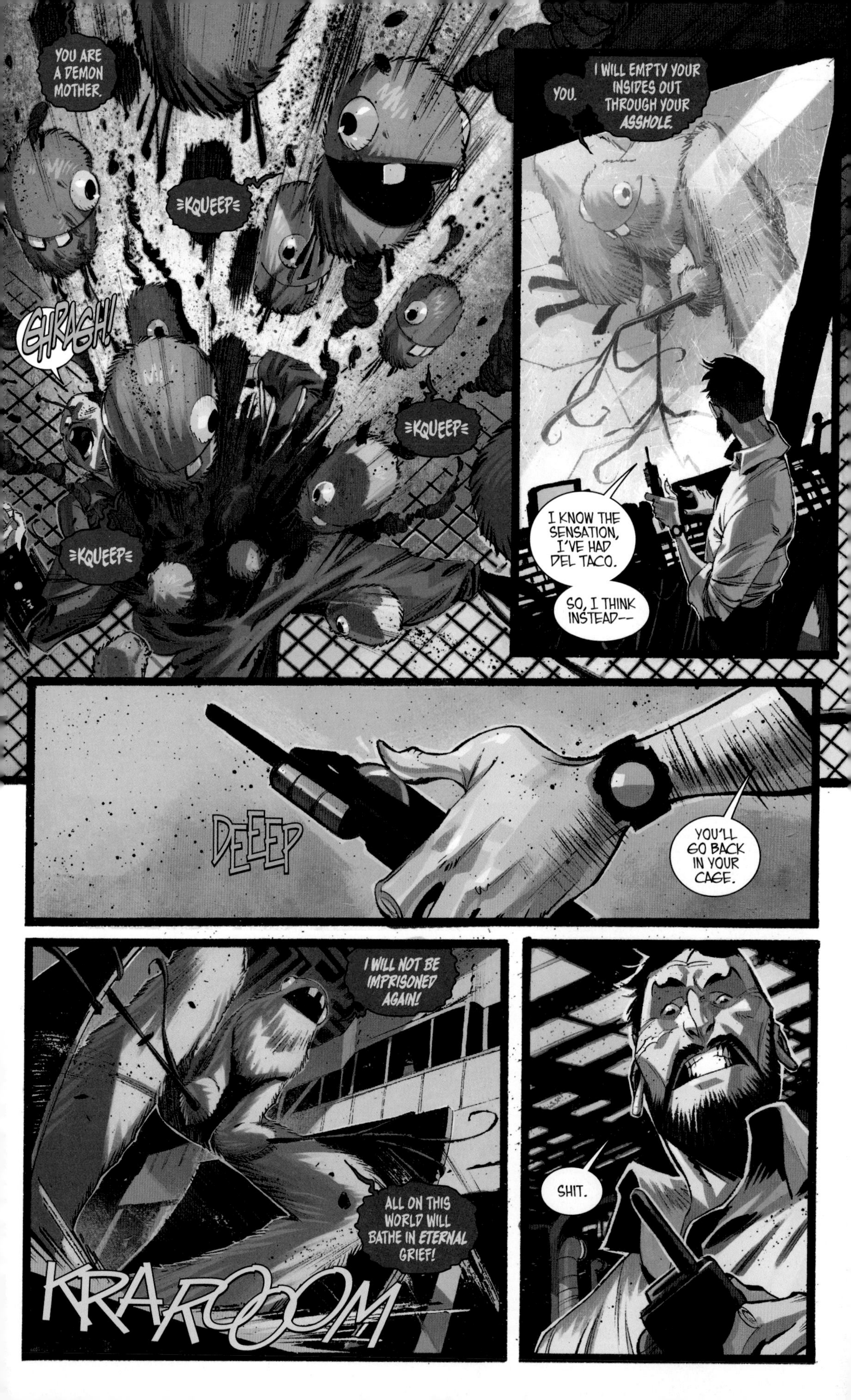

YOU ARE A DEMON MOTHER.
KQUEEP
GHRAGH!
KQUEEP
KQUEEP
YOU.
I WILL EMPTY YOUR INSIDES OUT THROUGH YOUR ASSHOLE.
I KNOW THE SENSATION, I'VE HAD DEL TACO.
SO, I THINK INSTEAD--
DEEEP
YOU'LL GO BACK IN YOUR CAGE.
I WILL NOT BE IMPRISONED AGAIN!
ALL ON THIS WORLD WILL BATHE IN ETERNAL GRIEF!
KRAROOOM
SHIT.

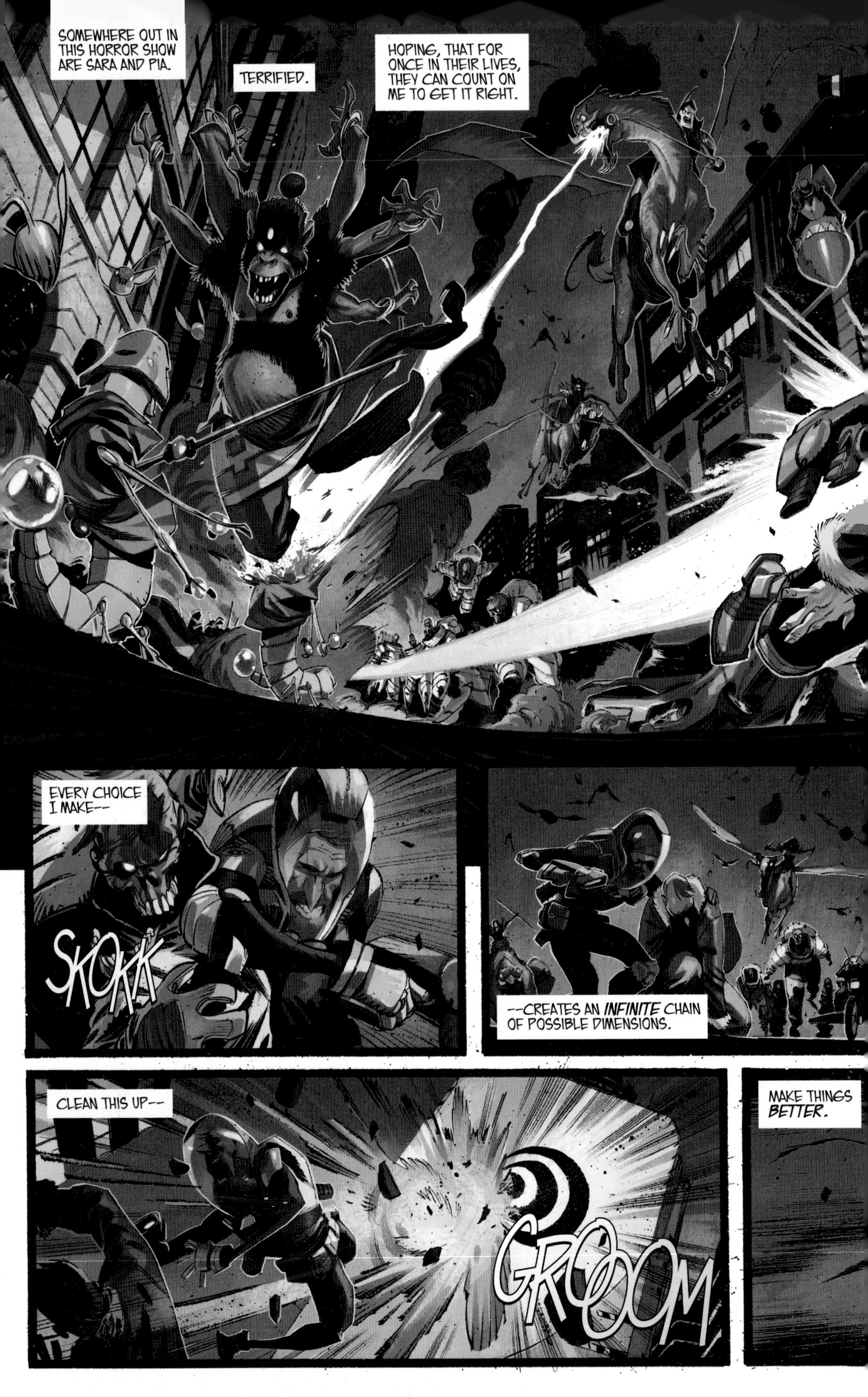
SOMEWHERE OUT IN THIS HORROR SHOW ARE SARA AND PIA.
TERRIFIED.
HOPING, THAT FOR ONCE IN THEIR LIVES, THEY CAN COUNT ON ME TO GET IT RIGHT.
EVERY CHOICE I MAKE--
SKOKK
--CREATES AN *INFINITE* CHAIN OF POSSIBLE DIMENSIONS.
CLEAN THIS UP--
GROOOM
MAKE THINGS *BETTER*.

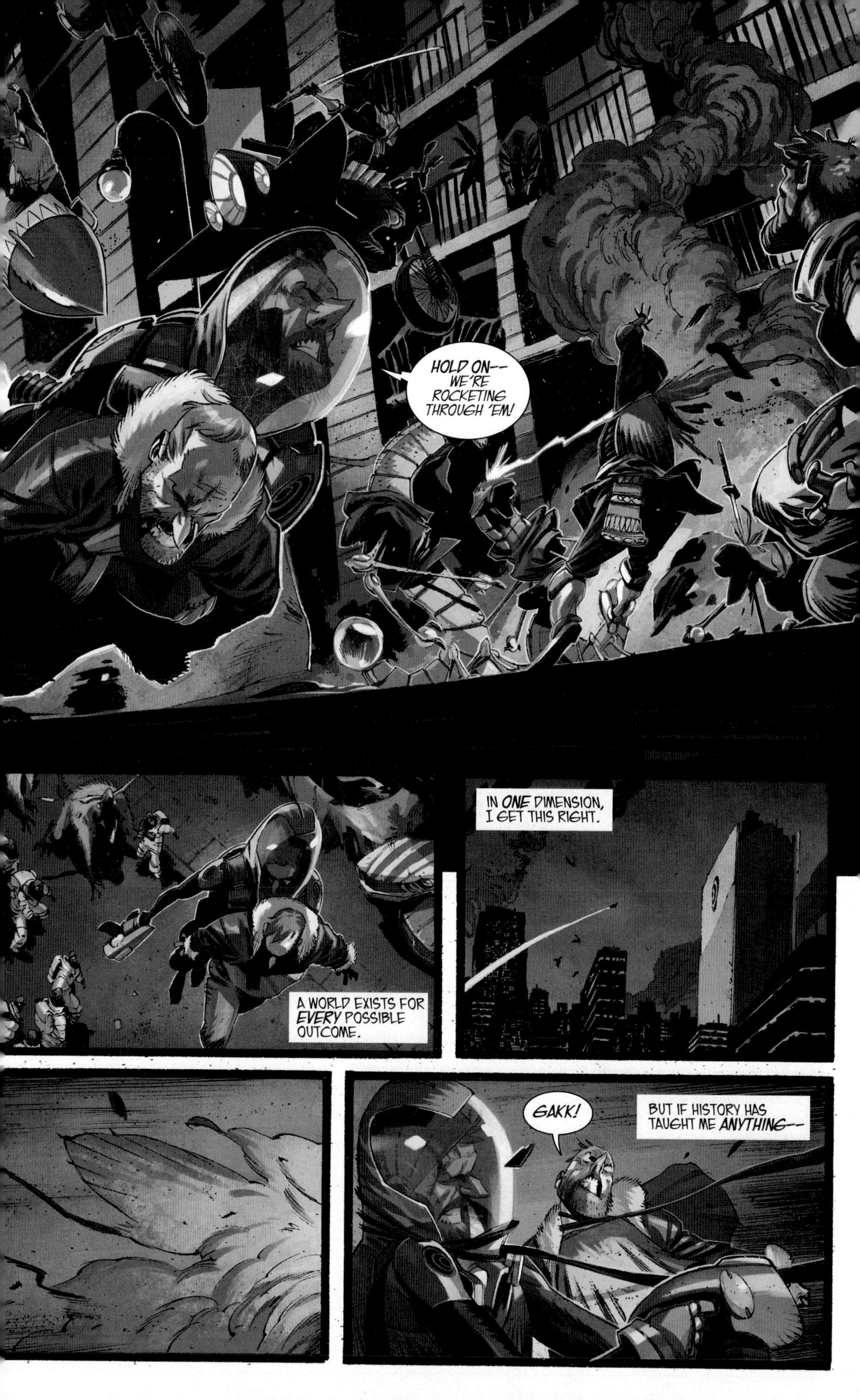
HOLD ON-- WE'RE ROCKETING THROUGH 'EM!
A WORLD EXISTS FOR EVERY POSSIBLE OUTCOME.
IN ONE DIMENSION, I GET THIS RIGHT.
GAKK!
BUT IF HISTORY HAS TAUGHT ME ANYTHING--

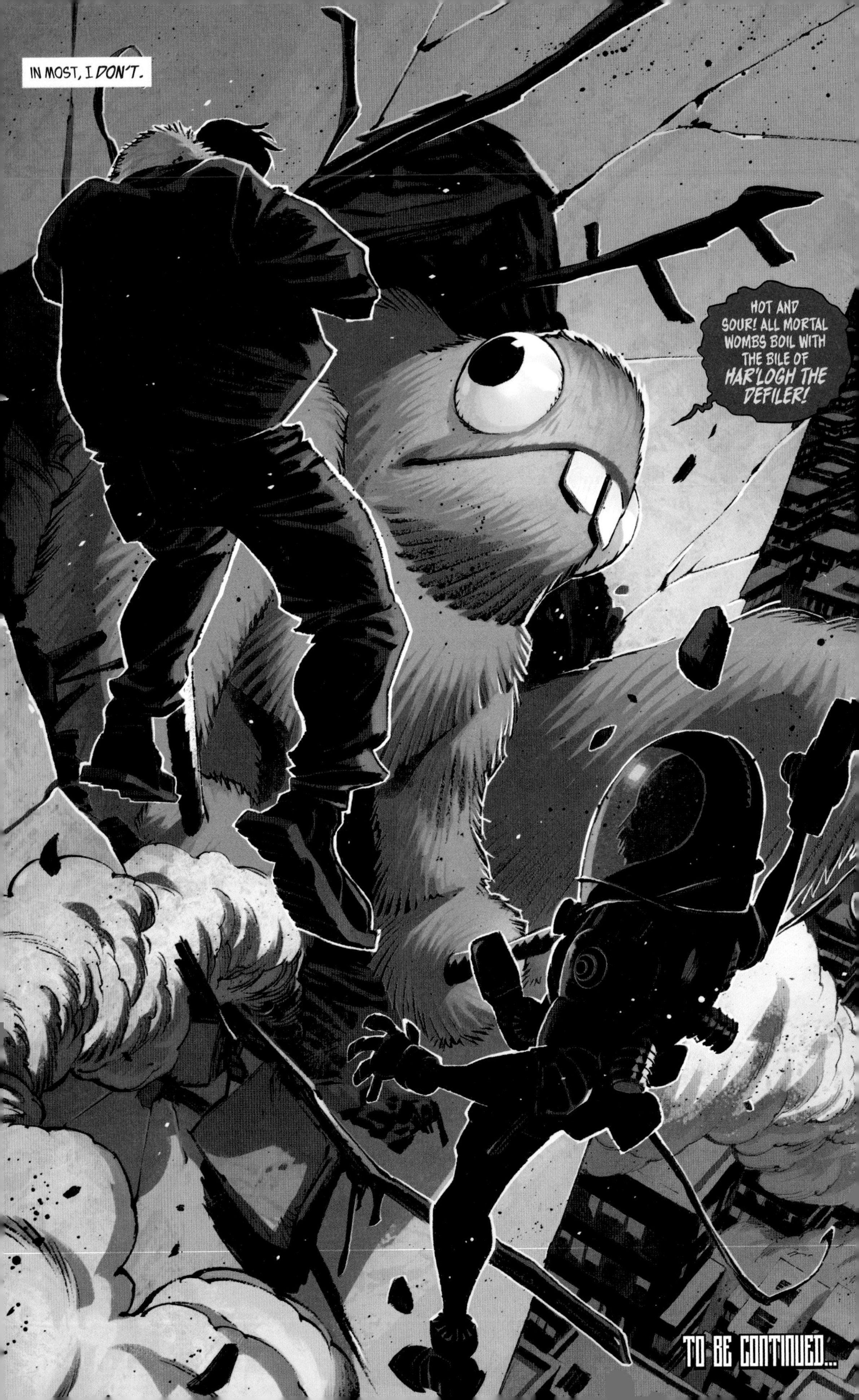
IN MOST, I DON'T.
HOT AND SOUR! ALL MORTAL WOMBS BOIL WITH THE BILE OF HAR'LOGH THE DEFILER!
TO BE CONTINUED...

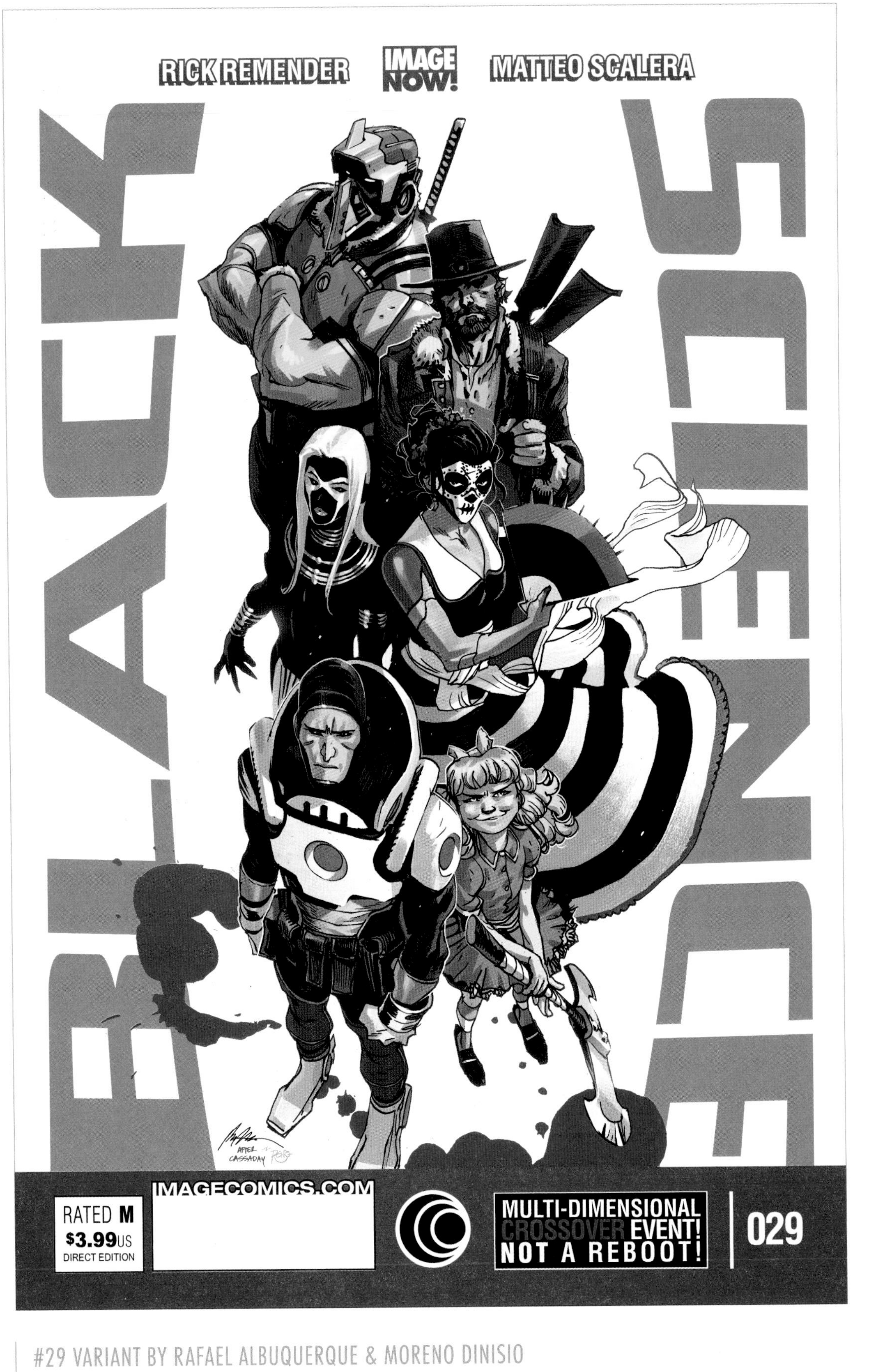
RICK REMENDER
IMAGE NOW!
MATTEO SCALERA
BLACK SCIENCE
IMAGECOMICS.COM
RATED M
$3.99US
DIRECT EDITION
MULTI-DIMENSIONAL CROSSOVER EVENT! NOT A REBOOT!
029

#29 VARIANT BY RAFAEL ALBUQUERQUE & MORENO DINISIO

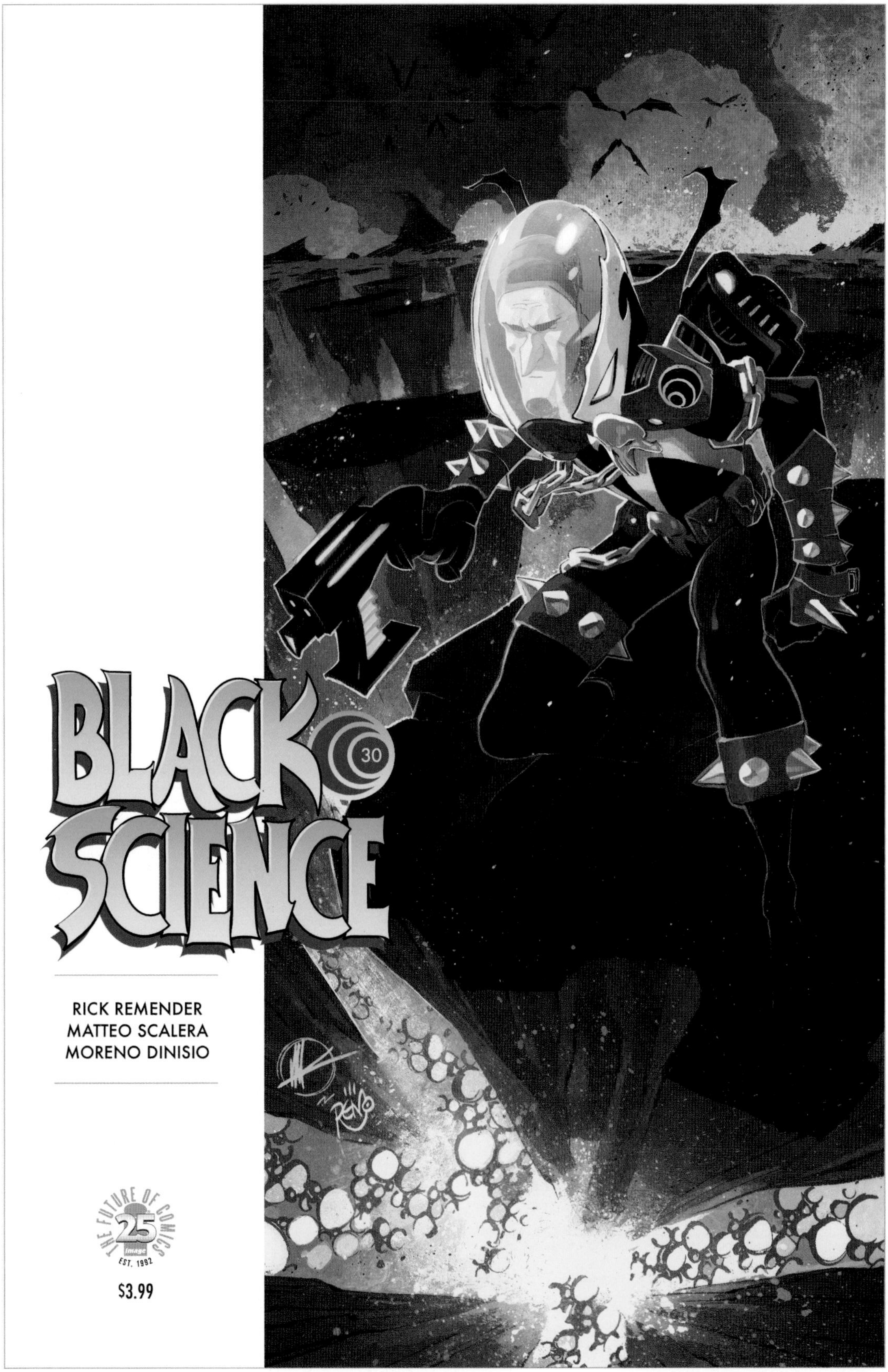
BLACK SCIENCE
30
RICK REMENDER
MATTEO SCALERA
MORENO DINISIO
THE FUTURE OF COMICS
25
EST. 1992
$3.99

#30 SPAWN VARIANT BY MATTEO SCALERA & MORENO DINISIO

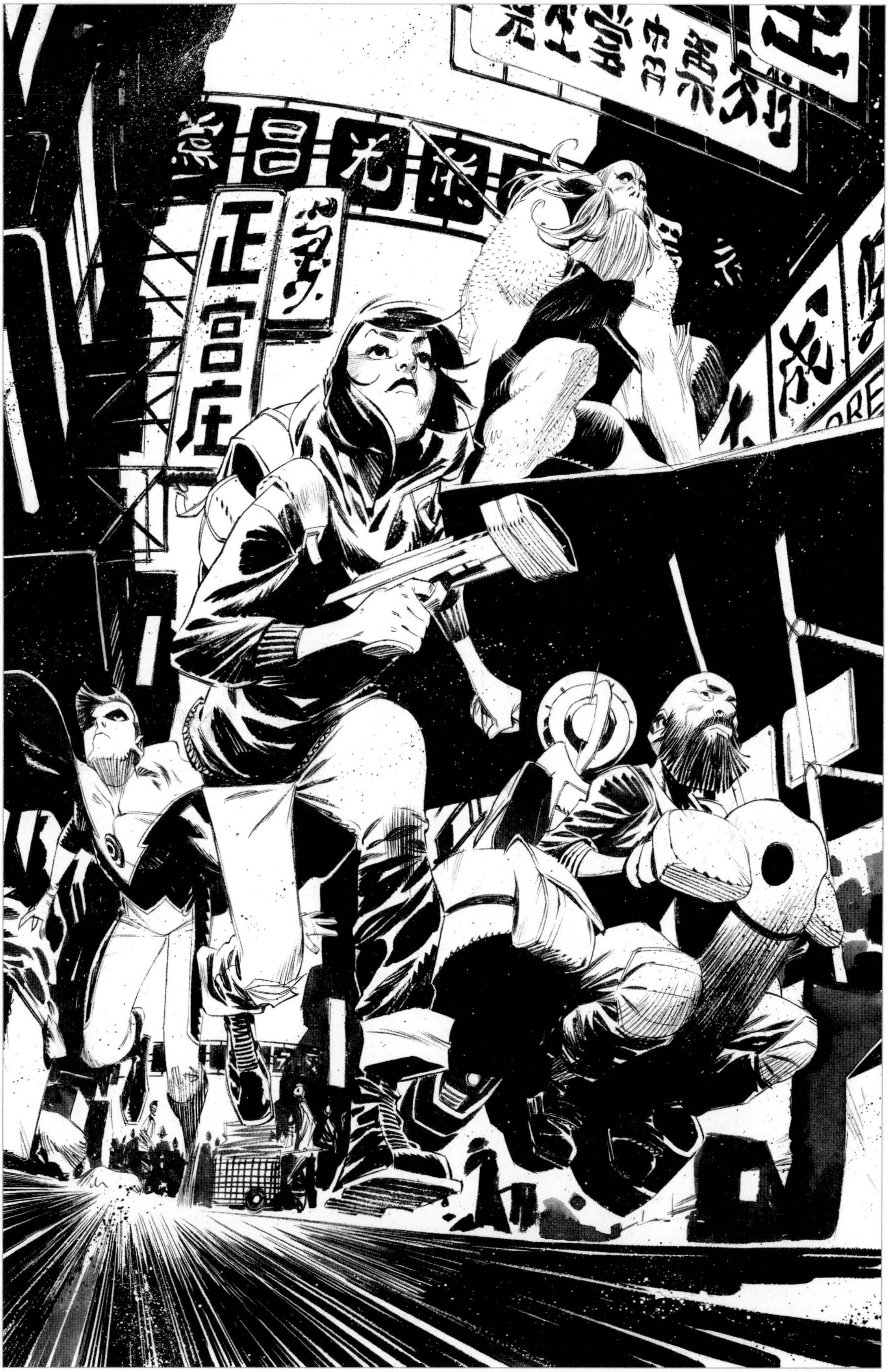

#27 PAGE 18 INKS

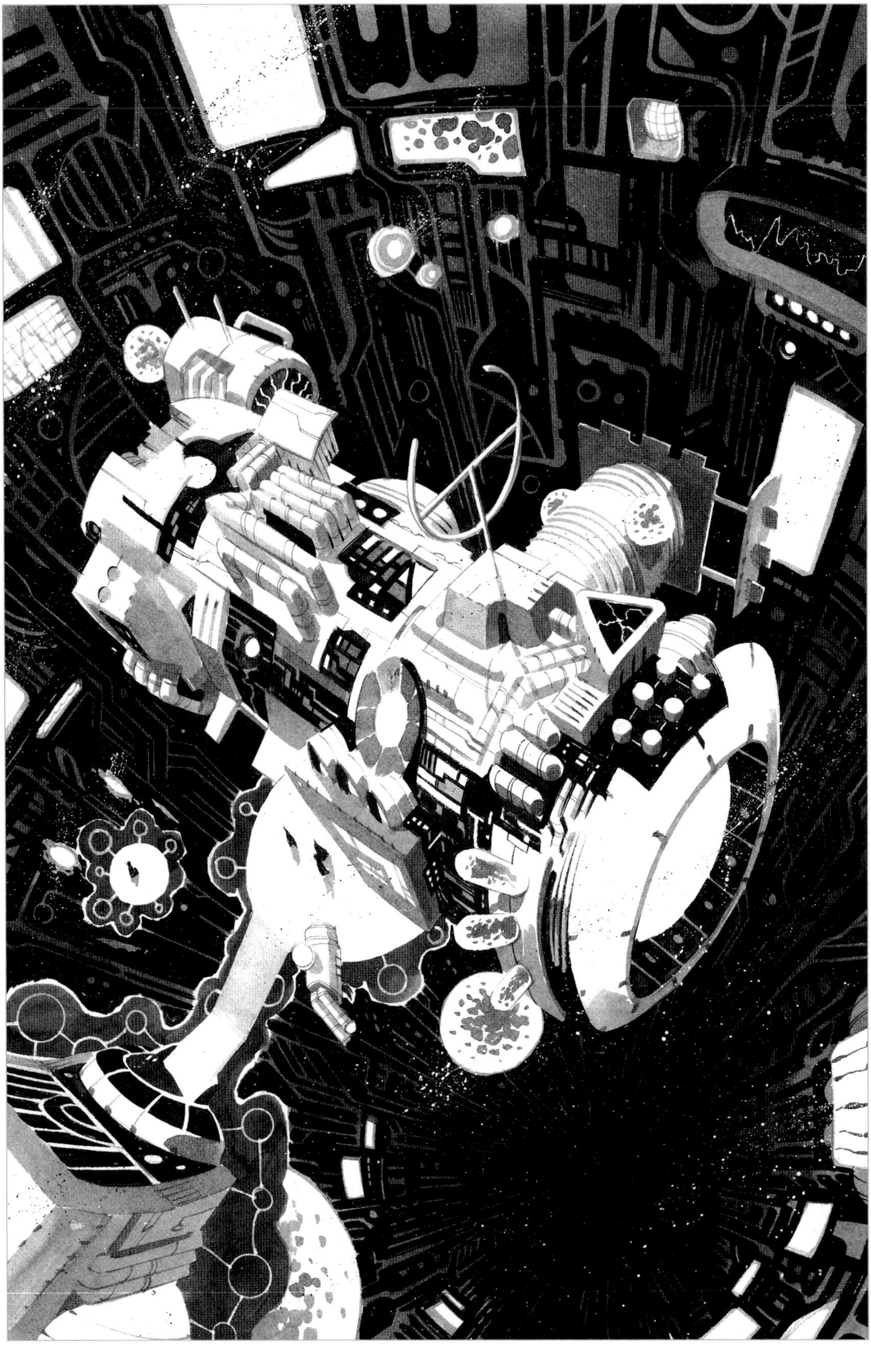

#28 PAGE 1 INKS

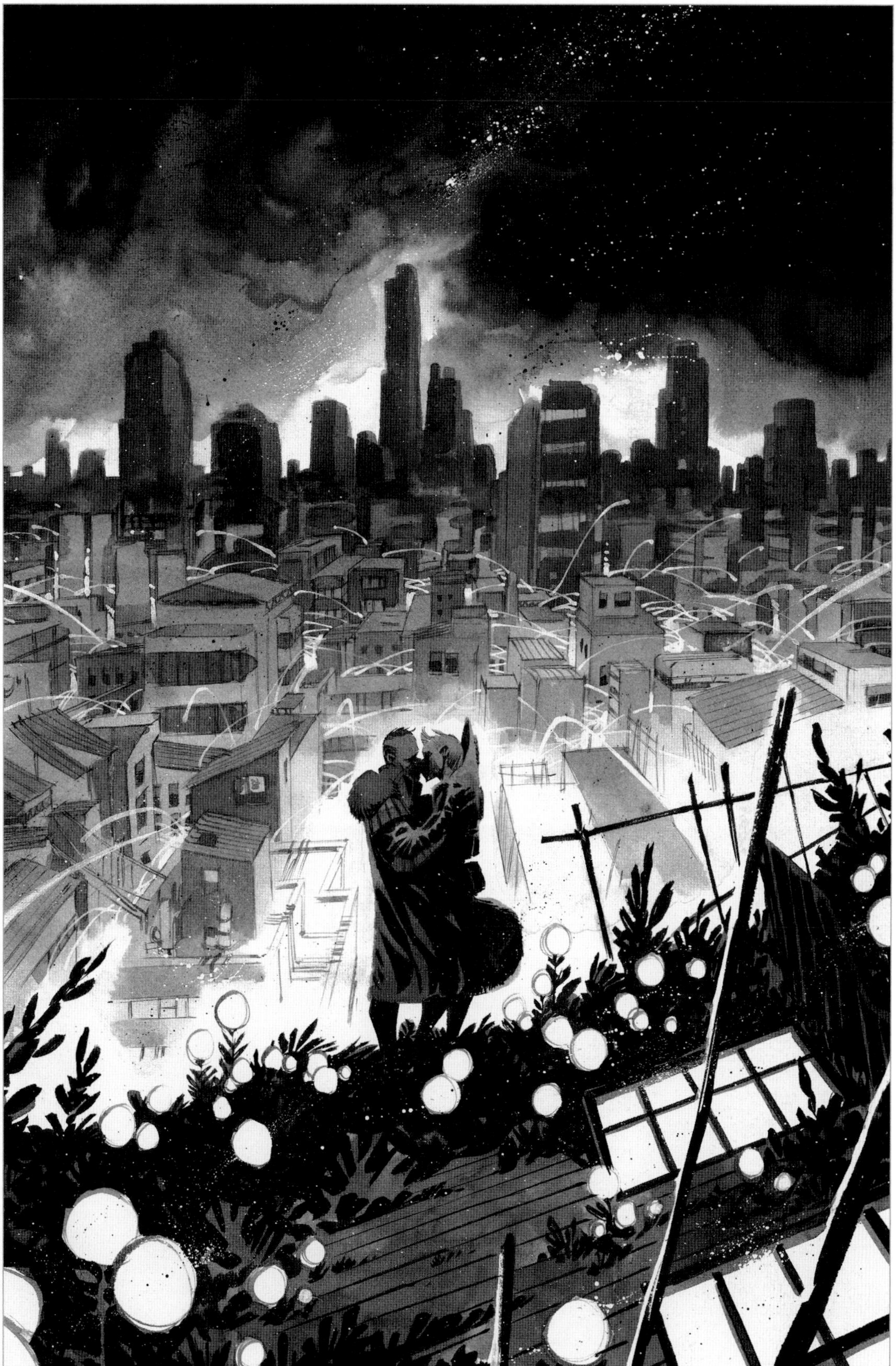

#30 PAGE 1 INKS

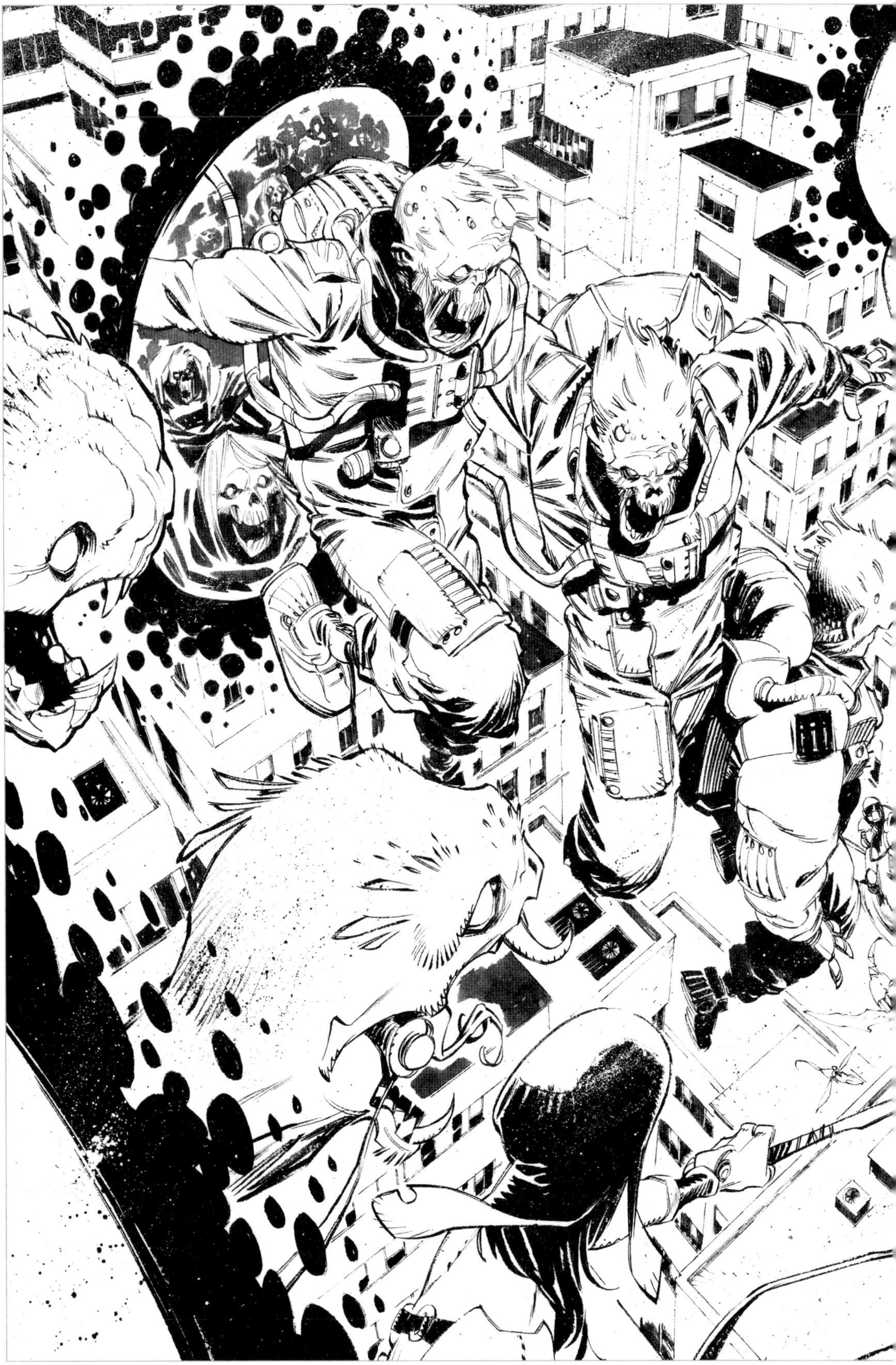

#30 PAGES 14-15 INKS

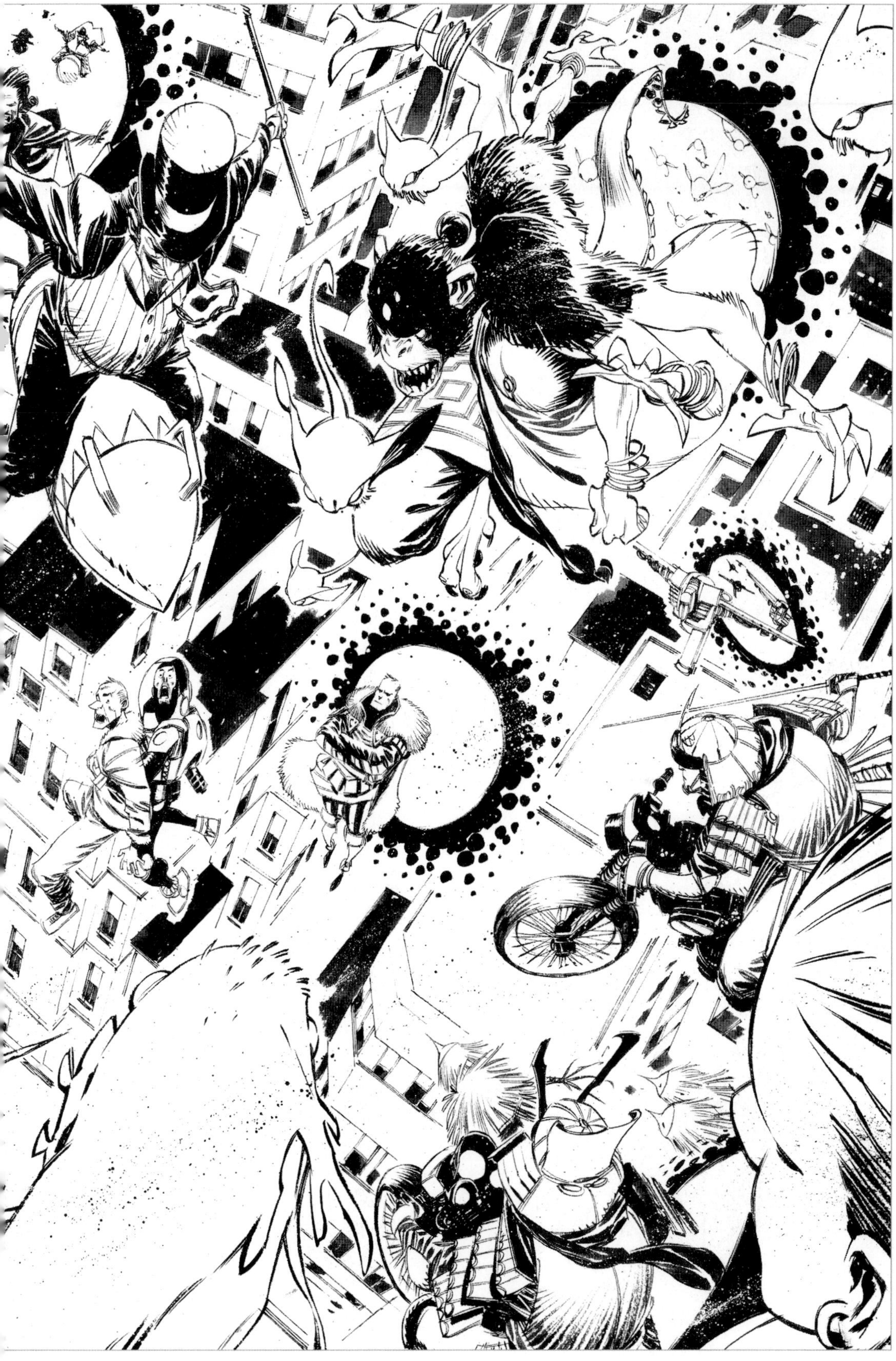

# BEHIND THE SCENES

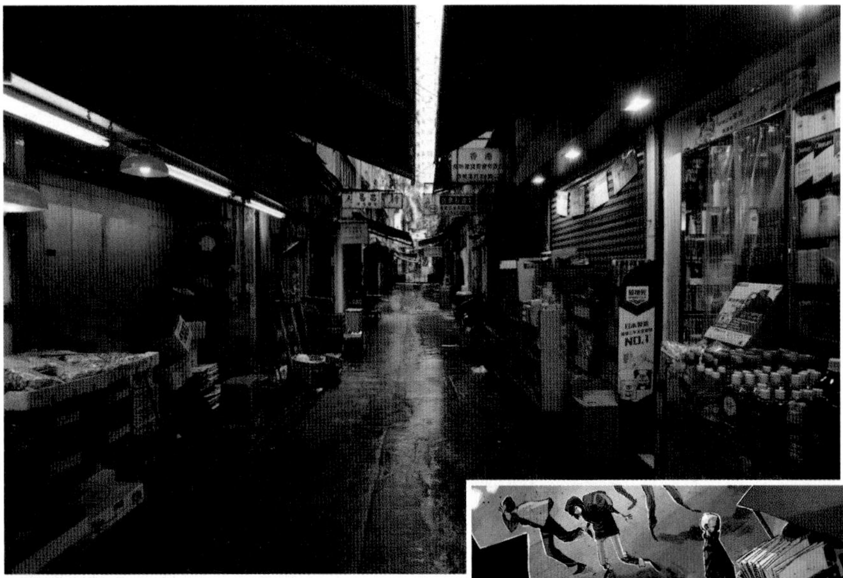

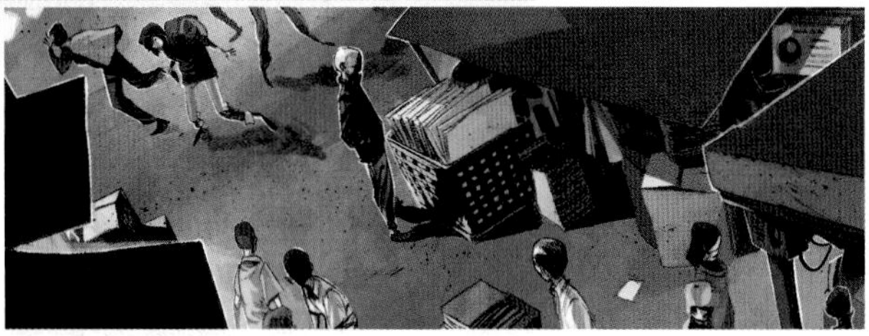

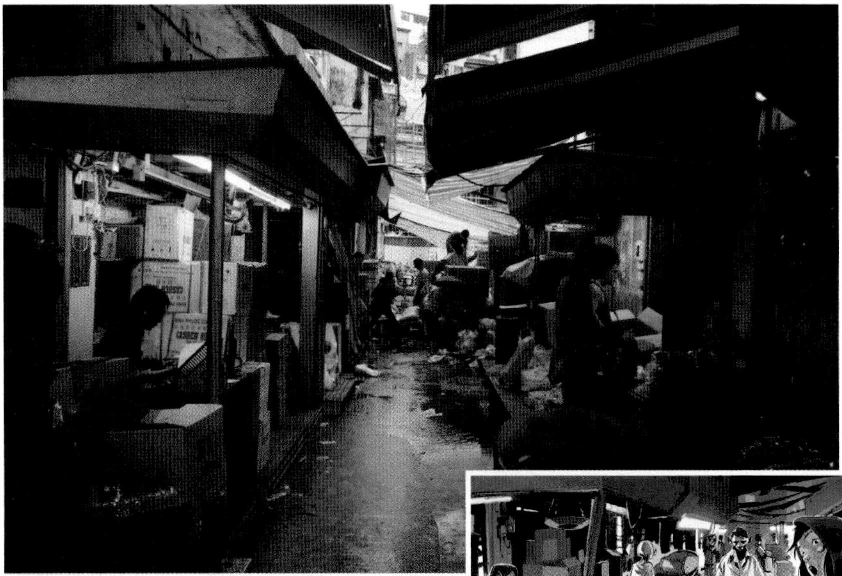

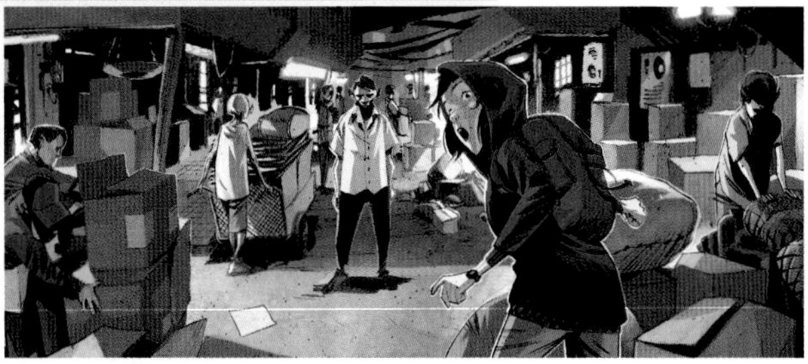

For Pia's adventure in Hong Kong in BLACK SCIENCE #26 and #27, Matteo was inspired by pictures taken by his friend and street photographer Tommaso Meli. Here you can see how the real-life streets of Hong Kong influenced the ones in BLACK SCIENCE.

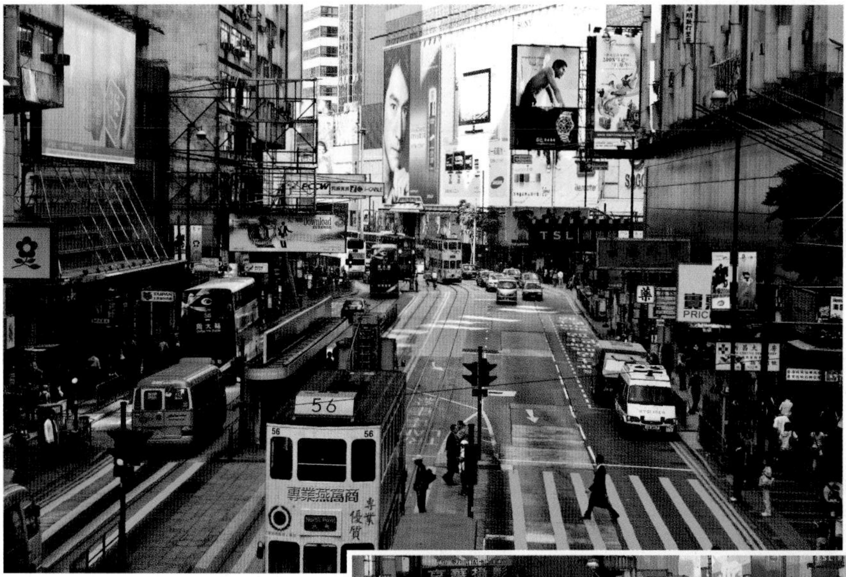
TSL
56
專業燕窩商

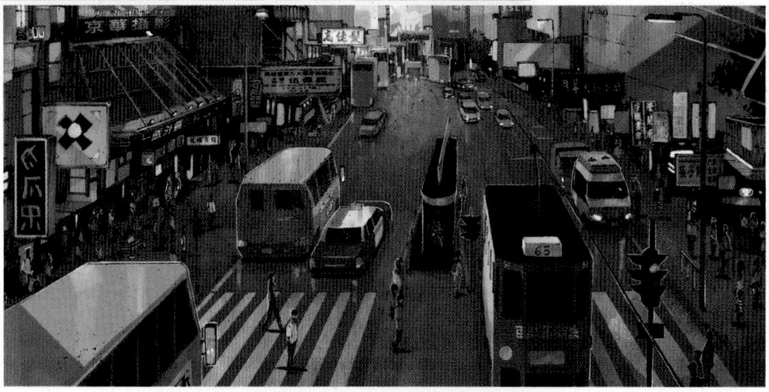
65

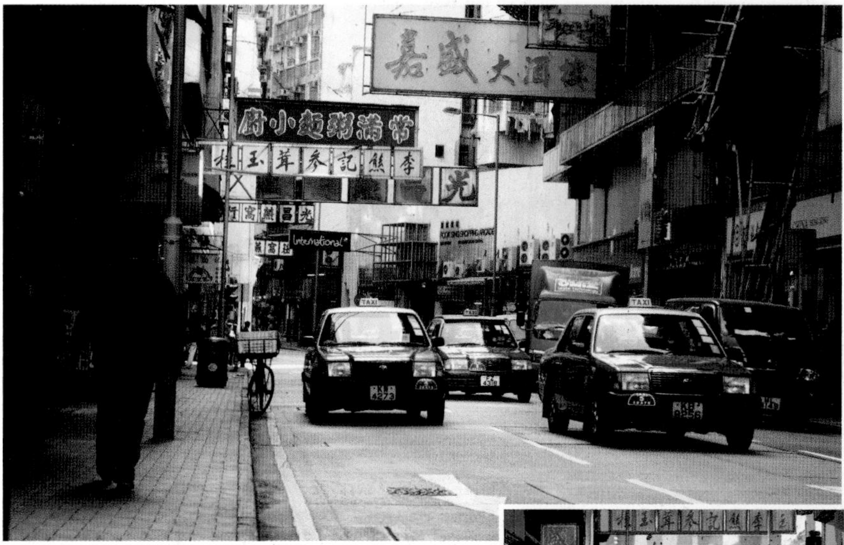
嘉盛大酒樓
International
TAXI

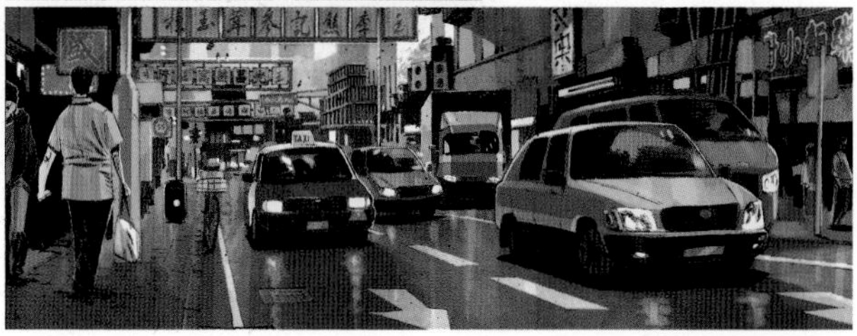

CHECK OUT MORE OF TOMMASO'S WORK HERE:
www.tommasomeli.com. and www.instagram.com/tommaso__meli/

## RICK REMENDER

Rick Remender is the writer/co-creator of comics such as *LOW*, *Fear Agent*, *Deadly Class*, *Tokyo Ghost*, and *Black Science*. For Marvel he has written titles such as *Uncanny Avengers*, *Captain America*, *Uncanny X-Force*, and *Venom*. He's written video games such as *Bulletstorm* and *Dead Space* and worked on films such as *The Iron Giant*, *Anastasia*, and *Titan A.E.* He and his tea-sipping wife, Danni, currently reside in Los Angeles raising two beautiful mischief monkeys.

## MATTEO SCALERA

Matteo Scalera was born in Parma, Italy, in 1982. His professional career started in 2007 with the publication of the miniseries *Hyperkinetic* for Image Comics. Over the next nine years, he has worked with all major U.S. publishers: Marvel (*Deadpool*, *Secret Avengers*, *Indestructible Hulk*), DC Comics (*Batman*), Boom! Studios (*Irredeemable*, *Valen the Outcast*, *Starborn*), and Skybound (*Dead Body Road*).

## MORENO CARMINE DINISIO

Born in 1987 in southern Italy and holding a pencil since year one thanks to a painter father, Moreno grew up with the aim of becoming a professional artist. After studying comic art in Milan, he went on to work as a comic and concept artist and character designer until 2013, when he crossed into American comics, coloring *Clown Fatale* and *Resurrectionists* (Dark Horse). Moreno first collaborated with Matteo Scalera on *Dead Body Road* (Skybound). With the release of *Black Science* in December 2014, he continues their fruitful partnership.